To Dian

Henrietta Alten West

A Fortress Steep and Mighty

Henrietta Alten West

LLOURETTIA GATES BOOKS • MARYLAND

This book is a work of fiction. Many of the names, places, characters, and incidents are products of the author's imagination or are used fictitiously. Any resemblance to actual events or locales or person living or dead is entirely coincidental.

Copyright © 2022 Llourettia Gates Books, LLC
All rights reserved. This book or any portion thereof may not be reproduced or used in any manner whatsoever without the express written permission of the publisher.

Llourettia Gates Books, LLC
P.O. Box #411
Fruitland, Maryland 21826

Hardcover ISBN: 978-1-953082-18-3
Paperback ISBN: 978-1-953082-19-0
eBook ISBN: 978-1-953082-20-6
Library of Congress Control Number: 2022914815

Photography by Andrea López Burns
Cover design by Zoe Malekzadeh and Jamie Tipton, Open Heart Designs
Interior design by Jamie Tipton, Open Heart Designs

This book is dedicated to the brave people of Ukraine who are fighting to save their country.

CONTENTS

Cast of Characters vii
Map of West & East Germany . . ix
Map of The Black Sea x
Prologue, 2021 xi

CHAPTER 1, 2021 1
CHAPTER 2, THE PAST 8
CHAPTER 3, 1958 13
CHAPTER 4, 2021 17
CHAPTER 5, THE PAST 23
CHAPTER 6, 2021 29
CHAPTER 7, THE PAST 33
CHAPTER 8, 2021 40
CHAPTER 9, THE PAST 45
CHAPTER 10, 2021 52
CHAPTER 11, THE PAST 60
CHAPTER 12, 2021 66
CHAPTER 13, THE PAST 75
CHAPTER 14, 2021 78
CHAPTER 15, 1965 87
CHAPTER 16, 1965 94
CHAPTER 17, 2021 102
CHAPTER 18, 2021 108
CHAPTER 19, 1945—1989 118
CHAPTER 20, 1965 128
CHAPTER 21, 1965 136

CHAPTER 22, 1965	146
CHAPTER 23, 1965	154
CHAPTER 24, 1965	161
CHAPTER 25, 2021	165
CHAPTER 26, 2021	174
CHAPTER 27, 2021	183
CHAPTER 28, 2021	193
CHAPTER 29, 2021	201
CHAPTER 30, 2021	211
CHAPTER 31, 2021–2022	216
CHAPTER 32, 1987–2022	222
CHAPTER 33, 2021–2022	231
CHAPTER 34, 2022	243
CHAPTER 35, 2022	253
CHAPTER 36, 2022	259
CHAPTER 37, 2022	264
CHAPTER 38, 2022	273
CHAPTER 39, 2022	281
CHAPTER 40, 2022	290
CHAPTER 41, 2022	298
CHAPTER 42, 2022	306
CHAPTER 43, 2022	316
CHAPTER 44, 2022	326
CHAPTER 45, 2022	333
CHAPTER 46, 2022	341
EPILOGUE, 2022	349
When Did I Grow Old?	352
Acknowledgments	355
About the Author	357

CAST OF CHARACTERS

Elizabeth and Richard Carpenter
Elizabeth and Richard live in a small town on the Eastern Shore of Maryland. Richard is a retired pathologist who did some work for the Philadelphia Medical Examiner's office many years ago. Elizabeth is a former college professor and CIA analyst.

Gretchen and Bailey MacDermott
Gretchen and Bailey live in Dallas, Texas. Bailey is a former IBM salesman, oil company executive, and Department of Defense intelligence agent. He currently is making another fortune selling commercial real estate. Gretchen works in the corporate world as the head of an HR department. Because she is so competent at everything she does, she actually runs the company she works for.

Tyler Merriman
Tyler lives in southern Colorado. Everyone suspects that Tyler flew the SR-71 Blackbird for the U.S. Air Force during his younger years. After he retired from the military, he made millions in commercial real estate. He flew his own plane around the country.

Sidney and Cameron Richardson
Sidney and Cameron have several homes and their own private plane. Cameron is a former IBM wunderkind who went out on his own to start several globally-known computer companies. Sidney is a retired profiling consultant who owned an innovative, successful, and fast-growing business before she married Cameron.

Isabelle and Matthew Ritter
Isabelle and Matthew live in Palm Springs, California. Matthew is a retired urologist, an avid quail hunter, and a movie buff. Isabelle has retired from her career as a clinical psychologist and now owns a popular high-end interior furnishings store and design business.

Olivia and J.D. Steele
Olivia and J.D. live in Saint Louis. J.D. is a lawyer who gave up his job as a prosecuting attorney to found his own extremely profitable trucking company. He is a logistics expert. Olivia is a former homecoming queen, a brilliant woman who worked as a mathematician and cypher specialist for the NSA.

Henley Breckenridge
Henley owns a ranch in Paso Robles, California. Her reputation as an expert with a gun draws her into an assassination plot that may save the world but threatens to destroy her.

Prologue

2021

The Camp Shoemaker boys from Cabin #1 were all war babies. Born in 1943, when the outcome of World War II was still uncertain, each one had made his entrance into a world of food and gasoline rationing, Rosie the Riveter, and war bonds. Many of their fathers were far away, fighting the Japanese or the Germans.

As boys, they were the "Duck and Cover Generation." All of them had lived with the threat of nuclear war hanging over their heads during every day of their childhood and every day of their lives for most of their adulthood. Once the Soviet Union had acquired the atomic bomb and the hydrogen bomb, these children had compliantly hidden under the flimsy wooden desks in their classrooms or filed to the basements of their elementary schools and assumed the position that civil defense experts said would protect them against an atomic blast. They knelt, one behind the other, on the linoleum floors, up against the concrete block walls, with their arms covering their heads. They practiced how to save their lives and survive the nuclear holocaust and a Third World War against the Soviet Union.

Two of the wives in the group were old enough to be war babies. These two also remembered and had participated in "Duck and Cover." The rest of the wives were younger, but all remembered the Cold War, the Berlin Wall, and the fall of the Evil Empire in December of 1991. For most of their days on earth, every one of the reunion crowd had believed that global annihilation might be just minutes away. Would they survive? Would there be a world worth living in after the nuclear catastrophe? This threat of death and total destruction had been an essential underpinning of their everyday lives.

The Camp Shoemaker reunion participants were meeting at the Woodbrier Resort this fall. None of them had ever visited the elegant and famous hostelry in White Sulphur Springs, West Virginia. They were eager to spend a few days relaxing at this extravagantly luxurious place that had great food. They were very much looking forward to having a tour of the Cold War bunker that had been built underneath the hotel in the late 1950s and early 1960s. This secret fortress of the Cold War was the stuff of legends for these men and women who had spent time during their childhoods preparing for a nuclear attack from the Soviet Union.

The bunker had been designed to house the entire United States Congress, both the House of Representatives and the Senate, in case of a nuclear war. The bunker's mission was to ensure continuity of government and to protect these servants of the people against radioactive fallout from an atomic blast. The bunker was well-equipped, and hopefully it had been built deep enough underground to shield the nation's elected representatives from the much-feared post-atomic-bomb radiation. The legislative branch of the government of the United States of America would be secure and able to continue to function in spite of an attack from the Soviet Union. The Woodbrier would save the day.

For these war babies, who had existed under the threat of nuclear war for most of their lives, the tour of the no-longer-needed facility would be fascinating. Each of these men and women, who had lived for the entire length of the Cold War and who were now in their late seventies, rejoiced that this bunker had never been called into service. It had been ready, but thank God it never had to be used.

The Camp Shoemaker boys, now approaching the end of the eighth decade of their lives, had met when they were all very young and had been assigned to cabin #1 at Camp Shoemaker located in the Ozark Mountains. After they had outgrown their years of attending summer camp, they'd lost touch. Years passed and the Camp Shoemaker boys grew older. More than a dozen years ago, Matthew Ritter had been inspired to invite his childhood friends and their wives and girlfriends to Palm Springs, California for a long weekend reunion. They'd all had the time of their lives. Every year since they'd reunited in Palm Springs, they had continued to celebrate their renewed friendship with a yearly reunion trip to someplace fun and interesting. Nobody wanted to miss the camaraderie and the stories these long weekends provided.

Mostly they just wanted to enjoy being with each other, but the places they chose to visit had to have outstanding food. The choice of the Woodbrier was exciting for all of the reunion goers. They said they were hoping for a peaceful week. The past several reunion trips had been more adventurous than relaxing. This group of friends had confronted villains from the past, and they had reached out to help and save the lives of others they'd met during the reunion trips. The Camp Shoemaker crowd said they hoped there would not be any drama this year. But they always seemed to be able to rise to the occasion and find the wherewithal to deal with the adventures and the challenges that just could not seem to leave them alone.

CHAPTER 1

2021

They had all survived a year of COVID spreading throughout the world and a year of social distancing and masking. Everyone in the group had been fully vaccinated and boosted, and they were all still alive. This was a year to celebrate many things. There had been some changes. Lilleth Dubois and Tyler Merriman decided to go their separate ways and had ended their five-year-long relationship. Lilleth took a new job in northwestern Arizona to continue her work with the Native American population. She would be missed at the reunion this year. Tyler was attending the reunion alone.

Olivia Steele had survived major surgery and several serious health crises. Her strength and determination were legendary among this group of friends. It was a huge disappointment that her physician had recommended she not attend the reunion. Olivia's doctor did not want her to be around crowds for fear of COVID and other things she might catch. Olivia's husband, J.D. Steele, decided to come alone. The men were going to outnumber the women this year. Everyone who was able to attend was looking forward to being a guest at this magnificent icon of hospitality located in the mountains of West Virginia.

Elizabeth and Richard Carpenter were driving to the resort from their home in Maryland. Isabelle and Matthew Ritter were combining a 50th wedding anniversary trip to Washington, D.C. with the reunion trip to the Woodbrier. Bailey and Gretchen MacDermott were flying to West Virginia from Texas. Gretchen was still working, and she would have to leave the reunion early. Bailey would stay on at the Woodbrier with his friends. Cameron and Sydney Richardson were flying on their private plane to this out-of-the-way location. This was going to be a reunion of gratitude. All were thankful they had survived the pandemic and were determined to have a great time in spite of it all.

Their first evening together was celebrated with dinner in the main dining room of the Woodbrier. Ahead of their dinner reservations, they gathered in the Lobby Bar, and everyone in the bar who was not a part of the reunion group was curious about who this energetic and fun crowd of older folks was. The Camp Shoemaker contingent literally took over the Lobby Bar with their toasts and their smiles and their delight at seeing each other again. They were a little bit loud and little bit boisterous. They were just so happy to be together. In spite of the hilarity, everybody was especially missing Olivia and wishing she were there to join the fun.

Matthew Ritter, their in-house expert on movies, pointed out that the magnificent chandelier in the Lobby Bar had been made for the movie *Gone with the Wind*. Debbie Reynolds, who had been a collector of movie memorabilia, had rescued the chandelier from the GWTW movie set and donated it to the Woodbrier. The group moved *en masse* from the Lobby Bar to the main dining room.

The main dining room of the Woodbrier was a majestic setting for their first dinner together. The Camp Shoemaker group was seated at a round table. Three seafood towers were ordered. These fabulous appetizers were presented on beds of crushed ice. The reunion goers dove into oysters on the half-shell, large gulf shrimp, chilled poached lobster tails, and healthy servings of jumbo lump crabmeat—compliments of the Mid-Atlantic blue crab. The cocktail sauce, remoulade sauce, mustard sauce, and other sauces for the seafood were served on the side. Celebratory drinks were ordered, and more toasts were offered.

Elizabeth's medium-rare lamb chops were more than a plateful. She could eat only one and gave the second one to Bailey. The Boursin whipped potatoes, the creamed spinach, and the hot and crispy onion straws went perfectly with all the entrees. Several ordered the poached Dover sole with a beurre blanc sauce. They were not disappointed. The Bananas Foster dessert was prepared tableside, and those who had ordered this extravagant and delicious concoction managed to eat almost every bite. Those who had chosen watermelon and mango sorbets were happy with their homemade frozen sweets.

Sidney had won first place in a fund-raiser dancing contest. Everyone wanted the details. Cameron attested to the fact that she had practiced religiously and truly had deserved her award. Sidney was gorgeous and graceful, and no one was surprised that she had been the best dancer at the fund raiser. Cameron had not slowed down or given a thought to retirement. He had stories of intrigue involving his company.

There was never a dull moment with Cameron. Sidney just shook her head and smiled.

Gretchen's company had survived the COVID pandemic and was charging ahead with renewed gusto. Matthew was playing a lot of tennis and watching many movies, as always. Isabelle's design and furniture business had grown by leaps and bounds during the fix-up-your-house craze that had accompanied the stay-at-home days of COVID isolation. She was way too busy. She and Matthew now had a third grandchild that they had just seen for the first time. The pandemic had kept them from traveling to visit the new baby until he was almost a year old, but they had kept up with his progress via weekly Zoom calls. Their lives were very full and busier than ever.

Tyler was somewhat quiet and did not mention Lilleth or anything about their break-up. No one was asking any questions. During the COVID pandemic and after Lilleth had moved to Arizona, Tyler had bought a new car and driven it from Colorado to California. His goal for the trip had been to visit everybody he'd been friends with from all phases of his life. Interesting!

Richard was writing the final chapters of his book about his ancestors and would give a brief talk to the group at the next salon about the role one of his ancestors had played in the U.S. war with Mexico. Elizabeth had written and written and written during the year of COVID, and she had several new mystery novels to show for her solitary and isolated days and nights.

Dinner continued long into the evening. At least two phone calls were made to Olivia. The Camp Shoemaker group was the last to leave the dining room, but finally, most of the reunion goers chose to retire to their beautifully decorated rooms and suites. Some were tired after traveling all day to reach the Woodbrier. It was not an easy place to get to. A couple of those who didn't want the evening to end decided to try their hands at blackjack in the hotel's casino. A table had been reserved in the main dining room for nine-thirty the following morning. Most of the men said they would be there for the breakfast buffet. Most of the women said they would be sleeping late.

A tour of the President's Cottage and a horse-drawn carriage ride were scheduled for their first day at the resort. Elizabeth knew she would not be able to climb up into the carriage, and the cottage was not wheelchair accessible. She opted to spend part of her day at the resort's world-renown spa. More than one-hundred fifty years earlier the Woodbrier had attracted guests who wanted to sample the famous spring waters that had made the resort famous. The springs had been a notable place to restore one's health for hundreds of years, since the days when Native Americans had discovered that the area's Sulphur-laced waters were cures for many ailments. Legends abounded about how the waters had given relief to those who suffered from rheumatism and arthritis, and Elizabeth hoped those rumors would turn out to be more than fantasies.

Masks were still required because of COVID. Everyone on the Woodbrier staff wore masks at all times. Masks were mandatory in the public rooms for guests but could be removed when one was eating or drinking. The Woodbrier was understaffed, like all hotels and restaurants were in this lingering phase of the COVID pandemic. Because the resort was short of employees, several of their restaurants were closed or were open only for a few days during the week. The members of the staff who were on hand were exceptional, however, and all went out of their way to help in any way they could.

The public rooms of the Woodbrier are large and airy and welcoming. The ceilings soar, and the windows give tremendous views of the acres of manicured gardens that surrounded the huge hotel. The colorful and inviting décor of each of the countless comfortable sitting areas couldn't help but make guests more cheerful. The rugs and carpets are exquisite and have obviously been designed for each particular room's size and function. The upholstered chairs that are found everywhere throughout the resort, number in the thousands. It was tempting to just to sit down in one of the luxuriously decorated lounges and glory in the beautiful space that has been created.

Elizabeth wondered how many full-time craftspeople were employed just to keep the upholstered furniture looking fresh and new. She could appreciate what an amazing feat it had to be to make sure the furniture alone remained in good shape at such a huge facility. Everywhere one looked was a feast for the eyes.

During and immediately after the war, the Woodbrier had served as a convalescent and rehabilitation hospital for World War II veterans. After the war, the resort's function as a hospital was discontinued, and the Woodbrier again became a luxury hotel open to the public. The famous and fabulous interior designer, Dorothy Draper, was hired to restore, redecorate, and revitalize the interiors of the Woodbrier as a first-class and elegant resort. Draper had set the post-war tone for the ambiance at the Woodbrier, and her sense of style still reigned.

The Woodbrier Resort has been called America's Resort. It is enormous. The hotel has been added onto many times over the years. As with any older building that has grown and sprawled in all directions, the elevators and the halls are not always where you think they should be or hope they might be. A first-time patron was guaranteed to be completely lost on their day of arrival. The resort provided excellent maps of the building that included the locations of elevators, restaurants, and bathrooms. Still, it was easy to lose one's way in the winding and meandering labyrinth. The Woodbrier concierges and other staff members were always there to help and guide guests to wherever they wanted to go.

The Carpenters were particularly challenged because Elizabeth was almost always riding in her wheelchair. The distances between destinations were often long and often circuitous. Richard got more than his usual workout as he pushed and pulled the wheelchair over the various kinds of flooring and up and down and on and off assorted ramps and lifts. The Carpenters miraculously almost always made it to the group's activities on time, thanks to the helpful employees of the Woodbrier. And the group of Camp Shoemaker friends were a tremendous help and took turns pushing Elizabeth when Richard was worn out.

Elizabeth remembered when she had ended up in the lake during their reunion at the Penmoor Resort in Colorado. An evil doctor had pushed Richard who in turn had pushed Elizabeth's wheelchair off the walkway and into the freezing water of the lake. She was thankful that none of the ramps at the Woodbrier were anywhere near the water.

CHAPTER 2

J.D. STEELE HAD BEEN AN athlete and a scholar in high school before he matriculated at the University of Oklahoma. He was handsome and outgoing as well as smart. He joined a fraternity and dated many women, but he also managed to make good grades, at least good enough for him to be admitted to the University of Oklahoma College of Law after he finished his four undergraduate years. After law school, J.D. fulfilled his obligation to Uncle Sam and was stationed in El Paso, Texas with the JAG Corps. J.D. had always wanted to be a prosecutor. He had a strong sense of right and wrong and wanted to help make sure the bad guys were found guilty and put in jail. He would devote twenty-five years of his life to this cause, and he became a legend in Tulsa legal circles. His specialty was trying the most complex and difficult criminal cases, including murder, rape, and drug cases. He was a relentless defender of justice and a dispenser of appropriate punishment. He was always prepared and performed brilliantly in front of the jury. J.D. seemed to thrive on convicting the worst of the worst, and he could count the cases he'd ever lost on one hand!

J.D. and his first wife were married just after they'd finished college. They were both very young, and neither of them was ready for marriage. The two had almost nothing in common, and after less than a year, they realized their union had been a mistake. They had no children and few assets, so their divorce was relatively amicable. They remained friends.

After his divorce, J.D. became one of Tulsa's most eligible bachelors and was quite the man-about-town for a few years until he met Signa Karlsson. It was a love match, and they married and had twins, a boy and a girl. Signa had her pilot's license and loved to fly. Both of their children had graduated from college when Signa was killed in a plane crash. She was a passenger in a friend's private plane. J.D. was devastated and terribly angry. He was convinced that if Signa had been flying the plane, there would not have been an accident. He didn't handle his enormous grief well and vowed never to marry again. He resigned abruptly from his job as an assistant district attorney, abandoned his beautiful Art Deco mansion without even cleaning out the refrigerator, told no one except his grown children goodbye, and left the country for French Polynesia.

This was where J.D.'s life and marital history became murky. Some say he married again on the rebound . . . two times! But no one is really sure whether he ever married again at all, or if he did, whether it was once, twice, three or even four times. Rumors flew, and J.D. wasn't talking about it. It didn't matter. J.D. never went back to Tulsa, and his house was sold. He eventually returned to the United States, and with the money he had saved, combined with an inheritance from his now-deceased, well-to-do parents, he bought a trucking company. The company's headquarters were in Missouri, and J.D. bought a condo in St. Louis.

He'd never thought he would enjoy anything as much as he'd enjoyed being a prosecuting attorney, but he found he loved running his own transportation empire. He was good at logistics and good with people, and RRD Trucking made him ten times more money than he'd ever dreamed he would make in his lifetime. He bought a cattle ranch. J.D. liked to travel to Washington, D.C. to lobby his legislators in person about transportation issues. It was on one of these trips to the nation's capital that he met Olivia Barrow Simmons.

Olivia Barrow had been a cheerleader and her high school's homecoming queen. She was beautiful and outgoing. She was the prettiest and the most popular girl in her school, and she was also very smart. After graduating from the University of North Carolina with a degree in mathematics, Olivia moved to Washington, D.C. where she shared an apartment with three other young women. Olivia had landed a job as a cypher specialist at the National Security Agency, so she wasn't able to talk to anybody about what she did at work.

Because Olivia was so attractive and had such a winsome personality, the NSA quickly identified her as a person who could represent the agency at Congressional hearings and other official public events. She always had all the answers, and although she would rather have been spending her time working on the complicated puzzles, mathematical constructs, and computer coding she loved, she was happy to be the pretty face of the No Such Agency. It was during one of her appearances before the Senate Select Committee on Intelligence that she was introduced to Bradford Simmons, the youngest man ever to be elected to the United States Senate. He was from Colorado, and he had a reputation as a womanizer.

Once he'd laid eyes on Olivia, he had to have her. She was young and vulnerable and flattered that a United States Senator wanted to date her. The women with whom she shared her apartment were envious and urged her to continue going out with Bradford. Olivia was eventually persuaded by the young senator's attentions, and within eighteen months, they were married. Olivia was devoted to her work and insisted on keeping her job at the NSA. Olivia and Bradford had three children, and Olivia chose to stay married to the senator until all three had graduated from college. Simmons had continued his womanizing behavior all during their miserable marriage, and Olivia had finally had all she could stand of the ridiculously handsome and adulterous cad. She divorced him.

Olivia vowed she would never marry again, and she focused her life on her children, her grandchildren, and the career she loved. Olivia had a very high security clearance and was a valuable employee at the NSA. Nobody could ever know exactly what she did, but whatever it was, she was very, very good at it. She knew lots of secrets about everything and everybody, but she was a person of the highest integrity. No one ever worried that she would suffer from "loose lips."

Many eligible bachelors in the nation's capital wanted to date her, but she was done with men . . . or so she said. Even in her late fifties, she was a beauty. She was a fascinating conversationalist, and everyone, men and women, wanted to sit next to her at dinner. It was at one such dinner party, hosted by her best friend, that Olivia was seated next to

J.D. Steele. The two hit it off immediately and were roaring with laughter before the main course was served. The hostess, who had known Olivia for decades, had thought J.D. and Olivia would appreciate each other's company, but she'd greatly underestimated the enormous amount of fun they would have together. For Olivia and for J.D., there was nobody else at the party.

They were inseparable from that night on. J.D. bought a townhouse in Georgetown and courted the woman who had swept him off his feet. He had never expected to fall in love like this so late in life, but he adored Olivia and didn't want to be away from her. Olivia was just as shocked to find herself head over heels in love with J.D. She liked men, but after her disastrous marriage, she wanted nothing more to do with romance. But these two were a match that was destined to be. They had such a good time in one another's company. Each of them had a wonderful sense of humor, and they could always make the other one laugh. Even their very skeptical grown children had to admit it was a beautiful thing to behold.

It was Olivia's idea to move closer to where J.D.'s business had its headquarters. The couple bought a house in St. Louis. She hated to leave her job at the NSA, but it was time to retire. Because Olivia insisted on spending one week out of every month near her children and grandchildren, who all lived in the Northern Virginia, Maryland, D.C. area, they kept the townhouse in the District. This was fine with J.D., and he usually came East with her. They traveled and enjoyed their lives. In spite of love and compatibility, Olivia was skeptical about marriage for many years. She didn't see why it was necessary. J.D. finally convinced Olivia that being married would not be the kiss of death, and they ended up tying the knot when they were both in their late 60s.

CHAPTER 3

1958

United States Congressman Masen Veudille was a former prosecuting attorney who had been elected to represent his Ohio constituency in the United States House of Representatives in Washington, D.C. in the 1950s. The Cincinnati Republican was a staunch conservative member of his party and a fierce advocate for taking a hard line against the Soviet Union. He had been to law school and was well-equipped to make the laws that govern the country.

Additionally, Veudille had an undergraduate degree in engineering and architecture, so he was particularly prepared to be one of the co-chairman of the Congressional committee that would oversee the building of a secret facility in West Virginia to protect his fellow members of Congress from the fallout of a nuclear war. The other co-chairman of the committee was a senator. The elaborate and secret underground hideaway would be designed and built to safeguard the country's elected representatives and ensure continuity of government in case of a nuclear attack by the Soviet Union.

A few members of Congress were aware that such a facility was under construction, but almost no one knew its location was to be underneath the new West Virginia Wing that was being built at the Woodbrier Resort in White Sulphur Springs, West Virginia. Building the West Virginia Wing at the Woodbrier would be the cover story for the secret construction project. The massive underground fallout shelter would be built in the sub-basement levels of the West Virginia Wing.

Cincinnati was close enough to the Woodbrier that Congressman Masen Veudille was periodically able to visit the site of the bunker to monitor the progress of the covert facility. The Woodbrier was about a six-hour drive from Veudille's home in Ohio. He wanted to check frequently on how the construction was proceeding and to consult with government architects.

The Congressman and his wife made many weekend visits to the Woodbrier during the three years the bunker was under construction. Mrs. Veudille spent her days at the spa and playing bridge. The Congressman told his wife he was playing golf all day, but in fact he was almost always touring the construction site. He donned a hard hat and made his way underground to where concrete was being poured and the Congressional hideout was being created. He consulted with the engineers, reviewed the plans, and made suggestions.

The Woodbrier had been a resort since before the 1830s. It had grown in size and popularity, and by the late 1950s, it was probably the best-known luxury resort in the United States. President Dwight Eisenhower became concerned, after the Soviet Union acquired nuclear weapons, that an attack on Washington D.C. by its former World War II ally would destroy the capital and cripple the ability of the United States to govern.

During World War II, the Woodbrier had been repurposed as a military rehabilitation hospital. After the war, Eisenhower had visited the Woodbrier several times while it was being used as a convalescent facility. When he became president of the United States, Eisenhower determined that the Woodbrier's remote location would be ideal for building a secret underground facility to house the U.S. government in case of a nuclear attack. The Woodbrier was a few hours' drive from the nation's capital, but it was essentially in the middle of nowhere in the Allegheny Mountains.

Because the facility would not be bombproof, it would not be able to sustain a direct hit by a nuclear weapon. The clandestine home for the United States Congress was designed essentially as an elaborate fallout shelter. Because the bunker in West Virginia was not a nuclear bomb shelter, it was absolutely essential that the location of this backup government complex, hidden beneath the Woodbrier, remain completely unknown. If the secret could be strictly maintained, the enemy would never target this location, a resort in the remote Allegheny Mountain range. The Woodbrier congressional hideaway was designed to protect the House of Representatives and the Senate from radioactive fallout for ninety days after an unthinkable attack.

In 1962, White Sulphur Springs was more than a four-hour train ride from the District of Columbia. At the time the bunker was designed and built, a nuclear attack on the United States would have arrived from the Soviet Union by way of aircraft that carried bombs over the North Pole. There would be hours, enough time, to evacuate the Congress and relocate them to the secret facility in West Virginia.

This underground government retreat was completed and ready in case of an emergency in the fall of 1962. The covert government headquarters remained completely unknown, a closely-guarded and highly-classified operation until *The Washington Post* outed it in a newspaper article written by journalist Ted Gup and published on Sunday, May 31, 1992. The secret of the well-hidden bunker, concealed in the side of a mountain, had been maintained for thirty years. Code named Project Greek Island, the massive living space had been kept ready to take care of the entire Congress in case of a nuclear war. The top-secret facility that had been built underneath the West Virginia Wing of the Woodbrier Resort was determined to be outdated and no longer needed. It was decommissioned in 1992.

Long before the bunker was decommissioned, intercontinental ballistic missiles had replaced aircraft as the means to deliver nuclear weapons. Cataclysmic destruction from halfway around the world could now arrive on U.S. soil within minutes rather than hours. Destruction would be almost instantaneous. Helicopters might be able to transport some members of Congress to the West Virginia mountain hideaway, but a four-hour train ride was ridiculously long and too slow and would not deliver the lawmakers to safety in time. White Sulphur Springs was now much too far away from Washington, D.C. Because destruction from a Soviet nuclear weapon delivered by an ICBM would arrive on U.S. soil within minutes rather than hours, there would no longer be sufficient time for the United States Congress to reach the Woodbrier.

CHAPTER 4

2021

*E*LIZABETH HAD SPENT THE MORNING at the Woodbrier spa. Several of the group who'd been on the carriage ride and the tour of the President's Cottage had decided to eat lunch at the Sam Snead Restaurant. Elizabeth hadn't been hungry for lunch so she opted to sit in the Trellis Lobby and people watch. This was one of her favorite pastimes, and she often found book material as she tried to figure out what was going on with the various people and groups she observed coming and going in public places. She was also known to occasionally drift off to sleep in her wheelchair.

A woman sank down into the cushions of one of the comfortable couches near where Elizabeth was sitting. The woman, who didn't notice Elizabeth, was in her own world. She was obviously terribly worried about something and was completely preoccupied with her troubles. Oblivious to her surroundings, tears began to stream down the woman's face. Most people who are lucky enough to be guests at the Woodbrier are able to put their cares aside, at least for the brief few days they spent enjoying this luxurious respite. Most people, who walked through the rooms and sat down near where Elizabeth was ensconced, were smiling and laughing. It was unusual to see someone crying. The crying didn't stop, and the woman finally began to sob. Elizabeth knew she should mind her own business, but she felt sorry for the woman and couldn't keep herself from speaking to her.

"Are you all right? Is there anything I can do to help?"

"I am not all right!" The woman was almost angry as she tried to speak through her sobs. "This was supposed to be one of the happiest times of my life, and it has turned out to be just horrible."

"What's happened? What's going on?"

The woman looked at Elizabeth and stared at the wheelchair. "I'm so sorry. I should be thankful for everything I have. I should not be feeling sorry for myself. But everything is going wrong. I hate weddings."

"Weddings are incredibly stressful." Elizabeth had three daughters, and years earlier she had orchestrated three enormous and elaborate wedding extravaganzas. She knew all about weddings and stress. She'd made a kind of joke about the fact that she had suffered from PTSD for years after her three daughters had all been married in a less than two-year time period. "Everybody is stressed. People are not at their best when it comes to a wedding. What's happened with your wedding?"

"It's my daughter's wedding, and you are exactly right. People are not at their best when it comes to a wedding. Why is that? My daughter is not speaking to me or to the groom. It's as if she has gone off the deep end and is angry with everybody."

Elizabeth had lived through one wedding like this, and after ten years of struggling and the birth of a wonderful grandson, the marriage had ended in a mess of recriminations and lawyers' bills. Elizabeth did not, however, feel the need to share this information with the distraught woman.

"I think the wedding is going to go ahead, in spite of my daughter's temper tantrums, but now my dress is missing. I spent way too much money on it to begin with, and now it has disappeared into the twilight zone . . . or who knows where it has disappeared."

"When was the last time you saw your dress?" Elizabeth was good at detecting and good at finding things, and she latched onto this problem as one that might be able to be solved. Nobody wanted to touch the dispute between the bride and groom or the dispute between the bride and her mother. That kind of problem solving was not in Elizabeth's repertoire.

"The last time I actually saw my dress was when I had a fitting at the store in Washington, D.C. My housekeeper, Maya, who is the most responsible person in the world, picked up the dress after the alterations were completed. She put the dress in a box and sent it to me via overnight mail two days ago. She carried the box to the post office herself and sent it certified mail, return receipt requested. We didn't want anything to go wrong, and of course now everything has gone completely wrong. When the dress did not arrive the next day, we got on the phone. USPS says they have a signed receipt for the dress. They say it was delivered here to the Woodbrier on time, and someone signed for it when it arrived."

"So the Woodbrier has lost the dress?"

"The Woodbrier says they have not lost it. But they don't know where it is. The USPS says *they* haven't lost it. Nobody will admit that they have lost the dress, but it is lost. The dress cost a fortune, but I don't even care about that at this point. I just want the dress in my hands. The wedding is Sunday afternoon. That's three days from now. I searched for months for the perfect dress and finally found it last week. I don't have time to shop for another dress and have it altered."

"It seems a little bit of detective work is in order. If somebody signed for the dress here at the Woodbrier, the concierge needs to track down the person who signed for the package and ask her or him where it is. How hard can that be?"

"I'm afraid I lost it with the concierge. I have been so upset about everything that I screamed at him. I said some things I should not have said. This is not his fault. He's said he would look into it, but I am afraid he thinks I have some screws loose. I am beginning to think I do, too. The resort is terribly understaffed because of COVID, and they are not able to hire enough people to fill all their positions in any of their departments. We are paying a lot of money to have the wedding here, and I am beginning to think it has been a huge and costly mistake."

"Do you have the name of the person who signed for the package when it arrived here?" Elizabeth believed in cutting to the chase. This poor mother of the bride had so much on her plate; she really was not able to focus on the task of tracking down her dress.

"My housekeeper just received the postcard they return to the sender. She can't read the writing on the receipt. She says the signature that is scrawled on the postcard is illegible."

"Does she have a cell phone that has a camera? Can she take a photo of the postcard with the signature and send it to you? If you have the signed receipt, you can take it to the concierge and tell him it is important to find out whose name is on the card. If you have a photo of the signature, it proves your package was delivered here. It also gives the concierge a place to begin to look to find out who signed for the dress."

"That's a great idea. I haven't been able to think straight the past few days. Of course, that will help the concierge. If I have a signed receipt to show him, he won't be able to ignore me or strike me off as belonging in the loony bin. I'm afraid that really is where I belong right now."

Elizabeth was not about to let the woman drown in self-pity. A minimum of directed action could get to the bottom of the mystery of the missing MOB dress. "Here's my card. I've written my room number on the back. Please call me on my cell phone and let me know what's going on." Elizabeth knew she should mind her own business. Richard was constantly reminding her not to get involved in other people's messes. But Elizabeth liked to help people, and she loved to solve a problem. She was intrigued by the mystery of the missing dress. This seemed like a problem that ought to be easily resolved.

"I'm Valerie Symington. I'm in room #3026. Thank you for listening to my whining and crying and for the suggestion about taking a photo of the signed receipt confirmation. I came to the Woodbrier several days before the wedding so I could be sure that everything was going to be perfect. Of course, there is no perfect. I know that. I have been in such a state. I wonder if I can even get through the next four days. Thanks for listening to me and allowing me to dump my problems on you. I will let you know what happens." Valerie had stopped crying and was on her way to see the concierge again. Elizabeth wondered what would happen with the not-so-happy couple. Maybe Valerie wouldn't need the MOB dress after all. Elizabeth had done what she could and drifted off to sleep.

Isabelle gently roused her from her slumber. "Time for montages. It's Cold War thrillers and chillers tonight. You were sound asleep."

"How was the carriage ride? I know the grounds are beautiful, and I'm sorry I had to miss that."

"The grounds are magnificent, and a few of the trees are just beginning to turn. But you would never have been able to get into the carriage. I almost couldn't get up there myself. They had a little set of steps, but it wasn't nearly tall enough for a short person. Matthew had to pull me up and into my seat. Here's your driver." Isabelle smiled as Richard came up behind her to push Elizabeth's wheelchair. Isabelle led the way to the Ritter's suite where Matthew was busy setting up to show his movie clips.

CHAPTER 5

THEY MET IN NEW ORLEANS when he was a fourth-year medical student at Tulane and she was a freshman at Newcomb College. They both had roots in Tennessee, albeit at different ends of that very long state. Their first few dates had long-term relationship written all over them. Isabelle Blackstone was considerably younger than Matthew Ritter, but he was committed to being eternally young and worked out every day to stay that way. They made a handsome couple. Isabelle was blonde and beautiful, and Matthew knew she was the one. He was in love, but he wasn't ready to settle down. He had places to go and people to see. He had an internship and a residency to do, and he had signed up to fulfill his obligations to his country by spending two years working for the United States Public Health Service. She had just finished her freshman year in college. Matthew was moving on to California for his internship, the next chapter in the long quest to become a urologist. Would Isabelle go with him or would she stay in New Orleans?

In the end, she decided he was worth it. She would transfer to UCLA and complete her undergraduate studies there. Her parents were not happy when their nineteen-year-old daughter told them she wanted to leave Newcomb College and move to California to complete her degree, but they trusted her and agreed to pay her tuition in California. She was an excellent student and worked hard to graduate with a dual degree in psychology and sociology. Isabelle and Matthew married after Isabelle finished her undergraduate studies, and they moved to the Phoenix area where Matthew served his two years in the Public Health Service, working on what was then called an Indian Reservation. While they lived near Phoenix, Isabelle earned a master's degree in clinical psychology at Arizona State University, and she later opened her own counseling practice in Palm Springs, the same year Matthew joined a thriving urology group in that California city.

The professional corporation Matthew Ritter joined was the leading group of urologists in Southern California. Movie actors and other famous people from Los Angeles drove to Palm Springs for medical care, especially when they had an embarrassing problem they didn't want anyone in L.A. to know about. Matthew was bound by the Hippocratic Oath and the covenant of professional confidentiality not to talk about his patients. And he never did. He kept many confidences about highly-placed people in all walks of life. As well as the Hollywood crowd, he treated wealthy businessmen and politicians, including two governors of Western states, several United States senators, and assorted congressmen and judges. His group was known for its medical expertise as well as for its discretion. Matthew knew many scandalous things, secrets quite a few famous people hoped he would carry to his grave. He would, but did they all trust that he would always abide by his commitment to confidentiality?

Isabelle likewise knew her clients' secrets. She was an effective therapist and a warm and caring human being. Her patients loved her. She had a successful practice within a year of hanging out her shingle and had to begin hiring additional counselors to join her. There was a lot of money in Palm Springs. There were also some very large egos in residence, a not unexpected circumstance. The very successful wanted to live, vacation, and retire in this golf course mecca that was reputed to have more sunny days than any other place in the United States. There was a great deal of infidelity, and many people came to her with problems that were associated with their addictions to drugs and alcohol. There was domestic abuse, and women, who did not want to be seen in public with a black eye or a broken arm, left Beverly Hills to hide out and seek counseling in Palm Springs. Isabelle listened and dispensed advice to the rich and famous.

Isabelle was sometimes called to testify in court, something she hated to do. She didn't like to break a confidence, but she was legally bound to respond to a subpoena to appear in court and to testify honestly when questioned under oath. She had almost been called to testify in the extraordinarily high-profile murder trial that involved a very famous football player and his second wife. Everyone knew the athlete had been beating up his wife on a regular basis. He'd finally killed her and was on trial for murder. Thankfully, Isabelle hadn't had to testify in that case. But there were other cases where her testimony had resulted in an unstable parent being denied custody of their child in a divorce. She had received direct and very personal threats as a result of some of these court cases.

Isabelle had struggled to work, at least part-time, while she raised the couple's two children. She had household and babysitting help, and she spent as much time in her office as she could. She knew she needed the stimulation of doing her own thing while dealing with diaper changes, wiping down counters, making endless peanut butter and jelly sandwiches, and driving her children to their after-school activities and numerous sports events. When her children graduated from high school, Isabelle realized she was burned out being a clinical psychologist, and she began to look for a new and less stressful career.

She found her next identity as an interior designer and owner of an elegant high-end shop that sold European antiques, lamps, and other wonderfully beautiful and expensive accessories for the home. Isabelle's store, Blackstone White, immediately became everybody's favorite place to find the perfect piece to make a room both interesting and classy.

What Isabelle had not expected was the extent to which being an interior designer and a store owner would call on her skills as a therapist. People came into the store to talk and sometimes to cry. Her clients had a great deal of money, but they did not always have much happiness or contentment. Isabelle was a good listener. She was patient and kind. People she barely knew poured out their hearts to her. If a husband was laundering money, his wife might express her disgust or her fear about his activities to Isabelle. If a boyfriend was involved in the drug trade, the girlfriend would confide in Isabelle. There were plenty of mafioso living in Palm Springs.

Isabelle sometimes helped a client disappear. It started with a woman who was a prolific shopper and regular customer of Isabelle's. The woman came into the store one day, terrified that her husband had sent his henchmen to kill her. She begged Isabelle to allow her to hide in the storage room at the back of Blackstone White. Isabell trusted her gut and helped the woman lie down, well concealed, behind a pallet of oriental rugs. Sure enough, two greasy looking tough guys with tattoos all over their arms arrived at the store, and without asking, searched high and low for the gangster's wife. Isabelle was frightened, but she was also angry. The mobsters were unable to find Isabelle's client, and as soon as they'd left, Isabelle called the police and reported the two for bursting into her store, turning everything topsy-turvy, and searching her property without her permission. She knew nothing would come of the police report she'd filed, but felt she had done the right thing.

Isabelle hid the frightened woman in her own home for several days and then drove her to Mexico. The woman had a secret bank account in L.A. and hoped to start a new life south of the border. The incident had been terrifying, but Isabelle had found a new calling. She was now an interior designer, store owner, and rescuer of the abused. It was a lot to take on, and Isabelle often asked herself if she had merely traded one stressful job for another even more stressful job.

The interior design part of her business was booming. Isabelle had excellent taste. Everybody wanted her help to design the addition to their house; consult with them about the space planning in their new kitchen; and do the paint, curtains, and new furniture in the family room renovation. She had more business than she could handle. She spent a lot of time in clients' homes and often drew on her counseling skills to settle disputes within their families. The husband, who was paying the bill for the redecorating project, didn't like white walls. The wife, who would be spending most of her waking hours in the room, wanted only white walls. He dug in his heels. She refused to talk about it. The interior designer/marriage counselor came to the rescue and brought a compromise and reconciliation. Isabelle often wondered how interior designers without experience in clinical counseling were ever able to accomplish anything.

Isabelle saw and heard many things she never wanted to see or hear. She kept her secrets, but she sometimes wondered if an angry father, who had been denied access to his children because of his mental illness, would remember her court testimony and come after her. She worried that the women she'd helped disappear would be found. Would the assistance Isabelle had given to rescue and hide these victims be exposed? Would an angry abuser come after her?

CHAPTER 6

2021

"Tonight it's clips from Cold War movies. Some of these are kind of silly and predictable, but I wanted to show a wide range of the movies that were produced during and about that period. All of these movies have well-known actors and actresses starring in them. We are going to see clips from *The Spy Who Came in From the Cold* which is in black and white, *Torn Curtain*, *The Man Who Knew Too Much*, *Funeral in Berlin*, *Berlin Airlift*, *Bridge of Spies*, and my personal favorite, *Dr. Strangelove*. Those of you who are familiar with these movies have figured out that they are mostly about spies and the threat of atomic bombs. That's what the Cold War was all about. We are having a tour of the Woodbrier bunker tomorrow morning, so I thought it would be interesting to delve into the Cold War with some montages tonight."

Who couldn't love performances by Richard Burton and Michael Caine? The pairing of Paul Newman and Julie Andrews had been an interesting and unusual choice. All agreed that the movie starring James Stewart and Doris

Day was really a showcase for the song "Que Sera Sera." Everybody loves Tom Hanks, and the brilliant trio of Peter Sellers, George C. Scott, and Slim Pickens had carried Matthew's favorite to the Oscar for Best Picture in 1965. The old movies, mostly from the 50s and 60s, resonated with this group of seniors, and they went to dinner at the Woodbrier's steakhouse humming old tunes and remembering when they and everybody else, even Jimmy Stewart, looked young.

Elizabeth and Richard had to access the steakhouse by way of a remote wheelchair lift. A concierge had graciously led them to the lift which they would never have been able to find on their own. The lift was not often used, and on this night it was being temperamental. It was small, and Richard could barely get on it with the wheelchair. Then it refused to go. Even the concierge had a difficult time figuring out what was wrong. It was a difficult arrival, and the usually unflappable Elizabeth was rattled by the experience. There had to be a better way.

French onion soup and lobster bisque were popular starters now that summer had retired and fall had taken over in West Virginia. They were in the mountains, and it was chilly at night. Soup was a good thing. Steaks were the obvious order of the evening, but many in the group ordered Arctic Char. The salmon-like fish was served with a creamy white wine sauce and rosemary roasted potatoes. It was steakhouse night so Richard ordered the giant porterhouse medium rare and shared it with Elizabeth and with several others. Side dishes at steakhouses are usually outstanding, and a couple of the women ordered a vegetarian array of creamed spinach, roasted Brussels sprouts, and loaded baked potatoes as their meal. The flourless chocolate cake, the chocolate soufflé, and dark chocolate gelato were the hands-down favorite desserts. Steaks and chocolate . . . what else could a human being wish for?

The highlight of the dinner, however, was the Facetime chat with Olivia over the phone. She looked healthy and was delighted to see everybody. The phone was handed around the table, and everyone had a chance to speak with her. She was thrilled when J.D. told her they'd toasted her at every meal. She was almost in tears that she'd had to miss the fun, but her friends promised to call her every night during dinner and pretend that she was there with them.

As they were leaving the steakhouse, there was one minor crisis when Elizabeth refused to ride on the lift again. She was worried that the lift would not be able to go at all or that it would go partway down and grind to a halt. When the manager of the steakhouse refused to allow her to ride on the employees' elevator instead, she grabbed her cane and propelled herself out of her wheelchair. Bailey gasped and murmured to himself, "Uhh-ohh!" Elizabeth hobbled to the short staircase and handed her cane to Richard who was holding his breath and praying.

She grabbed hold of the railings on both sides of the stairway, and thank goodness for those. She slowly and carefully walked down seven steps, hanging onto the railings for dear life. She secretly cheered for herself—for refusing to ride the lift and for being able to make it down the seven steps. She wanted to make sure that her crisis was short-lived. Those who had ever broken a leg or an ankle or who'd ever had a disabled grandparent in their charge would understand.

Bailey went to the casino again, much to Gretchen's dismay. She would never really know how much money

Bailey had lost, or won, at the blackjack tables. At least he was not wearing a ridiculous wig and a woman's dress—at least not yet. Gretchen was thankful for the small favors her life delivered to her.

CHAPTER 7

Bailey MacDermott graduated with an engineering degree from the University of Arkansas. He was hired by IBM directly out of college, and because of his outgoing personality and gift for gab, he quickly became one of Big Blue's best salesmen in his region. But Bailey was an independent guy, and he felt as if he was being smothered in the corporate world. He'd been selling computer systems to the oil industry, to help them with payroll and inventory and to keep track of where their oil was coming from and where it was going. Bailey let a couple of his clients know he was interested in making a change, and within a few weeks he had a job offer from a major oil company. He submitted his resignation at IBM and left his job in Chicago. Houston was calling, and Bailey was ready to conquer the oil business and earn some big money. Soon he was flying back and forth from Houston to the oil-rich kingdoms in the Middle East. Before long, he knew the countries and who the movers and shakers were in the world's wealthiest oil-producing nations.

When the Shah of Iran fell, the world, and especially the Middle East, was turned upside down. Previously ignored actors on the world's political and economic scene were on the march, and a few days after the hostages in Iran were taken, the U.S. Department of Defense was knocking on Bailey's door. He was a patriot and agreed to work with the DIA, one of the pentagon's spy agencies.

At first, he just met with other Americans in Riyadh and other Arab capitals. He carried the packages and papers these agents asked him to take back with him when he flew home to the U.S. Then he was asked to meet with foreign nationals and accompany them to safe houses. Once, in Lebanon, he had to rescue an American who was in desperate shape, running from Hezbollah, and suffering from serious gunshot wounds in his lower leg and thigh. Bailey drove the man to the airport in his rental car and slipped him aboard the oil company's plane. Bailey's assignments became more and more complex and more and more dangerous. He told himself he was doing all of this because he was helping to fight terrorism, but he also loved the rush he got from taking risks.

After a particularly harrowing mission, Bailey had to take some time off from his regular job with the oil company and from his special work for the DIA. He spent a month recuperating in Paris. He slept late and ate well. He also met and fell in love with an American woman he met at the Rodin Museum. Bailey had gone there to learn more about the sculpture. Marianna Archer was at the museum posing for magazine photographs. She was a gorgeous redhead who earned her living as a highly-paid fashion model. She was doing a photoshoot for an American fashion magazine and was dressed in very tight stretch stirrup pants, enormous earrings, and a sexy faux suede off-the-shoulder top. Bailey stumbled into the room where Marianna had her arms draped around *The Thinker*. That day Bailey completely missed seeing Rodin's most famous work of art, but he couldn't take his eyes off Marianna as she pranced and posed around the naked man made out of bronze.

It was the 1980s and Bailey MacDermott decided he had been a bachelor long enough. Marianna was a lonely ex-pat living in France, and she quickly succumbed to Bailey's warm and friendly personality. They spent a lot of time at her apartment getting acquainted, and before Bailey's month of vacation was over, the two were married. It was probably a mistake for them to marry, even under the best of circumstances. The complexity of their work lives and the travel both of their jobs required meant they spent a lot of time apart. Their time together was frenetic, and they never had a chance to really get to know each other.

What Bailey didn't know about Marianna was that she was manic-depressive, a mental illness that has since been renamed "bipolar 1 disorder." If she stayed on her meds, Marianna was mostly fine and a lot of fun. When she went off her meds, all bets were off. When they returned to the U.S., she realized she was pregnant. Bailey and Marianna's son was born in Houston, and Bailey was beside himself with joy. Marianna, on the other hand, lapsed into postpartum depression and a serious depressive phase of her mental illness. She reached the point where she didn't want to get out of bed at all.

Bailey and Marianna eventually divorced. She ceded custody of their son to Bailey, but Bailey was juggling too many things. He told the DoD he wasn't able to work for them anymore, and he quit his job working for the oil company because he didn't want to travel all the time. He began dealing in oil futures and was incredibly successful in this field. He made a lot of money, but the best part of his life at this time was that once he settled down in Dallas, he was able to make a home for himself and his son.

Before he met Gretchen, rumors flew that he had married again in haste twice and then quickly divorced twice! He didn't like to talk about what had happened in his love life during this period, and no one wanted to ask. It was clearly a painful subject for Bailey.

Gretchen Johanssen technically worked in human resources, but she was one of those people who was so competent that, wherever she worked, she eventually took over running much more than the HR department. She was petite and fit, and her good looks and style attracted attention. Once you got to know Gretchen and once you had worked with her for a while, because of her extraordinary competence, you forgot how small she was. Her abilities and her organizational skills belied her size, and she took on a significant presence in any room where she worked or spoke.

Gretchen had married twice and had two wonderful sons. She adopted and raised a foster daughter. Her daughter was still in graduate school, but after her second divorce and after her sons were launched, one into the military and the other to college, Gretchen decided to take a job with an international financial group. She had always wanted to travel and was excited to be sent to run the HR department at her company's office in Zurich.

As always happened when Gretchen arrived on the scene, her ability to get things accomplished was immediately recognized, and she took on more and more responsibilities, above and beyond her HR duties. She always attracted attention at a board meetings. When she made an outstanding presentation to a group of international businessmen, the head of one of Switzerland's wealthiest and most secretive banks noticed her. He wanted to date her and wanted to hire her to work for him. He offered her a salary three times what she was earning in her current job. She agreed to take the lucrative position as his special advisor, but she never mixed business and romance.

The Swiss banker was smart enough to agree to her terms, and Gretchen spent several years making top-level decisions in the arcane world of Swiss banking and international finance. She became fluent in German. She met arms dealers, heads of state, assassins, movie stars, Russians and Saudis, and people she was sure were mafia figures or drug dealers or both. She helped her employers invest their clients' riches. She knew the identities of many who had secret money and needed to conceal it.

When one of her ex-husbands was murdered, Gretchen returned to the United States. Her son, who was a Navy Seal, was involved in an almost-fatal car accident, and Gretchen wanted to spend time with him, helping him heal and boosting his spirits as he recovered. She was an accomplished corporate operator, but she was first and foremost a mother. It was while her son was recovering the use of his legs at a rehabilitation center in Texas that Gretchen met Bailey.

Bailey volunteered at the VA hospital where Gretchen's son was going for physical therapy. Bailey still made deals of all kinds. He had branched out from oil futures into commercial real estate, and it seemed that whatever he touched turned to gold. Volunteering to work with military personnel who were trying to get back on their feet was Bailey's way of giving back. He loved his work, but he loved working with the disabled vets even more. He spent time with Gretchen's son on an almost daily basis, and it was the young Navy Seal who introduced Bailey MacDermott to his mother.

Bailey and Gretchen had both been burned in the marriage department. Neither one was looking for a spouse. Each of them was happy living alone, but as they spent more and more time in each other's company, they realized how much they loved each other and wanted to spend the rest of their lives together.

Gretchen had taken a job with a company in Dallas, and in no time, she had, as she always did, made herself indispensable to her new company. She was the kind of employee who quickly became critical to the organization. When she mentioned the possibility of retirement, she was offered a large bonus to stay on for two more years. At the end of those two years, when the subject of retirement came up again, she was offered an even larger bonus, if she would just stay on a little longer. She might never retire because she was making too much money just by mentioning the word "retirement."

Bailey had moved into doing deals in international real estate, and this new clientele sometimes presented challenges. There were language barriers, although most people involved in the upper echelons of the business world spoke English. There were cultural differences, especially when it came to determining what was legal and ethical and what was not. Most of his clients were legitimate buyers who actually wanted to own a warehouse in Hong Kong or Mexico or an apartment building in Singapore. But a few clients who contacted Bailey were interested in buying real estate for the purposes of laundering money.

The schemes the money launderers devised were complicated and slick. Bailey found himself involved in a couple of these transactions before he caught on to what was happening. When he realized what these faux buyers were up to, he had to say no. He refused to participate in any money laundering intrigue. More than once, a disappointed money launderer had threatened Bailey's life. Bailey loved the rush and the risk of doing high-flying business transactions, but he definitely did not enjoy having a loaded gun pressed against his head. When one of these crooks tracked him to his home and threatened him, Bailey and Gretchen had to move to a different house. Bailey learned to be more discreet, but it was impossible for him to give up the thrill of making a deal. Now he was always wary when he took on a new client. In his early seventies, he was a vital and busy wheeler-dealer in the financial world.

CHAPTER 8

2021

Today was the big moment that Elizabeth and the rest of the Camp Shoemaker crowd had been looking forward to. Elizabeth suspected she was more excited than any of the others were, but everyone in the group had signed up for the bunker tour. They'd all heard so much about the bunker that had been built in the late 50s and early 60s, underneath the Woodbrier. They had read about it and seen documentaries about it, but now they were about to see it for themselves in person.

For those in their group who remembered the fear and daily drama of the Cold War, it was both curious and thrilling that President Eisenhower had planned for and built a facility so that the United States government would be able to function, even if Washington, D.C. was obliterated in a nuclear conflict. Those women in the reunion group who were younger might not fully understand what it had been like to have lived with the threat of the end of the world hanging over one's head every day of one's life. But they were all intrigued by the concept and the story of the bunker. The

Camp Shoemaker reunion group had gathered in the Trellis Lobby of the Woodbrier, and they were all waiting in line to pay for the tour.

Elizabeth heard the clanking and the jingle of the concho belt before she actually saw her. But, sure enough, there she was in line ahead of the Carpenters, right here at the Woodbrier Resort in White Sulphur Springs, West Virginia. Who would have ever guessed it? The last time Elizabeth had seen her had been the year before on the woman's ranch in Paso Robles, California. But here she was, and she was wearing her signature baggy blue jeans, her old leather purse, and her gorgeous silver and turquoise concho belt. Being at an elegant resort had not intimidated her into wearing different clothes. Elizabeth was thrilled to see Henley Breckenridge again.

"Henley? Henley Breckenridge, is that you?"

Henley turned around, looking suspicious. Who could possibly have spotted her here, where she was clearly out of her element? She thought she would be completely unknown to anyone and everyone at the Woodbrier. She turned around and spotted Elizabeth in her wheelchair, waiting behind her in the line to check in for the bunker tour.

"Well, Lord love a duck! Look who the heck is here at the Woodbrier! Elizabeth Carpenter, what *are* you doing here? You're a long way from home." She shouted at her across the room, not about to give up her place in line. The others waiting in the line must have already wondered who Henley was, and now they saw her shouting at the woman in the wheelchair. People in line between Elizabeth and Henley were preparing for a show. Henley would give it to them. Anyone who had ever met Henley could be certain of that.

"I'm here with the same group that traveled to Paso Robles last year. And guess who else is here, of course. Remember J.D. Steele? You pointed your shotgun at him and threatened to shoot him. He's in line here somewhere, or he will be. He'll be glad to see you." Elizabeth laughed. Henley knew her friend was teasing her.

"Well, J.D. was clearly trespassing on my ranch last year. I bought him a bottle of wine at the restaurant to apologize for the gun. How is my buddy J.D.?" Henley was laughing, too, at the memory of J.D. Steele, a rich businessman and former famous prosecutor from Oklahoma. Not usually intimidated by anyone, he'd seen his life flash before his eyes when he'd encountered Henley and her shotgun the year before in Central California.

He had trespassed on her property. That part of the story was absolutely true. J.D. and Cameron and the rest of the reunion group had been trying to save the life of a physician from Hong Kong. She'd left Communist China to become a whistleblower in the United States, but she had trusted the wrong person. She'd been kidnapped and tortured and had almost starved to death. Henley had seen the emaciated woman in J.D.'s arms. Henley had jumped to the conclusion that J.D. was involved in human trafficking when she found him lifting Sui Wai, the very ill and battered Chinese physician, out of his car. J.D. had been trying to save her, not hurt her, and it all got straightened out in the end. For weeks, Henley had cared for Sui Wai, the former Hong Kong physician, at her ranch outside Paso Robles, and Henley had brought the young Chinese woman back to health.

"J.D. is fine. We are all still alive . . . everyone in our group of friends, thank goodness. This COVID thing has really been something. We are all vaccinated and boosted. Several of us had breakthrough COVID, but because they'd been vaccinated, they weren't very sick. We're here for our yearly reunion. What are you doing here?" This was almost the last place on earth that Elizabeth had expected to see Henley Breckenridge.

"A wedding. My favorite niece begged me to come. I love this young woman, and I am here to keep a promise I made to her many years ago. I told her I would help to celebrate her nuptials, and here I am. I am also here to remind her not to let her fancy pants get the better of her. I personally think her deciding to get married here at the Woodbrier means her fancy pants are already running things, but here I am participating with both feet. I have to say, the staff here have all been incredibly nice and accommodating. I am beginning to think West Virginia has something going for it. It's my first time to visit 'Almost Heaven.'" Henley chuckled at her little joke.

"It is good to see you, Henley. You're obviously in line to register for the tour of the bunker. Our group is on your same tour. We'll have to have lunch or a drink or something and catch up. I want to hear about Sui Wai."

"I'd love that. I stay in touch with Sui Wai, you know. I'll tell you all about how she's doing. My niece has the next few days pretty booked up with wedding stuff for us to do, but I'd love an excuse to get away for a couple of hours."

"When's the wedding?"

"Day after tomorrow. Can we have lunch tomorrow? I need to get away from the wedding party once in a while. My niece is a great kid, and I actually think she's picked a keeper for a husband. Of course, I'd never tell him how much I really like him. His family is another story. They are very polite and very correct. They have way too much money, and they think they know everything. And they are driving me crazy. How about 12:30? We'll go to Draper's. You can meet me there." The others in the line were disappointed that they were not going to be able to hear the rest of the conversation, but it was time to stop shouting across the room.

The man who was taking the money for the bunker tour was ready for Henley to sit down in front of his computer so he could get her particulars and her credit card. Elizabeth had noticed that this man, who looked a lot like Wilford Brimley, everybody's favorite granddad, spent a good bit of time with each person or couple who paid. He definitely spent more time with each person than it would take to swipe a credit card. The reunion group was already on the list because they'd had to book their bunker tours several weeks in advance. It almost seemed to Elizabeth as if Brimley was interviewing the people who were paying to take the bunker tour. She would know more when it was her turn to pay.

Elizabeth looked forward to hearing how Sui Wai was doing and was delighted that Henley had kept in touch with her. Henley was a real character, and there was no question that she marched to her own drummer. She had an incredibly kind heart beneath her tough-talking exterior.

CHAPTER 9

When Elizabeth Emerson was a senior at Smith College in Northampton, Massachusetts, the CIA was actively recruiting from the Ivy League men's schools and from the Seven Sisters women's colleges. The spy agency had decided women had good brains after all and made good analysts. The CIA was especially interested in hiring economics majors because they'd found that people who understood economics had analytical minds, were able to process information in a systematic way, and could reach conclusions and solve problems. The CIA was not looking for covert operatives when they interviewed the college seniors. They were not hiring women to wear the classic fedora and trench coat spy outfit, lean against a lamppost in rainy, post-war Vienna, and wait for a rendezvous with a Russian double agent. The CIA wanted desk jockeys.

Elizabeth, an economics major, was of the duck-and-cover generation and had lived in the shadow of the Cold War all her life. She was intrigued by the pitch from the CIA and decided to look into what would be required for her to pursue a career with The Agency. She went to the initial meeting on the Smith campus and then made the trip to Boston with three other women from her college class. In Boston, the four were given a battery of tests, designed to evaluate their abilities to do the work the CIA would require of them. This was the first step in the application process. Those who passed the initial tests would be given more tests, some interviews, and then perhaps the offer of a job in Washington, D.C.

Elizabeth scored "off the charts" in the inductive reasoning part of the testing. Only one other person in CIA recruitment history had ever scored higher than she did in this one very important area, critical to the kind of work the CIA needed done. Although she had never realized it before, Elizabeth was told she could read and evaluate vast amounts of material in an incredibly short period of time and come up with an accurate analysis and conclusion. The testing people made a big deal over her, and this embarrassed the somewhat introverted Elizabeth. They singled her out, and she didn't like it. Since she'd never known she had this special skill, she wasn't that impressed with herself. She wondered what all the fuss was about.

Elizabeth had been seriously dating a graduate of Princeton who was now a first-year medical student at Tulane. Elizabeth was in love, and she thought Richard Carpenter was, too. It was 1966, and women married young. It was early in the women's liberation movement. Not all women, even very well-educated ones, had careers. Many became housewives and mothers. Elizabeth had always been very independent, but she couldn't imagine her life without Richard. Richard was not enthusiastic about her pursuing a career with the CIA. He didn't really understand that she wouldn't be in any danger, sitting in an office in Langley,

Virginia, reading newspapers and looking at data sets. He wanted her with him in New Orleans, although he'd not yet asked her to marry him.

When he did pop the question, Elizabeth said yes. They would be married that summer. The CIA was disappointed when Elizabeth turned down their offer of a position as an analyst. They pulled out all the stops and harassed her mercilessly for the remainder of her senior year. They played the "serving your country" card and everything else they could think of. Elizabeth did not waiver, and she and Richard were married in August. She got a job teaching in the New Orleans public schools, and the CIA became a distant memory. But the CIA kept its eyes on her, and years later when she decided to change careers, they welcomed her with open arms.

After she left New Orleans, Elizabeth went to graduate school. After spending two years on the faculty at the University of Texas at El Paso, she took a position teaching economics and economic history at a small college in Maryland. She was pressured to change a grade so that a failing student could become a "C" student. The student, who had not put forth any effort whatsoever in her class, had to have a "C" in order to maintain his eligibility to play basketball for the college team. The academic dean leaned on and threatened Elizabeth. Because she was only a part-time professor, the dean told her she could easily be fired from her position, if she didn't do as she was told and change the grade. Elizabeth refused to knuckle under to the threats and gave the student a "D." He had barely made the "D" and had just escaped failing her class by the skin of his teeth. After she'd turned in her grades, someone went to the registrar's office and changed the student's grade to a "C." The young man never missed a step or a dribble on the basketball court because of his failing academic work. Learning and getting an education had proven to be an afterthought, or given no thought at all, when it came to qualifying for a sports team.

Elizabeth thought she could hang on to her job, but she decided she did not want to be a part of the rotten system any more. She'd always known academia was fraught with politics, corrupted by competition to get ahead of one's colleagues, and filled with bloated and narcissistic egos. She decided life was short, and she didn't have to play the stupid games required to succeed in the university arena. She didn't want to be around the grasping and ambitious meanies any more.

She decided to take a job that she'd been offered years earlier. She made some phone calls and began the difficult task of hiring babysitters, drivers, and a housekeeper. She made complicated arrangements for her duties at home to be taken care of when she was gone. She began to build her cover story, that she was taking a research position at the Wharton School in Philadelphia. It was a three-hour commute one-way to her new job, and she would be away from home a couple of nights a week, sometimes more. It was a big commitment, but her new boss was willing to work with her to maintain the illusion of the imaginary job she supposedly had at the University of Pennsylvania. She was a valuable commodity, and the CIA helped her manage her home duties and her cover position in Philadelphia, as she committed to the more dangerous job she'd really been hired to do.

Most of her work was in Virginia, using the skills she'd demonstrated when the CIA had wanted to hire her years earlier. Occasionally she had to make trips overseas. None of her family or friends ever doubted for a minute that she was working at the Wharton School. They thought it was odd that she was gone from home so much, but by now, two of her children were away at boarding school in New England. Only one daughter was still at home. No one, not even Richard Carpenter, was allowed to know what Elizabeth did when she was out of town.

It was a rocky period in the Carpenters' marriage. Richard was consumed with his work as head of the surgical pathology department and clinical laboratory at the local hospital. He participated in the children's activities whenever he could, but he was pretty much oblivious to Elizabeth's needs at this time in their lives. He was angry that she wasn't around all the time, as she had always been before, but he was so preoccupied with his own career, he only noticed she wasn't there when something went wrong.

Richard Carpenter had risen to the top of his career and was the main partner in his pathology group, Richard Carpenter, M.D., P.A. He had done his internship and residency at the University of Pennsylvania, and during those years he'd had the opportunity to work with Philadelphia's medical examiner. In addition to spending his days accompanying the Chief Medical Examiner, Richard had done moonlighting for the medical examiner's office to earn extra money. The young doctor became a skilled and convincing expert witness. He was a favorite with prosecutors because juries loved his boyish looks and earnest, honest voice. When he was on the witness stand, members of the jury believed everything Richard Carpenter, M.D. had to say. If he gave evidence against someone in a murder trial, that person was always convicted. Vance Stillinger, M.D. was the Philadelphia Medical Examiner, and Richard Carpenter M.D. became his golden boy.

Carpenter's testimony had sent a number of very bad guys to prison. The child molesters, murderers, drug dealers, and drivers who had committed serial DUIs all should have known it was their own behavior that had caused them to be convicted. But bad boys and girls always want to find someone other than themselves to blame. Carpenter became a lightning rod for their anger, and some wanted to blame the blonde, cherub-faced scientist who had so convincingly swayed the juries that had convicted them. Occasionally, a defendant would shake his fist at Carpenter when he was on the witness stand.

Once a man stood up and shouted threats at Carpenter after he'd given his expert witness testimony. The defendant, who had been resoundingly drunk when he'd crossed the highway's median strip and run headlong into a van full of children, said Carpenter had misrepresented his blood alcohol level. The driver of the van and four of the children had died, and the defendant was sent to prison. The drunk vowed that when he got out of jail, he would hunt down Carpenter and kill him and his family.

Elizabeth Carpenter had just come home from the hospital after giving birth to the Carpenters' second child. Law enforcement took the threats against Carpenter and his family seriously, and until the convicted criminal was sentenced and safely locked away, the police kept a guard on Carpenter's rented house in the Philadelphia suburbs. Elizabeth wondered who would be there in a few years to watch out for her family when the man was released from prison.

Stillinger tried to convince his protégé to stay in Philadelphia and become a forensic pathologist, but Carpenter owed Uncle Sam two years of his life, serving in the U.S. Army. Furthermore, Carpenter had educational debts and needed and wanted to earn some money. He wanted more income than the salary of an urban medical examiner would pay him, and he didn't want to live in a city. The Army sent Carpenter to William Beaumont Army Medical Center in Texas for two years, and from there, Carpenter took a position at a hospital in a small town in Maryland where he built a successful pathology practice. He still testified as an expert witness, but the threats that had come his way when he was at the Philadelphia Medical Examiner's Office were long-forgotten. The question was, had the men he'd helped send to prison forgotten him?

CHAPTER 10

2021

When it was Elizabeth's and Richard's turn to pay for their tour, Wilford Brimley, who, when you got closer to him, actually looked more like an ex-military guy than a salesman for Quaker Oats, wanted to know all about them.

"You are listed here under Shoemaker, but you are the Carpenters. We have been trying to figure out who in your group is named Shoemaker. We have Steele, Richardson, MacDermott, Merriman, Ritter, and Carpenter. But we don't have any Shoemaker here." Brimley looked suspiciously at Richard Carpenter. Brimley was demanding answers.

"It's a long story about who Shoemaker is. The men in our group of friends all went to camp together back in the 1950s. The camp was called Camp Shoemaker. It's complicated. The person who made the reservations this year put down the name Shoemaker. It's not important. It's the name of a camp." Richard tried to explain and wondered if the man really wanted to know all of this.

Brimley looked closely at Elizabeth and Richard Carpenter. He decided they passed muster and were probably telling him the truth about who Shoemaker was, even though they hadn't really told him much of anything at all. Richard handed over his credit card, and they were given a badge and lot of instructions about what they could and could not take with them on the tour. They'd read the brochure ahead of time, and Elizabeth had left her purse in the safe in their room. Brimley looked closely at Elizabeth's wheelchair.

Elizabeth's radar had already gone up, even before they'd had to stand in line to pay for their tour of the bunker. Everything else went automatically onto the hotel bill, but this tour had to be paid for separately. Maybe a different system was needed because people who were not staying at the hotel could join the bunker tours.

Elizabeth had watched as Henley Breckenridge paid for her tickets to tour the bunker. When Elizabeth and Richard made it to Brimley's desk, Elizabeth definitely had the feeling she was being vetted. It was "vetted light" to be sure, but she thought she saw a very small camera positioned directly at the chairs where they were sitting. One chair had been moved out of the way to accommodate her wheelchair. They'd positioned the wheelchair very carefully. Hmmmm. Their tour guide was standing behind the older man who looked like Wilford Brimley and was taking credit cards. The handsome tour guide was carefully looking over everyone who was going to be on his tour. Elizabeth told herself she was being paranoid.

Everyone who had read the brochure about the bunker knew that no one was allowed to take a cell phone or a purse or bag of any kind on the bunker tour. If the place had been decommissioned in 1992, why did it matter if somebody took a cell phone photograph? Were the Russians or the Chinese really anxious to get a look at the 1960s-vintage bunk beds or the dated dining room with its mid-century modern plastic tables and orange chairs? Of course, everyone would comply or they would not be allowed to continue on the tour. It had been a long time since any of the reunion group had been asked to leave their cell phones and purses behind . . . for any reason.

Did Wilford Brimley really care where they were from? Was he just a friendly, chatty older man? A Walmart greeter type? Elizabeth didn't think so. The man with the mustache was ex-military. Elizabeth was certain of it. She chided herself. Lots of people were ex-military. Her own husband Richard was ex-military. In fact, every one of the Camp Shoemaker group was ex-military. No big deal.

The young man who was assigned to be their tour guide was excellent. In fact, he was too excellent. He was much better informed and too well-spoken to be a typical tour guide. He was definitely keeping an eye on Elizabeth's wheelchair and on Elizabeth. Did anyone think she was wearing an exploding vest underneath her windbreaker? She was chilly in the public rooms of the Woodbrier and figured the bunker in the basement of the West Virginia Wing was below ground and therefore would be even colder. She had a bulky sweater on underneath her jacket.

Did their tour guide think she had rigged her wheelchair to be some kind of spy camera or weapon? Did the metal rods that supported the back and arms of the wheelchair look like they could quickly be converted into rifles? Maybe they thought she had cameras rigged into the spoked wheels. She was, it was true, the only person on this particular tour who was riding in a wheelchair. But surely she was not the first or the only handicapped person to take the tour. She also had a cane with her. Could the cane be a pipe bomb in disguise? Elizabeth realized that now she was just being silly.

The other people on their tour appeared to be just like those of the reunion group. Nobody looked very different or weird or scary or anything like a terrorist. There were people of all ages, a total of about fifteen people on their tour. Henley was definitely a standout with her clanking concho belt. The guide was already telling the story of the bunker as they walked towards the elevators. Richard pushed Elizabeth's wheelchair through the hallways toward the West Virginia Wing of the hotel. The Carpenters room was directly above the bunker on the fourth floor of the West Virginia Wing. Apparently, all the rooms for handicapped people were located in that wing.

When they arrived at the huge blast-proof doors that would have sealed off the bunker in case of an attack, their guide told them they had to hand over any cell phones, bags, or purses anyone in the group might still have in their possession. He collected the errant items and deposited them in a locker. He explained why cell phones and bags were not allowed. Elizabeth thought the reason he gave for disallowing electronics and purses sounded pretty lame and quite frankly bogus. "CSX leases space from the Woodbrier. They keep the servers for several Fortune 500 companies here. So you can see this facility is still a high level and important place."

When Elizabeth heard Henley's voice, she held her breath. She knew Henley would not allow the guide to get away with much in the way of BS. Elizabeth had thought to herself that there was some duplicity to be found in the words of the tour guide. She couldn't exactly put her finger on what was bothering her. He was too polished and a little bit slick. He knew people didn't like having to leave their purses and their cell phones behind in a locker, and he had a whole spiel ready to tell them about why that had to happen.

Henley was not going to let him get away with his prepared speech. "I know and you know and everybody else knows that a cell phone is not going to do anything to interrupt the working of the servers or whatever you claim CSX is doing here. Did you take our bags and phones away to create a little drama for the tour? Or is there really something else going on here, something you don't want anybody to take a picture of with a phone? I can't begin to imagine what that might be."

Henley, bless her heart, intended to hold this cute guy's feet to the fire. The handsome, confident tour guide blanched. He looked as if he was not accustomed to any of his gaggle taking issue with having to give up their phones and put their things into a locker. He was not used to having his authority or his nice, neat prepared talk challenged. He didn't have a quick answer for Henley, but he rallied to try to answer her question.

"The Woodbrier leases the space to CSX, and it is at their request that we do not allow cell phones or any kind of bags inside the facility. We give tours to the public because there is great curiosity and tremendous interest about what was hidden here during the Cold War. These tours of the bunker attract the attention of tourists from all over the world. Visitors come here to see the secrets of this place for themselves. We are attempting to comply with the requests of our current tenant and at the same time allow the public in to see the sights."

"Well, I love seeing the sights and find this whole Cold War bunker thing incredibly fascinating. But as to what's going on here now and that whole CSX song and dance, I think you are feeding us a line of bull." Henley didn't mince words. She spoke her mind. Elizabeth put her hand in front of her face and tried not to let anyone see that she was laughing. She'd been thinking the same things that Henley was thinking, but Henley'd had the hutzpah to take on the tour guide and say them all out loud and to his face.

The guide had no response for Henley this time. He gulped and stared at her and moved on with his talk. "Moving on . . . to your left are the blast-proof doors. These doors are intended to protect the occupants of the bunker, and they are the doors that connect the bunker to the rest of the Woodbrier. Note how thick these metal barricades really are. Even more interesting, however, is how cleverly they are hidden behind a movable false wall. That wall is covered with wallpaper that matches that of the surrounding walls. If you were walking by or even looking closely at this wall, it would never catch your eye. Nothing would seem unusual. It would just appear to be a wall with wallpaper on it. It is essentially invisible . . . unless you know what is behind it. These doors were designed to protect those inside the bunker from radioactivity. They were designed to be closed and sealed in case of an attack."

The tour proceeded past the bulky but well-disguised doors that marked the entrance to the bunker. "We are now in the exhibition room. This area is actually part of the bunker and would have been sealed off during a nuclear attack. But this large room was also routinely used on a daily basis. When companies came to the Woodbrier for their trade shows, they used this space to set up booths and displays. Hundreds of corporate meetings used this room. We now have more modern convention spaces that provide companies with the electronics they need today, but back in the sixties and seventies and eighties, when the bunker was still a secret facility, this area was heavily used. It was a multi-functional space, and no one ever suspected that it was part of a nuclear war bunker. It was the perfect spot for companies to display their products of all kinds at a meeting or convention." Those taking the tour were allowed to walk around in this dated and empty room which still had its old-fashioned linoleum floor. There was not really much to see. There were many structural pillars that supported the rest of the building. There was a pile of mattresses stacked in one corner.

"There is another set of blast-proof doors on your left. These giant doors were the entrance through which the enormous volume of supplies of all kinds were brought into the bunker. Step this way." The tour group went through the doors and were outside in an alleyway. "Special trucks rolled down this ramp and stopped right outside this set of doors. The doors swung open so the trucks could be unloaded. Resupply of the facility was a massive and constant process. Think about what had to be done on an ongoing basis. Everything had to be prepared at all times and turn-key ready for instantaneous use. We never knew when the Soviets would attack. Everything had to be kept at a one-hundred percent level of readiness 24/7/365 . . . and it was . . . for decades."

"In case of attack, these doors would also be sealed. No more trucks would be coming down the ramp. No food or supplies of any kind would be coming through those doors for ninety days. Whatever was on hand inside the bunker when the doors were sealed would have to be sufficient to supply more than one thousand people's needs for three months. It was a gargantuan undertaking."

It was a fascinating tour to be sure, but Elizabeth definitely had the feeling, as Henley had openly questioned, that something else was going on here. They were seeing only a very small and highly contrived sliver of what this place had been like during the Cold War. It was an intriguing sliver, but it felt like a stage set. Elizabeth was reminded of the "rude bridge that arched the flood" that she had seen in Concord, Massachusetts. This was a museum display, a presentation for curious visitors. The public was not really being shown the magnanimity, the enormous scope of what had happened here in past decades. She also agreed with Henley that they were not being given a clue as to what was really going on here at the present time. Elizabeth was suspicious, but she would not have missed this tour for anything. Even if it was bogus, it was exciting and mysterious, especially for someone who was a war baby and a Cold War kid.

In one of the display rooms that the tour group was led through, there was a door with a glass top. The glass had "CSX" and "DO NOT ENTER" in big black letters embossed on the glass. The people on the tour could look through the glass top of the door, and everyone could see a staircase just inside. The tour guide pointed to the door with the glass top and put his finger to his lips in the classic hush, don't tell signal.

Isabelle leaned over Elizabeth's wheelchair and whispered to her, "If it's such a big secret, why is he pointing that out to us?" Elizabeth was wondering the same thing. She suspected he doth protest too much. She was waiting for Henley to say something outrageous to the tour guide about his performance vis à vis the glass door, but when she looked around, she realized that Henley had disappeared. Had Henley seen enough of the prescribed tour and gone back to the wedding festivities? Elizabeth hoped Henley had not decided to explore the bunker on her own, without supervision. How had she been able to slip away from the watchful eyes of their handsome guide? Elizabeth really liked Henley and didn't want her to get herself into trouble.

CHAPTER 11

Cameron Richardson had always loved to build things. From the time he was a child, he'd been taking things apart and putting them back together again. He loved to tinker. He loved to invent. He liked to change something, even just a little bit, to make it work better. That was the way his mind worked. There were stories of the rockets he and a friend had constructed launched; they were just in junior high school at the time. There were stories of gunpowder explosions in the woods and the resulting craters in the ground. Of course he would study science when he entered the small, exclusive southern college. He transferred to a university with an engineering program for his last two years, and upon graduation, he was immediately recruited by IBM.

Mastering the technology of computers opened up a whole new world to Cameron, and it wasn't long before he was out on his own, inventing and tinkering and making things better. He built an innovative and tremendously successful computer empire. Then he built a second revolutionary electronics enterprise. The man lived to challenge the status quo, and his head was always in the future.

Cameron's businesses dealt with enormous amounts of data, and thanks to computers, this data could be accessed relatively easily. It made him millions. It was inevitable that the U.S. federal government would, from time to time, come asking for help with something. Cameron was a straight shooter, a good guy. He was an entrepreneur of the first order, but he was also honest through and through his character and soul. He would not knowingly do something that was illegal or wrong. Sometimes he helped out the feds, and sometimes he didn't. He knew how to say no, even to Uncle Sam. When he said yes, it was never for his own gain but because he felt it was his patriotic duty to lend his expertise. He helped crack the cell phones that led to the arrests of terrorists. He helped out whenever he felt it was the right thing to do. He didn't want his part in any of these operations to become public, but there were some people who knew he had been instrumental in tracking down and gathering evidence on the bad guys. The question was, did any of the bad guys know that Cameron Richardson had helped to finger them and put them away?

There was no question about it. Cameron had information on everybody and everything. He didn't use it for nefarious purposes, but he did have it. Anybody who knew what his companies were all about knew he had the goods, and the bads. Anyone who has achieved the level of success that Cameron had, and anyone who has made the hard decisions about everything, including personnel, has acquired some enemies along the way. Because Cameron was a fair and benevolent boss, he'd made fewer enemies than most, but he had appropriately fired the dead wood that unfortunately but inevitably turned up, from time to time, among his employees. He'd made some people angry. He was cavalier about his own security, but his second wife Sidney worried about him.

Cameron had married for the first time when he was just out of college, and he'd married a woman several years older than himself. His friends had been puzzled about the union that, to those on the outside, seemed unusual. Were these two well-matched? Did they have anything at all in common? The guys loved their buddy and accepted his marital decision. Sometimes, love is strange. The marriage produced two children but eventually came to an end. The failure of the marriage wasn't anybody's fault.

After being a bachelor for a few years, Cameron met the love of his life. He had made his fortune and his reputation, and he finally had the time to invest in a relationship. Sidney Putnam insisted on it. She let Cameron know that, to make their marriage work, he needed to listen to what was important to her and spend time with her. He was wildly in love with Sidney, but she refused to marry him until he learned that she would be an equal partner in their marriage. She was not a back seat kind of woman.

Sidney's first marriage had also ended in divorce. She had one son, to whom she was devoted, and she'd been able to remain friends with her first husband, her son's father. Most people can't achieve this almost impossible feat, but Sidney had people skills that most people don't. Sidney had been the runner-up in her state's beauty pageant for the Miss America contest. She'd always had the looks, but more importantly, she had the smarts—of all kinds.

Sidney's most outstanding way of being smart was her gift for reading people. Her uncanny ability to know when someone was lying was an asset when she worked as a consultant for the Texas Department of Criminal Justice. She was the prosecutor's secret weapon. She consulted on jury selections and sat in on law enforcement interviews with suspects and witnesses. She was never wrong in her assessments. She didn't necessarily tell the authorities what they wanted to hear. She told the truth. And sometimes, nobody wanted to hear the truth. Sidney demanded that her assistance in criminal cases remain confidential, but she was almost too good to be true. Eventually, what she could do leaked out beyond the walls of the justice department, and she knew being exposed could put her in danger.

Her ability to vet people was invaluable to Sidney when she started her own business. As a single parent, she needed to support herself and her son. With her business, You Are Home, she identified a need that existed and built a business that responded to that need. Her first clients were corporations that frequently moved their employees from place to place. Corporations arranged to move their employee's household goods and paid for the packing and moving and unpacking. The gap in these employee benefits came when the wife, and it usually was the wife back in the day, had to put it all away and set up the new household. The husband, and it usually was the husband back in the day, was off doing his corporate thing, and the wife was at home with the kids, trying to find a place to put their stuff in the new kitchen and the unfamiliar closets.

Sidney's company was hired to come in and put their household goods away where they belonged. Her well-trained employees would organize the kitchen, at the housewife's direction, but with suggestions from the experts about the best kitchen logistics to make it fully functional. They put shelf paper in the drawers and on the shelves. They put away everybody's clothes—organizing, folding, and hanging everything in the most efficient and easy-to-access way. You Are Home would arrange for a room to be painted and would bring in other professionals to position furniture to its best advantage and hang art work. Sidney was good at this, and she taught her carefully-selected employees to be good at it, too. She charged high prices for her services, but there was a huge demand for what she was selling. Her company grew rapidly. She was a very successful entrepreneur in her own right when she literally ran into Cameron Richardson in a restaurant.

It was an expensive steak house in Fort Worth, and Sidney was there having lunch and closing a deal with a corporate client. It was summer, and she was dressed in a stunning white designer linen dress. She had a white cashmere cardigan sweater over her shoulders because the air conditioning was turned up so high in the steak house, to counter the July Texas heat. She got up to go to the ladies' room, and a tall, good-looking man didn't see her making her way through the tables in the dark, wood-paneled restaurant. The man pushed back his chair and stood up from his table with a large glass of iced tea in his hand. He ran straight into Sidney and spilled the entire glass of tea all over her dress, cashmere sweater, and expensive white high-heeled shoes. They were both stunned. He looked into the bright and beautiful eyes of the woman whose clothes he'd just ruined and couldn't turn away. To say it was love at first sight on his part would probably be the truth. She was angry that her outfit had been spoiled, but Cameron Richardson was so gracious about sending a car to drive her home to change her clothes. He insisted on paying for dry cleaning and replaced the clothes that could not be saved. Sidney had to soften her annoyance.

She had no idea who Cameron Richardson was, and they'd had several dates before Sidney fully grasped the extent of Cameron's wealth and success. Sidney was not looking for a relationship of any kind at this point in her life. She had a business to run and a child to raise. She was incredibly busy. But Cameron always went after what he wanted, and he usually got it. He went after Sidney like nothing he'd ever gone after in his life. Cameron pulled out all the stops to court the independent and strong-willed Sidney Putnam. The more she got to know him, the more she realized that Cameron was not only a success. He was also a kind and caring human being. She finally had to admit to herself that she'd fallen in love with the man.

CHAPTER 12

2021

The next day, the rest of the group was taking an afternoon walking tour of the gardens. An on-and-off drizzle of rain was falling, and it was too difficult in any weather to push a wheelchair on the grass and gravel paths of the Woodbrier's gardens. Elizabeth had an important lunch date anyway. Richard pushed Elizabeth's wheelchair to Draper's Restaurant before he joined the others. Henley had promised to return Elizabeth and her wheelchair to the room after they'd had lunch. Elizabeth had been wondering what had happened to Henley during the last part of the tour the day before, but she was not going to ask Henley anything about that.

Henley joined Elizabeth at their table for two at Draper's. "I think this is the best restaurant in the place. It's the only place open for lunch right now, except for Sam Snead's. That's mostly for golfers, and it's way over there in that other building. I had lunch here at Draper's the other day, and the chicken pot pie is exceptional. It's a little small, but I'm going to order it again. I know Dorothy Draper was a famous and fabulous interior designer and transformed the Woodbrier in the 1950s. She did a spectacular job with all of that. But, if she ever made a chicken pot pie in her life or if this is even her recipe, I'll eat my hat. Of course, my hat is back in my room. I've been informed that my hat is too disreputable to be seen in this fancy place. As soon as the wedding is over with, I'm going to be wearing my hat again." The menu did advertise and imply that the chicken pot pie had been Dorothy Draper's own creation. Both Henley and Elizabeth ordered the pot pie.

"How are the wedding events going? I know the rehearsal dinner is tonight."

"I avoid hanging out with those people as much as I can. I have to dress up for the dinner tonight as well as for the wedding tomorrow. I don't mind dressing up for the wedding, but I'd just as soon skip the rehearsal dinner. It's being hosted by my niece's future in-laws, and I don't like them. Anyway, I'm not going to waste my time or yours whining about the wedding. I want to tell you that Sui Wai has made a reasonably good recovery from her torture and starvation by those rotten Chinese Commies last year. She stayed with me for three weeks and told me everything. Sue Keely, the friend who helped her escape from Hong Kong, drove down from Ojai to pick her up. I hated to see poor Sui Wai leave, but the Keely woman seemed as if she was quite fond of Sui Wai and would take good care of her. After Sui Wai disappeared, when she was kidnapped, Sue Keely had believed for many weeks that she was dead. Keely hired a private investigator to try to find out what had happened to Sui Wai, but he found nothing. As you might imagine, she was overcome with emotion when she was reunited with Sui Wai." Henley paused and took a deep breath. Sui Wai's extreme torture and starvation by her Chinese kidnappers had touched something very deep inside Henley Breckenridge.

Henley continued, "But Sui Wai has not recovered mentally, I'm afraid, from her ordeal. She still wants to speak out and be the whistleblower she thinks she is, but she's very paranoid and doesn't feel as if she can trust anybody. It isn't any wonder she's short on trust after what she's been through. I'm trying to find somebody who will write her story for her, but nobody wants to touch what she has to say with a ten-foot pole. Everybody is afraid of the current state of politics in the U.S. right now. They're afraid to say the wrong thing, and/or maybe they're afraid of being taken out by the Chinese. Bunch of pussies in my opinion."

"Keep me posted about Sui Wai. I'm glad she has at least recovered her physical health, and I certainly understand why she is reluctant to trust anyone. They almost killed her when they kept her imprisoned at that building in Harmony, California."

"To look at that place now, you'd never know anything had happened there. The Feds swooped in and shut it all down. That corrugated iron building where Sui Wai was held for a month has been completely demolished and taken away. The weeds are already growing up around the foundation. The woods will more than take back the site in a year. You should have seen the to-do that was made over the motor home that ended up halfway inside the building. Apparently, the Steeles didn't want to lie and say the motorhome had been stolen. They said there had been an accident, which I guess is kind of close to the truth. And they told the company they'd rented the motorhome from just where to find it. My information is all according to local gossip, so I may not have it exactly right. I guess the Steeles had good insurance on the thing, so they didn't take too much of a financial hit when it was totally destroyed. The company that owned the motorhome tried to bring in a crane to separate the motorhome from the corrugated iron structure. The crane got stuck in the woods. Of course it did. What were they thinking? Anyway, they finally had to take the motorhome apart with a blowtorch to get it out of there. The vehicle was worthless after they did that, but maybe they can use it for parts. Ha!"

"The Steeles have never mentioned anything at all to me or to the others in the group about the motorhome. No one has asked them, either."

"You can't blame anybody for not talking about that. I'm not surprised there's not been a single word spoken about it, and I promise you, there will not be. Nobody wants to talk about that. I've heard, by way of the grapevine, that the reason the whole thing has been covered up is because somebody in the U.S. State Department doesn't want to stir up any trouble in international relations. Who do they think they're kidding? The Chinese Communist government hates us and everything about us. They'd like to destroy us. That's no secret to anybody that's still drawing breath. But somebody in the U.S. State Department wants to pretend that isn't true. Somebody in power does not want the U.S. public to know how awful Communist China really is. They also don't want us to know that the Chinese Communist Party is doing its dirty deeds inside this country and to our citizens. Sui Wai isn't a U.S. citizen, but that other scientist who was in the warehouse with her was born in the USA and lived here his whole life. This whole cover-up thing is not only bull; it's criminal. Those people ought to have to pay for what they did. They kidnapped two people and almost killed one of them. They should be prosecuted, but they never will be. But who's asking me? Nobody!"

"Do you still go to La Buona Ricetta? I love the food at that place."

"Of course I still go there. I'm one of the owners. I support my investments."

They ate in silence for a few minutes. Henley finally spoke up. "I have to confess that one of the reasons I wanted to come to the Woodbrier and to this wedding is because I've been curious about this place for a long time. I heard about the bunker many years ago, long before 1992 when that reporter from *The Washington Post* spilled the beans about what was hidden here under the West Virginia Wing."

"How could you possibly have heard about it that long ago? I thought the existence of this bunker was one of the U.S. government's best-kept secret operations."

"It was, but I did know all about it and a lot more than they will ever tell you on their forty-dollar tour of the place. I went off exploring on my own yesterday after I'd heard enough from that pretty boy tour guide of ours. I'll tell you what I found, but first, I want to tell you about the secrets of the Cold War bunker that Mr. Preppy Pants would never have been allowed to talk about."

Henley continued. "I had a guy who came to work for me at my ranch in the 1980s. He was retired military and had worked for the Army Corps of Engineers. He did construction work, and he was really good. I think he might have specialized in concrete, but he could do everything. He was more than able to do anything and everything I asked him to do in the construction and repairs department at my ranch. His name was Glen, and he was one of the people who helped build the bunker and the West Virginia Wing here at this resort. He was sworn to secrecy for life about what he'd been working on at the Woodbrier, and he was a loyal American patriot. But in his later years, he began to lose it mentally. I think he was in the early stages of dementia, or maybe he was just losing his social filters due to old age. I'm not a neurologist. Anyway, he was a hard worker, and he lived and worked at my ranch for years. I was fond of him, and he liked to tell me stories about things he'd done when he was in the military. He'd done secret building stuff for the Army Corps of Engineers all over the world. The work he did at the Woodbrier was a highlight for him. He was very proud of having participated in the work he did here. Of course, it was all super-secret, and he could have been imprisoned for life or even put to death for telling me all the things he told me. I never breathed a word of what he said to me about any of it. Glen died a few years after the newspaper story by Ted Gup came out. Before Glen died, he told me even more about what he'd worked on here at the Woodbrier and in other places."

"Did he tell you anything that *The Washington Post* didn't know about?"

"Of course he did, and I'm going to tell it all to you. Glen wanted to tell me about these things he'd done, I think, to have somebody to share his secrets with. He trusted me to keep his confidences. It's tough to keep a secret your whole life and never be able to tell anybody about any of it. Finally, at the end of his life, he wanted to talk about his secrets. It was kind of like a death bed confession, in a way. I'm not anywhere close to being at the end of my life, but since you are here and I am here, I'm going to tell you all about this place."

"I thought there was more going on here than the bunker tour and that song and dance about CSX. I can maybe see them not wanting cell phones in there and not wanting people to take pictures. But the whole thing with CSX feels and sounds like a cover story. They won't let you bring a purse in? Really?" Elizabeth let Henley know she also suspected something sketchy was going on with regard to the story the Woodbrier was telling about the bunker's current use.

Henley had more to tell and continued her story. "I know for sure there's something else going on here besides servers and CSX, but I have not for the life of me been able to find out what it is. More on that later. But now back to 1958 and the building of the bunker . . . and others." Henley knew she had Elizabeth's attention. Henley seemed to be relieved in a way and enjoyed being able to tell what she knew. "As you know, the bunker at the Woodbrier was built to house both houses of Congress in case of a nuclear attack from the Soviets. 'To ensure the continuity of government' was the official way they put it. EKT! Everybody knows that now. And, the Woodbrier even offers a tour to show you the bunk beds, the cafeteria, the offices, the decontamination showers, and all the rest of it." Henley was trying to keep her sarcasm at bay.

"Building and keeping the bunker at the ready every day for all those years had to be an overwhelming and prodigious undertaking. On the tour, we were even allowed to sit in the auditorium that was built in the bunker for the U.S. House of Representatives to hold its sessions. The reason for this fortress, for building the bunker in the first place was, we have been told, all about ensuring the continuity of government . . . supposedly. But, the question nobody asks, and I've always wondered why nobody ever asks it, is about what was supposed to happen to the other two branches of our government? Our Constitution was very specifically crafted to provide this country with three branches of government.

The Legislative Branch, the House and the Senate, is only one of the three branches. What about the Judicial Branch and the Executive Branch? If we are so concerned about ensuring 'the continuity of government,' what happens to the other branches in a nuclear attack? Were they chopped liver? In case of a nuclear attack, were they to be discarded? Or ignored? Why were provisions not made for the other two branches? General Dwight Eisenhower was a smart guy, and he knew all about the three branches. Hells bells! He was elected twice to be the POTUS, the CEO of the Executive Branch. He had to have given some thought to what was going to happen to the presidents who followed him into the White House, as well as to the nine guys who wore the black robes and sat over there at the Supreme Court."

Henley smiled. "I am happy to say that it is no longer nine guys in that hallowed chamber. There are also gals wearing those black robes now. And that didn't happen nearly soon enough in my opinion. But back to my story. Ike would not have neglected to provide a safe haven for the other two branches of government in case of a nuclear attack. We know there were no provisions for either of those other two branches of government here at the Woodbrier. Ted Gup never mentioned a word about them when he wrote his exposé revealing the secrets of the bunker at the Woodbrier. If there had been facilities for them here, that would have all been part of the story when the rest of it came out . . . about the Congress being kept safe in the underground facility here. So, what about the President, and what about the Supreme Court? Where were they supposed to go?"

"Actually, I had wondered about those other two branches of government and figured they would also have been sequestered someplace. I assumed they'd been provided for in a different location, another very secret place. It would be easier to build a bunker for nine men and their staffs and for the President and his staff than it would have been to build this enormous hideout for 535 members of Congress plus staff. Whatever that facility was, it would have been easier to build. It would not have taken nearly as long as this facility at the Woodbrier took to build. Being so much smaller in size, it would also have been a lot easier to keep it a secret. I assumed the facilities that were built for the Supreme Court and for the Executive Branch were just never discovered by the press. Nobody ever found out about them and wrote about them. So the public has never known where they were. They are still a secret."

"Bingo! Elizabeth, I knew the first time I laid eyes on you that you were smart. You are exactly correct. That is what I really wanted to tell you about. Glen, my former Army Corps of Engineers sergeant, worked here at the Woodbrier and helped to build the bunker and the West Virginia Wing. But he also did some work at the site of the other bunkers . . . the ones that have never been revealed." Henley was on a roll, and Elizabeth knew her part in this was to listen. What Henley had to tell her was fascinating, and Elizabeth had no trouble keeping her mouth shut and her ears open.

CHAPTER 13

TYLER MERRIMAN WAS A HIGH school football star. The Air Force Academy recruited Tyler to play football, and he played for one year before he was sidelined by a shoulder injury. Tyler stayed on and graduated. He subsequently earned an MBA from Stanford. He became a pilot for the United States Air Force and spent ten years flying military missions for the USA. He never talked about the years he'd spent in the USAF, but his closest friends speculated that he was flying the Lockheed SR-71, "the Blackbird" spy plane that supposedly had the capability to see the numbers and letters on the license plate of a car parked in Red Square. When anyone came right out and asked him if he'd flown the Blackbird, Tyler would hum a few bars of the Beatles' song of the same name and smile his enigmatic smile. If he had flown the Blackbird, he would have been able to see everything and everybody from way up there. But he would never tell.

Tyler had married, briefly, when he was in the military, but his wife was young and somewhat spoiled. She resented the time Tyler spent away from home, and they divorced when they'd been married for less than two years. Tyler moved to Northern California after he left the Air Force. He built a commercial real estate empire and became a wealthy man. Tyler dated well-known and glamorous women—movie actresses, anchorwomen who appeared on national television, and female politicos. He was very good looking and a much sought-after bachelor, but he successfully avoided the altar for decades after his first marriage ended.

Tyler Merriman had been smart and lucky in his business dealings, and he was a consummate athlete. He bought a condominium in Telluride, Colorado so he could ski for several months in the winter. Because he was such a skilled and outstanding performer on the slopes, it wasn't long before he was hired as a ski instructor. His time was his own, and he arranged his schedule so he could spend most of the winter in Telluride. He found he loved teaching others to ski. Tyler had his own plane and flew around the country to check on his commercial real estate empire. He hiked and biked and ran, and he even sometimes played squash when he couldn't be outdoors. Tyler was a very active guy. He decided he wanted to be closer to his condominium in Telluride and eventually relocated from California to Colorado.

Tyler had been attending the reunions for years and looked forward to seeing his old friends and their wives and girlfriends. He'd never brought a date or a partner to one of the events until he'd met Lilleth Dubois when he was in his early seventies. They had a long-term relationship, and Lilleth had attended several of the Camp Shoemaker reunions. Tyler wasn't sharing the details of their breakup, and no one was asking any questions. But Lilleth and Tyler were no longer a couple, and Lilleth would not be attending any more reunions. Tyler was still athletic and energetic. He was still a force on the ski slopes and in other demanding athletic arenas. Who knew what the future might hold in terms of romance for Tyler Merriman?

CHAPTER 14

2021

Henley Breckenridge proceeded to tell the story of the other bunkers, the places that had been constructed as refuges for the United States Supreme Court and the executive branch of government in case of a nuclear attack from the Soviet Union. "Think about it for a minute. If continuity of government is the ultimate goal here, all three branches of government have to communicate with each other. The Congress passes laws, but the President has to sign them. There are rules and a whole process for how that happens. Civics 101. If a law is passed and signed but then is thought to be unconstitutional, it is challenged in the courts. Eventually the law could go to the Supreme Court which takes it under review and votes on it. There's a whole process and procedure for that, too. So, the Congress cannot act in isolation. The three branches have to be in contact with each other, and they have to act together to make it all work." Henley paused. "Of course lately with the whole executive order thing, it sure seems to me as if the executive branch wants to circumvent the entire Constitution. And they all do it. All of those arrogant

SOBs do it, no matter what party they belong to. They want what they want when they want it. They act like Czars. The heck with the Constitution!"

Henley continued. "I happen to think the whole bunker construction was a good idea, as an idea. And if there had been an attack from the Russians, it might have worked, kind of, for a very short period of time. And thank goodness nobody ever had to try to use it. It was really a theoretical concept which, thank God, they never had to put to the test of implementing in the real world. I think it was a worthy effort for lots of reasons, at least for the few years the Ruskies planned to deliver their bombs by way of airplanes. It might have been possible to get some members of the Congress to White Sulphur Springs in time to keep them safe. But once ICBMs were invented, and missiles became the way to deliver the bomb, the bunker at the Woodbrier became completely obsolete. With intercontinental ballistic missiles, there was not nearly enough time to get anybody to the Woodbrier. They might, might have had time to bring a few members here by helicopter. When you consider the logistics of it all, it seems ridiculously archaic in today's world, doesn't it? I think the government spent a lot of money to reassure themselves that there would still be a world and a United States of America after a significant nuclear exchange. It was, for the powers that be, a way of whistling past the graveyard. That's just my opinion."

Elizabeth agreed with Henley's assessment about the building of the bunker. "I've often thought that this very costly and very secretive fortress was more of a hedge against catastrophe and not very realistic. It was earnest but naïve. Like everybody else in the world, I am very thankful it never had to be tested. It remains a sort of monument to what we were afraid might have been and to what we hoped would never be." Elizabeth, like everybody else, was more than thankful there had never been an attack. She had thought about that possibility every day of her life until Christmas of 1991 when the Soviet Union finally collapsed.

"In a way the United States government was operating in a fantasy world. And the insanity was more widespread than just building this bunker here at the Woodbrier. I have an even more unbelievable story to tell you about. And you really might not believe me. I'm not sure I believe it all either." Henley paused and sighed. "Because the three branches of government are supposed to communicate, they have to be somewhat close to each other. Telephone lines and television cables could be buried, and I am sure a lot of them were laid underground in the 1960s. But engineers knew, even back then, that a nuclear blast would be able to take out, and probably would take out, all of the existing means of communication. If direct communication was required among all three branches of the Federal Government, the bunkers for all three branches would have to be in relatively close proximity. Guess what other very fancy resort is located less than an hour's drive from the Woodbrier?"

"I've never been there, but I have good friends who love the place. The Grovestead is now owned by Omni Hotels and Resorts, but I know it is a terrific hotel. It's in Hot Springs, Virginia. I don't know exactly where Hot Springs is, but I'll take your word for it that The Grovestead is less than an hour's drive from here."

"Bingo again! You are going to get an A+ on this quiz, Elizabeth. The Grovestead Resort is now just 49 minutes from here by car and less than four hours from Washington, D.C. That's in theory. The traffic in and around D.C. is totally impossible, and that I-66 mess . . . unbelievable! Anyway, getting a few Supremes and their people and the president and his people to Hot Springs would have been a much, much easier task than transporting the entire Congress to the Woodbrier. The other two branches could have easily gone to The Grovestead from D.C. by helicopter and might actually have made it there in time before the world blew up.

"According to Glen, my Army Corps of Engineers sergeant, The Grovestead is where the other bunkers were built. They were much nicer and more luxurious than the massive and rather primitive facility here at the Woodbrier that was built for the Congress. No bunk beds at the Grovestead! I believed Glen when he told me about the Grovestead bunkers. That all sounded perfectly reasonable . . . or at least reasonable for the times when those bunkers were being planned and built. The building of the bunkers at The Grovestead is not the insane part of the story. The craziness part of all of this is what Glen says he worked on after the bunkers here and at the Grovestead were completed. Remember, he was old when he told me this last part of the story. He was not well physically, and he was suffering from mental decline. I always have taken what he told me about The Grovestead with several grains of salt. I always believed everything he told me about his work here at the Woodbrier. He told me all of that back in the 80s. But, at the end of his life, he also told me that he'd worked on building an underground tunnel that was intended to connect The Woodbrier with The Grovestead.

"Driving from the Grovestead to the Woodbrier and back would have been impossible after a nuclear war. Even if anybody was still alive and hiding in their various bunkers, the roads would have been completely destroyed, not to mention that everything in sight would have been radioactive. You would never have been able to travel on surface roads between White Sulphur Springs, West Virginia and Hot Springs, Virginia. The only way to get from the Congressional bunker to the two bunkers that were located at The Grovestead would have been, in the opinion of some decision makers, through an underground tunnel. This sounds like a great idea until you look at a map of the terrain between the two places. Or, if you actually drive between the two places, you can't help but notice that most of the terrain is mountains. The underground tunnel would have had to be built under and through the mountains. That would have been an almost impossible task under any circumstance, but somebody thought it would be a good idea . . . back in the day. The fact that responsible people thought it was possible to build such a tunnel and that it was a good idea to try to build it, gives us an idea about the fear and paranoia that were overriding forces driving governmental decisions at the time.

"It is true that there were a lot of miners in West Virginia sixty years ago, when all of this was being proposed and engineered. There were more miners in West Virginia in the 1960s than there are now. Still. Was it realistic to expect miners, who extract coal out of the earth, to be able to hack out a tunnel from solid rock? I don't know about that. It sounds to me like it would have been an impossible task, and as it turns out, it was an impossible task. It just could not be done. It was too far and too deep, and it was solid rock most of the way. The underground tunnel between the two facilities was eventually abandoned in the late 1960s. The Cold War still raged. The Berlin Wall had been built to try to keep people in East Germany from escaping their Soviet worker's paradise. Many of the Germans who were stuck behind the Iron Curtain wanted to leave their rotten Communist disaster behind and live in the decadent West." Henley thought for a minute. "I have always wondered why we didn't put our efforts into building tunnels between East Berlin and West Berlin. And I have good reason to believe that in fact we really did that, that we actually did build those tunnels. That's a story for another day. I'll tell you about it some time. But back to our fancy resorts and their bunkers. There was never going to be a tunnel between The Woodbrier and The Grovestead."

"I am fascinated but not entirely surprised by your story. It has always amazed me that those who worked on building and maintaining these bunkers, were able to keep their mouths shut for as long as they did. There were an enormous number of people involved in building the bunker and a huge number of people required on a daily basis to manage it and keep it fully supplied and ready at any moment for the Congress. Even with threats of prison, I think it is remarkable that these secrets were kept for so long. In the current day, the public still doesn't know anything about The Grovestead's bunkers or the tunnel under the mountains that was begun but never completed. Of course, most of the people who worked on building these bunkers and the tunnel are probably dead by now. It was a different world then, Henley. It was my world. I grew up in that world. I scarcely recognize the world as it is today. The Soviet Union dissolved, but the current president of Russia is doing everything he possibly can to try to put it back together again. Georgia, Crimea, Ukraine. We are giving it back to him piece by piece."

"Don't get me started down that road. I will have a stroke." Henley clearly did not like the current president of Russia.

Elizabeth wanted to say more about this very disturbing and disturbed man. "What is wrong with that man? He is creepy and so dangerous. He said that the greatest tragedy of the twentieth century was the dissolution of the Soviet Union. I can't believe he actually said that, but his behavior ever since he came to power certainly indicates that he believes it to be true."

"I absolutely know what's wrong with the guy. After I saw those ridiculous and nauseating pictures of him bare chested riding on that little horse, I knew exactly what his problem was. I mean who even does that in the first place? And then he has somebody take pictures of that kind of mess? Really? Ugh! He has to have an inferiority complex of the worst kind. My theory is that he must have an incredibly tiny, little . . ."

"Henley, stop. No need to go into those details. I'm sure everybody who has seen those pictures of him thinks the same thing."

"I never would have figured you to be a prude. I don't think I am saying anything the world doesn't either know for certain or at least suspect."

"I'm not a prude, but we are eating lunch. I want to enjoy my lunch."

"You're right. I should keep my lunch-time conversation away from my often too-graphic anatomical criticisms. I'm a vet. I breed cattle and horses. I think about sperm counts and whether or not my animals can perform. I think about their abilities to reproduce. I'm used to thinking about these things and talking about them . . . even at lunch." Henley paused and saw that Elizabeth had stopped eating. "Sorry. I forget that I'm not on the ranch right now. I really am not fit for polite company, at least not in a fancy place like this. But I still say, that little Russian guy who is their president . . . sorry. He couldn't make it as a secret agent in the KGB, so they kicked him upstairs and put him in charge of propaganda or something like that. He is seriously nutso, in my opinion. The Russians have had a lot of terrible strong-man-type leaders over the years, but this one has nuclear weapons that I'm afraid he's more than willing to use. This one is very dangerous."

Elizabeth had a graduate degree in history. She knew some things about the history of Russian aggression. "The Russians have been causing trouble in the world for centuries. They got into a war with Japan in the early 1900s, fighting over who was going to control Manchuria. Manchuria was in China, but Russia and Japan got into a war about who was going to get to be in charge in part of a country that didn't belong to either one of them. Who does that? And that was even before Lenin came on the scene. That was back when feudalism still reigned, for all intents and purposes, in Russia . . . and in Japan. The tsars were in power in Russia, and the samurai and an emperor were in power in Japan. Russia, in spite of having an incredibly huge land mass, has always had imperialistic ambitions. It is a bizarre thing, but it continued all through the Communist era and continues to this very day with their current disastrous leader."

"I still say he feels inferior about his. . . ." Henley paused and searched for another word that would not offend Elizabeth. "He is not confident about his manhood, and this goofy stuff with the horses is all about that. I fear that his arrogance in international affairs is also based on his feelings of inferiority. He's a bully. Bullies feel inferior. They try to make themselves feel important by putting others down and by trying to control them. Mark my words, when they do an autopsy on this Russian president, they will find his . . . his anatomy . . . wanting. He wouldn't be doing all of this if he didn't have a tiny little pecker."

Elizabeth interrupted. "Okay, changing the subject for a minute. Tell me what you are wearing to the wedding. Are you wearing a dress?"

"Oh, yes, I am wearing a dress. My niece knows I haven't put a dress on this body for years, but she particularly requested that I wear one to the wedding. I think she was afraid I would show up in my jeans. I know better than that, but she doesn't think I know what's appropriate. Even if I don't pay attention to conventional manners, I know what they are. I just choose not to live that way. I have a beautiful navy blue dress with matching shoes . . . if you can believe that . . . to wear to the wedding. I am having my hair done later this afternoon for the rehearsal dinner. You will not recognize me." Henley sighed a deep sigh. "I can't wait to get back home to the ranch and live my normal life again. It has been a tremendous break in the wedding action for me to run into you, Elizabeth. I hope you will come back to Paso Robles one of these days."

"It has been great to see you again, Henley. We need to stay in touch."

CHAPTER 15

1965

WHENEVER CONGRESSMAN MASEN VEUDILLE VISITED the Woodbrier, he ate his meals in the main dining room. Sherrod Jefferson always waited on Masen's table, and over the years, they had built a warm relationship. Sherrod took very seriously his profession as a first-class waiter in one of the world's first-class resorts. He was smart and funny and had all the social graces. He was a master at what he did. Sherrod had begun his career working in the kitchen and in the dining car of one of the Chesapeake and Ohio Railroad's premier overnight sleeper trains. If you've learned to serve an elegant dinner on a moving train, being the perfect waiter in a luxury hotel was easy.

Masen Veudille tipped generously. He was an outgoing and friendly person and appreciated the attention and excellent service he received from Sherrod. After the work on the bunker was completed and the rooms in the Woodbrier's new West Virginia Wing were filled with customers, Masen continued to visit the Woodbrier. Managing the bunker and keeping it supplied was a major undertaking. Masen wanted to check on things to make sure the facility was running as expected and that the bunker was being kept at the ready. He made several trips to the Woodbrier every year. If he wasn't flying home to Ohio, he usually drove down to West Virginia for a long weekend when Congress was in session in Washington, D.C. One Friday night, he arrived later than usual. He thought about going straight to his room and ordering room service, but decided to dine in the main dining room as he usually did. He sat at his reserved table and was looking at the menu when Sherrod Jefferson came to take his drink order. Sherrod was gracious and always delighted to have Masen make an appearance in the dining room. Masen noticed that Sherrod was not himself tonight. There was something different about his tone of voice when he greeted Masen.

"Is everything all right, Sherrod? Are you feeling okay? You are not yourself tonight."

"I'm fine, Congressman, sir, just fine, thanks." Sherrod was trying hard to be his usual cheerful self, but Masen knew his heart wasn't in it. Something was bothering Sherrod.

Masen ordered tomato bullion soup and the Dover sole Hollandaise with whipped potatoes and French green beans. Sherrod brought his meal but had little to say. He was not able to keep up his usual banter. Masen ordered a slice of carrot cake for dessert, and Sherrod brought him a piece of cherry pie instead. Masen knew there was something very wrong with Sherrod tonight. He had never made a mistake and brought the wrong food. Sherrod's attention to his profession had always been impeccable.

Masen did not want to mention that Sherrod had brought him the wrong dessert. Masen loved cherry pie, so it was fine. But when Sherrod came to the table to refill Masen's coffee, he looked at the plate of pie and hung his head.

"I am so sorry, sir." Sherrod was clearly devastated, even ashamed, to have served Masen something he hadn't ordered. "I just noticed I brought you cherry pie instead a the cake you wanted. I'll bring the cake right away. If you want, I'll put it in a box, and you can take it with you back to the room. I'm so very, very sorry. I never makes mistakes like this. I especially don't make a mistake like this with my favorite customer."

"Tell me what's bothering you, Sherrod. This is not like you. I love cherry pie, so it doesn't matter a bit that you brought me the pie for dessert."

Sherrod hung his head, clearly embarrassed and distraught. "I'm so very, very sorry, sir. Please forgive me."

"There's nothing to forgive. Sherrod, this is not a tragedy. It's okay, really it is. Don't beat yourself up about it. You are a superb waiter. You're just having a bad day. It happens to all of us."

Sherrod looked as if he might break down and cry. "Sir, I . . . I . . . things have happened. It is not your concern, and I shouldna have allowed anythin' to interfere with my service. Please forgive me."

"Sherrod, you and I have been friends for a long time. You have taken care of me for years. Whenever I come to the Woodbrier, you are my waiter. I always look forward to seeing you and having a chat. I am going to insist that you tell me what is bothering you. You are obviously terribly upset about something, and I want to know what's wrong. I want to help if I can."

"I need help. Somethin' real bad has happened, and I don't know what to do 'bout it. I can't talk 'bout this here, and I really shouldn't be talking 'bout it with you at all. One of the things the Woodbrier tells all us waiters is that we're not to discuss anythin' unpleasant or anythin' personal with our guests."

"I don't care about what the Woodbrier has said. I want to know what's going on."

"It is somethin' very serious, and it isn't really personal, or not exactly. It has to do with security here at the hotel. I am very worried about it. I need to talk to somebody 'bout it. Somethin' needs to be done about the situation, but I don't know what to do."

"I want to know all about whatever it is that has got you so upset. I might be able to help. If it has to do with security here at the Woodbrier, it is doubly important to me."

At first, Sherrod was silent and didn't say anything. Then he made a decision and began to speak. He dropped his voice to just above a whisper. It was late, and there was only one other table still occupied. It was all the way at the other end of the dining room. No one could possibly hear what Sherrod was saying to Masen, but he kept his soft Virginia drawl low anyway. "I am goin' to tell you somethin' I am not supposed to tell you." The waiter paused, considering how much he was willing to say. "I know about what is goin' on here . . . underneath the West Virginia Wing. I help with the resupply of that area. I know you come here to check on things. Nobody told me that about you, but I figured it out for myself. Once when I was working down there, in the bunker, I saw you. So I know you are one of the people who is in on what is happnin' here."

Masen Veudille was not shocked that Sherrod Jefferson was one of the members of the Woodbrier staff who had been chosen to help with the work of maintaining the bunker. He was also not surprised that Sherrod was aware of his own role in supervising what happened with the bunker. He was surprised that Sherrod would breach the confidentiality agreement he'd signed and admit to Masen that he worked in the extremely secret facility that no one at all was supposed to know anything about. Masen knew Sherrod well enough to realize that only something of vital importance would ever move this fine man to break the rules.

"I am going back to my room now. When you have finished your shift and are on your own time, I am going to insist that you come to my room and talk to me. I want to know about everything that's happened and about everything that is clearly so disturbing to you."

"Another one of the rules here is that I am not allowed to come to your room, or to any guest's room, unless I am comin' to your room as a part of my job. I can't come to your room."

"I understand that you will have to break a rule to come to my room to talk to me, but you have to do it. It is that important. I know it is that important because I know you, Sherrod. I will take the responsibility for insisting that you come to talk to me. If there is a way for you to reach my room without being seen by anybody, so much the better. We will keep this just between the two of us. If you have to wear a uniform or push a cart or carry a tray to give you an excuse to walk through the halls to come to my room, do that. But we must talk tonight. Will you promise to tell me all about whatever this is . . . as soon as possible?"

Sherrod seemed to almost collapse with relief. "I have been carryin' a terrible burden. It will be such a liftin' of my troubles if I can tell you what I know." I will come to your room at ten o'clock. There's an employee's elevator I can use that comes to your floor, and it's not very far from your room."

"How do you know where my room is?"

"I earn extra money workin' room service at night, after I am finished waitin' tables here in the main dining room. I know you always stay in one of two rooms. When you come with Mrs. Veudille, you stay in the suite. When you come by yourself, you stay in the room next door to the suite. If you order room service, I always make sure they get your order just right. That's how I know what room you're in."

Masen had to laugh at that. "I'm glad you know where my room is located. I'd thought I might have been getting some extra special service with my room service. You do a good job with everything you do, Sherrod. I look forward to seeing you at ten o'clock tonight. You know where to find me."

"Thank you, Sir. This means the world to me. I've been sick to my stomach over worryin' about this, and it'll be a great relief to tell you what I know. You have power. Maybe you can do somethin' about it. I'm a waiter. I don't have no power at all. Nobody would ever listen to me or believe what I had to say. But, I trust you, and I know you will believe me. Thank you, sir, thank you."

Sherrod became his professional self again and asked if he could get the congressman anything more. Masen asked for the check. He finished his coffee and left the dining room. He was very anxious to hear what Sherrod Jefferson had to tell him.

Just at ten o'clock there was a soft knock on the door of his room. Masen Veudille opened the door to Sherrod Jefferson who was standing in the hall with a room service cart.

Masen wasn't hungry, but Sherrod had brought a plate of sandwiches and a plate of petit fours on the cart which also held a silver coffeepot, cups and saucers, and cream and sugar. "If somebody stopped me and wanted to know what I was bringing you, there had to be some kind of food or drink on the cart." Sherrod smiled. He pushed the cart into the room, and Masen closed the door behind him. Masen thought about putting the security chain on the door but decided against it.

"Well, I'm not hungry right now, but this might be very welcome later as a midnight snack. Have you eaten? Please help yourself."

"Oh, no thank you. They feeds us real good here at the Woodbrier. Look at this uniform. I'm always havin' to ask for a bigger size."

"Sit down, Sherrod. I can't talk to you while you're standing up. I know the Woodbrier probably tells you not to sit down when you are in the room with the guests, but this is just you and me here now. Nobody knows you're here, and we are going to have a heart-to-heart talk. You are not my waiter now. You have important information for me, information I need to know. We are going to work together on this problem, whatever it is. So relax and sit down here with me at the table." There were two chairs that were pulled up to a small table by one of the windows in the bedroom. Sherrod reluctantly sat down on one of the chairs. "Tell me your story."

"I don't know how or where to begin."

"Just tell it to me in your own words. There's no right or wrong way to tell this. Just let it come."

CHAPTER 16

1965

"I'VE BEEN WORKIN' PART-TIME IN the bunker since before it was finished. Supplyin' food for that place is a mighty big job. You can imagine. But we have a real organized system to keep the food from goin' bad. The system, it work just fine. Makin' sure the food gets rotated in and out of the bunker is part a my job. The refrigerators and the freezers have to be stocked full at all times, but the food's gotta be kept for only so long a time. That isn't easy to do. We try to move food in and out of the bunker so there's as little waste as possible. It's a complicated thing, and we have to stay on schedule to be sure nothin' gets overlooked. There are several of us who do that work, and we all have been investigated and investigated. We've had lots of interviews and had to sign papers in front of witnesses. It was a very big thing to be able to qualify to get a clearance to do the work I do. I understand how important it is that nobody ever know anythin' about the bunker. Nobody can ever know what I'm doin' when I'm not in the main dining room."

Masen was quiet. He wanted Sherrod to tell the story and get to the point in his own way and in his own time. Masen felt for this good man who was trying so hard to do the right thing.

"The fish can only stay in the freezer for two months. The meat can only stay in there for six months. Then it has to come out and new food has to go in. We use as much as we can in the kitchens of the Woodbrier's restaurants. You'd be surprised that ham tastes just as good after it's been frozen for six months as it does bought new at the store. The chefs here work magic with that ham. It's ground up and it become ham salad for tea sandwiches. It go into green beans and baked beans. It go into all kinds of soups, and it get fried for breakfast. No ham ever go to waste. No sir. The filet beef is made into beef pot pies and beef stroganoff . . . very fancy and very delicious. Anyway, we rotates the food, and the chefs use as much of what comes from the bunker as they can. What the Woodbrier don't use, we takes to the Baptist church in Lewisburg. The minister there, he run a big soup kitchen and give out groceries to people who need food. We keep him supplied. He don't ever ask no questions. He just know the food come from the Woodbrier, and he's happy to get it. We don't want to waste anything or just throw the food away, so we try to make it all work. But, you really don't want to hear 'bout what a delicious recipe the Woodbrier has for ham and scalloped potatoes do you?" Sherrod chuckled a little bit and realized he might be getting off the subject.

"I am tellin' you all of this to splain how I know 'bout the bunker and what my job is on the bunker food detail. My younger brother, Warner, works here at the Woodbrier, too, and he also work in the bunker. Part of his job is to drive the food we can't use here to the church in Lewisburg. He has been through all the security checks like I have, and he's got other jobs he does in the bunker. It's really my brother who found out somethin' kind of by accident, somethin' he really didn't want to know nothin' about. He told me what he'd heard, and neither one of the two of us knows what to do with any of it. My brother stumbled into somethin' he shouldn't have just a few days ago, and now we are both worried to death about what to do."

"What did your brother stumble into?"

"He thinks and I think it too, that he stumbled onto a spy. That might sound to you like I'm makin' this up, but there's a reason we both think there's spyin' goin' on. It has to do with somebody talkin' about the bunker with somebody they shouldn't be talkin' to and about Russians who don't belong around here. But I'm gettin' ahead a myself."

"Your brother thinks he's stumbled onto a spy who is talking about the bunker. And Russians?"

"I know it sounds like I'm makin' this up. I know it does. But after I tell you all about it, I think you're goin' to agree with me." Sherrod looked the Congressman in the eye, and Masen knew the waiter was telling him the truth from his heart. "Warner drives the van that delivers the food the Woodbrier can't use. He goes to the church in Lewisburg on his runs, twice a week at least. Last Tuesday, he stopped at the diner on Rt. 60 to get hisself some lunch. He was sittin' in a booth at the back of the diner. Black folks are allowed to eat in this diner, but we have to sit in the back, in a special section. Warner saw a man who works in the bunker with him come in the diner, and that man sat down in the booth right next to where Warner was eatin' his lunch. Back in the Negro section of the diner. The guy from the bunker can't see Warner, where Warner is sittin'. Warner don't really know that man; he just know the man work in the bunker. But Warner is curious. A few minutes later, a guy that Warner don't know comes in the diner. He sits down in the booth with the guy who works in the bunker. They start to talk, and they are speakin' in Russian."

"Russian? Really?" How in the world did Warner know they were speaking Russian?"

"Warner fought in World War II. He's ten years younger than I am. I tried to join up, too, but I'm older, and they didn't want me. He joined up with the U.S. Army in 1943 when he turned eighteen. He was captured in 1944 in Italy, and he spent the rest of the war in a Nazi prison camp in Poland. It wasn't a good thing. It's a long story how he got there. He almost starved to death, and he almost froze to death. But there were plenty of Russian soldiers in the camp with him, so he learned how to speak a little bit a Russian. At least he learned to understand it, and he learned it enough so that he could talk with the Russian prisoners. Of course he didn't write it or read it or anythin' like that. I think he understands it more than he can speak it. And it's been a long time since 1945. He's forgotten a lot a that Russian. But he knew enough to know the men were speaking Russian in the diner. Warner was so surprised to hear them speakin' in Russian. He hadn't heard anybody speakin' Russian for such a long time. They were trying to be real quiet and speak real soft. But Warner, he try real hard to hear what they're sayin'. He knew it was real wrong for somebody who work in the bunker to be talkin' to a guy who's a Russian."

"Was Warner able to understand what the men were saying to each other?" Masen's interest level in the story Sherrod was telling him had just moved into the stratosphere.

"He understood part a what they were sayin', and Warner, he say the guy who works in the bunker is a spy. The Russian was askin' the man who works in the bunker, the spy, all about the bunker—exactly what parts of the Woodbrier the bunker is under, what it's for, how many people can stay there, how often the bunker has to be resupplied, how many days' worth of food and water they have, how the air is moved around that circulate inside a the bunker, and everythin' else about it. The Russian was also askin' the traitor, the spy from the bunker, things my brother don't know nothin' about. He was askin' about how many feet below the surface the bunker goes, how thick the blast doors are, how bombproof is the bunker, how protected is it from radiation, and other technical things my brother don't really understand."

"So the Russian was asking the guy who works in the bunker questions about everything he knows he's not supposed to talk about. And the Russian is definitely someone who is not supposed to have this information. And they are speaking to each other in Russian. Of course, as you know, no one is even supposed to know there is any such thing as the bunker anywhere close to the Woodbrier. Nobody is supposed to talk about any of it . . . in any language. It is one of the most critical things our government wants to keep a secret."

"I know that, and my brother, he know that, too. That's why we been so worried. We want to tell somebody 'bout this, but we don't know who we otta tell. We don't know who's safe to trust, and we don't think nobody will believe our story anyway. Knowin' about all this has been tearin' both of us up these past few days. This all just happened on Tuesday."

"I can certainly understand why you and Warner have been upset. This is a major breach of national security, to be sure. And, it is always difficult to know where to place one's trust. Of course, I understand why you didn't know what to do with this information. Hardly anybody would have known what to do in a situation like this. But how fortunate that Warner was able to understand Russian and understand most of what those two men were saying to each other."

"He want to follow the other man to see where he was goin' to go and who else he was goin' to talk to 'bout this. But because he stayed in the diner to listen in on that conversation, Warner was already goin' to be late gettin' back to his job here."

"Does your brother know the name of the spy, the traitor, the man who works in the bunker and was talking to the Russian man about the bunker?"

"The man who work in the bunker is Johnny Bidwell. He's a local. His family lives in Dickson. He's an American, a white man. I can't understand why he'd want to be a traitor and tell the Russians anythin' 'bout the bunker. He signed all the same papers, just like the rest of us signed. He promised not to talk 'bout the bunker. If he went against his promise not to talk, he's a traitor in my book."

"You did the right thing, Sherrod, bringing this information to me. I will be sure that the right people hear every detail of what you've told me. I'm afraid I'm going to have to mention your brother's name. I'm sure the FBI will want to talk to him and ask him more questions. They may show him some photographs or have him try to give them a really accurate description of what that other man in the diner looks like, the Russian guy. They may ask him to meet with a sketch artist who will try to draw a picture of the Russian. I will try to keep your name out of it, but since Warner is the one who actually heard the conversation, the FBI will have to talk to him. I'm sorry."

"We just don't wannna lose our jobs over this. I called Warner 'fore I came up here to talk to you. I told him I was gonna tell you everything. He said it was okay, that it was for the best. I think he already know somebody from the gov'ment gonna want to talk to him about what he overheard."

"I will be calling someone about this tonight. You might want to give Warner another call and tell him what we talked about. You both have absolutely done a very brave thing by coming forward. This is extremely important information, and I have to act on it immediately. Someone might even come to Warner's house in the middle of the night . . . tonight. I don't know for sure about that, but I don't want him to be frightened if someone knocks on his door in a couple of hours. He did the right thing, and so did you. You are both patriots and are to be congratulated because you were willing to tell me what you found out. As a representative of the American people, I am very grateful to you for your courage. Not everyone would have been willing to step up like you and Warner have done."

"I've got to go and make that phone call to Warner, and then I've got to get home. I'm on the breakfast shift at seven in the mornin'. That means I have to be here by five o'clock. Thank you, Congressman. I've had a thousand pounds a worry and lament lifted off my shoulders tonight since I told you my story."

"I'm the one who should be thanking you." Masen shook hands with Sherrod.

Sherrod walked to the door. He opened it and looked around to see if anyone else was in the hall. "I'm goin' to leave the room service cart here. But I can't let anyone see me walkin' through the halls without a reason for bein' up here. The Woodbrier is good to its employees, but they expect us to follow the rules. I've broken more than a few of 'em tonight, but my heart's lighter. I will have to be careful. If any employee wanders around where they aren't supposed to be, they be reprimanded. But I'm a black man. If I am wanderin' around where I'm not supposed to be, I will probably lose my job. Wish me luck." He slipped out the door.

Masen Veudille stepped quickly into the hall and stopped Sherrod before he could hurry away out of sight. "You will never lose your job here as long as I have anything to do with it. You don't need to worry about that, and neither does Warner. Be sure to tell him."

Masen watched Sherrod disappear down the hall and finally closed his door and put on the security chain. He made a few notes on the scratch pad beside his bed and picked up the receiver of the room telephone. It was going to be a long night.

CHAPTER 17

2021

"So back to the present day. I'm sure there is something secret still going on here now, here at the Woodbrier, something other than CSX and Fortune 500 servers. But I have no idea what. How could anyone figure it out from the bunker tour? We really didn't see very much of that whole thing. The real bunker was built as a mighty fortress and had to be huge in size and a huge operation, much more than the little bit we were allowed to see today." Henley was understandably suspicious about current activities at the Woodbrier. Elizabeth had been fascinated by the bunker tour, but she, too, was not satisfied that they'd been told the whole truth.

Henley continued. "I don't know what's going on here now. But something is definitely going on. I just hope they're not doing some kind of crazy secret Gain-of-Function research on viruses in some freakin' mountain laboratory."

Elizabeth's jaw dropped. She knew Henley was a veterinarian, but Gain-of-Function research? In amazement, she stared at Henley with wide eyes.

"What?" Henley couldn't help but notice Elizabeth's look of incredulity. "I majored in biology at Stanford. Then I went to vet school at UC Davis. I still know how to read, and I read all the time. I know about these things."

"Of course you do. Henley, I know you're smart. Don't misunderstand me. I just wasn't even thinking along those lines, that we might be doing stuff we've been so outraged at the Chinese for doing."

"Don't kid yourself. We just have a lot better quality control and security than the Commies do." Henley chuckled. "That's not what's going on at the Woodbrier anyway. Don't you think West Virginia would have tried to keep that from happening here? The resort is owned by a local billionaire now, not by a railroad company that has to do what the government tells them to do. You said you looked for me, and I wasn't there. You're right, I did slip away from the tour, you know." Henley's eyes twinkled with the knowledge that she had been able to put one over on the adorable and charming tour guide. "Of course, I had a back-up phone with me, and I took some photos. I'll send them to you. I always come prepared. Glen, my Army Corps of Engineers sergeant, told me about some of the secret places here. Most of them have been closed off and walled up, but they've kept the special elevators working. In fact, one of those special elevators goes to your floor and is right next to your room. It says "freight elevator" on it or "employees only," or something like that. But it actually goes from the bunker up to certain floors in the West Virginia Wing. That elevator next to your room goes right down into the bowels of the bunker. It doesn't stop at every floor, which is why I know it isn't really a freight elevator. A freight elevator would have to stop at every floor. For some reason, whoever put in that elevator wanted to have access from the bunker directly to some of the floors of the West Virginia Wing."

"You know, I think all the handicap rooms are in the West Virginia Wing. And I haven't seen anybody else, not another guest, at all on our floor. The bathroom has a great shower. In most handicap showers in motels and hotels, the drains aren't made right, and the water goes out all over the floor of the bathroom. But that doesn't happen in our well-designed bathroom in the West Virginia Wing. The shower floor is perfectly made, and no water gets outside the shower area, even without a shower curtain or a shower door. It's a wonderful room." Elizabeth was thinking about other anomalies on the fourth floor. "Another odd thing is that they don't want us to get our own ice. They are very strict about this and have told us to call room service if we want any ice. Of course, Richard doesn't pay any attention to that. When he wants ice, he just goes and gets it. He went exploring one day and found where on our floor they keep the ice. After he found that out, he didn't bother to call room service anymore. He didn't like waiting for them to bring it. But once, when he went to get the ice on his own, he got caught by one of the maintenance people. The guy scolded him a little, and reminded Richard that he was supposed to call room service when he wanted ice. But the maintenance man said he wouldn't tell on Richard. He kind of made a joke about it. But he cautioned Richard about wandering around and getting his own ice in the future. Of course, Richard hasn't paid any attention to that, but he does look around to see if anybody is out in the hall or watching before he goes for ice now."

"They probably don't really care about the ice. They just don't want you wandering around in the halls or getting on that bunker elevator by mistake. They don't want you to end up down in the bunker and finding your way to someplace where you don't belong."

"So what did you find when you left the tour and went off on your own?"

"I found your room on the fourth floor of the West Virginia wing." Henley laughed. "Other than that, I didn't find much of anything. There were some obscure doorways that were locked up tight. None of that glass doors with signs on them BS. That was all for show, a part of the performance. But I definitely found some no-go areas. I am really curious, but I don't have the time to continue any sleuthing. Tonight is the rehearsal dinner, and tomorrow is the wedding. These are both command performances for me, so I will be there in my best bib and tucker. You know, one of the reasons I agreed to come to my niece's wedding was so I could come here and get a look at this place for myself. After hearing from Glen about the bunker and how elegant and wonderful the Woodbrier was, I had to see it once in my lifetime. And now I've seen it. But I have not seen it all, and you haven't either. Can I count on you to keep on trying to figure out what is happening here? I'm leaving on Sunday morning to go back to California. I don't have time to do any more exploring on my own. But I do have a little map, a rough drawing that Glen made for me years ago. Glen told me about some places and marked them on a map of the Woodbrier bunker for me. The map shows where there are secret rooms and hallways and hidden nooks and crannies . . . other places of interest in the bunker that he's drawn on it. I will make a copy of my map and put the copy in an envelope. I'll slip it under the door of your room. Look for it. Will you try to investigate some of these places? I know it's difficult for you in a wheelchair, but you might be able to find out more about what's happening here."

"I have some time on my hands while the others are out doing hiking and biking and those kinds of things. It will cut into my people-watching time, but I'll try to investigate. Leave the map for me. I know J.D. Steele will want to investigate the places shown on the map, even if I can't." Elizabeth smiled. After their encounter in Paso Robles, she knew Henley had a soft spot in her heart for J.D.

Henley laughed. "So I am sorry to say I probably won't see you again until you come to Paso Robles the next time. And please don't bring any more of those Chinese Communist trouble makers with you when you come in the future." Henley laughed again. "I know you don't want to have anything to do with those people either. I've already paid the bill for lunch, so all I have to do is put you on the non-secret elevator and push you back to the fourth floor of the West Virginia Wing. We will go right by that 'special elevator.' I'll show you on the way back to your room."

Elizabeth was ready for a nap after hearing all that Henley had told her. They exchanged hugs and emails and phone numbers for texting. Elizabeth told Henley to enjoy the wedding as much as she could. Elizabeth was sad to see Henley go. She liked the rough-and-ready ranch owner and thought the woman with the exquisite concho belt and the baggy jeans was fascinating company.

Elizabeth couldn't walk long distances, and the Woodbrier was sprawling —with lots of hallways. Long distances were the norm. It would not be easy for anybody to explore the whole place, even the parts where guests were allowed to go. She wondered if Henley would really be able to give up her search for the Woodbrier's secrets. Elizabeth knew that Henley would much prefer to be sneaking and snooping around the no-go zones in the bunker than she would attending the rehearsal dinner and a wedding reception with her niece's extra fancy in-laws. Elizabeth looked forward to seeing the map Henley had promised to leave for her. She was sorry to say goodbye to Henley.

CHAPTER 18

2021

ELIZABETH WAS NOT EXPECTING TO have Henley swoop down on her after dinner that night. But Henley was waiting for her as the Camp Shoemaker group left The Forum, the Woodbrier's Italian restaurant. Because several of the restaurants were understaffed due to COVID and the reunion goers had a large group, they'd had to wait for their table for seven. It had been worth the wait, and they'd had a large round table. Round tables are great table for being able to talk to everybody. Most of the reunion goers ordered pizza, but Elizabeth had been happy with her order of veal Milanese with a side of spaghetti marinara. The group had passed around their dessert orders of spumoni and various versions of Italian cream cake—lemon, vanilla, and almond.

Gretchen had left the Woodbrier immediately after the bunker tour the day before. She had a business meeting to attend in Los Angeles. Cameron and Sidney had intended to stay another day, but the Richardsons had left early because of a crisis at one of Cameron's companies. An employee, who had come highly recommended and who had done great work for Cameron, had been discovered defrauding Cameron's company. Cameron was having a difficult time believing he had been fooled, but the evidence against the employee was overwhelming. He had called a special meeting of his staff for the following morning. He was going to confront the guilty party, and he was going to have to fire her. He and Sidney said a regretful goodbye to their friends after breakfast that morning. The Camp Shoemaker crowd was now down to seven.

As they left The Forum, Henley Breckenridge hurried over to speak to Elizabeth who was in her wheelchair. Henley knew J.D. Steele from Paso Robles, but she didn't really know any of the other members of the reunion group. She'd seen them together at the restaurant, La Buona Ricetta, in Paso Robles, but she didn't know their names. Henley was dressed in an expensive, bright blue silk pants suit and looked very elegant. Her usually wild and unruly, long and curly gray hair had been contained and tamed into a chignon that rested neatly at the back of her neck. She wore a colorful scarf and a beautiful strand of pearls. Elizabeth almost didn't recognize her.

"Henley, you look gorgeous. I've never seen you in anything except blue jeans. You clean up real good, girl." Elizabeth was surprised, shocked really, to see how really lovely Henley looked in her rehearsal dinner get-up.

But Henley didn't have time for any compliments. She had a strained and serious look on her face. She clearly wanted to speak with Elizabeth, and Elizabeth was betting that Henley didn't want to discuss the rehearsal dinner or the wedding or her hairdo.

"I need to talk to you, Elizabeth." Henley turned to Richard and stuck out her hand. "I'm Henley Breckenridge. I know your wife from Paso Robles. That's where I'm from.

I'd love to talk to you, Richard, but right now I need to borrow Elizabeth for a while. I hope you don't mind." Without any real apologies or explanations, Henley took possession of Elizabeth's wheelchair and began to push her away from the restaurant. Richard didn't know what to say and certainly did not want to challenge this bold and confident woman he'd only heard about.

"I know I was rude to your husband and rude to the rest of your friends. I'm sorry about that. But I need to talk to you tonight and ask your opinion about some things. There is not much time, and it has to be now."

"My opinion? Since when have you wondered about anybody else's opinion other than your own?" Elizabeth let Henley know she was annoyed with her and didn't like how discourteous Henley had been when she'd swept her away from the others. Henley pushed Elizabeth's wheelchair in the direction of a bar near the casino. Elizabeth was tired and ready to go to bed. She didn't want to go to a bar, and she didn't want to transfer from the wheelchair to a chair at a table like she usually did when she went into a restaurant. Elizabeth insisted on staying in her wheelchair. She ordered a ginger ale when the waiter came to take their order. Henley ordered an Irish whisky straight. Elizabeth demanded to know. "What is so urgent, Henley?"

"I have to talk to you, and this is my only chance to do it. Today at lunch we were talking about a certain Russian guy, the one I suspect has a little tiny you-know-what. At the risk of sounding like Sigmund Freud, whom I despise, I think that's the reason why the man, who likes to have his photo taken bare-chested and riding on the little horse, has been doing the other awful things that he's been doing. Some people believe that the Russian president is mentally ill or has a brain tumor. They claim that's why he is behaving in such an aggressive and reckless manner. Most of the world thinks he's acting really goofy, frighteningly goofy. Makes no sense. Anyway, I don't have time to explain to you about all the things I know or how I know all the things I know. But I will give you a couple of hints." Henley was on a roll, and Elizabeth knew she was not going to be able to get to bed any time soon.

Henley continued. "I'm a crackerjack markswoman. I was an Olympic gold medal winner way back a long time ago. I can shoot anything. I am the Annie Oakley of Paso Robles. I may even be the Annie Oakley of California. I still practice my shooting every day at the ranch. I don't shoot people or critters or even birds. I just shoot targets. Well, to be honest with you, once in a while I do shoot critters. I've bagged a few rabid foxes and a few sick skunks. Anyway, I'm very good, and I don't miss."

"This revelation does not surprise me at all, Henley. When I saw you with your shotgun, ready to put some buckshot into my friend J.D., I knew you meant business and would not miss hitting whatever it was you aimed at."

"I don't have much time, so please bear with me. This is not about bragging about my gold medals." Henley sighed and seemed to hesitate. She was undecided about whether to continue the conversation with Elizabeth. Elizabeth had never seen Henley undecided or hesitant. Henley's reticence was surprising and troubling to Elizabeth. But Henley's reluctance didn't last long, and she plunged ahead. "That very, very bad man we have talked about is planning some more very, very bad things in his part of the world. He already took Crimea, and nobody said 'boo' about his doing that. They just let him get away with it. Actually the world just handed him Crimea on a platter, but that's another story. Most people now understand that the Crimean disaster was a terrible foreign policy failure and was one of the early steps in this bad man's march to reconstruct the Soviet Union. He is obsessed with this mission, and he has to be stopped. He has already begun working on his next country. Everybody knows he has had Ukraine in his sights and has been messing in things there for years. He believes Ukraine is still a part of Russia. He has publicly said many times that Ukraine is not a country. I'll bet you the Ukrainian people would strongly disagree with him. But everybody is afraid to say anything about it, let alone take any steps to stop him. Ukraine wants to be admitted to NATO and to the European Union. It has not quite made the grade to be allowed into those two clubs, and this has made them even more vulnerable to Russian aggression. The former KGB thug who now has Russia in his clutches will invade Ukraine in the coming months. Don't ask me how I know this, but I know it with absolute certainty. No one in the U.S. or NATO or the UN or anyplace else in the world is going to do anything to stop him. Bunch of pussies in Washington right now, in my opinion, but I digress." Henley paused to get her breath.

Elizabeth took the opportunity to get a word in. "I am aware of this problem. I've been asking myself, 'Where is the Mossad when we need them?'" Elizabeth was listening carefully to all that Henley had to say, but she wanted Henley to know she was well-informed about the situation in Ukraine. Henley didn't have to spend her time explaining any of that to her. "Golda Meir had the right idea when she initiated Operation Wrath of God and sent her operatives out to seek justice for the Israeli athletes who were murdered in 1972. Hooray for Golda."

"My thoughts exactly. I wonder if any man, even in Israel, would have had the gorgonzolas to order such an operation."

Henley continued. "I seriously wonder to what extent Bad Vlad really has the Russian people and the Russian military behind him in his quest for more territory and more power. He is pretty much a one-man band with a really bad band leader. He seems determined to go to war against Ukraine. Things will develop over the next several months, but in the end, he is determined to take back Ukraine for Russia. Then he will set his sights on the Baltic States. No one has the courage to stand up to him, least of all the idiots we've had running things lately. The last several idiots. I don't pick parties. I dislike them all. Excuse my French, but that's the way I feel about it. I like you, Elizabeth. I respect your opinion, and I am glad to know where you stand on this. I trust you, and I do not trust people easily. I may not see you again after this weekend. I am going on a mission. It is something I feel very strongly about. I can only compare this conversation I am having with you right now to the deathbed confessions of my sergeant major friend, Glen, who helped to build the bunker here."

Henley had more to say. "Do you think you would have been able to shoot Hitler if you'd had the chance to do it? Before he killed six million Jews? Could you have pulled the trigger? Would you have had the moral courage to murder someone evil? What about Stalin? Could you have taken a gun in your hand and shot him?"

Henley had asked her several questions, but Elizabeth knew Henley was not going to pause in her monologue long enough to allow Elizabeth to answer any of them. Elizabeth interrupted her. "Wait a minute, Henley. You have asked me some questions, but you won't allow me to answer them. I guess you meant them to be rhetorical questions, but I am going to answer them anyway. First of all, I know nothing about guns. The last time I held a gun of any kind in my hands was when I was eighteen years old. I fired an antique pump-action rifle loaded with blanks into the balcony of my high school's auditorium." Elizabeth smiled when she saw the confused look on Henley's face. "It was the high school musical. We did *Annie Get Your Gun*, and I played Annie Oakley. Of course, I was merely the Annie Oakley of Bexley High School." Elizabeth looked at Henley who smiled a faint smile at the reference to what she had said about being Annie Oakley and her own marksmanship abilities. "I mostly sang, but I also had to learn to fire the old-fashioned gun because I was pretending to be that excellent markswoman . . . in the musical. Anyway, I've not had a single gun in my hands since then. So I don't know how it might feel to shoot real bullets from a gun or to kill something . . . even a rabbit. There is no question that I wish somebody had killed Hitler or Stalin. Is there anybody who knows anything about history that doesn't wish someone had taken out those two evil people before they had a chance to wreak havoc upon the world? I wish somebody had done it, but I don't know if I would have had the courage to do it myself. I guess I would like to think I would have been brave enough and unselfish enough to sacrifice myself and my life to do the world a favor. This is all very hypothetical. But I will tell you that I am not opposed to the death penalty. I think there are a few monsters out there who deserve to be destroyed. I guess if I'd had the opportunity to get rid of Hitler or Stalin, I'd like to think I would have done it."

"I knew you would feel that way. I just needed to talk to somebody about some of these things."

"What's going on with you, Henley? I'm worried about you. You are not yourself."

"I'm not myself, and I can't tell you anything more. I have already told you too much." Henley obviously spoke with a heavy heart as she continued. "I am going to put a letter addressed to you in the safe deposit box at my bank in Paso Robles. It explains everything. There will also be a letter to my daughter in the safe deposit box. If I don't make it through this mission that I've decided to undertake and I die, my lawyer will retrieve the letters from the bank. He will contact you and send you the letters. I trust you to do what I would want you to do with them. It will all be made clear to you when you read my letter to you. But this will happen only if I am already dead." Henley paused. "I know this sounds terribly ominous and overly dramatic, and it really is . . . ominous. What I am saying is not overly dramatic. Do you understand what I am trying to tell you?"

Elizabeth really didn't understand, and she had a hundred questions. She was alarmed by the things Henley had said. She really didn't know what to think about any of it. She had suspicions about what Henley was trying to say to her without actually having to say any of it out loud. Elizabeth decided she would not ask Henley any of her many questions. She didn't think Henley would answer them anyway.

"Wish me luck. You might not hear anything from me for a long time. Or maybe you will never hear from me again. I've enjoyed knowing you, Elizabeth. Don't ask me anything. Don't say anything. I won't be able to tell you anything more. I've already said way too much to you. I wanted you to know about the letter I've written so you won't be completely shocked if and when my lawyer contacts you."

Elizabeth's concern was obvious on her face. Still she didn't speak. Henley continued. "I'm sorry to put this on you. But you are the only person I know with the smarts and the courage who is responsible and grown up enough to handle it. I have chosen you. You may not want to be chosen, but you have been. One of the reasons I have put this burden on you is because nobody knows I know you. You are not one of my family members or one of my employees. Nobody will ever be able to link you with me. You will not be at risk, and because I have decided to speak to you about this, my family and the people I know and love in Paso Robles will not be at risk. They will know nothing. Even if my name becomes public, which I hope it will not, my usual circle of acquaintances will know nothing. And, you are old. Nobody will blame you for speaking out for me, if you choose to do so. Thank you. I have to go now. Don't try to contact me. After the wedding tomorrow, I will be completely incommunicado. Don't ask. Don't tell. My choosing you is the highest compliment I can possibly pay to anyone. My own daughter would be second on my list. I trust her, but she has two daughters to raise. I can't take the chance of involving her and putting her at risk while her kids are still young."

Henley stood up and pushed Elizabeth's wheelchair out of the bar and towards the nearby concierge desk. "Tell the concierge to push you to your room or call your husband to come and get you. I have to go now. I hope I will see you again someday . . . somewhere. I will tell you all about it in person—if I ever can. Goodbye, Elizabeth." Henley squeezed Elizabeth's shoulder, and then she was gone.

Elizabeth called Richard on her cell phone. He agreed to come and get her at the concierge desk. Elizabeth was a bit in shock after her conversation with Henley. She needed time to absorb the jumble of things Henley had just said to her. She knew Henley was a brave and resourceful woman, but she feared that Henley might also be prone to taking imprudent chances. Henley was super smart, but Elizabeth worried that she might have a reckless streak. Elizabeth did not know exactly what Henley intended to do, but she had her suspicions. Elizabeth was afraid her friend was planning to jump off the deep end. She was afraid Henley was heading down a very dangerous road to a place from which it might not be possible for her to return. Henley didn't seem to be that afraid, but Elizabeth was definitely afraid for her.

Elizabeth was completely wiped out after Henley's revelations. Elizabeth and Richard would drive back to their home in Maryland on Tuesday. This was just Friday night. Elizabeth wondered if she would be able to sleep at all tonight. She knew it was useless to try to reason with Henley, to question her, or to try to talk her out of doing something she was determined to do.

Elizabeth really wondered why Henley had trusted her with her cryptic hints about whatever it was she was about to do. Henley was not as old as Elizabeth, but Elizabeth felt her friend was too old to take on any kind of a crazy mission. It made sense that Henley did not want to involve her own daughter who had two young children. Elizabeth would not have wanted to add to the burdens of her own daughters in a similar situation. Of course, Elizabeth did not really know what the situation was. She had a lot of suspicious and a lot to speculate about, but Henley had not really told her anything definitive.

CHAPTER 19

1945—1989

NIKITA KHRUSHCHEV, THE SOVIET UNION'S arrogant and brutish First Secretery of the Communist Party from 1953 until 1964, was the man who had pounded his shoe on the table at the 902nd Plenary Meeting of the United Nations General Assembly held in New York City on October 12, 1960. Khrushchev began building the Berlin Wall in August of 1961.

After World War II, Germany was divided into four sectors. The United States, Britain, France, and the USSR, the four major allies who had triumphed over the Nazis, each was awarded a sector. To be fair to the four victorious countries, the Nazi capital of Berlin was also divided into four sectors, and a sector of the city was given to each of the victors. Each of the four allied countries was allowed to control a sector of Berlin. But, the dictates of geography had to be accommodated. Berlin was in the eastern part of Germany and was completely surrounded by the sector of the country that had been awarded to the USSR. The Western Allies insisted on having access to their sectors of Berlin. Roadways and railways and air corridors were agreed on and provided for to allow the required access between West Germany and West Berlin.

A few years later, the barriers between the sectors of the three NATO countries disappeared, and West Germany became a united entity. Likewise, the three sectors of Berlin that were controlled by the NATO countries became West Berlin, the free part of the city that faced off against the Communist Russian sector known as East Berlin. The division between the countries that were free and the countries that were under authoritarian Communist rule became known as the Iron Curtain.

The Yalta Conference of 1945 divided war-torn Europe among the countries that had defeated Germany. As a result of this unfortunate division of the spoils of war, unlucky East Germany, Poland, Hungary, Czechoslovakia, Estonia, Latvia, Lithuania, Bulgaria, Romania, Albania, Yugoslavia, and others had the extreme bad luck to be given to the Union of Soviet Socialist Republics and its bloodthirsty leader Joseph Stalin. The hapless victims of this gross but seemingly unavoidable post-war travesty, the citizens of these ill-fated countries, fell under the tyranny of the USSR. Known as the Eastern Bloc, the people who had hoped for better after Hitler's Nazis were defeated, were forced to live for decades under the oppression of the debased Communist system with its accompanying poverty and injustices. These citizens of the Eastern Bloc had endured the criminality and brutality of the Nazis, and then they were forced to endure the criminality and brutality of the Reds. These ill-fated ones, forced to live within the realm of Soviet domination, struggled to survive under the stranglehold of the economic and political control of the cruel and corrupt Communist system.

It was a horrible system. Nothing reveals a system's flaws more accurately than the intensity of the desire of those who are trapped within it to escape from it. Hungary and Czechoslovakia tried revolutions and reforms, and they were crushed into submission beneath the Soviet boot. Many of those who were held captive in East Germany wanted to escape and live in the West. Droves of the brightest and best, who were caught behind the Iron Curtain, were leaving the warped, brutal, and failing Communist world behind.

The totalitarians who ruled the USSR could not allow this behavior to continue. East Germany was suffering from a fatal brain drain. Those who wanted to live in freedom were abandoning the sinking ship that was Communist East Germany. The Soviets and their puppets, who ruled the pathetic state of the DDR, had to stomp out freedom and force the people who lived in all Soviet satellite countries to remain behind the Iron Curtain and work for Communism. Nowhere was this desire to keep one's citizens imprisoned more intense than it was in Berlin. To prevent its citizens from escaping to freedom in the West, the Communist leaders of East Germany felt they had no alternative but to build an ever larger, ever taller, and ever stronger wall to force its people to stay inside their country. Khrushchev was determined to keep the East German people in chains by building a fortress, steep and mighty. The Berlin Wall would become a cruel fortification of infamy.

East Germany began to build the Berlin Wall in 1961. The wall was constructed, not just in Berlin, but all along the border that the Communist country shared with the West. The overriding goal was to keep the people of East Germany from escaping to freedom in West Germany. The most obvious example of the Soviet Wall of Shame was in

Berlin. In spite of the construction which consisted of massive concrete, barbed wire, and every other kind of barrier, those who wanted to escape the totalitarian state and live in freedom continued to try to escape and continued to succeed in escaping. The stories of their willingness to risk everything in their desperation to flee the brutal Soviet Union became legend.

In spite of towers containing armed soldiers, who were ordered to shoot to kill anyone who tried to go over the wall to the West, people determined to escape Communism continued to put their lives on the line in their attempts to get over the wall. To give their progeny a chance to live in freedom, parents took tremendous chances and went to great lengths to drop their infants and their children out of windows close to the wall. These parents were willing to demonstrate, with these extreme efforts of self-sacrifice, the hope that their children would be able to live in the free part of Berlin, the free part of the world. More than 100,000 people attempted to escape from Communism over the Berlin Wall. Countless brave human beings, who sought to live in freedom, were shot and died as they tried to escape the tyranny of the Soviet State.

The wall came down in 1989. The Soviet Union finally gasped its last breath and blessedly collapsed in 1991. Countries that had endured decades of the repression and poverty that socialism always brings, were finally free. But generations of Germans and others had lived and died under the brutality of Soviet attempts to keep their people in chains. The Berlin Wall was one of the most aggressive and blatant symbols of those terrible years.

In the early 1960s, an American soldier fell in love with a young German woman who became trapped behind the wall. Only eighteen years old when he joined the military, Johnny was willing to become a traitor to the United States because of his passion for the woman he loved. Johnny Bidwell of Dickson, West Virginia had been too young to fight in World War II. He joined the U. S. Army in 1960 and was sent to Germany to serve his country. While stationed in Berlin, he met and fell in love with Frieda Schultz who worked as a waitress in the West Berlin *biergarten* where Johnny liked to eat his meals and drink beer when he was off duty.

Frieda lived in East Berlin but had a work permit to travel to West Berlin for her job at her uncle's *biergarten*. She returned to her home and her family in the East every night. In 1961, when the Berlin Wall was built, Frieda was caught behind the Iron Curtain. She was no longer able to travel back and forth to work in West Berlin. She was a prisoner, along with millions of others, in Communist East Berlin.

Johnny did everything he could to try to get Frieda out of East Berlin. But he was as powerless as everyone else who wanted to free a loved one from "the other side of the wall." The U.S. Army was not able to do anything to help him rescue his girlfriend. Johnny tried for months and years to find a way to be reunited with Frieda. After his tour of active duty in Germany, he returned to the United States in 1963. He left the Army an embittered and angry young man. He and Frieda had intended to marry. Johnny was willing to do anything, to go to any lengths, to find a way for his beloved Frieda to escape from the East.

It was never exactly clear, even to Johnny, how he had become connected with the Russians. He had talked to so many people who had promised to help him bring Frieda out of East Berlin. He had begged. He talked to whoever would listen to his sad story. From the way he behaved and the way he talked, it seemed that he was willing to sell his soul to be reunited with Frieda. When he was picked up for questioning in 1965, Johnny explained to the FBI that he had "kind of stumbled into his relationship" with the Russian spy who wanted the secrets of the Woodbrier bunker.

The Soviet agent found Johnny and became his Russian handler. The Soviets knew all about his love for Frieda and the lengths to which Johnny had gone to be reunited with her. The Russian handler hoped to convince Johnny to tell him everything he knew about the bunker at the Woodbrier. He wanted Johnny to find out very specific details about the secret facility. In return, the Soviet agent agreed to arrange for Frieda Shultz to be allowed to leave Communist East Germany. Once Johnny had given the Russians all the information they wanted, the Stasi promised they would deliver Frieda to West Berlin where she and Johnny would be reunited.

Johnny knew he was doing something that was very wrong. He had signed papers and promised never to reveal anything about the secret project that was being undertaken at the Woodbrier. But the offer his handler had made him, to deliver his beloved Frieda from East Berlin to the safety of his arms in the West, was more than the young man could resist. He decided to become a traitor and put his life at risk for love. He felt guilty about what he had agreed to do, but his feelings for his East German girlfriend won the day.

What Johnny Bidwell did not know was that an employee from the Woodbrier had overheard him talking to the Russian agent at a local diner. A coworker from the Woodbrier, who by chance also happened to know the Russian language, had overheard Bidwell being asked to hand over important information about the very secret government installation at the West Virginia resort. This fellow employee heard Johnny agree to turn his back on the agreement he had signed—his solemn promise not to reveal information about the bunker. The man who'd recognized Johnny at the diner had overheard him agree to break his oath and betray his country.

Although Johnny had agreed to break this promise and had agreed to reveal information about the bunker, he had not yet told the Russians anything. A special contingent from the FBI appeared at Johnny's door in Dickson, West Virginia in the middle of the night and arrested him for treason. The FBI knew all about his relationship with the Russian handler and knew he had agreed to reveal secrets about the Woodbrier to the Soviets. Johnny was handcuffed and taken from his home. The FBI drove him to a non-descript government building where they grilled him for many hours about his association with the Soviet Union.

Johnny was scared to death. He had not wanted to betray his country. He had thought only of rescuing Frieda from East Berlin. His passion for Frieda had been more important than his oath not to reveal the Woodbrier's secrets. The promise of being reunited with Frieda had been his sole motivation for agreeing to make a deal with the Soviets.

The three FBI agents who questioned Johnny Bidwell when he was arrested used a sketch artist to compose a likeness of the Russian man Bidwell had met with in the diner. This was Johnny's handler, the man who had promised him Frieda would be allowed to come to the West. Johnny trusted the Russian to deliver on his promise, but Johnny knew very little about the geopolitics of the day or about the duplicity of spies who promise things but do not deliver on their promises. The FBI wasted no time letting Johnny Bidwell know that his Russian handler never had any intentions of delivering Frieda. The FBI told him honestly that, once Johnny had told the Russians everything they wanted to know, both he and Frieda would probably be killed. Johnny believed the FBI when they told him what would happen to him and to Frieda, once he had betrayed his country to the Russians.

Even though Johnny was now terribly afraid of both his Russian handler and of his FBI inquisitors, he agreed to accept the deal the FBI offered him. He agreed to continue to meet with the Russian. Johnny would feed his handler false information, created by the FBI, about the secrets at the Woodbrier and the underground bunker. The relationship between Johnny and his handler would remain intact, but the Soviets would not know that Johnny Bidwell had become a double agent.

Johnny agreed to all of this duplicity and to take all the risks involved on one condition. The one condition was that the FBI and the U. S. government would do everything in their considerable powers to rescue Frieda Schultz and bring her to the West. Johnny was frightened, but he was still willing to do everything he could to save the woman he loved. He was willing to put himself at risk, being a double agent and pretending to cooperate with the Russians, in order to be reunited with Frieda Shultz. The FBI promised to do what they could to get Frieda out of East Germany.

Once the FBI had a picture of Johnny's Russian contact, it did not take them long to hunt down and identify the man. Foreigners tended to stick out in small towns in West Virginia. The FBI chose not to arrest the Soviet agent immediately but decided instead to follow him. They wanted to watch Johnny's contact to see who the Russian communicated with. They wanted Johnny's local handler to pass along the false information he obtained from Johnny. They knew Johnny's contact would deliver the information Johnny had told him to someone higher up in the hierarchy of agents. Johnny's misinformation about the Woodbrier would be handed on and eventually would end up in Moscow.

The FBI held off arresting Johnny's contact because they felt he could lead them to other Russians currently spying in the USA. There were plenty of Russian spies and even some Soviet sympathizers in the U.S. in those days, and the FBI wanted to identify as many of them as possible.

Johnny's instructions as a double agent were to pass along false information and to lead the FBI to more Soviet spies. Johnny was told to continue to meet with the Russian agent at the diner. The FBI promised him that he would always be protected by watchers—U.S. operatives who would be present but disguised, during Johnny's meetings with his handler. These agents would follow the Russian when he left the diner to see with whom he was meeting and to whom he was passing along the information he had just learned from Johnny.

The FBI was stumped about how Johnny Bidwell of Dickson, West Virginia had been able to learn the Russian language. Johnny had a great personality and many friends, but he had barely been able to make it through high school before he'd joined the Army and been sent to boot camp and then to Germany for active duty.

Frieda wanted to practice her English when she was with Johnny, so she refused to speak German with him. She almost always insisted on speaking English when she was with Johnny. He had been able to learn a little bit of German, eating and drinking in the *biergarten* and hanging out in West Berlin.

Johnny told the FBI that Frieda had been forced to learn Russian in the schools she'd attended in East Germany. Everyone had to learn the Russian language if they wanted to make any advances in the East German educational system. Frieda was fluent in Russian. In spite of refusing to speak German with Johnny, she made one exception when it came to speaking Russian with him. Frieda had made a kind of game out of teaching Russian to Johnny. She demanded, as a kind of joke, that Johnny always make love to her in Russian. Consequently, Johnny had been highly motivated to learn his Russian quickly.

The FBI was understandably skeptical of Johnny's abilities to be a successful spy. They realized he was not that intelligent, and of course, he'd had no training at all to be a spy. But he was very motivated to be reunited with Frieda. As long as he believed the FBI was trying to get her out of East Berlin, he was going to do his best to try to be the double agent the FBI wanted him to be. Johnny did not really understand exactly what a double agent was, but he was going to do, to the very best of his abilities, everything his FBI handlers told him to do. The man had a one-track mind. He would deliver for the FBI if the FBI would deliver Frieda.

CHAPTER 20

1965

THERE WAS A TUNNEL UNDER the Berlin Wall. In fact there were several tunnels under the wall. It would have been an easy thing to bring Frieda out of East Belin through one of these tunnels. But military regulations and strict security and secrecy concerns made it impossible for Frieda to leave East Germany through one of these escape routes. Even under extraordinary circumstances, those in power would not agree to Frieda's quick exit via the tunnels. No one except those with very high security clearances could ever know about the existence, let alone the locations, of the Berlin tunnels. To reveal that such escape routes existed to an East German woman would be the height of stupidity. She might not be able to keep a secret, or she herself might be a spy.

The FBI realized that as soon as Frieda had made it to the West, Johnny would no longer have any reason to continue to act as a counterspy for them. They could threaten him with prison and even with execution for betraying his country. But the agents who were handling Johnny Bidwell quickly realized that he was willing to go to jail and even to die for love. The plan to rescue Frieda would have to be drawn out and delayed in order for the FBI's plan to work. The FBI wanted to continue to use Johnny Bidwell to track possible high-level Soviet agents for as long as he would work for them.

The summer of 1965 was targeted as the time period for the operation to begin to bring Frieda to the West. A very tall American, who said he was from Texas and wore a big ten-gallon white hat and handmade alligator-skin cowboy boots to prove it, hung out in the railway stations of West Germany. Hanging out in train stations was part of his job, and his cover story was that he was a rich Texan who was seeing Europe that summer.

His immediate assignment was to be on the lookout for a young woman who resembled Frieda Schultz, a female of her same approximate age, build, and face. Tex was willing to attempt to recruit a Brit, a Dane, a Swede, an Irishwoman, a woman from Switzerland, or anyone at all who could be convincing as Frieda's double.

He felt very lucky when he discovered the group of four American girls at the train station in Munich. One of the four looked so much like Frieda, she could have been the young woman's twin sister. She was blonde and blue-eyed and perfect. Tex decided he would do whatever he had to do to convince Frieda's doppelganger to help save Frieda.

The four girls were all very attractive young women. They were so obviously Americans, wearing their black London Fog raincoats and carrying their Samsonite and American Tourister suitcases. They looked as if they were from well-to-do families, so money would not be one of the recruitment tools Tex would use with this group. He would have to appeal to their patriotism.

The girl who so closely resembled Frieda looked like she was the shyest of the group. She also looked like she was the most observant. She had noticed Tex sitting on the bench in the waiting room of the train station. She had been curious about him and had looked him over carefully. Tex was able to fool most people, but he knew he was not fooling this newly found "Frieda." The shy girl in the group of four knew he was not exactly what he seemed to be. Maybe he had overdone it with the big cowboy hat. She would be the most difficult of the four to win over. They all looked smart, but he wondered if the shy one already suspected he was CIA. He had not really wanted a group of four girls. Two would have been ideal. But the girl he needed was definitely one of four. He thought he could work with that.

Tex figured they were waiting to board the train to Frankfurt. They had a couple of hours to wait for the train. They would probably decide to have a meal in the station's café. The food in Germany's train stations was good, and it was cheap. Sure enough, they went into the dining room and sat at a table for four. There were not that many people in the *Bahnhof* this late at night, so Tex was able to get a table close to theirs and eavesdrop on their conversation.

They were hungry. They'd run into friends from the U.S. at the Hofbrau House the night before and had stayed up too late. They'd overslept and missed the breakfast that came with their room at the youth hostel. They'd had to find a bakery and pay for their breakfast that morning. They had missed the chiming of the Munich Glockenspiel at eleven and had returned to Marienplatz for the Clock Tower show at noon. They'd tried to cram all of their sightseeing into the rest of the day. Because breakfast had been late, they'd had a late lunch. They had not really been hungry for dinner at the usual hour. It was way past time for the evening meal, and now they were starving.

They ordered pork schnitzel and tomaten salat, the usual things Americans ordered in Germany. One of the girls ordered the rotisserie chicken that came with roasted potatoes. They ordered Rhine wine. No one could face any more beer after their night at the Hofbrauhaus. They kept close watch on their purses and suitcases while they ate their dinner. The group appeared to be a little too smart and a little too well-heeled for Tex, but the shy girl in the group looked so much like Frieda Shultz, he had to have her.

Tex ordered food, and when the girls were getting ready to leave, he turned around to face their table and struck up a conversation with them. He was tall and good looking, and he hoped they might welcome a chance to chat with someone from the good ole' U.S. of A.

"Hey, ladies. I hope you don't think I'm bein' rude, but I couldn't help overhearin' your conversation. I have to say it sure was the most pleasant of sounds to hear American being spoken at the table right next to mine. You young woman look like you are pretty seasoned travelers, and it sounds like you are havin' the time of your lives on your European trip."

The girl with the red hair was the most confident one of the group. Her name was Alice. "And who are you?" She demanded. She was the self-imposed protector of the group, her mission being to keep her friends from falling in with possible predators of the opposite sex.

"Excuse me all to pieces, ladies, what has happened to my manners? What would my Mammy say about me bein' uncouth? I'm Tex, and I'm from Dallas. You might have been able to guess that from my accent." The shy girl, whose name was

Jane Ellen, rolled her eyes. She was suspicious of him, and the red-haired girl was going to continue to challenge him. Kate, the tall and really beautiful girl in the group of four looked like she was probably a fashion model and probably had at least one boyfriend, and probably several, at home in the States. She had pale skin, long dark hair, and dark eyes. She ignored him completely and continued writing postcards. She was not interested in anything the tall Texan had to say. The fourth girl had brown hair that she wore in a ponytail, and she had a mischievous glint in her eye. This was Susie, and she looked like she would be up for an adventure. She looked like she would be a lot of fun. Tex knew this might be a tough group to break into and make friends with. They were either ignoring him or were very wary of his approach.

"Are y'all intendin' to head for Berlin on your trip?" Tex knew they were. All the young Americans who came to Europe for the summer since the wall had gone up were curious about Berlin. They wanted to experience the ride on the locked train that traveled through the Eastern sector, the Communist sector, from Koln to Berlin, without stopping. The trip smacked of a little bit of danger, traveling through big, bad Communist territory. They knew they were safe inside the train that sped through the summer night and would only stop and unlock its doors once it reached safety in West Berlin.

Susie, the girl who looked like she would be fun and like she would laugh a lot, was the one who answered him. "Yes, we are taking a ride on the Rhine for the day, and then we will take the train from Koln to Berlin. We have Eurail passes."

"The Eurail pass is the best bargain around. You can always go first class, and always get a wagon lit. I usually visit

Berlin but probably won't go there on this trip. I'm here on business, and of course, that takes priority."

"What kind of business are you in?" The shy one was going to try to trip him up. She didn't believe his cover story for a minute. She was the one he had to win over, and he was going to have to tone down the Texas drawl and the whole cowboy thing in order to win her trust. He might even have to tell the truth about what he really did in order to convince this one.

"I'm in the oil business. We sell a lot of Texas oil to the Europeans. We want to give them a good deal and make sure none of these countries do any business with the Ruskies. You know what I mean?"

The shy one was weighing his answer. It would be just his luck if she was majoring in economics or something like that. Why couldn't she be a nice art history major or even a zoology major? This one might actually know something about the economics of oil, and she might know that most of the oil European countries used was imported from the Middle East.

Tex decided to take a chance. "I also do work, kind of on the side, to help refugees from the Eastern Block get to the West. Some want to go to the United States and begin new lives." He'd had to say this. These four were smarter than he'd even pegged them for, but he thought he'd finally found their soft spot. He sensed that they cared about refugees and people escaping from the Communists. "It's hard enough to get these poor folks across the wall in the first place. We have a few ways of going around the wall, but it gets harder and harder as the East Germans close more and more of our secret escape routes." All four were listening to him now, and he knew he had them. "Once they finally escape, they need all kinds of help. They've pretty much left everything they own behind, except for the clothes they're wearing. They might have been able to bring a little bit of money out, but of course marks from East Germany aren't worth anything in the West. Nothing to back them up, and the coins are made out of aluminum. Worthless!"

He had a completely captive audience now. "The escapees with family in the West don't need us and usually go directly to their new lives. Most of the others want to stay in West Germany, as you might expect. But a few want to go to England and to the United States. Some want to go to Scandinavia. Those are the ones we try to help. We get them a hotel room and give them some money. We make sure they have enough to eat and some clothes. All of these folks have suffered hardships and have even been shot at, trying the get over the wall. Depending on their ages and their skills, and especially their language skills, of course, we try to find them new homes. We respect their bravery and want to do what we can to help them get settled in a free country."

The shy one had questions. "Do you work through the Red Cross or some kind of a religious organization? The work you do sounds wonderful, but who funds all of this and handles all the official paperwork and red tape? I know it's complicated to be granted political asylum in the United States. But those who risk their lives coming over the wall certainly deserve to have help once they make it to freedom."

Tex was encouraged, but he didn't want to have to answer any questions about his lack of associations with other organizations. He felt he now knew how to get to the shy one. She was smart, but she was idealistic. He thought he finally had her hooked. He looked at his watch and stood up to leave.

"I sure do hate to have to interrupt this interesting discussion I've been havin' with you lovely ladies, but I've got to be on my way. It's been real nice gettin' to know y'all. I'm going to give each one of you my business card. You all seem to be such capable and independent young women, you probably won't ever need any help with anything. But just in case you do, while you're on your European grand tour, remember you can always contact ole Tex for help. Just call that number on the card, and you'll be connected with my office in Texas. Reverse the charges. My office staff always knows where to find me, even when I'm in Germany. I'd be honored and flattered if you ever need to call me for anything at all. Y'all take care of yourselves now." Tex dropped a U.S. hundred dollar bill on his table, tipped his hat to the four American girls, and swaggered off in the direction of the Frankfurt train.

CHAPTER 21

1965

They were not aware that they were being watched, but someone kept an eye on the four American females while they continued their travels through Germany. They made their way to Heidelberg and then to the Rhine River cruise that was so popular. It was a beautiful day, and they ate wurst and potato salad and drank dark beer. On the river boat, they met some boys from Bowdoin College and had dinner with them in Koln before boarding the train to West Berlin. It was also possible to fly or drive to West Berlin, but the plane fare was too expensive. They didn't have a car. They did have Eurail Passes. They would take the train. The train would take them through Communist East Germany to West Berlin.

In 1965, the Berlin Wall was well established. East Berlin and East Germany existed behind the Iron Curtain. Barriers had been built to try to keep people from leaving the East. What kind of a system has to go to these extraordinary measures to make their country into a prison in order to convince its people to stay?

The train to Berlin was locked before it was allowed to enter the East sector. The train would not be allowed to stop or even slow down while it traveled through Communist East Germany to reach Berlin. This was the agreement between the East and the West. Tourists would be allowed to visit West Berlin, but the train could not slow down or stop because the East German government did not want any of its citizens to be able to board the train to freedom—the train that was headed for free West Berlin.

There was a sense of danger and even a sense of doing something forbidden when one rode the nighttime train to Berlin. For the American girls, it seemed very odd and against human nature for their train to be racing through a country where they were not wanted. They wondered what would happen if there was a breakdown or a train wreck. What if the East Germans and the Russians decided to block or shut down the railway lines while they were on the train?

Each of them was familiar with the days of the Berlin Airlift, originally known as the Berlin Blockade, when the Communists had decided they wanted all of Berlin for themselves. The young women had been small children at the time of the Berlin Airlift, but they remembered their parents talking about it. They'd learned early in their lives that the East Germans and the Russians were the Evil Empire.

During the Berlin Airlift, the Soviets blockaded all rail and road access to the free zones of West Berlin. It became impossible to travel by roadway or by railway between free West Germany and free West Berlin. The Communist objective was to starve and freeze the citizens of West Berlin, to cut off everything the free Berliners needed to live. Without a constant resupply of food and fuel from the West, the USSR hoped that Berlin would fall to them. But the free nations of the world refused to allow this to happen. The countries of NATO refused to allow West Berlin to give in to the brutes of the East. It was about saving the lives of the citizens of West Berlin, but it was about so much more than that. It was a crusade, a symbolic mission, about which system, which culture had the staying power to prevail against the other. It was about freedom versus evil.

The countries of NATO refused to allow East Germany and their puppet masters, the men in Moscow, to have their way. The countries of the West rallied to the cause and used the only route left to them to keep free West Berlin alive... the airways. To shoot down a plane that was bringing fuel oil and gasoline and food and clothing to West Berlin would be to ignite World War III. Russia decided it was not worth it to go to war against its former allies. They already knew first-hand about the determination of the Americans and the other free nations of the world. The Communists in Berlin and in Moscow again were forced to learn hard lessons about the power of freedom.

After more than a year of flying life-saving supplies to West Berlin, the NATO countries triumphed. The Russians realized they had been defeated in their attempts to bring West Berlin to its knees and to conscript the entire city as its own. They gave up and decided to once again allow land route access to Berlin from West Germany. The Berlin Airlift had prevailed over Communist aggression. The Russians had failed. Communism and repression had failed.

In the end, freedom will always win. Freedom is the natural state of the human condition. Freedom lives in the hearts and minds of men and women everywhere. Dictators and oppressors do not want to admit that this is true. They continue, at their peril, on their foolish path to try to dominate and hold the human spirit captive. Tyrants will fail. Tyrants will fall.

The four American girls felt their part in this struggle acutely as they rode the train through Communist East Germany. They were part of the defiance against a system that suppressed and imprisoned. Making a decision to be on that night train to Berlin was more than just a train ride. It was an act of solidarity with the free people of the world. The locked train, speeding towards West Berlin, was a symbol of that solidarity. It represented the continuation of the imperative and unbreakable links among people who are free.

West Berlin was thriving and prosperous in the mid-1960s. East Berlin was impoverished, and much of it was still in ruins from Hitler's war. The four young women from the United States wanted to see the miracle that was West Berlin, a city that had risen from the ashes of defeat and become a beacon of liberty in the darkness of totalitarianism. West Berlin was thriving, an economic success, a symbol of what freedom and private enterprise could offer.

The young woman also wanted to visit mysterious and forbidden East Berlin. They wanted to experience a Communist country for themselves. They had heard about Communism all their lives. They now had the opportunity to actually see one of those treacherous places first hand.

They arrived in West Berlin and celebrated the progress and success that city represented. It was no wonder everyone who was held captive in East Berlin wanted to escape and come to the West. But curiosity and the lure of potential but unlikely danger tempted them to make several trips into the Communist controlled sector of Berlin.

The women knew that when they traveled into East Berlin, they would have to trade five West German marks, which were hard currency and had actual buying power, for five East German marks that were essentially worthless and made of aluminum. The East German marks were like feathers in one's hand. They had no substance, no weight, no value. The coins were like the promises of Communism and Socialism . . . relics in the dust.

On their first trip to East Berlin, the girls rode the subway to the checkpoint where they had to show their passports multiple times and exchanged their hard currency for the worthless East German *Deutschmarks*. The young women were not intimidated by the questioning they received from Communist interrogators or by the close looks they received from the East German authorities. They were not frightened by the scrutiny. The four American girls had nothing to hide. They were who their passports said they were. These young women held citizenship in the greatest country in the world. They were free to come and go. The military guards who examined their papers and who questioned them at length were not free. They could not leave their Communist prison that was East Germany.

The four briefly walked around the area close to the barriers between the East and the West. When they left East Berlin after that short walking tour and returned to West Berlin on the subway, they did not get their money back. It was illegal to take East German money out of East Germany. They had to leave all of their unspent feather-weight East German marks behind. They realized they had in fact made a donation of hard currency to the DDR, the People's

Republic of Germany, the corrupt East German government that robbed its people of prosperity and freedom. Besides, the East Germans did not want the rest of the world to see how truly worthless their currency was. They had to hide their money. Their flimsy coins could not be allowed to see the light of day.

The four young women were curious about what lay beyond the immediate area of the border, what the rest of East Berlin was like on the other side of the wall. The only way they would be able to see more of Berlin was on a special sight-seeing tour, on an East German tour bus, sponsored, supervised, and carefully controlled by the East German authorities. They signed up to take the bus tour scheduled for the next day, their second foray into the Eastern sector.

The tour was on an old East German bus. The seats had been reupholstered in ugly, dark, scratchy fabric to try to make a better impression on Western tourists. The bus smelled old. Unlike Greyhound buses in the West, there was no bathroom on the bus. Once again, West German marks were exchanged for the strange East German coins. Those on the tour were urged to spend their coins while they were in East Berlin. There would be only one stop on the tour, just one opportunity to spend those coins on anything. East German money would, once again, be collected at the end of the tour. It could not be taken back to the West.

After the Western sightseers boarded the bus at the East-West checkpoint, the stocky East German Brunhilde, who would act as their tour guide, collected the passports of everyone on the tour bus. The passports would be held by this tour guide while they toured East Berlin. No one on the bus liked having to hand over a passport to the East Germans, even for a few hours. But everyone on the bus tour gave up their passport and crossed their fingers that the passports would be returned at the end of the day.

The American girls were alarmed by the confiscation. It was one thing to give one's passport to a hotel manager or the administrator of a youth hostel in a free country. It was an entirely different thing to hand over one's U.S. passport to a Communist government agent who pretended to be a tour guide.

The tour bus traveled through the rubble left by the war. The bunker where Hitler was said to have committed suicide was in East Berlin. That bunker was a favorite stopping place on the tour. No one was allowed to disembark from the bus. But the bus did stop in the general area of the location where the tour guide told them that Hitler had died. The people on the tour bus could look out the windows. Of course the bunker was below ground, and it was only possible to view a pile of concrete debris that lay strewn around on top of the bunker. In fact, there was nothing to see. They could have been anywhere. It was only the word of the East German tour guide, who spoke to the people on the bus through a crackly microphone, that assured them Hitler's suicide bunker was indeed underneath the pile of rubble they were looking at.

The four young woman wondered among themselves why the East Germans had not cleared away more of the war rubble and rebuilt the city. If they wanted to convince the world that Communism and Socialism were the way to go, a paradise for the people, they should have made their part of Berlin look better. Twenty years after the war had ended, much of what their bus tour of East Berlin had to show them was of a city still in ruins. The few places they were allowed to see that had been rebuilt were extraordinarily ugly. Apartment buildings made of cement blocks and the square office buildings constructed of uninspiring and already crumbling cement with tiny windows were horribly depressing. What kind of a place was this? No wonder the people of East Berlin and East Germany wanted to escape to the West.

Near the end of the day, they arrived at the Soviet War Memorial, the high point of the tour and the one place where tourists could spend their lightweight East German aluminum coins. At the war memorial, two of the American girls bought postcards, and two of the four spent their coins on what they thought were soft drinks. The postcards had been outrageously expensive, but those costly cards had been the better choice. The only postcards one could buy, of course, were cards that showed various photographic views of the Soviet War Memorial. But the drinks were room temperature and sickly sweet. The flavor could not be discerned, but supposedly they were something fruity. The drinks were terrible. The girls wondered if the East Germans kept these especially disgusting drinks for foreign tourists or if the people of Berlin were also forced to buy and consume the small and dreadful juices in waxed paper cartons. Ugh! They threw the containers and their expensive and putrid contents into the closest trash bin.

The Soviet war memorial was the last stop on the tour. When they returned to the bus, Brunhilde began to hand back their passports. The reason for the confiscation became clear to the Americans. Brunhilde gave most of the passports back after she closely compared the face on the passport with the face of the live human person seated on the bus. One man, however, did not resemble his passport picture as closely as Brunhilde thought he should. Mr. Baxter was accused of not being Mr. Baxter. An argument ensued. Brunhilde was fierce. The departure from the war memorial was delayed by the argument over the face on the passport.

It occurred to the shy American girl in the quartet that indeed the Mr. Baxter who had left the bus to view the Russian tourist site might not be the same Mr. Baxter who'd returned to the bus after spending forty-five minutes at the Soviet war memorial. This would be one way to try to get people in and out of the East Bloc. For the substitution to work, the picture on the passport would have to have a close resemblance to the live person. Brunhilde was suspicious. Mr. Baxter stood his ground. Finally the bus left and traveled the short distance back to West Berlin where those who had just visited East Berlin were happy to disembark from the bus and bid Brunhilde *auf Wiedersehen*. All the tourists were delighted to be back in West Berlin, back to freedom.

Most of the rest of the sightseers on the bus were either sufficiently intimidated or bored by the tour of rubble. Most of them would not be returning to East Berlin any time soon. But the curiosity of the four American girls had been piqued. They wanted to see more of East Germany. They would be back the next day to apply for the required travel permits that would allow them to take the train through the East German countryside from East Berlin to Rostock in Mecklenburg, East Germany where they would board a ferry for Denmark.

They waited in an East German bureaucrat's office for most of the following day. They filled out forms. Each of the women was interviewed twice. The questions were routine about where they had been born and where they had grown up in the United States. The answers to the questions probably did not mean anything to these agents of the Communist state, but a certain amount of harassment was required before the four would be allowed to travel on an East German train from Berlin to Rostock. From there, Westerners who had been thoroughly vetted and sufficiently harassed would be allowed to leave the train and board the ferry that would cross a part of the Baltic Sea to reach Denmark.

The four eventually overcame all the hurdles and obtained the necessary papers to make the journey. It had been a long day, most of it spent waiting in the office of the East German official who screened the applicants and stamped the papers of those who were worthy. The wait and the experience of interacting with the Communist East German government had been instructive. The young women ended the day being even more thankful than they had been at the beginning of the day that they lived in the United States of America. The people they had encountered had been very polite and nice, for the most part. But the systems that the Russians had imposed on East Germany had brought a new realization of how incredibly lucky they were to be Americans and how sad they were for the people trapped behind the Iron Curtain.

CHAPTER 22

1965

After they had visited the war memorial on the bus tour and after they had spent the day waiting in the East German bureaucratic office mess, trying to get their travel permits, Tex knew he had them. He now had to figure a way to get the shy girl alone. She was his target, and Tex had to convince her to agree to his plan to help Frieda Shultz escape to the West. He had to make his pitch directly to her. Separating the shy one from her three traveling companions would not be easy. They were bound together like glue. They were staying at a youth hostel style hotel in West Berlin. Tex would have to bribe the manager of the hostel to be able to talk to the shy girl alone.

The manager of the youth hostel asked to speak to the shy girl whose name was Jane Ellen. He told her there was a problem with her passport. A look of fear and confusion passed over her face when he said these words to her, and he felt guilty that he was causing this sweet young American such obvious distress. There was nothing wrong with her passport, but he had been paid a lot of money to bring her to his office where Tex could speak to her. Tex insisted on complete privacy for his talk with the shy girl, and he had paid the hostel manager generously to provide that privacy.

Tex reassured her immediately about her passport. "I apologize for scarin' you about the news that your passport wasn't just right. Your passport is fine. I had to find a way to talk to you in private, without your three friends listening in to what I had to say."

The shy girl's expression had changed rather quickly from fear to annoyance and then to anger. She had been annoyed to see Tex in the hostel manager's office. She hadn't trusted him when she'd seen him for the first time in the Munich train station, and she trusted him even less now that he had turned up in Berlin.

"Please don't be angry, and please hear me out." Tex could see that this young woman did not like him and was ready to walk out before he'd even begun his pitch. "I work for the United States government, and your country needs you."

When the shy girl gave him a look of disgust, Tex realized he was not making his case very well. She thought he was making a pass at her and was claiming to be a government agent to get a date with her. She stood up to leave the room.

"Please, Jane, I'm telling you the truth. I am not trying to seduce you or date you. I need your help. You are uniquely qualified to help me with a very important operation."

"Is this more baloney? Somehow I think that is all that comes out of your mouth . . . baloney."

"This is not baloney. It is a plea to your patriotism and your good character."

"I have experienced a lot of lines from boys and men in my life, but I have to say this one you are putting out there is a first for me. Patriotism and good character . . . what are you talking about? You don't even know me."

"I know quite a bit about you, Jane Ellen Gilbert. I know that you grew up in Columbus, Ohio and attend a very prestigious girls' college in New England. Your father is a doctor, and you are an only child. Shall I go on?"

"I am offended that you have looked into my background so completely, but now you have triggered my curiosity. Why am I uniquely qualified to help you in your operation? I just turned twenty-one years old. I am a student. I am not really very worldly, although I try to pretend that I am. You are scaring me. Do you really work for the U.S. government?"

"I really do work for the U.S. government. You are uniquely qualified to help me because you look very much like a young woman that I am trying to smuggle out of East Germany and into the West. Will you help me?"

Jane Ellen Gilbert stared at Tex. She was weighing whether or not to trust him and whether or not she wanted to risk going along with what initially sounded like either a scam or an illusory and dangerous plan. "I have no way of knowing whether or not you are telling me the truth. I want you to know that my parents' closest friends back in Ohio are a United States Congressman and his wife. I am best friends with his oldest daughter. He will cause an international incident if anything happens to me while I am out of the United States. He will hunt you down and put you in jail if anything happens to me. I trust him to do all of that for me. What do you have to say to that?"

"I know your Congressman friend, and I promise that he would urge you to help me extricate this woman from Communist East Germany. This young German woman very much wants to leave the East, and it is of critical importance that we get her out of East Berlin. You have the chance to do your country a great service. Please. It will not be much of a risk to you, and it will mean everything to her."

Jane Ellen was a patriot. She wanted to do something for her country. She felt terrible for the East Germans who were not allowed to leave their Communist country to find freedom and a better life. Especially after the wall had gone up, she had shared with all her fellow Americans the agony of seeing people held against their will in a brutal Communist state. She made the decision to help. If she could bring even one poor soul from tyranny to freedom, she would do it.

"What do I tell my friends, my traveling companions? Are they in on this, too, or is it just me all alone?"

"I will leave that up to you. I will explain to you in detail everything that you have to do. If you think you need to bring your friends into the plan, that is fine with me. I trust you to know them and to have good judgment. Whatever you think will make your part in this easier and help with the woman's escape, that is what I want you to do."

"Of course you know I am not a spy and could easily make a mess of this. If I screw up, will I die or will your important person die? I don't want to go to prison, and I don't want anybody to be hurt."

"We think we have quite a foolproof plan. You might be somewhat at risk, but for only a very few minutes. Our woman who will be impersonating you briefly is the one who will be at risk. You will hang onto your own passport, and you only need to always be yourself. She will be the one who takes the chances. We have provided her with a real United States of America passport, and we think it will pass muster. But you never know with these Communists."

Tex was elated and was certain that shy Jane Ellen was going to agree to help bring Frieda Shultz to freedom. He continued. "Let me explain what we want to happen. After you have heard all the details of the plan, you can decide if you feel you can carry it out. Or you can decide that it is too much for you. You can change your mind and forget the whole thing. You can forget you ever met me."

Tex proceeded to explain to Jane Ellen what was going to happen. He laid it out for her in great detail. She had a lot of questions. Tex answered them all. She finally agreed to take on the challenge. It didn't seem to her as if she would be in any great danger. She thought she might have to tell her friends what was going on, but she decided she would wait until the last minute to tell them anything. That way they would not be able to argue with her or get nervous about what was happening.

Tex gave Jane Ellen a shopping bag of clothes. He told her she had to wear the outfit that was in the shopping bag when she rode on the train the next day. Tex assured her that everything would fit, including the shoes she was to wear. She shook hands with Tex and left the hostel manager's office. Tex wished her luck. Jane Ellen returned to the room she shared with her three friends. She assured them that all the problems with her passport had been resolved. It had been a mistake. Everything had been cleared up. It had mostly been a pain in the ass.

They had specific instructions about where they were to meet the train that would take them to Rostock and how they were to get to the train. The time table was strict, and the directions were very precise. They were to take a certain subway from the West that would deliver them to East Berlin. They then would board another subway that would take them to the *Bahnhof* from which the long distance train would depart.

Only two of the four American travelers were able to arrive on time to make the departure of the first subway. The shy girl and the beautiful fashion model, Jane Ellen and Kate, were on time. Alice and Susie had overslept and did not make the subway in time. The East Germans waited for no one. The two late sleepers would miss the train ride through East Germany. They would have to find another way to get to Copenhagen.

When the subway from the Western sector traveled to the Eastern sector, there was a great deal of passport scrutiny and shuffling of paperwork, even before they were allowed to get off the subway. East German soldiers with machine guns stood on either side of the exit door of the subway from the West. These armed guards stood shoulder to shoulder and formed a tight pathway for the two women to follow to board the East German subway. There would be no deviation from the way they were to walk. Anyone who was not aboard the first subway and who had not had their travel papers checked and rechecked would not be allowed to get into the line of passengers headed for the second subway.

After a brief ride on the East Berlin subway, they reached the East Berlin *Bahnhof*. Papers were examined and reexamined at every transfer. Finally the two young American female travelers were allowed to make their way to the East German long-distance train bound for Rostock. They had reserved seats and boarded the nearly-empty train car. There were a few other passengers on board, but the train was far from full. Not many people were making the trip from East Berlin to Rostock or Denmark today.

One of the other passengers in their car struck up a conversation with the two Americans. The young woman said she and her aunt were Danish and were going home after visiting relatives in East Berlin. The young girl spoke excellent English and was quick to tell the two American women that she'd learned her English in school. She was traveling with her aunt whose English was not as good. The young woman spoke for both of them. Most people took off their coats when they settled into their seats on the train. The Danish girl kept her raincoat on, and Jane Ellen noticed that. She wondered if the Danish girl was cold. It was July, but it was Germany. It seemed odd to Jane Ellen that she had not taken off her coat.

Jane Ellen's friend Kate asked her about the clothes she was wearing that day. Kate said she'd not seen Jane Ellen wear that outfit before. The friends had been traveling together for nearly two months. Kate thought she had seen all the items in Jane Ellen's travel wardrobe . . . many times. The pleated plaid skirt, the white blouse with the Peter Pan collar, and the navy blue cardigan sweater made an outfit with a very American look. Kate had seen the white socks before, but Jane Ellen's penny loafers looked new. Jane Ellen told her friend she would explain the new clothes to her when they were on the Danish ferry. Kate gave Jane Ellen a funny look and shrugged her shoulders. They'd been friends all their lives. Kate knew that Jane Ellen sometimes did off-beat things. This was probably one of them.

The train ride was long. They ate the ham and cheese sandwiches they'd brought with them. They had been warned that there would be not be any food service on the East German train. They had also brought bottled water and a few pieces of fruit in their string bags. They looked out the window at the countryside that could have been someplace in Ohio. They fell asleep.

The train stopped at what seemed to be some kind of a military facility, not a train station. Soldiers boarded the train. Two guards questioned each passenger in the train car. It seemed as if the questions took a lot of time. The guards were clearly members of the East German military. There were many questions. Jane Ellen and Kate were not used to be interrogated so intensely. The guards were polite enough, and their English was excellent. They were not threatening, but they were very insistent and very thorough. After the soldiers had interviewed everyone and left the train, the car was locked.

Ellen and Kate watched through the train's windows as soldiers with machine guns crawled under the train and searched everywhere for anyone who might be brave enough or stupid enough to try to escape from the DDR. The soldiers searched relentlessly. They had special mirrors on long handles that allowed them to see underneath the railroad cars where they could not go themselves. They searched everywhere and everything again. And then they searched again. No one would be able to slip onto the ferry to escape their Communist prison and make it to the free world today. Only those with foreign passports would be able to travel to Denmark on the ferry to freedom.

CHAPTER 23

1965

When she looked around, Jane Ellen noticed that the girl from Denmark and her aunt were no longer anywhere in sight. Jane Ellen knew this was the moment when she had to tell Kate what was happening and what was going to happen.

"I'm going into the bathroom. Someone else, who will be dressed exactly like I am, will come out of the bathroom and sit down next to you . . . in my seat. Don't talk to her. Just pretend that I am the person who is sitting beside you, just like I am now. The train will move ahead slowly, a little bit closer to the pier where the ferry is docked. The cars that are still part of the train will pull up closer to the water and the gangway entrance to the ferry. The guards will unlock the train car. A soldier will get on our train car and give directions. Do exactly what he tells you to do. Everyone on this car will get off the train and walk through a checkpoint with their luggage. Your passport will be checked. You are an American, so you won't have any trouble. The girl you don't know, the girl that is supposed to look like me and is dressed like me, will walk beside you to the checkpoint. She will follow behind you through the checkpoint and will also have her passport inspected. Ignore her. You will appear to be traveling together, but you should not talk to her. As soon as you are on board the ferry, go to the dining room. Find a table and order something to drink or something to eat. I will join you there. Don't worry. You are not at risk. You are not in any danger. I will explain it all to you once we are on the ferry. Just walk with the unknown girl, like you would walk with me. You are not responsible for her. She is escaping to freedom by pretending to be me. You will have helped her leave East Germany. Again, there is no danger to you. Just keep walking and get onto the ferry. As soon as you are on the ferry, that girl who walked onto the ferry behind you will go in a different direction. She will disappear. I repeat, don't talk to her or pay any attention to her or to what she does. You will never see her again. You have no responsibility for her. So, don't worry."

Kate was furious, as Jane Ellen knew she would be. "What do you think you are doing? What the heck have you gotten yourself involved in now? I don't want to have anything to do with any part of this. Why didn't you tell me about this before?"

"Later. I will tell you everything. I didn't want to give you a chance to get nervous and give it all away. I have to go now." Jane Ellen ducked into the train car's bathroom. A few minutes later, a young woman who had an uncanny resemblance to Kate's life-long friend, Jane Ellen, came out of the bathroom. She wore the exact same clothes and shoes that Jane Ellen had been wearing and sat down beside Kate. Kate was angry and frantically worried about what had happened to her unpredictable and crazy friend Jane Ellen.

At that moment, the train moved ahead a few hundred yards, just as Jane Ellen had said it would. The military men with automatic weapons unlocked the doors of the train car. One of them came aboard and explained in German, French, Danish, English, and Russian that everyone in the railroad car was to exit and follow him to the checkpoint. Passports would be examined. Everyone should have their papers ready to hand over to the authorities. All luggage was to be made available, in case there was a need to search it. Travelers were to keep moving and were not to step out of line. "Please keep moving ahead after you have cleared passport control. Move onto the gangway in a timely way and board the ferry for Denmark."

Angry and frightened, Kate walked forward as directed towards passport control. The young woman she didn't know walked beside her. She carried a suitcase that was the exact replica of the suitcase Jane Ellen had carried with her all summer, all across Europe. When they reached the passport control kiosk, Kate stepped ahead of the unknown woman and handed her passport to the soldier. He looked at her closely and looked closely at her passport. "United States?" he asked.

Kate replied, "Yes." The soldier motioned her on through the gates. She picked up her suitcase and walked ahead towards the ferry entrance. She never looked back, never turned around to see if the young woman behind her would also pass inspection and be allowed to board the boat. Kate hadn't realized that she was holding her breath until she stepped off the gangway and onto the ferry itself. She finally exhaled and took a deep breath. She followed the arrows that directed her towards the restaurant. She was out of East Germany, or at least she thought she was.

The woman behind her handed her passport to the soldier in the kiosk. He looked closely at her face and closely at her passport. "United States?" He asked.

The young woman in the plaid pleated skirt and penny loafers nodded her head and said, "Yes." The guard waved her through the gates. She stepped onto the gangway and then onto the Danish ferry. She carried her suitcase down a hallway that led away from the ship's restaurant.

A man approached her and took her suitcase from her. He said, "Follow me." He led her down another hallway and then another. He unlocked a door. She stepped into a stateroom that held four bunk beds. The man opened a compartment underneath one of the sets of bunkbeds. It did not look like there was room for a person inside the small space, but the man motioned for her to climb into it. Sure enough, she fit, but barely. It was claustrophobic, but she would do whatever it took. She would soon be free. She would soon be on her way to her boyfriend Johnny's arms.

Jane Ellen entered the train car's tiny bathroom. It was empty. Something had gone wrong. Where was the woman who was supposed to take her place and escape on the ferry to Denmark? There would scarcely have been room for both of them in the cramped bathroom anyway. Jane Ellen knew she had to stay inside the bathroom for at least ten full minutes. She checked her watch. She would follow her instructions and could not worry about whether or not her doppelganger had been able to get off the train and onto the boat that would cross a part of the Baltic Sea to freedom in Denmark. She knew the train would move ahead a few hundred yards.

Five minutes after she heard the announcement in five languages that gave directions for everyone to exit the train car, she could leave the bathroom and leave the train.

It seemed like hours rather than minutes elapsed while she waited. Jane Ellen never saw the girl who wore the same exact clothes she was wearing, the girl who carried a U.S. passport and a suitcase identical to her own. She couldn't worry about that now. She was more worried about Kate's fury than she was about being arrested by the Stasi. She could only hope that the woman she was trying to help would make it onto the ferry and would be able to continue her journey to freedom . . . wherever that happened to be.

She heard the announcement, and finally it was time. Jane Ellen left the bathroom. She grabbed her suitcase and her raincoat and hurried down the steps of the East German train. She ran forward a little bit, as if she was afraid she would miss the ferry's departure. She had her passport in her hand.

"I forgot my raincoat and had to go back for it. I had to go back to the train." She explained, out of breath, to the soldier in the kiosk." This would be the moment of truth. She would either be allowed to pass and board the ferry or she wouldn't. The soldier glared at her. He scrutinized her passport and scrutinized her face. Jane Ellen knew he was puzzled. He knew that this same young woman had just passed through his checkpoint. He had seen her only a few minutes earlier. How was it that she was here again, coming through his checkpoint a second time? She'd muttered something about her raincoat. She said she had forgotten her raincoat on the train and had gone back for it.

She was indeed the person whose picture was on the U.S. passport. The ferry was sounding its whistle. It was a mystery, but he had no real reason to stop or question this woman or her papers. She had all the necessary travel documents and most importantly, she held the coveted passport from the United States of America. He motioned her and her suitcase on ahead through the gate . . . for the second time in just minutes.

"You must hurry. The ferry is leaving. You will miss it." Jane Ellen was gone and hurrying up the gangway and towards the restaurant. Now she had to try to placate and explain it all to her friend Kate. As soon as the ferry pulled away from the port in East Germany, they would be safe. Maybe. Jane Ellen had been told that East German undercover agents traveled on this ferry to discover if East German citizens had been able to somehow sneak aboard to try to travel to Denmark. Jane Ellen looked around and saw a few men she thought might be East German agents. She would be discreet and keep her voice down as she explained to Kate what had just occurred. Jane Ellen had her fingers crossed that the woman whose fate had been briefly in her hands had successfully been able to make her escape.

Jane Ellen slipped into a chair at the table where Kate was sitting. Kate was eating a large plate of Scandinavian open-faced roast beef sandwiches with potato salad. Kate had ordered a Coca Cola, a budget buster anywhere and everywhere in Europe. It was Kate's act of defiance. She was angry and did not look up from her food when Jane Ellen sat down at the table. Jane Ellen knew that in time, after Kate had heard the entire story, she would forgive her. After she had been given an explanation about what was going on, Kate would be proud that she, too, had played a part in helping someone escape to the West.

Both Kate and Jane Ellen would again rejoice that they had been born in the most wonderful country in the world, and they would be grateful that they could come and go whenever and wherever they wanted. They could travel and see the world. Today, they would be more thankful than they had ever been that they lived in a free country.

CHAPTER 24

1965

A FEW HOURS LATER WHEN THE Danish ferry docked, one of the mysterious men who had stowed her inside the compartment under the bunk beds returned and helped Frieda out of her claustrophobic hiding place. The man handed her a nun's habit. The habit included a long tunic-style black dress and a long black veil complete with white coif and wimple. The man told her to change into the nun's outfit and to be quick about it. He told her to use the bathroom as it would be a long time before facilities would be available to her again. He left her in the stateroom to put on the nun's complicated clothing. In a few minutes, there was a knock at the door. Frieda was ready. She opened the door to find a man in priest's garb standing there. He picked up Frieda's suitcase, and they quickly made their way to the ferry's exit.

A sedan, that had a sign on it that said it was a taxi, was waiting at the bottom of the gangway, and the two people dressed in religious clothing slipped into the waiting car. The priest had never spoken a word to Frieda, and she had also refrained from speaking. They drove a long way in the taxi that was not really a taxi and finally arrived at some kind of military installation. There was a gate, and there were several guards. The driver of their pretend taxi communicated with these soldiers in Danish. They had arrived at a NATO airbase. They drove directly onto the tarmac where a large cargo plane was waiting. A man in a United States Airforce uniform opened the car door and held out his hand to Frieda. She stepped out of the sedan and walked with the uniformed soldier to the rear of the transport plane. The U.S. solider carried her suitcase. They walked up a ramp, and the soldier asked her if she spoke English. She replied that of course she spoke English. Frieda was frightened, but she followed directions and strapped herself into the primitive seat on the cargo plane. She was the only passenger on the plane, as far as she could tell.

The man in uniform asked her if she was hungry or thirsty. Frieda was both but refused to eat or drink anything. She did ask for the bathroom. She fell asleep and woke up just as the plane was taking off from the NATO airbase in Denmark. Frieda was certain she would soon be reunited with Johnny Bidwell. They would be married and raise a family in Johnny's hometown of Dickson, West Virginia. Her life would be perfect with Johnny in the United States of America.

What Frieda did not know was that Johnny Bidwell had disappeared. The FBI had been tracking him closely while he continued to meet with his Russian handler. The handler had specific questions he wanted Johnny to answer about the secret facilities at the Woodbrier. The FBI knew that Johnny had been able to pass along some important misinformation as answers to these questions. The FBI had watched the Russian as he communicated the false information to his own bosses.

The FBI did not know how it happened, but one day Johnny suddenly disappeared from the diner where he routinely met with the Soviet agent. Johnny had excused himself from the table to use the restroom, and he never returned. Eventually the Russian had also left the diner. The FBI searched desperately for Johnny but could not find any trace of him. He had vanished completely. The FBI was frantic to locate him. Johnny's precious Frieda was scheduled to arrive in West Virginia the next day.

Now that Johnny had disappeared, the Soviet agent had no reason to stay in Dickson, West Virginia. The FBI continued to follow the Russian. When he left West Virginia to drive to Washington, D.C., they arrested him before he could get to his superiors and before he could reach the Russian Embassy and be sent back to Moscow. The Russian agent would be tried in a secret U.S. court and spend the rest of his life in prison. Once he was in custody, he was questioned closely by the FBI about what had happened to Johnny Bidwell. Johnny's former handler claimed to know nothing of Johnny's whereabouts. No one who questioned the Russian believed this, but he maintained his ignorance throughout his days and weeks of incarceration. The Russian agent died during a knife fight in a federal prison. Whatever he might have known about Johnny Bidwell's disappearance died with him.

Johnny was never found. The FBI wondered if he had grown tired of waiting for Frieda to escape from East Berlin and decided to defect to Communism and live in Russia. Maybe he had not trusted the U.S. authorities to bring Frieda to the West. Maybe he had returned to East Germany to try to find her. The FBI wondered if Johnny had been kidnapped and murdered. They never found a trace of Johnny after he'd left his table at the West Virginia diner.

Frieda arrived in Dickson believing she would be reunited with her beloved Johnny. She didn't discover that he had disappeared until she arrived at Johnny's house and realized it was deserted. She was sure he had not abandoned her, and she kept asking law enforcement officials to try to find him. Frieda held out hope for two years. Johnny's brother, Tommy, had been by her side since she'd arrived in West Virginia. After two years of searching and hoping and waiting, and with not a single sign of Johnny, Frieda gave up all hope of ever seeing him again. She had fallen in love with Tommy, and he had fallen in love with her.

Thomas Bidwell was angry with his brother for being willing to betray his country. He was even angrier with Johnny for deserting the beautiful woman who'd risked her life to escape from East Germany. Tommy had grown to love this woman who had traveled thousands of miles to live in Dickson, West Virginia. Frieda and Tommy married and had four children together. Frieda became a United States citizen and was hired by the Woodbrier resort in White Sulphur Springs. She worked in food services for four decades. Tommy Bidwell died three days after they celebrated their forty-fifth wedding anniversary.

CHAPTER 25

2021

THAT LATE SEPTEMBER SATURDAY MORNING in the mountains of West Virginia promised a perfect day. The drizzle of the day before had ended, leaving sunshine and seventy-degree weather. The Ritters had signed up for an intensive private horticulture lecture and tour of the Woodbrier's gardens and grounds, and they would be busy all day. Elizabeth was exhausted and needed to rest after having been kept up late by her friend Henley Breckenridge.

Elizabeth had been quite concerned by Henley's words and behavior. Even though Elizabeth had been worn out when she'd arrived back in her room the night before, she had not been able to keep her mind from racing. She'd not been able to stop speculating about what Henley had become involved in. Elizabeth couldn't go to sleep until she finally dropped off around four o'clock in the morning. She needed to sleep late the next morning. She would order lunch from room service and spend the day resting. Richard and three other Camp Shoemaker reunion attendees were meeting for breakfast. They thought they might take a walk around the grounds after they'd eaten.

When he woke up on Saturday morning, Richard found the map that Henley had slipped under the door of their room, and he was intrigued. Elizabeth was sound asleep when Richard picked up the envelope that held the map. The envelope did not have a name on the outside and wasn't addressed to anyone in particular. Richard stuck it in his pocket and would look it over at breakfast. He joined J.D., Bailey, and Tyler in the main dining room of the Woodbrier. With no wives to encourage healthy eating, they all ordered pancakes and waffles and sausage. Tyler even ordered a Bloody Mary to enjoy with his "Mountaineer's Morning Special" that included pancakes and steak and eggs. Almost heaven!

Richard was looking closely at the photocopy of a yellowed piece of paper that was a rough, hand-drawn map. The map had been made years earlier by Henley Breckenridge's now long-deceased employee and friend from the Army Corps of Engineers. The map had been drawn to show the secret spaces that could be found in the bunker à la the early 1960s. Richard doubted that anything on the old map existed any longer. The entire bunker would have been redone by now. Everything must have changed after all these years had gone by—except maybe for the elevators. Elevators were almost impossible to change after they'd once been installed. Richard's friends were curious about what he was studying so closely, and he'd had to share the map with them. Everyone at the table had an opinion about the map and about what they should or could do with it.

The gang of four took a walk around the grounds of the resort, but the copy of the old map of the bunker had piqued their curiosity. They were tempted by the elevator next to the Carpenter's room and the possibilities presented by the map. They, too, had not been convinced by the story about CSX and the Fortune 500 servers. The Camp Shoemaker boys wanted to investigate on their own. This reunion had been much too tame for some of them. They wanted an adventure.

Several weddings were taking place at the Woodbrier on this beautiful Saturday. The resort charged a lot of money for couples who wanted to be married at this exclusive venue. The receptions were elegant and first class, and so were the prices. Whether it was a garden wedding or a wedding in the ballroom, Saturdays at the Woodbrier, while the weather was still cooperating, were always matrimony central. All of this connubial bliss further stressed the staffing resources of the resort that were already stretched thin due to the COVID pandemic. Much of the Woodbrier's staff would be occupied with chairs and tables and wedding guests and all of the confusion and chaos that weddings inevitably entail. There was a great deal of hustle and bustle going on in the hotel. Who was going to notice four older men if they were snooping around in spots that were usually off-limits to guests?

Richard had learned about the "freight elevator" next to their room and the fact that it connected directly with the underground bunker because Henley had told Elizabeth about it. Elizabeth had shared with Richard a few, but certainly not all, of the secret things Henley had told her about the Woodbrier. The group of elderly friends decided to throw caution to the winds and investigate the areas that were marked on Henley's map. Richard knew his only chance to do anything about the old map might be that day before Elizabeth woke up. She might not approve of the inclinations of the others in the group, including those of her husband, who wanted to explore the forbidden parts of the West Virginia Wing's basement levels to try to find out what was really going on in the decommissioned bunker. Several of the Camp Shoemaker crowd had expressed aloud their doubts about the CSX story and the reasons given for the restriction against cell phones on the bunker tour. They were ready to take some risks. They were ready to venture into the bunker without a guide. The four set out to find the map's secret places that the official tour of the bunker had chosen not to include.

They got on the "freight elevator" just outside the Carpenter's room on the 4th floor of the West Virginia Wing and rode it down to its lowest level. When they stepped off the old elevator and fumbled for the light switch, they found themselves in a storage room full of cleaning equipment and boxes and other things nobody knew what to do with or wanted any more. The place did not look very exciting or the least bit mysterious. It looked abandoned and cluttered and dusty. Surely no one would care if they wanted to take photos of this stuff with their cell phones. Not one of the Camp Shoemaker boys took a single picture.

They gathered their courage and decided to leave the storage room, but they were locked in. That in itself was puzzling. Tyler suggested that maybe the door was locked in case someone took the freight elevator by mistake. The only option they would have after arriving in the basement storeroom by mistake would be to get back on the elevator and ride it back up to where they belonged.

Fortunately or unfortunately, J.D. had brought along his set of lock picks, and he began to work on the lock of the storage room door. When J.D. brought out his lock picks, Bailey always cheered him on and couldn't wait to enter whatever place J.D. was trying to break into or out of. Seeing the lock picks come out made Richard nervous because he knew he was participating in some kind of a break-in. Richard did not want to be caught. Tyler was also nervous about what J.D. was doing, but he always watched closely. He secretly wished he had a set of lock picks of his own and wished he knew how to use them. J.D. soon cracked the lock, and the door opened.

They left the storage room and found themselves in a long, narrow hallway. There were doors on both sides of the hall, and there was no lighting overhead. Each of the four men had a cell phone, and each cell phone had a flashlight included as one of its features. Three of the four knew how to turn on this flashlight function, and two of the four knew how to turn off the flashlight. They were good to go.

They checked all the doors that were at their end of the hall. Each of the doors they tried in the long, dark corridor was locked. J.D. got out his lock picks again and worked to open one of the doors. Finally, he had the door open, and they were inside. They could not find a light to turn on inside this room. From what they could see with their phone flashlights, the room was filled with metal filing cabinets. There must have been more than one hundred filing cabinets in the room, and they were packed very close together. The filing cabinets were in rows, separated by narrow spaces that looked like they were just wide enough to allow the filing cabinet drawers to be opened. There was barely enough space for all four of them to squeeze into the dark room.

"Well, this doesn't look very exciting to me. It looks like just what it is . . . a bunch of old filing cabinets full of old files." J.D. was disappointed about their discovery.

Richard had his cell phone flashlight positioned on the filing cabinets as he tried to read what was written on the labels on the fronts of the file drawers. "These labels are not very illuminating. The labels on the drawers are just a long string of letters and numbers. There aren't any words. I guess somebody knows what these numbers and letters mean." He studied one of the labels more closely. "I think part of what's on the label is a date." He moved onto the drawer below. "Yes, each of these labels includes a date and some cryptic letters. The dates on this filing cabinet are all from 1962. I guess the files inside are something somebody thought was worth keeping from 1962."

Bailey was examining another filing cabinet. "These filing cabinets back here are from the NSA. These labels have the letters NSA as part of the numbers and letters on the file drawers."

"Do you think these files really are National Security Agency files? Why would they store them here? I thought everything the government wanted to keep had been digitized by now. I didn't know any agency of the government still kept filing cabinets full of files." Tyler had a friend who had participated in the enormous task of digitizing government records. "I guess the NSA didn't participate in that program. Or maybe these are things they don't want anybody to know about."

They wondered if all the other rooms along the dark hall were also filled with filing cabinets. And what was so important that it needed to be stored in a secret part of a bunker inside a mountain and in a room that was under lock and key without any lights? Bailey could not wait to get his hands on the files in the filing cabinets to find out what important secrets they held.

Bailey had tried every drawer on almost every filing cabinet, hoping to find at least one that had been left open by mistake or one which had a broken lock. He was way in the back of the room fiddling with the lock on a filing cabinet drawer. He was sitting on the floor when he yelled, "I've got one open, and boy is it a doozy. It's photos of Marilyn Monroe with some very important people. Wow! Come and look at these!"

The three other men tried to squeeze in between the rows of metal filing cabinets, hoping to see the unexpected and previously unpublished photographs of the sex symbol of their teenage years. It was difficult to see anything in the dark room with only the flashlights from three cell phones as illumination, but they all made a valiant attempt to get a glimpse of the glamorous and seductive woman that all of them remembered from their youth.

"I think this is where the NSA has decided to keep the photos and the other stuff they don't want to get rid of but also don't want anybody with a computer to have access to." Richard was getting nervous. "Think about it. They've got all this information from their surveillance . . . photographs, phone conversations, never-seen documents about leaders from all over the world. This is where the dirty little secrets are being kept. But why? Most of these people who misbehaved in the 1960s and 1970s are probably dead by now. Why keep all this stuff? Why not just get rid of it if you don't want anybody to see it?"

J.D., the guy with the lock picks and the guy who knew how to use them, had a sudden attack of panic. "I think we need to get out of here right now. I don't think anybody was ever supposed to find these files or see any of those pictures. I think, if we are found in here, we could be in really serious trouble. This is what the Woodbrier doesn't want us to see. Everybody has a camera on their cell phone these days. They don't want anybody taking photos of any of these documents or any of these old photographs with their phones. The heck with the CSX servers. That's just a bull shit cover story. You can bet your bippy that the clean-cut tour guide who gave us the bunker tour doesn't have the slightest idea what is really stored down here. I will bet you there are miles of these hallways and miles of these rooms full of filing cabinets. There could be years' and years' worth of NSA discoveries and secrets stored here." J.D. was not exactly frightened, but he was ready to get out of this room filled with trouble.

Bailey was having a great time, leafing through the files and the photos of the forbidden. Tyler and Richard lifted him by his arms up off the floor where he was enjoying the various photo arrays of Marilyn Monroe. Richard was on the same page with J.D. "I agree, we need to get out of here now. We have left a ton of fingerprints, but who is going to ever know to come in here and check for them? We can't be found here. We need to leave immediately." Richard knew that if they were caught, he would not only be in big trouble with the United States government, he would also be in big trouble with his wife. He was the one with the map and the one who knew about the "freight elevator" that didn't carry any freight. He had led his friends to this prohibited spot.

They almost had to carry Bailey out of the room. He was having a great time sitting on the floor and looking through all kinds of materials that had been procured surreptitiously by the No Such Agency. The other three put the files away and closed the drawer Bailey had found so easy to open. They tried to make the room look exactly as it had before they had broken into it. They didn't try to wipe down their fingerprints, counting on the fact that no one had been in this room for many years and would probably not be in it again for many years to come.

Tyler held his cell phone up to try to give J.D. enough light to fix the lock on the door of the room. When J.D. was satisfied that he had left everything the way he'd found it, the four hurried back down the hallway towards the storeroom and the elevator. They would immediately go back up the freight elevator to safety. No one would ever know they'd been nosing around down in the basement of the West Virginia Wing of the Woodbrier.

CHAPTER 26

2021

Just as they entered the storage room, locked the door to the hallway behind them, and pushed the button for the elevator, there was a loud rumble. Then there was an ear-splitting boom. It sounded as if something had exploded. Then there was a huge tremor, and the storage room moved and shook. They hit the ground as debris from the walls and ceiling, as well as the miscellaneous contents of the room, tumbled down around them. A cabinet full of outdated cleaning supplies opened and spilled its contents on them and on the floor. Then the entire cabinet that had been attached to the wall, was torn away from the wall and fell on top of Tyler. He was momentarily stunned as the old metal cabinet knocked him down and banged against his head.

"It's an earthquake." Richard yelled to the others, trying to be heard above the loud rumbling and the shaking. "There was an earth tremor like this when we lived in Philadelphia, and it sounded like an explosion, just like this. This is worse, though. Things are falling off the walls. The walls are crumbling." The room they were in went suddenly dark, and when they tried the elevator again, they found it was not working. The electricity had gone out, or maybe the elevator was just old and had given up the ghost. Because the light switch wasn't working either, they decided it was the electricity. They held out hope that when the electricity was restored, the elevator would also come back to life.

They all had plaster dust and bits of plaster in their hair. Tyler's head was bleeding, just a little bit. He said he wasn't really hurt. The three who were not injured managed to push the cabinet, that had once been attached to the wall and had held cleaning supplies, off Tyler's body. "You are damn lucky this heavy thing didn't actually land on your head. And, you are going to be very sore tomorrow. That is, if we ever get out of this place." Richard was the doctor on the scene as well as the geology expert.

"Holy cow. What are we going to do now? We need to get out of here. We aren't supposed to be here in the first place. Are you sure the elevator isn't working?" Bailey often rushed in without fear of consequences, but he was worried now.

J.D. had his phone out and was using the flashlight on his phone to examine the damage to the walls of the storage room. "Holy crap! Will you look at what the earthquake uncovered when the wall fell down?!" He was shining his phone flashlight onto the wall that the metal cabinet had been attached to before the plaster walls had crumbled. The room was so dark and full of dust, it was almost impossible to see what J.D. was looking at. "Can't you see it? It's a skeleton! A skeleton with clothes on it, or clothes kind of hanging onto it. There's been a person plastered up in the wall behind where that cabinet used to be. Or, he used to be a person. It looks like somebody plastered over the body and then hung the cabinet on the wall. Whoever those bones belong to has been in that wall for a long time. He's just skin and bones; oh, excuse me, he's just bones. J.D. was a former prosecutor and had been used to seeing dead bodies. He was not easily freaked out. Today he was freaked. He had not been expecting to find a skeleton stuck in the wall of a room where he knew he was not supposed to be anyway.

Richard was a retired pathologist. He had seen a lot of dead bodies in his day, but he'd rarely seen a skeleton. And this skeleton was not all cleaned up and on display in an anatomy lab. This skeleton had been put into the wall when it had been a whole human being. Richard could only hope that the human being who'd been plastered into the wall had been dead when he had been entombed. It was possible for Richard to see that when the plaster had been packed into the wall around the body, the body had not been a skeleton. It had been a whole, intact body with muscle and other tissue.

Because Richard had worked for the Philadelphia Medical Examiner's Office during his residency at the Hospital of the University of Pennsylvania, he knew without a doubt that this was a crime scene. He knew about preserving evidence. He knew they could not touch anything, especially the skeleton or the area around the skeleton. "Don't touch anything. This is a crime scene. That guy did not plaster himself up in the wall. Somebody killed him and hid his body. Then whoever did this attached a metal cabinet to the wall in front of where they'd put the body. Even though this is a crime that happened decades ago, it is still a crime. Even though the perpetrator is probably dead by now, it is still a murder."

But Richard was very curious about this skeleton that used to be a living, breathing person. All four of the men in the closet were curious, but none of the others wanted to get close to the skeleton. It was just too spooky. Richard was not as frightened of death as his non-medical friends were.

"You can see he was buried in the plaster with his clothes on. As his muscle mass disappeared, some of his clothes fell down around his ankles. See the belt buckle and the leather belt down around his feet? His trousers have fallen down there, too. I'd love to see if there is a wallet in the trousers, but the police will have to determine that. I don't want to touch anything or disturb the scene in any way."

Richard got up close to the skull of the skeleton. He directed his flashlight onto the bones. "This guy has a chain around his neck, and the chain has a ring on it. That might help identify him, even if he doesn't have a wallet. The chain is black. It's tarnished, so it's probably silver. Gold wouldn't tarnish like this. But the ring on the chain isn't tarnished. So it's not silver. The ring looks like it might be aluminum." Richard was not afraid of the skeleton, and the investigator part of him had taken over. He wanted to find out as much as he could before his phone's flashlight gave out. "Whoever plastered this guy up in the wall probably thought no one would ever find him behind that metal cabinet. And no one ever would have, if it hadn't been for the earth tremor. I sure hope they can figure out who this poor dude is. He would have disappeared without a trace. You can't help wonder if he had a family and how long somebody might have been looking for him and wondering what in the world had happened to him."

Richard's friends were not really wondering about anything except about how they were going to get out of the closet and out of the mess they now found themselves in.

"What the heck are we going to do now? We have to report this body, or what used to be a body, to the authorities. Somebody must have been wondering what happened to this guy. He's been in here a long time. Does anybody's cell phone work down here? Can we call for help?" Bailey's voice had only a trace of panic in it when his cell phone didn't have a signal. Nobody else's cell phone could get a signal either. There were no lights. The electricity was gone. The elevator wasn't moving. They were in trouble.

Tyler concurred. "I sure as heck am not going to touch the skeleton or anything else in this place. I just want to get out of here and turn this situation over to somebody else. I wish I'd never been here." He paused. "How much trouble do you think we are really in . . . I mean, for being down here where we don't belong?"

Nobody could answer that question for Tyler, but they were all wondering the same thing. Not one of them had any idea how to get out of the utility closet. Not one of them knew what was happening in the floors above the bunker. Had the earthquake destroyed the entire Woodbrier? Was the building still standing? When the earthquake had happened, they'd been inside a basement that had been constructed to withstand the aftermath of a nuclear war. Bailey was hoping that Gretchen never learned anything about this latest misadventure that he'd gotten himself into. He was always in trouble with his wife, and it was always his own doing.

Richard was terrified about what might have happened to Elizabeth during the earthquake. Had she been hurt? He knew she would have a difficult time getting to the elevator that hotel guests were allowed to use. And would that elevator even be working? Was she trapped in the room? Would anyone be able to get to her to help her in case she was hurt?

Whatever might have happened in the rest of the Woodbrier was a complete mystery to them. None of their cell phones could send or receive signals down in the depths of the bunker. J.D. wondered if it was because they were so far below the surface of the earth or because, for some reason, there was a jamming device at work down here . . . maybe thanks to CSX or the NSA. He just knew that he couldn't send a text or an email or make a phone call. The only things that worked on his phone right now were the flashlight, Solitaire, and Word Cookies. When his battery died, he would have nothing.

J.D. was a lawyer and had been giving serious thought to the trouble they might be in. "We might be down here for a long time, and we need to think very carefully about all of this. We need to plan what we are going to say when we are questioned about what's happened. And you can be certain that every one of us will be questioned. Because the electricity has gone out, we are not going to be able to get out of this place until the power is restored. We don't have any idea how badly damaged the rest of the hotel might be. More specifically for our own purposes, we don't know how badly damaged this elevator and this elevator shaft might be. We are going to have to somehow contact people who run the hotel for help to get us out of here. Even if this skeleton had not turned up unexpectedly, we would have been scolded and probably questioned about what we were doing down here. So think about what we are going to say about why we were down here in the first place. We were not supposed to ride on that elevator. We are not supposed to be here at all."

J.D. let his friends think about all of that for a minute. "And because of the skeleton in the wall, this is now a crime scene. Richard agrees with me that it is . . . a crime scene, and eventually there will be law enforcement people swarming all over this place. A person was murdered, and the killer hid the body by plastering his victim up in the wall. Then the perpetrator of the crime went to the effort, and took a considerable risk, spending all the time it required, to hang a metal supply cabinet on the plaster wall to further obscure his crime. This is a big deal and will be a bigger deal. Don't doubt that for a minute."

J.D. looked at his friends to see if they were taking all of this as seriously as he thought they should be. He was the Dutch uncle telling them what was going to happen. Their eyes were wide, and he was relieved that they were listening closely to every word. Richard Carpenter had even turned up his hearing aids so he would not miss anything J.D. had to say. "This closet will be investigated as the scene of a crime. Nobody is going to think, of course, that we had anything to do with the murder of this victim. It happened long ago. That is perfectly obvious to everyone. However, the authorities will want to know what the heck we were doing down here, down here in the bunker basement where we are not supposed to be. They are going to want to know how the wall came down. Of course, we know the wall came down because of the earthquake. The authorities may want to know if we tampered with the metal storage cabinet or tampered with the plaster wall. We know we did not, but because we were down here in forbidden territory in the first place, they might have some doubts about us. We have to be sure they believe our story about how the wall and that metal cabinet came down. We all know exactly what happened here in this closet when the earthquake hit, and we must all tell the authorities exactly the same story . . . the truth."

J.D. continued, "However, whatever you do and whatever you say, do not for one minute even think about mentioning anything whatsoever about the fact that we ever left this closet. My lock picks do not exist and never existed. Not one of you can ever say a word about that hallway that we know is outside this closet or about that room we broke into or about those filing cabinets or anything at all about any of that. None of us were ever there. None of us were ever outside this storage closet. We have been locked in here, in this room, ever since we came down in the elevator. Have you all got that?"

Bailey nodded his head in enthusiastic agreement that certain things were never to be mentioned. They all nodded their heads in agreement. J.D. was reassured, from the looks on his friends' faces, that no one would ever dare to mention that other part of this disaster . . . ever and for the rest of their lives. They knew the chips were down. They knew that if they ever got out of this place, they shared a secret that could never be revealed.

Their immediate problem was to figure how to get out of the basement. They could only tell somebody about the skeleton in the closet if they themselves were able to be rescued. What a mess they were in!

Richard realized that some of his friends might be close to panic. "Elizabeth will raise the alarm. She will realize I am not answering her texts. She will try calling me and will become worried when she can't reach me. She will try calling the three of you to see if you know where I am. When she can't reach any of us, she will know something is wrong. She will get together with the Ritters to see if they know where we are. They won't know anything either. The three of them will contact hotel security, and they will begin to search for us. Of course, Elizabeth has no idea where we are. She has no idea we took the elevator down here to this forbidden part of the bunker. But because there are four of us missing, and three of our friends will be making a fuss about our being missing, the hotel will have to pay attention. It may be a while before we are rescued, but we will be rescued. I am certain of it. So don't panic."

Usually there is a stairway next to or close by an elevator. These nearby backup staircases had saved many lives in both World Trade Center bombings in New York City. But there was no staircase next to this antiquated elevator. No one was supposed to use this elevator. This elevator had been installed when the West Virginia Wing was built in the early 1960s and had never been intended for use by the public. There had been no need for a backup evacuation staircase next to this elevator. No one had any idea the four of them were down there where they were not supposed to be. What if nobody made the effort to repair the never-used freight elevator and no one ever found them? Would they end up like their fellow closet-dweller . . . five skeletons in the room instead of one?

CHAPTER 27

2021

Fortunately, the rest of the Woodbrier had come through the earthquake relatively unscathed. There had been some loud booms, and the building had trembled. Some glassware had tumbled off tables and shelves. Most of the guests at the resort had experienced similar tremors at some time in their lives, and they immediately realized what was happening. No one panicked. No walls fell down, and after some minor cleanup and reassurances by the various concierges, everything went on as if nothing had happened. The electricity had gone out in parts of the building, but backup generators quickly took over. All weddings in progress had continued after brief interruptions.

When Elizabeth awakened, she was surprised that she had slept until after twelve o'clock noon. She knew that Richard planned to spend the day with his friends, so she didn't expect to see him in their room. She sent a text to Richard to let him know she was awake, and she asked him where he was and what he and his buddies were up to. She'd thought Richard would text her back immediately, and she was surprised when that didn't happen.

She was hungry. She looked at the room service menu and ordered a turkey club sandwich on sour dough toast with French fries and a large unsweetened iced tea with lemon and mint and extra ice. While she was brushing her teeth, the earthquake hit. She knew exactly what was happening. She grabbed the sink and held on tight until the rumbling stopped. The lights flickered briefly, and the generators had immediately responded. The lights came back on quickly in this part of the hotel. Elizabeth worked her way carefully back to the bedroom. Her room service lunch was delayed.

When the waiter brought her sandwich and tea to the room, they discussed the earthquake. Elizabeth was relieved to hear that there had been very little damage to the resort either inside or outside. It seemed the Woodbrier had experienced earthquakes in the past, but they were few and far between. An earthquake the magnitude of the one that had happened that day had not occurred at the Woodbrier since the late 1950s. The Woodbrier building was solid as a rock, and thank goodness for that. The electricity had come back on throughout the hotel, and pretty much everything had returned to close to normal. The waiter joked that there would have to be some new glassware ordered to replace what had fallen off the shelves and broken. Otherwise, the mild earth tremor had not been much of an event that day in White Sulphur Springs.

Elizabeth finished her lunch and drank her iced tea. She was ready to go down to the elegant main rooms of the resort for more people watching. With all the weddings going on at the Woodbrier today, there would for sure be a lot of interesting people to see. There would also probably be some unplanned drama. Wedding festivities always provided drama. Family members who had not seen each other for years, old family feuds revived, freely flowing alcohol, romances blossoming between bridesmaids and groomsmen, a last-minute spat between the bride and groom, cold feet, Republicans marrying Democrats, old boyfriends and girlfriends who might have been included on the guest list—there were so many opportunities for drama at a wedding.

Elizabeth still had not heard anything from Richard which was somewhat disturbing. He usually answered her texts within a few minutes, even if he was busy. She texted him again to say that she had eaten lunch and would like to join him and the other three . . . whatever they were doing. She thought she would hear right back from her husband, but she continued to hear nothing. She called Richard, and her call went directly to his voice mail. He always picked up when she called. She was becoming more concerned.

Maybe the earth tremor, that had seemed so minor on the fourth floor of the West Virginia Wing, had been more serious in other parts of the hotel. She sent a text to J.D., and then she called to ask him if he was with Richard and if they were all right. When she phoned J.D., her call went to his voice mail, too. She left J.D. a message that she was contacting him because Richard was not answering any of her texts or phone calls. She thought maybe Richard's phone was turned off or that his battery had died. She waited and waited for some kind of a reply, but she had no response from either Richard or from J.D.

She tried calling Tyler and Bailey, and again her calls went immediately to voice mail. She sent a text to the Ritters, asking if they'd heard anything from the gang of four who were now incommunicado. Isabelle Ritter texted back that they'd not heard anything from anyone, but their extensive botany tour of the Woodbrier grounds had been spectacular.

Just then, Elizabeth received a text. She hoped it was from Richard, but it was from Henley.

> Did you get the map I slipped under your door this morning? It was a copy of the map that was drawn by my ACOE employee years ago. It shows some of the places I scoped out after I left the official bunker tour. Start at the "freight elevator" next to your room. Going to the wedding now. Wish me luck. HB

Elizabeth opened the door to her room and checked the hall for Henley's map. There was nothing either outside or inside the room. There was nothing on the desk or the dresser and nothing on her bedside table. Elizabeth figured Richard must have found the map on the floor when he'd left their room to go to breakfast with his friends. Elizabeth texted Henley back and told her she'd not received the map. She asked Henley to send her a phone photo of the original map. Elizabeth was certain that a copy of the mysterious homemade map that Henley had slipped under her door that morning was now in Richard's hands.

Elizabeth realized Henley would be attending the wedding ceremony at this moment and would not have a chance to read and respond to her text for a while. Elizabeth called the Ritters and asked if they would come to her room in the West Virginia Wing when their tour was finished. She told them she was becoming increasingly concerned about Richard and the others. Richard's phone might be turned off. But when she'd also tried to reach J.D., Bailey, and Tyler, and had received no replies from any of them, she realized something was very wrong. If everything had been all right, one of their group would have answered her text or called her. When all she heard was crickets, the usually unflappable Elizabeth began to seriously worry.

When the Ritters arrived at the room, Elizabeth told them that she'd not been able to reach any of the others from their group. No one had responded to her texts. All of her phone calls had gone to voice mail. Elizabeth didn't think Isabelle and Matthew were showing as much concern as they should about their missing friends.

The Ritters had all the news about what had sustained damage at the resort. Matthew Ritter told her he'd learned the electricity had been knocked out briefly in various places around the resort when the earth tremor had hit. The Woodbrier had a serious and extensive generator system, so nothing was ever down for very long. But apparently a few remote locations at the resort were not hooked up to any backup generator. The bunker, ironically, was no longer covered by a generator, so bunker tours had been delayed until the power came back on. It was mostly glassware sitting on open shelving that had taken a hit. No one had reported any serious destruction to the hotel or the grounds. The Ritters had not heard that anyone had been injured. It had pretty much been a non-event for most of the resort. Isabelle tried calling their missing friends from her phone. Then Matthew became concerned, and he also tried to call. No one was picking up the phone. The three debated what to do.

They knew that because it was a Saturday, there would be several weddings underway. These special events demanded time away from the duties of the regular staff that was already stretched very thin. With all the disruptions of COVID, it had become increasingly difficult to hire all the people the Woodbrier needed to take care of the resort as well as provide staff for weddings and other special events. Elizabeth, Isabelle, and Matthew decided they needed to talk to security about trying to locate their four missing friends.

Matthew pushed Elizabeth's wheelchair, and they walked to the desk of the hotel's main concierge. They approached the concierge, Sherrod Jefferson, to ask where the security office of the Woodbrier was located. He listened carefully to everything Elizabeth and Isabelle and Matthew Ritter had to say. He was honestly and obviously concerned that they were unable to contact four members of their group. Elizabeth wanted to know if power had been restored to all parts of the resort. She also wanted to know if there were places in the resort where cell phones didn't work.

"We think power has been restored to all areas where it went out. That was a top priority after the earthquake. There are places in the resort that do not have good cell phone coverage. But almost all of those are in the bunker and other basement areas. Bunker tours were suspended while the electricity went down. Your friends would have no reason to be in any of those areas. They are not open to the public except for official tours."

Elizabeth was thinking about the map that Henley said she had slipped under the door that morning. It was a map Elizabeth had never seen, but she suspected that her husband had picked it up and taken it with him to breakfast. She knew Bailey, and she knew he loved an adventure. She was worried that the four friends had seen Henley's map and had not been able to resist it. She was afraid they might have decided they would go exploring. That would probably have been fine, and under normal circumstances, they would have been able to explore the no-go zones of the bunker and get away with it. But there had been an unexpected earthquake. It had been a minor one to be sure, but the power had gone out. What if they were stuck in an elevator somewhere or stuck in the underground bunker somewhere? If they had wandered into an area that wasn't open to the public, would anyone even think to look for them in a place where they were not supposed to be?

Elizabeth didn't want to tattletale on her husband and her friends, if indeed they had gone to places in the bunker where they were not allowed to go. But, from her point of view, their safety was much more important than any fear of being scolded for possible trespassing sins by the concierge or by a chief of security. She wondered how much to say to Sherrod Jefferson about Henley's map and what she now suspected might have happened to Richard and his cohorts. Sometimes when the campers got together, they forgot they were almost eighty years old and momentarily thought they were just eight years old again. That's what could have happened today. She decided to take the plunge and tell this nice young man, Sherrod Jefferson, what she suspected might have happened.

"I have some concerns that my husband and his friends might have gone exploring on their own . . . maybe down into the bunker . . . maybe where they don't belong. I'm not certain of anything, but because I can't reach any of them, I am afraid they are some place where they are not supposed to be. I know they were very curious about the elevator next to our room in the West Virginia Wing. I'm afraid they might have ridden it down to the basement, even though they knew they were not supposed to use that elevator."

"What makes you think they might have used the elevator? Or gone to parts of the bunker where the public is not allowed to go?"

"I'm not sure of anything. I am just generating random thoughts right now, based on what I know about this group. They might consider a 'do not enter' sign as a challenge rather than a direction to be obeyed. They talked about not believing the CSX story they were told regarding the use of cell phones and locking up bags and purses . . . when we took the tour yesterday. I'm just offering this as a possibility about where they might be. Is there any place that might be especially vulnerable to the earthquake, anyplace they might be trapped and can't get out of?"

Sherrod Jefferson knew the Woodbrier resort like he knew the back of his hand. His grandfather, the now-deceased Sherrod Jefferson for whom the head concierge had been named, had been a waiter in the main dining room of the hotel for decades. The head concierge's great uncle had also worked at the resort to keep the bunker supplied during the secret years when it was ready and waiting for the Congress to take refuge during a possible nuclear holocaust. As a child, Sherrod had visited often and sometimes played here at the hotel. He knew exactly where the elevator outside the Carpenter's room went when it descended into the basement of the West Virginia Wing. He could not imagine anyone taking the creaky old elevator anywhere, let alone down into the bunker. Why would anyone want to do that? Why would they want to stay down there and not come back up? But the elevator could be a place to start to look for the missing men.

"Let's go to the fourth floor of the West Virginia Wing and see what is going on with that elevator." Sherrod led the way, and the others followed.

The group stood in the hallway while Sherrod tried to summon the elevator. "You are exactly right. Power has not been restored to this elevator. It is on its own circuit, separate from the electrical boxes that serve the rooms and the other elevators in this wing. Because this elevator communicates with the bunker directly, it has its own power source. At the time the West Virginia Wing and the bunker were built, that made sense. Now it really doesn't. Because no one ever uses this elevator any more, no one would have thought to check it . . . to see if it had lost power. It's so old, the electrical box that controls this elevator uses fuses. No one would have bothered to see about, let alone replace, the fuses in that fuse box. I will have to hunt for the fuse box that controls this elevator, and then I will have to hunt for some fuses to replace the ones that must have been blown during the earthquake. It may take a while. And, of course, your husband and your friends may not be anywhere near this elevator. I can't make any promises, but it's worth checking out. I will do my best. Meanwhile, I am going to alert security that four people have gone missing. Can you please write down their names for me? Do any of you have photos of these men?" Isabelle began to search her phone for pictures she'd taken the night before. She found them and sent them to Sherrod's cell phone.

The Ritters and Elizabeth decided to wait in the Carpenter's hotel room. It was kind of a mini suite and had a nice sitting area. It had been a long and stressful time since lunch, and they decided to order a full cream tea from room service to be brought to the room. Matthew also asked for a glass of white wine to be included with the tea. He'd thought about ordering a whisky, but decided since it was tea, he would make do with a glass of wine. He thought white wine might go better with cucumber sandwiches and petit fours than whisky anyway.

It was close to five o'clock when Sherrod returned with the news that he thought the elevator was working again. It was difficult to find fuses these days. Most buildings in the resort had upgraded to circuit breakers. He did not want Elizabeth or either of the Ritters to ride down in the elevator with him. He promised he would let them know what he found as soon as and if he found anything in the bunker basement. No sightings of the missing men had been reported anywhere at the resort . . . inside or outside. Elizabeth was desperately hoping Sherrod would find something in the bunker. Even if it was bad news, she had to know what had happened to Richard and the others.

CHAPTER 28

2021

Fuses had been found, and the elevator was working again. Sherrod Jefferson rode the elevator all the way to its bottom floor. He was not entirely shocked, when the doors to the elevator opened, to find four older men covered in plaster dust and looking very sheepish but very relieved to see him. He smiled at them, and they were overjoyed that he knew who they were. "You are the Camp Shoemaker bunch, I gather. I'm Sherrod Jefferson, head concierge at the Woodbrier. We've been looking everywhere for you. There are some people upstairs who have been very worried. They will be delighted and relieved to know that you are okay. You are all okay, aren't you? How long have you been down here?"

None of the four wanted to speak up. Finally Richard Carpenter decided that no one else was going to say anything, so he answered Sherrod's question. They had already decided that, if they were rescued, they were not going to mention having fiddled with the lock to get out of the utility closet. They were not going to say anything to anybody, ever, about the hallway outside the closet and the room filled with filing cabinets. That had never happened. No one would ever in a million years hear anything about that. They knew they were already in enough trouble, just being in this room . . . not to mention the skeleton that was hanging on the wall in the plaster, behind where the metal cupboard had been before the earthquake. "We have been here about four hours, I think. We'd just ridden the elevator down when the earthquake hit." Richard knew that, if anyone bothered to check the security cameras he was sure were all over the hallways of the hotel, they would realize he was lying about their timeline. He did not want to have to reveal that they had broken out of the utility closet and gone exploring down the hall or anything at all about that part of their misadventure. "We know we are not supposed to be down here." Richard's strategy was to admit to wrongdoing and then immediately begin talking about the skeleton.

They could be blamed for being in a place they were not supposed to be, but they could not be blamed for the skeleton in the wall. The earthquake had knocked the metal cupboard of cleaning supplies off the wall and brought down the plaster wall that revealed the long-buried mystery man . . . or woman. The skeleton had been here for many years before the Camp Shoemaker group had checked into the Woodbrier. Richard felt the discovery of the body, really just the bones, would be the attention grabber necessary to deflect any, or at least most, of the recriminations about their being in the bunker.

The lights were back on in the storage closet, and Sherrod Jefferson immediately saw the skeleton hanging in the wall, still half-encased in its plaster tomb. The fallen metal supply cupboard lying on the floor in front of the skeleton made it obvious what had happened when the earthquake had occurred. Sherrod realized the skeleton must have been hiding in the plaster wall behind the cupboard for decades. The concierge knew at once that this closet was now a crime scene. Nobody plasters themselves up into a wall and then attaches a cupboard to the front of the wall.

There had been foul play in the bunker and an almost perfectly successful attempt to cover up a crime. It would have been the perfect murder, if there had not been an earthquake that had shaken loose the metal storage cabinet and the plaster wall. The authorities would have to be involved. These older men had uncovered a hornet's nest as well as a long-dead somebody. Sherrod knew the next hours and days would be tedious and complicated. He addressed the four tired and disheveled-looking fellows.

"Looks like you found a friend down here to keep you company." Sherrod wasn't smiling. "This is now a crime scene, and you guys will have to get out of here ASAP. I'm taking you back up. The elevator is working, but my cell phone won't work down here any better than yours did. The five men crowded into the rickety elevator and rode it up to the fourth floor. "Elizabeth Carpenter and Dr. and Mrs. Ritter are in your room, Dr. Carpenter. I know these three people will be very glad to see all of you. You will have to be questioned by the authorities about how this event transpired. You will have to tell them how and why you happened to be where you were and exactly how the skeleton in the closet made its appearance." Sherrod couldn't help but smile to himself, even though he knew he had a long night ahead of him cleaning up the skeleton trouble. "Don't even think about checking out of the hotel until after the FBI or the West Virginia State Police, or both, have taken statements from each one of you. I am going to call them now."

Sherrod knocked on the door to the Carpenter's room. Matthew Ritter answered, and his mouth dropped open when he saw his four friends in the hall looking dusty and dirty and very sheepish. Elizabeth immediately saw Richard, and she didn't know whether to put on her "I love you, and I am thrilled you are all right" face or her "what the hell did you think you were doing?" face. She decided he looked guilty enough and smiled her "I love you" smile. He was too covered with plaster dust for her to be tempted to hug him, but she was very relieved that her husband of more than fifty-five years had been found.

The four didn't have much to say about what had happened. They were dusty and dirty and embarrassed and had to use the bathroom. They were tired and thirsty and hungry. They didn't want to talk about it. Each one of the explorers could not wait to gulp down a couple of bottles of cold water and take a hot shower.

After everyone else had left to return to their own rooms, Richard pulled Henley's map from his pocket and handed it to Elizabeth. He couldn't look her in the eyes. But Elizabeth looked pointedly at Richard. "She texted me today and asked if I'd found the map she'd LEFT FOR ME!" Richard had nothing to say in his defense. He went to take a shower and get rid of some of the plaster dust.

The Ritters invited the remaining reunion goers to their suite for a room service dinner and wine. They'd had a reservation at the Sam Snead restaurant at the golf club that night, but none of them wanted to leave the hotel to go to another building for dinner. They were tired and wanted to go to bed early. In spite of the fact that they had discovered a long-dead body, a skeleton, during their foray into the unknown alcoves of the Woodbrier's bunker, the four who had been in the utility closet were not ready to have a discussion about what had happened to them. The experience had been traumatic, and they had been held captive in the small space with that skeleton for hours. Elizabeth and the Ritters were more than eager to hear about every detail of their friends' exploits into forbidden territory, but they were not successful convincing the others to say anything about it.

They ate their delicious room service steaks and shrimp cocktails, drank more wine than usual, and retired early to their rooms. Three of them were happy they did not have to confront and explain to wives or girlfriends about what they had done that day. Richard knew that sooner or later, he would end up telling Elizabeth everything. But he was not ready to do that tonight. After all, it had been Elizabeth's map that he'd "borrowed" which had led to their troubles.

Sherrod Jefferson had been scheduled to leave the Woodbrier this Saturday at five o'clock. But after the discovery of the skeleton in the supply closet in the basement of the West Virginia Wing, he knew that was not going to happen. He knew his night was just beginning. He didn't mind working long hours or working overtime, but the discovery of a decades-old crime scene on his watch and what to do when you found a skeleton hidden in the wall was something they'd not taught him at Cornell.

Sherrod had been a straight-A student in high school, and he had graduated second in his class from Lewisburg High. He had always wanted to work in the hotel industry, and he earned a full scholarship to attend the Cornell Hotel School. He'd excelled at the Ivy League university and gone on to the Wharton Business School for his MBA. He had worked at several hotels in New York City until he finally was hired to work his dream job as head concierge at the Woodbrier Resort.

Sherrod Jefferson's father had been killed in Vietnam, and his mother had died of breast cancer when Sherrod was six years old. Sherrod had been raised by his grandfather. His grandfather had been a waiter at the Woodbrier. He'd been named Sherrod, too. The grandfather had been extremely proud of his grandson's success. He'd been older when his grandson was born, but he had lived to see the boy hired at the Woodbrier. The Jeffersons had come a long way in three generations.

The younger Sherrod missed his grandfather every day and wished the old man could have been around to see how well his only grandchild was handling his responsibilities at the Woodbrier. He wished his grandfather was here with him tonight. His grandfather had always done the right thing and always known how to handle any kind of problem. The younger Sherrod Jefferson could have used his grandfather's advice in this current bizarre situation.

The authorities arrived, and by the next morning, there was yellow crime scene tape across the doors of the elevator next to the Carpenter's room. Elizabeth had heard people coming and going in the hallway all night long. She'd heard the old elevator creaking as it carried the crime scene investigators up and down and to and from the supply closet and the skeleton. Always anxious to solve a mystery, she thought she would have liked to see the crime scene and the skeleton hanging in the plaster. But maybe that would not have been as interesting in real life as it was in a mystery novel. Richard had shared a little bit of his adventure with her, but he had not shared it all. Elizabeth knew the elevator and the supply closet had previously been off limits to Woodbrier guests, and they would continue to be off limits for the foreseeable future.

Elizabeth intended to make a point of getting to know Sherrod Jefferson better. He would be her best source of reliable information about who the poor victim was. Everyone was now assuming the skeleton was male because of the bits of clothing that had been found in the wall with him. If the skeleton had been hanging in the closet for as long as everyone believed he'd been hanging there, it might be an impossible task to figure out his identity. No one might ever know who had been sealed up behind that metal supply cabinet. Elizabeth thought of Edgar Allan Poe's short story "The Cask of Amontillado."

The next day was Sunday. Elizabeth planned to spend time hanging out in the luxurious public rooms of the Woodbrier. People would be coming and going. There would inevitably be leaks about what had been found in the non-public, off-limits part of the bunker. News like this could not be kept quiet. Everyone would know about the skeleton by noon on Sunday. Elizabeth wanted the straight story from Sherrod Jefferson, but she also wanted to know what the gossip was, the scuttlebutt about who had been found hanging in the plaster wall.

Elizabeth knew Henley was planning to leave the Woodbrier early Sunday morning to fly home to California. She knew Henley would love to have been at the Woodbrier to hear about the skeleton. Henley would have relished the thought that her employee's roughly-drawn sketch of a map might have inadvertently led to the discovery of the guy behind the metal cabinet. Henley had been so outspoken and adamant about there being more to the bunker than was presented on the official tour. The discovery in the supply closet would have at least partly confirmed her suspicions. Once Elizabeth was able to discover the identity of the skeleton, she would text or email Henley all about the excitement she had missed.

CHAPTER 29

2021

Late Sunday morning, those who were still left from the Camp Shoemaker crowd gathered in the Woodbrier's main dining room for the elaborate Sunday brunch. It was delicious and opulent, and they enjoyed every minute of it.

The crêpes station was a particular favorite. Two expert chefs made quite a show of flipping over and turning out the thin pancakes, one after another without a pause. Guests could select sweet or savory fillings and sauces. The Camp Shoemaker crowd as a group tried one of every flavor and one of every filling. Elizabeth loved her choice, chunks of lobster in a lemon beurre blanc sauce. It was so rich and delicious, she couldn't finish her dessert crêpe stuffed with sour cherries and almond-flavored mascarpone. They washed it all down with the complimentary champagne.

The disasters of the day before had seemingly been forgotten, and they were pretending that none of it had happened. Elizabeth suspected that every one of them was dying to know if the skeleton had been identified and if the authorities had been able to determine when and how he had died. But nobody brought up the subject. They focused on the food and where they would meet the following year.

The Ritters were leaving early Monday morning to drive to Dulles Airport to fly home to Palm Springs. The Carpenters would drive back to Maryland on Tuesday, assuming the authorities had taken a statement from Richard by then and given him the okay to leave. The other three Camp Shoemaker boys were also subject to being questioned by law enforcement about their discovery of the skeleton. They planned to leave to fly back to their various hometowns on Tuesday morning.

It was early afternoon, and Richard was pushing Elizabeth's wheelchair through the hallway when she saw Valerie Symington, the mother of the bride who had lost the dress she'd intended to wear to her daughter's wedding. Elizabeth had been wondering what had happened with Valerie and her search for the missing MOB dress. "Valerie! Valerie Symington!" Elizabeth called out to the woman who was now dressed in a gorgeous French blue floor-length beaded gown. It looked like it had cost a great deal of money. Elizabeth wondered if this was Valerie's lost dress or if she'd been forced to buy another one.

Valerie turned around and recognized Elizabeth. She rushed over and grabbed Elizabeth's hand. "The wedding has finally happened, and I am just taking a short break from the reception. How do you like my dress? I followed your advice, and sure enough the dress was found . . . and in time . . . in one of the hotel's freezers. Can you believe it?"

"Your dress is absolutely spectacular, but . . . it was in the hotel's freezer? What in the world happened? How did it get into the freezer? How did you ever find it?" Elizabeth was delighted with the news that the dress had been located in time, but she couldn't imagine how it had found its way into the Woodbrier's freezer.

"My housekeeper, Maya, sent the dress in a box she found in my attic. Something that was frozen had been sent to me in that box, a gift of steaks, I think, and on the outside of the box it said 'put in freezer immediately.' It was a nice, sturdy box, so I'd saved it. Maya found the box in the attic. It was a good mailing box and just the right size. After she picked up the dress from the seamstress, Maya packed my dress in the box to send to me. Of course when the box arrived at the Woodbrier, and it did arrive overnight as it should have, someone sent it directly to the kitchens. They saw the warning on the outside of the box that said 'put in freezer immediately,' and that is what they did. No one really bothered to look closely at the address on the box, to read the name of the person it was actually sent to. They rushed the box to the freezer. The man who signed for the box was in food services. The concierge tracked him down, and eventually the dress was located. Pretty cool, huh?" Valerie laughed at her little joke. "The hotel steamed out the wrinkles for me, and I was able to wear it to the wedding today."

"That's quite a story. It's a beautiful dress. I don't blame you for wanting to find it. I'm so glad it was located in time. I'd been thinking of you and wondering what had happened."

"Thank you for listening to me cry and for your practical advice about how to go about tracking down the package. I was at my wits end and not thinking clearly. You put me back on track. I'm not sure my daughter is on track or that this marriage is on track, but I did my best. I've got to get back to the reception. Thanks again for all your help."

Elizabeth was relieved that at least one mystery had been solved. Now all she had to do was find out who had been plastered in the wall. It had happened so many years ago. She was trying to come to terms with the fact that she might never have an answer to this one. No one might ever know who had been hanging in the supply closet or how he had ended up there.

Three of the Camp Shoemaker boys had gone to the hotel's casino, and Richard had joined the Ritters for a walk around the grounds. It was a perfect late September day, sunny but cool. The end of the summer flowers were vibrant in the Woodbrier's gardens. Elizabeth would have loved to have been able to accompany her husband and her friends on their walk. She didn't often feel sad that she couldn't do the things she used to be able to do. Today she regretted that she could not accompany the others in their stroll through the Woodbrier's magnificent grounds. Richard had offered to try to push her in the wheelchair, but she knew it would be difficult to negotiate the gravel paths. She knew she would slow down the others. She'd chosen to stay inside.

She decided to hang out in the Garden Room, perhaps to be able to pretend that she was actually outside in the garden. She loved this room because it not only had a great view of the Woodbrier's grounds, it also had a great view of the Lobby Bar, the place where everybody came sooner or later. So far, she'd not heard a single word about the skeleton. Sherrod Jefferson had done a masterful job of keeping the whole thing under wraps. It was a disappointment to Elizabeth. She had counted on hearing some gossip. She decided she should have gone on the walk around the gardens with Richard. She moved her wheelchair to the cozy library alcove off the Garden Room. This was the Victorian Writing Room, her very favorite spot. The writing room also had an excellent view of the Lobby Bar. She would not miss a thing. Elizabeth nodded off to sleep.

The sound of a woman crying startled her out of her nap. The woman who was crying appeared to be about Elizabeth's own age. She had gray hair and was being consoled by a young man who was in early middle age, about the age of Elizabeth's own daughters. He looked young to Elizabeth. But everybody looked young to Elizabeth these days. The young man was obviously worried about the older woman, and Elizabeth was sure the woman who was crying was the young man's mother. He was holding his mother's hand and talking with her in earnest. Elizabeth strained to overhear what they were saying. This was the second woman she'd encountered who was crying in the public rooms at the Woodbrier. This was supposed to be a happy place. What was going on?

"Are you absolutely certain that it was Uncle Johnny?" The young man had doubt in his voice.

It was almost impossible for Elizabeth to understand what the woman was saying. She was farther away than her son was from where Elizabeth was sitting, and she was speaking and crying at the same time. The woman was nodding her head and seemed to be insisting that she knew what she was talking about. Elizabeth quietly moved her wheelchair a little closer so she could better hear what the woman was talking about.

"He had my ring on the chain around his neck. I gave Johnny that ring the last time we were together in West Berlin. We were going to marry, but I didn't know if I would ever see him again. The wall was almost completed, and closing everybody in. We all knew it was just a matter of time, and we would not be allowed to move freely back and forth with the western part of our city. Johnny begged me not to go back to the Russian sector. He warned me that I might not be able to leave again. And he was right."

"Why did you go back? Why didn't you stay in West Berlin?" The young man could not understand why his mother hadn't followed her heart and stayed with the man she loved.

"I had my whole family still living in the eastern sector of the city. My parents were still alive. My grandparents were still alive. They wouldn't leave their home. They did not believe the wall would ever be completed or that the Russians would be successful in keeping people prisoners in East Germany. They were so wrong."

"So what is this about the ring? Did my dad know about the ring?"

"Of course your father knew about the ring. I held nothing back from him. I told him everything. We were desperate to find Johnny. There were no secrets between us." The woman paused and cried again for a while. "I'd had the ring made . . . out of aluminum. The woman who made it for me said it had been fabricated from the wreckage of an allied plane that was shot down over Germany during World War II. This jeweler friend of mine was making rings from the aluminum she'd been able to salvage from that downed plane. The rings became symbols of resistance to the Russian occupation of our country and the cruel Stasi that enforced the Russian laws. To wear one of these rings was a subtle but obvious way that let others know you were protesting and resisting the occupation and the repression and the building of the wall."

"And you gave the ring to Uncle Johnny?" The woman's son was trying to understand the meaning of the ring and what his mother had done with it.

"I was in love with Johnny. I told him the ring was a pledge of my love. It didn't fit his finger, as it had been made to fit my own much smaller finger. He promised he would put it on a chain and wear it around his neck—always. He said he would keep it close to his heart until he could exchange it for the wedding ring I would give to him in the future. Now I know that aluminum ring was still around his neck when he died . . . when he was murdered. I knew he hadn't left me. I knew something terrible had happened to him. The FBI kept telling me there was no trace of him, that he had just disappeared."

"Mom, that was all true. There was no trace of him. He had just disappeared."

"They tried to tell me that he might have defected to Russia. They tried to tell me he'd grown impatient waiting for me to escape from East Germany. They said he had gone over to the Communists. I knew none of that was true. Because he had briefly kind of been a Communist agent and he'd agreed to tell the Russians secrets about the Woodbrier and because he had a Russian handler, they didn't spend much time looking for him. They had already decided he was a traitor and had gone to Russia. They said he had abandoned me." She stopped crying, and her anger took over. "And now we know that absolutely none of that was true. He never abandoned me. He never was a traitor. He never became a Communist or went to Russia. He was here, in the basement of the Woodbrier all along, all these years. Poor Johnny."

"I wish Dad were still alive to know what happened to his brother. I know at the time it was devastating for you that Uncle Johnny disappeared. But you must have had your doubts, even just a few doubts, that maybe he had abandoned you. As horrible as Uncle Johnny's death is, and now we know he was actually murdered, it worked out for you in the end. It was a good thing that you and Dad tried so hard to find him. You never gave up, and then the two of you fell in love. You had a happy life with Dad. I would not be here if Uncle Johnny hadn't been murdered."

"Yes, my darling son. I have had a happy life. I loved your Uncle Johnny when I was very young, and then I grew to love your father with all my heart. Your father stood by me and saw me through the most difficult time of my life. I had just arrived in this country, and my fiancée, who had promised to wait for me and love me forever, was nowhere to be found. Your father accepted me and comforted me. Then he fell in love with me, and I fell in love with him."

"What do we do now?"

"This is a murder case. Things are no longer in our hands. I have told the authorities that I am quite certain I know who the man in the plaster coffin is. I have identified him on the basis of the ring on the chain around his neck. They cannot just take my word for it, of course. They will have to do tests. I don't know if it is possible to retrieve DNA from bones, but I know they will do their best to try to identify this person and solve the mystery."

"Don't you think whoever murdered Uncle Johnny is probably dead?"

"If Johnny's body was buried in that wall in the summer of 1965, yes, whoever killed him is probably dead by now. Or, they are so old they would not be worth prosecuting. I don't think the FBI will spend too much time looking for the perpetrator of this crime. I would like to know how Johnny died. I hope it was not a painful death. I may never know *why* he died. I suppose his death must have had something to do with his association with the Communist spies. Yes, poor Johnny. He did it all for love. He loved this country. He did not want to betray the USA. But he was so in love with me. He would have done anything to be with me. He would have done anything to get me out of East Berlin. The FBI told me, and your father also told me, that Johnny agreed to violate his agreement never to talk about the bunker here at the Woodbrier. Information about the bunker was what the Russians wanted to find out from him. They promised to allow me to leave the Russian sector of Berlin if Johnny would tell them all about the Woodbrier's bunker. Johnny was naïve. The East German authorities would never have allowed me to leave, but Johnny believed them. When he had told them all he knew, they would have killed him. I know they did it. I know the Russians killed him. Who else would have wanted Johnny dead?"

"Dad said Johnny had agreed to become a double agent. He was giving false information to his Russian handler. That was what he'd agreed to do in return for the U.S. government bringing you here."

"Yes, that was the deal. He was going to be an agent for the U.S., and our government promised to get me out of East Germany. The government kept their part of the bargain, and because he had disappeared, they thought Johnny had not kept his part. They gave me a hard time at first. They thought I knew something about Johnny's disappearance. I think they even suspected that I was an East German spy for a while. Finally, when they realized how destroyed I was by Johnny's apparent abandonment, they relented and realized I knew nothing about what they believed was his defection. Now they will have to admit that he did not defect."

"There is a lot of satisfaction that Johnny's name has been cleared. His reputation has been restored. The authorities now know he didn't leave and go to Russia. He did not betray his country."

"All of the people who worked on his case in the late 1960s are long gone. None of the people who will be investigating the skeleton in the closet will know or care anything about what happened in 1965. That's just the way life is. But, yes, I am glad that your Uncle Johnny's name has been cleared. I never doubted him. In my mind and in your father's mind, he was never a traitor."

"Now we can give Uncle Johnny a funeral and a proper burial. We can bury him beside Dad. Is that what you want to have happen?"

"Oh, yes. That is certainly what I want to have happen. Let's go now. We will have to speak with all these official people again and again, I'm sure. But I'm tired and need to go home. After this is all over, will you ask someone if I can have that ring back, the one from around Johnny's neck? It's a relic of the past, the only thing I really ever gave your Uncle Johnny.

CHAPTER 30

2021

ELIZABETH HAD HEARD ALL SHE needed to hear. The woman and her son left, and Elizabeth was pondering the story they'd had to tell. Hanging out in her wheelchair was never boring, but today she'd really hit the jackpot. People ignore the elderly, the quiet woman sitting in her wheelchair, nodding off to sleep. The handicapped are often regarded as almost non-people. Even though they might not be able to get around very well, they still have eyes and ears. Many people fail to think about that fact. Elizabeth had realized this when she'd become disabled. But she didn't whine. She had turned her disability into an excellent cover for finding out secrets and overhearing confidences. She had learned to fade into the woodwork. She had made lemonade out of her lemons. Today's coup was one of her best discoveries ever.

She couldn't wait to tell the others in the group about what she'd just found out. The four men who had trespassed where they weren't supposed to go had been too embarrassed to speak of the incident. Elizabeth would bring up the subject and fill them all in about exactly who the person was that they'd found hanging in the plaster. She reminded herself to ask her pathologist husband if there was any chance, after all these years had gone by, that DNA could be recovered from a skeleton's bones.

Elizabeth wanted to tell Henley all about the skeleton and everything she'd discovered about who was in the wall, but she was worried about Henley. She was concerned that Henley had made a decision to do something reckless. Elizabeth decided she would wait a while and tell Henley all about it after Uncle Johnny's cause of death had been determined. Henley would want to know the details. Elizabeth would be sure she had them all before she shared this adventure with her friend.

This was the last night together before the Camp Shoemaker group went their separate ways, back to their own lives all over the United States. They had decided to meet in Phoenix the following November. September in Arizona was still too hot to be comfortable. Even October could be a challenge. By November, the weather in Phoenix would be perfect. The Ritters suggested one of their favorite places, The Mimosa Inn, an elegant resort in Paradise Valley, Arizona. It was luxurious and secluded. They would be pampered, and breakfast, accompanied every morning by, guess what . . . mimosas, was included. It was expensive, but they could afford it. It had great food. One night, they would have dinner in the wine cellar. It sounded perfect. They reserved their casitas at the Mimosa Inn and were already looking forward to seeing each other again.

The Ritters left early Monday morning to drive to Dulles Airport. The four witnesses to the accidental discovery of the skeleton in the storage closet were interviewed by the authorities on Monday. They were given the okay to leave town. Elizabeth made a point of speaking with Sherrod Jefferson about the dead man. She did not reveal how she had come by the information she already knew, but she managed to glean some additional tidbits from the head concierge.

Elizabeth learned that Uncle Johnny's last name was Bidwell. His skeleton had been identified immediately. His wallet had been taken, but an old-fashioned Woodbrier ID card that was found in the pocket of the man's trousers had identified him as Johnny Bidwell. Whoever had murdered him had probably stolen his wallet. Money might not have been the motive. Johnny Bidwell would not have been expected to have much money. It was more likely that the wallet was taken to make the murder look like a robbery gone bad. Elizabeth was guessing that Johnny had probably been murdered because of his association with the Russians. Maybe they'd gained all the information they thought Johnny had to tell them, and he'd become a liability. Or maybe, the Russians had found out that Johnny had turned on them and had become a double agent. They might have discovered that he was passing them false information.

For whatever reason, the wallet was gone. Whoever had killed Johnny had not checked all of his pockets. They probably figured no one would ever discover his body, so it didn't matter what he might still have in his pockets. Nobody would ever find Johnny in the wall of the bunker's basement. No one would ever find a body they needed to identify. But somebody had found Johnny, and they had found the identity card with his name on it. Johnny's sister-in-law, Frieda, was called in by the police to see if she could identify a skeleton that nobody could possibly identify and to claim what was left of a body that had already been buried for more than fifty-five years.

Frieda Bidwell had worked at the Woodbrier for decades and was known to the head concierge, Sherrod Jefferson. She was now retired. Frieda had been able to positively identify the body, because of a ring the skeleton had on a chain around his neck. Further tests were being done to confirm the identification. The cause of death had not yet been determined, but an autopsy was being performed by a forensic anthropologist. Strangulation was suspected because preliminary findings showed that the skeleton's hyoid bone had been fractured. Elizabeth was sorry to hear this. It had not been a painless death as Frieda had hoped. When Frieda heard about the cause of death, she would be sad again.

Johnny Bidwell had been murdered in the summer of 1965. Whoever had ended his life had plastered him into the wall and hung the metal supply cabinet on the wall over the impromptu crypt. Sherrod Jefferson believed that the murderer had been certain the body would never be discovered. Although he was reluctant to admit it, Sherrod suspected that the person who had murdered Johnny Bidwell was probably someone who worked at the Woodbrier. Sherrod doubted it could have been a guest. It had to have been someone who had access to the bunker and the bogus "freight elevator." The murderer would have needed time to mix the plaster and allow it to dry sufficiently. It would have taken time to install the metal cabinet on the wall. It would have been a several day effort to accomplish all of this. It had probably been an inside-the-Woodbrier job.

Sherrod Jefferson never mentioned to Elizabeth that Richard Carpenter and his compadres had been in a part of the Woodbrier where they were not supposed to be. That was a moot point now, and Sherrod was well aware that Elizabeth knew her husband had been in an area that was off-limits to the public. But Elizabeth was bold enough to mention to the concierge that the mystery of Johnny Bidwell's disappearance might never have been solved if it had not been for the four bad boys who'd found themselves locked in the supply closet.

Sherrod Jefferson nodded his head and smiled a weak smile. He made no comment out loud. Elizabeth thanked him for listening to her when she'd come to him about her missing husband. If she'd not raised the alarm, she pointed out, they might still be down there in the bunker. "You might have eventually found five skeletons in your closet, Sherrod."

CHAPTER 31

2021–2022

When she returned from the wedding, Henley told her family and her employees at the ranch near Paso Robles that she was going on a trip around the world. Everyone who knew her was shocked and thought she must be completely out of her mind. Henley loved her ranch and her restaurant and her life in Paso Robles. She never wanted to leave the place. It had been almost impossible to talk her into flying to West Virginia to attend her niece's wedding at the Woodbrier. And now all of a sudden, she was going on a trip around the world? Really? It didn't make any sense. Nobody believed the around-the-world story for a minute. But sure enough, when Henley arrived home from her trip to West Virginia, she packed up her stuff, had a big goodbye dinner at La Buona Ricetta with her family and ranch employees, gave everybody tearful hugs, and left town. Nobody could figure it out.

Henley's daughter had pleaded with her mother to tell her the truth about what the heck was going on. Was Henley sick with some fatal disease? Had she met a boyfriend and was running off to live with him? Henley's daughter was beyond being upset by Henley's erratic behavior. Long ago she had accepted that her mother marched to a unique drummer, but this was too much. Her daughter felt as if Henley was deserting her. The way Henley had hugged her granddaughters when she'd told them goodbye had alarmed her daughter. It was as if Henley never expected to see any of them again. But all who loved Henley knew in their hearts that it would be useless to try to talk her out of what she intended to do. It always had been useless to reason with Henley, and it always would be.

Henley left Paso Robles in late October. No one knew where she was after that, although Henley sent occasional emails and text messages to let her family and her staff at the ranch know she was all right. When she had been gone for four months, the communications stopped.

Henley had never known exactly how she had been recruited into this very secret group that had taken on a nearly impossible mission. She assumed that someone who had known about her prowess as a markswoman had recommended her. She figured that her skill with guns was the reason she'd been approached to be part of the operation. The group had formed as an ad hoc coming together of those who believed that action had to be taken to prevent a possible nuclear holocaust in the world. They had a one-time-only goal. After they had accomplished their objective, the group would immediately disband.

The recruiting techniques and the training techniques, in fact all of the stages and pieces of the intricate planning, were shrouded in secrecy. The most important rule was security and protecting the real identities of those who had been chosen to participate. No one was allowed to speak with anyone else in the group about their real name or anything at all about their real lives as they had existed before the mission. Hopefully they would all be able to return to these previous lives after their objective had been sucessfully completed.

Everyone involved was completely anonymous. There were many levels in the recruitment process, so each person who agreed to participate was completely protected. This protection was considered essential to the success of the mission as well as essential to the safety of those who were willing to put their lives on the line. Taking risks was required, but each man and woman who signed on wanted to be able to return to their normal lives after it was all over.

Henley was willing to abide by all the rules of secrecy and anonymity. She was thankful for them, and she trusted that all of the others with whom she was training and working were likewise committed to the rules. She thought overall that they had a brilliant plan, and she was honored to have been chosen to be a part of it. Henley worked hard. Everyone worked hard. Every detail was carefully thought out. Every detail was practiced over and over again. When the time came, there would not be any do-overs. There would be one—and only one—chance to get it right.

When her training was complete and it was time for the plan to be put into action, Henley felt she was ready. There were some aspects of the plan she did not particularly like, but she had agreed to this mission and was eager to end the training and take the fight into the real world. The elaborate arrangements were all in place, and she knew she could do this. The difficult part for her would not be the shooting or the escape. The difficult part would be the waiting and the pretending. She admitted to herself that overall, it really was an ingenious plan, and she'd agreed to go along with all of it, even with the parts of it she didn't like. She would force herself to wait and to pretend.

Traveling to any place in Russia at this particular time in history was not a smart thing to do. Nobody in their right mind would dare venture into that snake pit of a country. It was not the Russian people's fault. It seems as if it they were once again being forced to live under another tyrannical ruler. In this most recent case, their tyrannical leader was even more of a nut job than the previous ones had been. He had changed the Russian constitution so the Russian people had no way to vote him out of office and into obscurity. He had made himself president for life. UGH! The people were already suffering from the sanctions imposed on them by the rest of the world because of their president's hapless and disastrous foray into a war with Ukraine. Things in Russia were a mess, and the unfortunate people of the Rodina were left to suffer—again.

The leader of their country was already the richest man in the world, having squirreled away billions in oil money that he had stolen from Russia's citizens. The oil money belonged to the Russian people, but Bad Vlad had appropriated it as his own. In addition to countless secret bank accounts he had stashed around the world, he'd used some of these pilfered funds to build himself a vacation house. And what a vacation house it was. The man had built a 1.4 billion dollar dacha on the Black Sea. The ridiculously excessive and extravagantly overdone estate near Gelendzhik and Sochi was a testimony to the Russian leader's hubris, narcissism, megalomania, and bad taste.

Because of his paranoia, the Russian president had chosen to hunker down in his billion-dollar folly during his grossly ill-advised aggression towards Ukraine. Rather than stay in Moscow, this madman had decided to manage, from his beach house, the war that was his and his alone. In fact Ukraine was dangerously close to the bloated dacha. If this foolish man wanted to be even closer to the conflict, he could take a boat out into the Black Sea and keep an eye on his catastrophic military operation from the water.

The misguided leader thought Ukraine should be returned to Russia. Ukraine had been forced to be a part of the Soviet Union in the first place, and the man who was trying to reconstruct the failed fantasy of the USSR believed Ukraine had always belonged to Russia. The Russian president believed that Russia was entitled to its breadbasket, and he was determined to make it so again. If he'd had any idea his war to take the country back would turn out to be such a disaster, one has to wonder if he might have chosen to build his vacation house in a different location, not so close to the borders of Ukraine, so close to his war.

He must have felt safe in the dacha, at least safer than he felt in Moscow. The former KGB thug's dacha had become the most heavily fortified place in the world. Fort Knox in the United States had never been as well guarded. War planes flew over the Black Sea property 24/7. Any unidentified plane that flew even close to the grounds of the estate would be shot down without warning. Armed helicopters hovered over the buildings. Only the most trusted soldiers manned the grounds, and these heavily-armed loyalists stood ten feet apart along the perimeter, around the mansion, and on every road and pathway.

The dacha's location, on a cliff high above the water, had excellent views. There was limited and nearly impossible access to the sea below. The compound had been built by a man who realized he had many enemies and was hated by the world. It was a pumped-up, puffed-up twenty-first millennium version of Berchtesgaden. It was a fortress, steep and mighty.

The man who inhabited this fortress trusted no one. He had fired his staff and his military generals . . . several times. He said they were incompetent, and maybe they were. Or maybe they were not just not that engaged with their assignment to invade another country on this mad man's whim.

CHAPTER 32

1987–2022

The one person the mad man had not fired was his cook. His cook was a genius in the kitchen. Trained in Paris, the cook had been discovered by the Russian leader at the Astoria Hotel in St. Petersburg. Ilya Baranov had been ordered to quit his job as head chef at the hotel and move at once to Moscow. It was considered to be a great honor to be singled out by the nation's president, and Ilya could not refuse the order to accept the position. Baranov's job required that he accompany his new employer wherever he went, whether the president was presiding over the Kremlin in Moscow or was traveling or was hiding out in his vacation home on the shores of the Black Sea.

Ilya Baranov had quickly learned the likes and dislikes of his new boss. He knew how to please the man's palate and at the same time was able to keep him relatively slim. The cook made his food and personally served every meal to the man. He tasted each dish in front of the Russian president before he allowed his boss to eat the first bite. Bad Vlad trusted his cook with his life. The cook was one employee who would never be fired.

Ilya Baranov appeared to be a man above reproach. But Ilya had a secret that, for many years, only he had known about. He had once, a very long time ago, been in love with a Ukrainian woman. His fiancée had been from Odessa. The two had met in Paris when they were attending Le Cordon Bleu cooking school. Sasha Zakharov was an ardent and out-spoken anti-Communist. She had left Ukraine when it was still a part of the Soviet Union, and she vowed that she would never live on Russian-controlled territory again. Ilya and Sasha were good enough at what they did that they knew they could make their way as chefs in the West. They made plans to find jobs in the United States.

Sasha had never wanted to talk about the family she had left behind in Ukraine. She had implied to Ilya that they were all dead, murdered because of their anti-Soviet political views. Sasha was obviously well-educated and cultured. She had come from a good family. She always grew silent and sad whenever people around her were discussing their families. She didn't have a family any more. Ilya suspected that the woman he loved was living in Paris and attending cooking school under a name that was not her own. He suspected that she was in hiding under a false identity.

Sasha had rejoiced when the Soviet Union collapsed in December of 1991. For several years, she had felt relatively safe living in France until the current leader seized control of Russia in 2000. Ilya noticed that Sasha became much more paranoid and much more careful after the former KGB's creepy horseman had pushed representative government to the side in Russia and taken on the role of a modern day Joseph Stalin.

After Alexander Litvinenko was poisoned with polonium while living in England and subsequently died a horrible and painful death, Sasha refused to leave their Paris apartment. She became obsessed with not eating and not drinking. She was terrified that her food or her wine or her tea were poisoned.

Ilya found her behavior disturbing and excessive. He did not know whether her life really was in danger. He wondered if Sasha's paranoia was just her imagination or perhaps was exaggerated because of incidents from the past. He was at a loss about what to do to help her. She could not work and would not eat. Ilya didn't know if Sasha's fears were real or if she was suffering from mental illness.

When he came home one day and found his beloved murdered and dismembered on the floor of their flat, he was forced to acknowledge that he had not taken Sasha seriously enough and had failed to protect her. Through his devastation, he berated himself for having stayed in Paris. He felt he should have made more of an effort to find employment in the United States for himself and Sasha. He had thought they had time, but they had waited too long. Ilya was crushed by grief over the loss of his young love. He didn't know for sure who had murdered Sasha, but he suspected it had something to do with the family she had always refused to talk about. He suspected her death had been some kind of a revenge killing. She had predicted her death and had spoken of it often. He had soothed her and told her she was ridiculous to be so fearful. Sasha had been right to be afraid for her life, and Ilya had been wrong to ignore her fears.

He was never able to discover what it was about Sasha's background that had caused her to live in fear or caused her to die a horribly painful and agonizing death. He had his suspicions, but that is all they were . . . suspicions. He had no clues, no real facts about who had murdered his fiancée.

The Paris police, likewise, were never able to find any leads to Sasha's killer. Law enforcement ran into dead ends at every turn. The brutality of the crime haunted them, and initially they had devoted many resources in their efforts to find the murderers. They always said they'd never been able to turn up a single suspect. It had been a professional hit, an almost perfect crime. The police had interviewed Ilya countless times. They had implied to him that they thought the murder was politically motivated, but they were hesitant to cast anyone in the role of the perpetrator. As time went by, Ilya began to feel as if the French authorities were not telling him everything they knew. He had a sense that law enforcement was afraid to solve the case.

He could not stay in Paris. Every street in the City of Light and every place in France reminded him of his loss. He never spent another night in the flat he had shared with Sasha. It had been closed off as a crime scene for weeks. Ilya never wanted to go back inside. He did not want to be reminded of his last grisly encounter there, the brutal scene of the death of the woman he'd loved so dearly. He found he could no longer live in Paris or in France. Every vista, every meal, every piece of music he heard reminded him of Sasha. His grief and his guilt threatened to destroy him.

He was angry all the time, but he did not know where to direct his anger. He loved to cook, and working at his profession was his refuge, the only thing he could turn to for solace. He let his colleagues know that he wanted to leave France and was looking for a new position. He was extraordinarily talented, even as a young man, and he knew he could find a new and desirable position in a place that did not constantly remind him of Sasha.

He had not intended to return to Russia at all, especially after his relationship with Sasha. Sasha had hated Russia. But a coveted job as head chef at the Astoria Hotel in Saint

Petersburg opened up, and Ilya applied for the position. He was made an offer he could not refuse. St. Petersburg had always been the most westernized city in Russia. Close to Finland, even during the Soviet Era when it had been called Leningrad, the hotels in the city had catered to western tastes and visitors from abroad. Now the city was St. Petersburg again, and the Astoria Hotel was calling him. He decided to accept the offer, and he moved to St. Petersburg.

While he was working at the Astoria, Ilya had the misfortune to capture the attention of the most powerful man in Russia. Ilya received another offer he could not refuse, for very different reasons. The cook did what he had to do. He had no choice. He went to Moscow and became the chef and the food and drink police for the world's richest and most powerful low-life bag man. Ilya loved to cook and to be creative with food. He had no problem doing the job, even though he despised the man he cooked for, the man whose food and drink he tasted, the man whose life he saved every day.

No one in Russia knew anything about Ilya's relationship with Sasha. Ilya's background had been checked before he'd begun to cook for Russia's president, but it was a cursory check. The Federal Security Service (FSB) knew he'd been born in Russia and had gone to France to study in his chosen field. He had an exemplary record at the Paris cooking school, and his employers throughout Paris lauded both his cooking skills and his easy-going personality.

Investigators had no idea he'd once loved a Ukrainian woman, his fiancée who had died a horrible death because of her hidden past. The Russian leader was so enthusiastic about hiring Ilya to cook for him that no one delved too deeply into his background. Ilya's past life appeared on the surface to check all the right boxes. His security clearance was quick and superficial. No one who investigated him ever heard about Sasha. She was just a woman, a mere girlfriend, after all. She was of little notice or importance to anyone on the misogynistic staff composed of former KGB employees.

Ilya's deep-seated anger continued to build within him during the years the Russian leader became more and more aggressive towards Ukraine. But the cook never breathed a word about his anger or the underlying reason why he had come to hate Russian foreign policy. He was a cook. International politics was not his concern.

Ilya had been cooking for Russia's leader for several years when he happened to run into a former friend, another student at Le Cordon Bleu from his Paris days. Ilya's colleague, Otto Bauer, was sitting at a table at a coffeehouse in Moscow, and the two chefs were astonished to see each other. Otto had stayed in France, and now worked at a five-star hotel in Lyon. He had been a good friend to Sasha and to Ilya. Sasha had also been Otto's fellow student at the esteemed cooking school. Otto knew that Ilya and Sasha had intended to marry. He knew that Ilya had left Paris because of his grief over Sasha's horrible murder.

Otto had information for Ilya. The information was not proven. It was really just scuttlebutt that had floated around among the people who cooked in Paris. Otto told Ilya that Sasha's name had not in fact been either Sasha or Zakharov. Otto did not know what her real name was, but he knew that Sasha Zakharov had been a false name that she had adopted to hide her real identity.

Although Otto did not know Sasha's Ukrainian name, he'd heard via the grapevine that she had been the only surviving member of a once-powerful Ukrainian family from Odessa. The family were fervent Ukrainian nationalists and had spoken out against Russian meddling in Ukrainian affairs. They had all been murdered. Sasha had been away at boarding school in Switzerland at the time her entire family was killed. She never returned to Ukraine and was secretly given assistance in moving to France, changing her name, and obscuring her identity and her past. But, she had always known she was unfinished business for the Soviets.

When the current Russian leader came to power, she knew she would be on the hit list. The president's gang of neo-Soviets, the thugs of the FSB, were now in power and wanted revenge. They had changed the name from KGB, but their love for murdering their enemies and their other brutal tactics had not changed. Sasha had known she was a target. She was in the sights of the FSB, and in the sights of Russia's current autocratic leader who was pretending for the moment that he was not a despot and wearing his disguise of democratic clothing. The former KGB gangster who ruled Russia wanted Sasha in the ground with the rest of her troublesome family. She'd had to be eliminated.

Ilya had long suspected what Otto told him. Ilya had been too distraught at the time to think things through or ask many questions about Sasha's former life or about her death. The recent news from Otto had confirmed his suspicions about many things. Ilya had always wondered, if Sasha and her family had hated the Russians so much, why they had given their daughter a name with a Russian origin. Sasha was a very Russian name. Ilya now wondered if she had chosen a Russian name as part of her cover, a way of distancing herself from her former Ukrainian life and her family's position in that country.

Otto also told Ilya that the French authorities had backed off from their investigation of Sasha's death when they'd realized their clues to her killer were pointing them in the direction of the highest echelons of a foreign power. It had been a state-ordered torture, mutilation, and assassination. The gendarmes on the streets of the City of Light did not want to get involved in that kind of trouble. Sasha's murder was allowed to become a cold case. No one cared any more. Life had moved on.

But Ilya had not forgotten. And he'd just had confirmation from Otto about the things he had been mulling over in his mind for years. The combination of Otto's visit and the information he'd brought to Ilya's attention, in addition to Moscow's increasing aggression against Ukraine, finally pushed Ilya over the edge. But he was extremely careful. No one would ever guess that anything at all had changed for the popular chef. He continued on as always, behaving as the perfect employee and the perfect protector of the Russian head of state.

Deep down inside, Ilya Baranov was cooking up his plans for revenge. He was a patient man and never spoke of his desire to seek justice for Sasha. He knew his employer was a bully and a boor and a brute, but Ilya also knew he would never be able to leave his position as the chef and food taster for the Russian president. He knew he was stuck in his job for as long as the most powerful person in the country wanted him to remain where he was.

When the Russians shot down Malaysian Airlines Flight #17 over eastern Ukraine, Ilya knew it was time to become active. He was sickened at the loss of all those innocent lives. Many things had led up to his going over the edge, but the downing of the airliner was the final straw. Ilya knew the only way was for his employer to die. More and more despicable events would occur in Russia and in

Ukraine. These additional straws of Russian tyranny added to Ilya's determination to avenge Sasha. He did not care if he perished in the attempt, but he needed help with his plan. Ilya bided his time. He wanted to be certain that he was successful, that even if he died in the attempt, it was not in vain.

CHAPTER 33

2021–2022

It was illegal and considered to be immoral for any government to target another country's leader for assassination. No matter how much the nations of the world might want a certain dangerous and evil head of state to disappear from the land of the living, they could not officially take any action to end his or her life. The Israelis' Operation Wrath of God had been a governmentally sanctioned mission of assassination, but this very secret project didn't target a head of state. Ilya did not have the okay from any official government. He suspected that quite a few members of the group, which had formed around the operation that hopefully would end the life of the man who was trying to destroy the world, had connections to more than one government.

Russia's invasion and struggle in Ukraine in 2022 had added impetus to the desire of people in all countries of the world to get rid of Russia's leader. Millions believed the man was deranged. Everyone realized that he was terribly dangerous. The man was revealed for the soulless and despicable person that he truly was. His evil was now on display for all to see. Money flowed to Ilya's cause as it never had before. Ilya was concerned that too many people knew about their effort. It seemed as if the entire world wanted to join in the conspiracy to destroy this devil. But it was important that they remain as small an organization as possible. Everything they planned had to be kept completely secret, or Ilya and others would die.

They needed an older woman to complete their plot. Things had been delayed because they had not been able to find the right person to actually pull the trigger. But finally they had her, and she had gone through a rigorous training process. She was perfect for the job, and she was ready. All the pieces were in place.

It was disappointing that the operation had been delayed until after the man had actually invaded Ukraine and begun his thermobaric bombing, his cluster bombing, and the countless other means he had to wage his war. His determination to utterly destroy the country he had invaded was horrifying. He had proven himself to be the worst kind of war criminal in the eyes of the entire planet. Many had perished because the timetable to eliminate this disgusting villain had been delayed. Ilya was relieved when the plans were finally set, and the operation was a go.

Ilya had been adopted as an infant, so his relatives from Krasnodar, the people who had raised him and been his family, were not linked to him with DNA. This could became a significant point because he felt certain that after his mission was accomplished, the Russians would be tracking and testing DNA to try to find the culprit. They would never be able to prove that Ilya had anything to do with any of it. Ilya had prepared and tasted the bad man's food for years. He had always been a favorite and was above reproach.

He would be in the clear. The assassin would also be in the clear. The real person she was and the real life she had would never be associated with her role as a killer and a savior of the world.

Ilya had been talking about bringing his elderly aunt to live with him for many months. She was in ill health, and even though she had a daily caretaker, she was struggling to live in her own home. Things were not working well, even though Ilya had the resources to hire around-the-clock help for her.

Ilya's boss, the Russian leader, no longer felt safe in Moscow. He had relocated to Gelendvisk for the duration of his war. Gelendvisk and Sochi were close to Krasnodar, the city where Ilya had been born and grown up. This would be the perfect time for Ilya to move his ninety-three-year-old aunt to live with him on the Russian leader's estate. Ilya had insisted on having his own separate housing on the property. He did not want to live in the dacha itself. He had good reasons for this, and he was such a favorite of his employer that he got what he wanted. His cottage was small, but there was room for his aunt and her caretaker to move in with him.

Ilya really did have an elderly aunt. Before she was allowed to move into the Russian leader's compound, her entire background was closely scrutinized. She had dementia and no longer recognized Ilya or had any idea who he was. This had been well-documented by her own physicians and by the physicians who were hired by the FSB to investigate this person who was going to be living so close to the Russian president. Mila Fedorov's life had been an open book. There were no red flags. She would be welcome at the high-security villa near Gelendvisk and Sochi. Confined to a wheelchair, she was not a threat to anybody.

Likewise, Mila's caretaker was extensively investigated and found to be a solid Russian patriot with an unremarkable past. What investigators didn't discover was that Mila's caretaker despised Russia's current leader. She had hated Communism and rejoiced when Russia was finally free. She was desolate again when the most recent despot had seized power and tried to destroy her country. She was not outspoken, so the vetting process would never expose anything about her true feelings. She had taken care of Mila Federov for years, so Ilya knew the woman's political views. He knew she would be willing to do whatever was required of her to help destroy the evil man who held Russia in his grasp. Without incident, Mila and her caretaker moved to Ilya's cottage in March of 2022.

What only Ilya, the caretaker, and a few others knew was that Mila Fedorov never made the journey to live in Ilya's cottage on the Russian president's estate. The day before officials began the elaborate process of moving Ilya's aunt from Krasnodar to the grounds of the dacha, another woman who closely resembled Mila, had moved into Mila's home in Krasnodar. This substitute aunt, an imposter who really did not have dementia, was the woman who was moved in Mila's place to the cook's cottage by the Black Sea.

The real Mila Federov, who had been so carefully and extensively vetted and had been determined to be no risk to anyone living on the grounds of the Russian leader's mansion, had been secretly and quietly whisked away from her residence in Krasnodar. She surreptitiously traveled by private plane to Geneva and went to live in a very expensive care home for the aged in Switzerland. She arrived at the exclusive facility in the mountains outside Geneva and was content to live in this beautiful place under a name that was not her own.

Mila no longer spoke, so no one knew her by any other name than the one under which she had been admitted to the Swiss nursing home. No one ever suspected that the old woman was not who the paperwork claimed she was. Mila would never contradict the staff who called her by a name unknown to her. The woman who would live and eventually die in Switzerland had been assigned a false moniker late in life. In her declining weeks and months, she was given the highest level of care any person could hope to have. She spent her last days as happy as she could be and in good hands. As a condition of his cooperation and participation in the operation, Ilya had insisted that his aunt be treated with respect and given first-class treatment.

The pretend Mila Federov, along with Mila's long-time caretaker, was moved to the dacha near Sochi, into Ilya Baranov's cottage. The woman who claimed to be the ninety-three-year old Mila Federov would live in the cottage with her nurse and her nephew for only eight days before Ilya told his staff that his aunt had suffered a massive stroke and had been transferred to a hospital in Krasnodar. The pretend Mila Federov had not really had a stroke, but Ilya sadly reported all the details of this shocking and sudden medical event to the kitchen staff at the dacha. He tried to be philosophical. No one lives forever. Mila was at the end of her very long and very good run.

It was a few weeks before Mila was recovered sufficiently from her 'stroke,' and Ilya was able to arrange for his aunt to return to the cottage on the compound. When she returned from her stay at the hospital, Mila seemed more debilitated than she had before she'd had the stroke. This was an anticipated outcome for an elderly person in her nineties who had managed to live through such a potentially catastrophic ordeal. No one was paying much attention to Ilya as he lamented to his co-workers in the kitchen about his aunt's failing health and how difficult it was for him to see her in her current state. Thank goodness for her wonderful caretaker who was a godsend and did all the heavy lifting in caring for this woman who was at the end of her life.

Things were moving quickly now. In fact, a woman who was in her sixties had become the second substitute for Mila Federov. She was an American and did not speak or understand a word of Russian. She was a well-trained assassin, and she was now at last in place to accomplish a task almost everyone in the world supported in theory but no one was able or willing to undertake.

Before the previous stand-in Mila Federov had been taken to the hospital weeks earlier with a stroke, for the few days she had lived at the dacha, every morning her devoted caretaker had pushed her wheelchair along the neat paths of the elaborately landscaped grounds of the estate. The old woman and her caretaker liked to go to a particular spot and stay for a while in a location that overlooked the Black Sea. Mila had always loved the water, and Ilya insisted that she be allowed access to the views that her current location afforded her.

The terrain around the dacha was formidable. It was rocky, and the cliffs fell off sharply to the sea. At this particular spot at the edge of a precipice, where Mila's caretaker pushed her wheelchair every day, there was no sandy beach to tempt swimmers or dog walkers. It was hundreds of feet straight down a very steep rock face to get to the water. Even without the guards armed with machine guns and killer Rottweiler dogs, who were in place day and night to keep visitors off the private estate, no one would ever have been tempted to go for a swim by way of this unforgiving approach to the water.

The location for the vacation house had been chosen partly because it would have been impossible for anyone to climb the cliffs that surrounded and protected the dacha. Not even the men who'd scaled the heights in the movie, *The Guns of Navarone,* would have been able to reach these craggy summits.

There were pathways that meandered through the gardens of the dacha and led to some of the world's most spectacular views of the cliffs and the Black Sea in the distance. Mila's caretaker had taken pains to establish her frequent presence in one specific location, by taking her charge who was confined to a wheelchair, on walks along the cliffs. After Mila returned from the hospital in Krasnodar and was recovering from the stroke, her caretaker resumed her daily walks with the old woman along the perimeter of the cliffs. The guards were used to seeing the caretaker and the old woman in the wheelchair. They became invisible.

The man who lived in the dacha had become so paranoid, he scarcely allowed himself to go outside the confines of his palace any more. Even though his grounds were more secure than any other place on earth, he was still afraid. Since the war had begun, he only went outside on the terrace above his swimming pool very early in the day—to spend a few moments drinking his tea in the morning sun.

The plan for the assassination was to do this thing as soon as possible after "Mila" returned from being treated for her stroke at the hospital. The longer they waited, the more chance there was that they would be discovered. But the weather had not been good for several days, and the Russian leader had chosen not to have his tea outside on the terrace. The war was not going well for him. Those who wanted to see the man in his grave hoped he would not hide in his house forever. They hoped that the reason this loser had not ventured out onto his terrace was because the sun wasn't shining. Those in on the plot were desperately hoping that the man would come back outside once again—when there was sunshine on the terrace.

Ilya always brought the glass of tea, wherever the man decided to drink it. When he stayed in his bedroom, Ilya went to the bedroom and drank from the glass before his employer drank from it. When the weather was nice, this ritual took place on the terrace that overlooked the Black Sea. On the morning in question, there would be at most a ten-minute opportunity when the Russian leader would be visible to the markswoman who would be waiting, several hundred yards away at the edge of the cliff, to take her kill shot.

It was a difficult shot. There was one and only one location on the land from which it was possible to shoot a person who was relaxing on the dacha's terrace. Many possible shots could be made from the air and from the water, but these places were patrolled and heavily guarded at all times. No one thought about the site on the cliffs to the south of the terrace. Because only those who had been carefully screened would ever be allowed on the estate itself, there was no need to look for danger on the dacha's grounds. It was only from this difficult and unique position at the cliff's edge that it was possible to shoot the Russian ruler.

Mila Federov and her caretaker always had to be out very early for their morning walk. They would have to reach the cliffs in plenty of time before the Russian president began drinking his daily glass of tea. They were hoping to be in position on the fifth morning after Ilya's "aunt" had returned from the hospital.

The Mila who was now installed in the cottage would keep her head down. She would wear a wig that was a perfect copy of the hair of the woman who had left the cottage a few weeks earlier for the hospital. The elderly woman in a wheelchair would wear a shawl over her shoulders and another shawl over her head to hide her face. She would be swathed in wool coverings of various kinds. Old women are cold all the time. You never see a person who is in their nineties without layers of warm clothes. Mila would be covered head to toe with warmth. No one would ever suspect that the woman in Mila's wheelchair was not as elderly as everyone believed. The woman in the wheelchair was nearly thirty years younger than ninety-three-year-old Mila Federov, the woman she was pretending to be.

The wheelchair, that the caretaker would use to push the assassin to the location from which she would take her shot, was in fact much more than just a wheelchair. It looked like a wheelchair and functioned like a wheelchair, but it was also a rifle and a parachute. The metal pipes that made up the structure of the wheelchair came apart and could be quickly reassembled to function as a high-powered rifle. The assassin had practiced hundreds of times, taking the wheelchair apart and putting it back together as a gun. She could do it with ease in less than thirty seconds.

The soft portions of the wheelchair and the remaining structural pieces that had not been used to build the gun were designed to unfold and disappear into a cleverly conceived parachute. The shooter would have an additional minute to assemble these remaining pieces of the wheelchair into her escape vehicle. The special parachute was designed to carry the assassin over the side of the steep cliff to splashdown in the Black Sea.

After she had taken her shots, two air canisters, concealed under the wheelchair's seat, would be secured in place on the assassin's back. She would strap herself into the parachute, put her regulator in her mouth, and leap from the cliff. No trace of the woman or the wheelchair would remain behind. The assassin had practiced assembling the parachute and making her flying escape many times.

The caretaker would drop the blankets and shawls that had been wrapped around the woman, over the side of the cliff. These coverings already had bullet holes shot through them. They had been soaked in human blood which had dried. The blood would seep into the sea water, and the fabric would be shredded even more after being tossed from the cliffs and dragged along the rocky shore. Mila Federov and her wheelchair would be completely gone . . . off the cliff and down into the waters of the Black Sea.

The caretaker would run for help. She would tell the story of the bullet that had struck Ilya's aunt in the head and propelled the woman and her wheelchair off the cliff down onto the jagged rocks below. She would tell of her horror as she watched the old woman's head explode from the powerful rifle shot. Two people would be found dead that day. One old woman, who nobody knew and hardly anybody cared about, would be declared to be deceased when her body was found in the shallow waters close to the shore of the Black Sea. One man the whole world knew and despised would be shot and declared to be deceased.

The entire scenario was designed to make the world believe that both deaths were at the hands of a single assassin. This assassin, everyone would be led to believe, had been positioned off the coast of the dacha, somewhere on the waters of the Black Sea.

The body of a ninety-three-year-old Russian woman and her wheelchair would be found floating in the water at the bottom of the steep cliff. These sad remains would be identified as those of Ilya Baranov's elderly aunt who had finally died of unnatural causes. The dead corpse would have a gunshot wound to the head, and her DNA might or might not be tested. She had never had any DNA link to Ilya because he was adopted. The DNA testing would be a formality and a useless task. The test would show that the woman had Russian and Slavic ancestors.

The plan was for the assassin to successfully leap from the edge of the cliff, holding on to her rifle, the liquidation weapon. As she'd ridden in her wheelchair to the assassin's nest, she would be dressed in a wet suit under the old woman's disguise of voluminous shawls and blankets. She would land in the Black Sea and remain under the surface of the water. The specially designed air canisters would allow her to stay underwater until her mini submarine rescue arrived.

The assassin had been a scuba diver earlier in her life. In recent months, she had relentlessly practiced hundreds of times, her leap from the cliff, her descent through the air to the surface of the water, and her submersion into the sea. She had worked hard to get herself into shape so this part of her escape would be flawless and, in spite of her age, would cause little or no harm to her body. She knew what to do with the parachute once it had served its purpose. In case she was separated from the parachute when she impacted the water, there was a tracking device on the parachute that would allow the minisub to find it and pick it up and take it away from the scene. She could do it all with her eyes closed. She was ready.

In theory, it was a perfect plan. But hardly anything ever works in the real world as it has been planned ahead of time. The assassin had high hopes that she would successfully survive her leap from the cliff and would have enough air in her tanks to last under the water until the mini submarine arrived to take her to safety. She knew her part of it would be executed perfectly. She did not like the idea of having to wait for the minisub to pick her up underwater. She was suspect about the parts of the plan that were not under her control.

CHAPTER 34

2022

ON THAT FATAL DAY, THE target was scheduled to drink his tea on the terrace outside his dacha. The operation was a go for the morning. The assassin dressed in her wet suit and checked out the wheelchair that comprised all of her equipment. She ate a hearty breakfast. Who knew when she would have her next meal? The woman who was her caretaker wrapped a blanket around her legs and covered her shoulders with a shawl. They adjusted the white and gray wig and checked the assassin's makeup in case one of the multitude of security cameras took close-up pictures of her face. They wrapped another shawl around her head. The assassin was prepared, and they were on their way.

The timing had to be precise. The target would spend only a few minutes outside on the terrace drinking his tea. Ilya was going to try to talk him into staying outside a little longer today, but he didn't want to make his employer suspicious. The assassin reached her spot on the cliff and dismantled her wheelchair. She thought of this as her James Bond moment, when she was able to turn something into something it wasn't and fly away from danger to safety. In less than a minute, her rifle was loaded and ready. The remaining parts of the wheelchair were made into a parachute and waited on the ground beside her. All she had to do was put the air tanks on her back, strap herself into the parachute, secure the regulator in her mouth, and grab her weapon. The wheelchair that had been made into other things would disappear completely. The assassin would also disappear completely. Timing was everything.

She stood ready, waiting for the man to appear on the terrace. Finally he did, and she took aim. It was a difficult shot, no matter how many times she had practiced it. She waited. She waited. Finally, she took the shot and then she immediately took a second shot. Both shots reached their mark, and she watched this current-day Russian Hitler's head explode into a thousand pieces. She had hit her target. The man was most assuredly dead.

Now she had to save herself. She fired a third shot into the air. This was the shot that would be blamed for Mila Federov's death. She strapped on the air tanks and the parachute and adjusted her equipment. Her regulator was in place. She picked up the empty ammunition cartridges from the ground, and she held her rifle in her hand. Everything was good to go. She took a few steps to the edge of the cliff and jumped off into the air. She floated down, down, down towards the water. She activated her parachute. The parachute and the assassin's wet suit were pale blue-gray, the color of the sky and the sea. If someone was watching and thought they'd seen something fall or fly from the cliff, they would later learn that what they must have seen was the old woman and her wheelchair as they careened over the cliff and into the water. Or maybe they had only seen a bird.

The assassin hoped that the hackers had been successful, even for just a few minutes, in disabling the cameras that kept a constant watch on the old man's hideout. If the hackers had done their job, nobody would ever be able to prove that anyone had jumped from the cliff, floated to the surface of the water, and disappeared into the depths of the Black Sea. The hope was that no camera would record a parachute anywhere in the neighborhood skies today.

Disabling the cameras was important for several reasons. It was important that the security forces who watched the areas around the dacha never know that anyone had jumped from the cliffs and gone into the water. It was just as important that these cameras never record the assassin's face. If the cameras were not functioning when she took her shot and when she jumped from the cliff with a parachute, she could live the rest of her life knowing that no one at the Russian dacha had ever seen her face or her escape. No one would have spotted anyone floating down into the water using a parachute. As she flew off the cliff and headed for the sea, she sang to herself: "Ding Dong the witch is dead. The witch is dead. The witch is dead. Ding Dong, the wicked witch is dead."

The parachute opened as planned, but then something went terribly wrong. Had someone tampered with her parachute? Had someone booby-trapped her escape? She briefly wondered if the people she'd been working with had decided she was somehow a threat to them and had to die. The assassin slammed into the Black Sea with much greater force than she had experienced during her practice jumps. She lost consciousness when she landed hard in the water. The tanks stayed on her back, but the rifle flew out of her hands and fell to the bottom of the sea. She had weights in her dive vest that guaranteed her body would not float on the water's surface. Her regulator miraculously stayed in her mouth as she sank further and further down into the depths.

As she was parachuting toward the surface of the water and before the impact that caused her to lose consciousness, she had been able to catch a glimpse of the ragged and rocky shore at the bottom of the cliffs. Sure enough, there was the crumpled wheelchair that had, weeks earlier, been dropped from a cliff in Montana and had been brought to the scene of the assassination and deposited into the shallow water by the minisub.

The assassin was relieved to see that there was a body lying tangled with the broken wheelchair close to the shore. The body was that of a ninety-three-year-old woman who had died of natural causes. After she'd died, her body been dropped off the same cliff in Montana that the wheelchair had been dropped from. The body and the wheelchair were sufficiently mangled, as they might have expected to be. The woman had been posthumously shot in the head, with the same gun, with the same batch of ammunition, and in exactly the same way as the main target that the assassin's gun had just dispatched. Then the body had been kept in a refrigerator, ready and waiting for the occasion. The scene was staged to look as though the Russian president and Ilya's Aunt Mila Federov had both been targets of an unknown assassin's bullets.

There were many flaws in the next part of the plan. Believability depended on how scrupulous a medical examiner would be about doing an autopsy and how long the body of the old woman and her wheelchair would remain in the shallow water of the Black Sea before they were recovered. It was very possible that someone could figure out the old woman's body had been hanging around in a refrigerator for a while before it had appeared just off the rocky beach. It was also very probable that someone would figure out that the gunshot to the woman's head had been fired after she was dead.

Those who had planned the assassination did not really care about exactly what the autopsy might show. Their mission would be accomplished with the target's death. Any autopsy would come days after that. Who were they going to hold responsible? Who were they going to punish? There was never going to be any kind of evidence presented at a trial. By the time an autopsy was performed on anybody, the perpetrators of the assassination would be long gone and very far away.

Ilya's aunt's caretaker would be so distraught by the experience, she would be too upset to talk to the authorities with any kind of rationality about what had happened. The caretaker had been carefully vetted before she'd been allowed to accompany Mila Federov and live inside the Russian leader's compound. She was above suspicion. The caretaker would be hysterical with shock, shame, and failure for a few days. She would repeat over and over again in a terrified voice that she, too, could have been shot and killed. She would say she knew that Mila had been much too close to the edge of the cliff, but the old woman always wanted to be close to the overhang so she was able to look down at the water. The caretaker would blame herself for allowing the wheelchair to be too close to the edge of the cliff, for allowing Mila to be targeted. And why would Mila have been targeted anyway? She was an old woman. There was no reason.

Then the caretaker would disappear forever. At first her story would be believed. What happened in the long run did not really matter to her or to those who had planned the operation. The caretaker would be untouchable in her disappearance, and she would be safe.

The only person who would be forced to remain behind and who would inevitably be on the hot seat was Ilya, the chef. He would take refuge in the shock and dismay over the brutal slayings—his aunt's, as well as his employer's. He had witnessed in person the murder of the Russian leader. Ilya would exhibit all the stages of grief. He would be speechless and in shock. He would be in denial. He would be in disbelief. He would be angry and demand revenge for the senseless deaths.

Eventually, he too would be gone. He had been employed by the Russian president to be his personal chef. Because the president was dead, Ilya would no longer have a position. He would bide his time and play it all out as it developed. One day, when things had settled down and he thought he could make a graceful exit, he would move on to take back his job at the Astoria Hotel in St. Petersburg. Ilya was above reproach. No one would ever suspect the man who put his life on the line several times a day to safeguard the Russian president's life. Ilya would never be able to hold his beloved Sasha, or whatever her name had been, in his arms again, but she would be avenged at last.

The headlines and the twenty-four hour news stations screamed the news. The man the world feared and despised was dead. That was the only thing that anyone knew for certain. The most secure and heavily guarded location in the world had been breached. How could that have happened?

No one had any idea who had pulled the trigger. Speculation ran wild as every possible terrorist group, every criminal organization, every nation that had ever had a beef with Russia, was offered up as a possible culprit. It had to be Ukrainians who were behind the assassination. The Russian leader's ex-wife, his girlfriend, and his boyfriend were all put forward as potential suspects. The crime had involved tremendous planning, courage, and audacity.

For a long time, investigators believed that the kill shots had come from an assassin who was positioned offshore, someplace out on the water. That is what the organizers of the assassination wanted the Russians to think. Those who were trying to figure out what had happened and were attempting to solve the crime were certain the shots could not possibly have come from the land or from any place within the dacha's compound.

To help confuse investigators even further and to try to convince them that the assassin had been positioned off the coast, somewhere on the waters of the Black Sea, Ilya made a couple of quick adjustments, immediately after the shooting, to the furniture and to the position of the body. When he was alone on the terrace with the Russian president's freshly dead corpse and before bodyguards came running, Ilya changed some things as he had been instructed to do.

The trajectory of the bullet and exactly where the shots had entered the target's head were vital pieces of information in determining where the assassin had been. If Ilya moved the body and the chairs around, just a little and in just the right way, investigators would at first continue to believe that the shots had come from the direction of the water. The deception would initially be convincing. A really good investigative team would, in time, uncover the discrepancies and realize that the body had been moved after it was shot. If Ilya were ever asked, he would of course report that in his panic, he had tried to save the Russian president's life and might have moved the body or the furniture in his panic, in his futile efforts to save his boss. No one believed that the investigation would be carried to those lengths.

The minisub had done part of its job and deposited the body of the old woman and the broken pieces of her wheelchair close to the shore. These would be easy to find because the wheelchair and the body were dropped in shallow water. Hopefully, it would be days or weeks before the body of the old woman was examined with an autopsy. Maybe that autopsy would never be considered a priority. The minisub had successfully recovered the remains of the assassin's parachute. It had a tracker attached to it and had been designed to sink into the shallow water.

The rifle was another critical piece that had to be recovered. It could not be found anywhere close to the shore. The rifle had a homing device embedded in its stock and was easily found and recovered by the minisub. The homing device was removed, and the rifle was dropped into the deeper waters of the Black Sea, at a significant distance from the shore. If it was ever found one day, its location might lend credence to the fact that when the Russian president was killed, the assassin had been firing from somewhere far out in that body of water.

When the assassin had been falling into the Black Sea, much more rapidly than had been planned, she had briefly wondered, before she lost consciousness, if someone had sabotaged her escape. She knew she was lost if she was not able to be found by the minisub that planned to rescue her from the water. She'd known all along that this mission was a dangerous one. She'd known there was a high probability that she would not come out of it alive. She was resigned to her death. She had accomplished her critical objective, a mission that was of importance to the world. What better way to go out than to have done what she had been able to do. Even if no one else ever knew what she had done, she knew. That was enough. She was content that she had been able to accomplish her courageous act. She could die knowing she had been something of a hero, even if she was a hero only to herself. She gave herself up to the sea.

The assassin had performed her job perfectly, but she had not been recovered according to plan. The minisub had not found her where she was supposed to be. The minisub did not have the luxury of time to search for her. Everyone who knew what she had just accomplished assumed that she had died when she'd flown off the cliff into the water. A few who had been close to the assassin wondered silently to themselves if her death had been intentional. Had her existence been too great a risk to someone? Had someone or a few in the group felt it was too dangerous to allow the assassin to live, considering what she had done and everything she knew. Had someone with access to her equipment decided she knew too much? Did someone consider her a threat? Had someone sabotaged her parachute or some part of her dive gear? Had she been considered a loose end that needed to be tidied up at the end of the mission?

The assassin's death had not been part of the plan, at least as the plan had been known to most of the participants. Ostensibly, the planners had gone to great and elaborate lengths to keep the assassin alive and to ensure her recovery after she had accomplished her part of the operation. Had a rogue subgroup or individual within the larger group decided differently and determined that she had to die?

No one could ask these questions, and no one could answer them. The organization that had planned and executed the assassination plot had agreed to disband immediately after their mission was completed. Each participant had a specific, secret, and detailed escape plan. They'd agreed never to contact one another again. The assassination had been a one-time thing. It had been a project of tragic and immediate necessity, to take out the insane man who had threatened to use his nuclear weapons and destroy humanity.

They had all come together using names other than their own real ones. No one had revealed where they lived or anything about their identities, their families, their occupations, or their backgrounds. They had planned and acted with complete secrecy and the total anonymity of each participant. The assassin was missing and presumed drowned in the Black Sea. The mission had been accomplished. It was over.

CHAPTER 35

2022

Fishing in the black sea had become a sore subject. Because the Black Sea has been overfished for so many years, quite a few of the varieties of fish, that had once been found in abundance in its waters, were on their way to becoming extinct. In an effort to revitalize the dwindling fish populations, commercial fishing became heavily regulated by all the countries that border the Black Sea. All of these countries have fishermen who depend on that body of water for their livelihoods. Not all fishermen are able to get permits to fish. Many of those who cannot afford the licenses or the necessary bribes and do not have family connections that can get them a permit, go ahead and fish the waters illegally.

Bulgaria is a member of the EU and is required to obey restrictions imposed by that organization for fishing in the Black Sea. Boiko Dragomir was a fisherman who could not afford a commercial fishing license and did not have family connections. But he had customers for his fish, and he knew the waters of the Black Sea. He only fished at night. He knew where he could hide his boat along the coast. He was a ghost among fishermen. No one ever saw him fishing on those forbidden waters, but he continued to supply fish to his customers, even without a license. He knew how to hide, how to be invisible. He struggled to survive.

Boiko never expected to find a woman floating near his boat in the waters off the Turkish coast. She was quite a long way from any land. Boiko was not exactly within Russia's territorial waters, and he was not exactly within Turkey's territorial waters. He convinced himself he was in a kind of no man's land, or really in a kind of no man's waters. Boiko's rationalizations were constant and necessary to sustain his pirate-like fishing career. He dragged the woman from the sea, assuming of course that she was dead. There might be jewelry or money on the body. It would be a shame, Boiko thought, for all of that to go to waste. It would be finders keepers. But he also felt compelled to check to be certain she actually was dead. Once he had determined that she was a corpse and had checked for valuables, he intended to throw her body overboard, back into the water. His conscience would be clear.

He was shocked and dismayed to discover that the woman he had pulled into his small boat was still alive. She had a weak pulse. He had enough scruples that he knew he had to try to save her life. As soon as he found she had a pulse, he compressed her chest. His skills with CPR were almost nonexistent, but he made a primitive effort to get the water out of her lungs. He was able to get her to vomit sea water and to begin gasping for breath.

His life would have been a lot easier if the woman had been dead when he'd brought her on board. His life would have been a lot easier if he had been able, in good conscience, to allow her to die. A live woman on board his fishing boat was the last thing Boiko needed. He had his catch and was just about to head back to his secret and deserted landing spot off the coast of Bulgaria. Now he had a nearly-dead woman on board the boat with him and his fish. He had no idea what in the world he was going to do with her.

She was wearing a wet suit, dressed as if she had been scuba diving. She had on a dive vest, but she did not have any air tanks. Boiko could not understand how this woman had reached the location where he had found her. He had never encountered any divers, dead or alive, in all his years of fishing these waters. It was a mystery to be sure, but here she was, a real, still-alive, but barely-breathing woman.

Boiko had never married. He was afraid and suspicious of women and did not like them. He avoided them as much as he avoided all human contact. He only interacted with his customers. He lived alone in a tiny hut in the woods, miles outside of a remote Bulgarian village. His only family was one brother from whom he was currently estranged. What was he going to do now?

It was impossible to tell what nationality the woman was. In diving gear, everyone looked the same. Boiko thought the woman in his boat looked like she was European. Her skin was white, and her diving outfit looked expensive. He suspected she was English or American. They were the ones who bought glamorous wetsuits and could afford to go scuba diving.

Boiko spoke no English. He was barely able to speak a crude and obscure dialect of the Bulgarian language. He spoke to so few people and so infrequently, his speech was primitive and halting. Boiko had no idea how to communicate with this mermaid he had dragged from the sea. The woman's hair had recently been shaved, and it had begun to grow back. She had stubble on her head now, and it was gray and white. Boiko realized his mermaid was really an older woman.

He brought a blanket from the cabin. It was dirty and smelled of mackerel and fuel oil, but he thought it might help warm the woman after she had spent hours in the cold sea. He got a cup of water from his fresh water supply and held her head up so she could drink it. She sputtered and spit most of the water out, but Boiko thought she had swallowed a little bit. Her eyelids fluttered. She reached out for the cup of water. He held it up to her lips again. She drank with more enthusiasm. Finally her eyes opened, and she stared at Boiko.

She wondered momentarily if she had entered heaven or hell. Wherever it was, it smelled like fish. She liked fish, but this was too much. She was so thirsty. Her body hurt all over. There was a very odd-looking fellow staring down at her. She was rocking from side to side. She knew she must be in a boat, a very small boat. She saw that she was dressed in a dive suit and that the dive suit was wet. Her skin was shriveled, so she knew she must have been in the water for a long time. She tried to figure out what had happened to her, but she could not remember how she'd gotten to where she was or what in the world she was doing here, wherever here was.

Nearly dead when the fisherman dragged her body from the sea, she remembered nothing about how or why she had ended up in the water. Even though she'd been unconscious, her regulator and her air tanks had stayed in place long enough to keep her alive. The woman remembered nothing about her air tanks or her regulator, and they were gone now. When she had lost the air tanks, she had floated to the surface and drifted toward the coast of Turkey. The first thing she had become aware of was the smell of fish. Then someone had been forcing her to drink water from a cup. She realized she was thirsty and wanted to drink more of the life-saving elixir. Every inch of her body, inside and outside, hurt like the dickens.

When she regained consciousness from time to time, she realized she had no memory of what her life had been before this moment. She tried to think. She must have hit her head. Or perhaps her brain had been deprived of oxygen. She could remember nothing. When she woke up, all that mattered to her was that she was incredibly thirsty. She lost consciousness. When she woke up again, she still could not remember anything. The odd-looking fellow was still looking down at her.

She spoke to him, but he didn't understand anything she said. She motioned to him that she wanted more to drink. The fellow brought her more water. It tasted like fish, but it was the best thing she had ever put in her mouth. She drank all of the water the man brought her, and she went to sleep again.

When she would momentarily regain consciousness, she felt brief moments of panic because she did not know who she was or why she found herself in a fishing boat in the middle of a large body of water. Who was this strange and smelly man? She motioned for more water. She knew she was in trouble, but drinking water seemed to help. She said thank you in English to the man who reeked of fish. She lapsed into unconsciousness again, too drained and battered to force herself to stay awake any longer.

Boiko let her sleep. What else was he going to do with her? He thought she had thanked him for the water. He thought she had thanked him in English. He did not know for sure what language she had spoken, but it sounded like what he imagined English sounded like. Maybe she was American or British. Or, she could be from Canada or from some other place where people spoke English. Boiko set his small boat in the direction of the Bulgarian coast. His first priority was to unload his catch and deliver his fish to his customers. After he had taken care of business, he would think about what he was going to do with this strange woman he had dragged from the sea.

CHAPTER 36

2022

Boiko lived in a one-room hut. There was no room in the hut for the woman, and he had no way to transport her from his fishing boat to the hut. She would have to stay in the boat. He tied up his boat as close to the shore as he could. He had a piece of canvas he could put over the boat to keep out the weather. This impromptu tent might help protect the sick woman from the the wind and rain. After one night, Boiko realized he couldn't leave the woman in his boat. He would have to take her to the hut, no matter how small it was. He fashioned a kind of sled and managed to drag her from the boat to his hut in the woods.

Boiko had known he was in over his head when he had rescued the woman. Now he was desperate. He needed help to deal with this unanticipated person who had so rudely and unexpectedly entered his life. He realized he was going to have to contact his brother Timotei. He needed Timotei's help. Boiko knew his brother was smarter than he was. He thought Timotei also might know a little bit of English. Maybe Timotei would be able to talk to the woman.

Boiko had promised himself he was never going to speak to his brother again, but now he was going to have to ask him for help. Boiko and his brother had fallen out over Boiko's failure to follow the rules about fishing. Timotei wanted Boiko to obey the regulations the European Union had set for fishing in the Black Sea. Boiko had refused to obtain the proper licenses. The two brothers had stopped speaking to each other, but now Boiko was going to have to swallow his pride and ask his brother to help him with the woman.

The next thing she knew, she was inside a house. It was a very small house, and it smelled bad. It smelled of fish and human body odor. Maybe she really had died and gone to hell, and now she knew that hell smelled like fish. Everything around her smelled like fish. She opened her eyes. A scruffy-looking man with unkempt hair was bending over her. She looked up into a frightening face with deep set dark eyes and eyebrows the size of small bushes. The odors that emanated from his person were those of fish and more fish and the scent of someone who had never really bathed. He was staring at her head.

She put her hand up to her scalp to try to figure out what the man found so curious. Her shoulder screamed with pain as she raised her arm to try to touch her hair. She hoped the pain was from torn tendons and not from a shoulder dislocation. Her hand finally found the stubble on her head. Her head had been shaved. Why would that have happened? Who had done that to her? When she was able to painfully lower her arm and look at her hand, she saw that her fingers were covered with blood. Her head was bleeding. Her shoulder was killing her. She passed out again.

Timotei Dragomir realized the woman needed care, and he knew his brother Boiko was incapable of adequately providing her with the help she needed. Timotei was a fisherman, but he also kept a flock of sheep. He was more prosperous than Boiko and had more land around his hut. And he had a cart. He did not have an animal to pull his cart. He pulled his cart himself. Timotei strapped the cart to his shoulders and pulled the cart behind him when he walked. The woman was unconscious when Timotei and Boiko loaded her into the cart and moved her to Timotei's hut.

She was vaguely aware of being transported in a small cart over a very rough road. The journey made every one of her muscles throb with pain. When she woke up again she was in a different hut. This place smelled like fish and sheep. A different odd-looking fellow looked down at her in the new place. This fellow looked a little bit like the first odd-looking fellow, but this one had a brighter look in his eyes. The woman could only hope that he was smarter than the other one. Neither one of these peculiar men spoke English or understood a word she said to them. She still had no memory of any former life or any clue about who she was or what her name might be. She was indeed a mystery woman, even to herself.

Both Timotei and Boiko lived in a very rural and almost inaccessible part of Bulgaria. There were few roads here. There were almost no cars. There was no railroad service in this part of the country. Boiko and Timotei were both peasants who had never been to school. They chose to live in the woods, away from their fellow human beings. They eschewed all modern conveniences. Their huts were without electricity or indoor plumbing.

Timotei's hut had two rooms. He did not have a wife or a family, except for Boiko. Timotei put the woman in the room he used as a kitchen. He had nowhere else to put her. The hut was not very clean, but Timotei made a bed for her under his kitchen table. He gathered a load of straw that he'd planned to use for his sheep. He found a blanket to put on top of the straw. The woman would have to recover on the bed of straw. This was the best he could do for the unwanted guest his brother had thrust upon him. He would try to take care of her until he could figure out what to do with her.

War raged in neighboring Ukraine, and the demand for his fish had soared. People were hungry. Timotei had hoped to spend more time fishing and was looking forward to making more money because of the increased demand. Once again Boiko had thrown a monkey wrench into his plans, but Timotei felt obliged to help the woman if he could.

The woman was still unconscious most of the time. She woke sporadically and was able to communicate to Timotei that she wanted water. Timotei understood the English word for water, and he gave the woman water when he knew she wanted it. Inside his house, he had a small fireplace that he used for warmth in the winter. But now it was summer, and he never used his fireplace in the summer. He had slaughtered a sheep and prepared some lamb broth on the fire pit outside his house. He offered the woman small sips of the broth, and she was able to swallow this little bit of nourishment. Most of the time she slept.

Because Timotei had no indoor plumbing, he had left a bucket in the kitchen for the woman. At first she had been too dehydrated to have to use it. After a couple of days of drinking water and broth, Timotei realized the woman had been able to rouse herself enough to be able to use the bucket. She was getting better.

He knew this unknown woman was from an English-speaking country. He guessed that she was probably American, Canadian, or British. Why she had turned up nearly dead in the Black Sea was a mystery he might never unravel. He wished his brother had left her to die and had not brought her into his boat. His brother Boiko was always dumping his problems onto him. But now that he had her, he felt he had to help her. Such was his bad luck. He had no idea how he was going to get her out of his life and back to where she belonged.

The woman gained strength slowly. She began to eat solid food when Timotei offered it to her. Using sign language, one day she asked for some clothes. The wet suit she'd been wearing since she was found in the water was soiled and had become ragged. She needed shoes. Timotei asked a friend for some used clothes, cast-offs he thought would fit the woman. They were men's clothes, but they were relatively clean. The old shoes Timotei found were too large, but the woman was thrilled to have them.

Timotei wondered why he had not confided in anyone that he had this strange woman, with whom he was largely unable to communicate, living with him at his house. He had not asked anyone he knew for help about how to keep her alive or what to do about her. For some reason, he'd chosen to keep her existence in his life a secret.

CHAPTER 37

2022

It was as if her life had begun when she had awakened in the small fishing boat. She still remembered nothing about who she was or where she was or why or how she had ended up in the water. She remembered nothing about a parachute or a dangerous hard landing in the sea. She remembered nothing about the impact to her body that had also destroyed her memory. Timotei had been able to communicate to her that the body of water in which Boiko had found her was the Black Sea. All recollections of her fall into the Black Sea had been wiped from her brain.

This man had taken her into his home. He had given her water. He had given her lamb broth. Then he gave her food. She slept, and she ate a little bit at a time. She tried to communicate with her caretaker but had very little luck with that. She began to be able to walk again, and she regained some of her strength. She smiled at her caretaker, but he was clearly not happy to have her on his hands or in his house. She did not want to be here either, but she had no idea what to do about any of it or how to remedy her situation.

The mysterious woman was still recovering when one of Timotei's sheep became ill. He brought the ewe to his house. This odd man carried his sick sheep into the kitchen where the woman slept. The woman was walking around a little bit every day. When she saw the sheep in Timotei's arms, a light came on in the woman's eyes. She was clearly interested in the animal and seemed concerned about its health.

The woman immediately knew what was wrong with the ewe and what to do about it. She had no idea why or how she knew what to do to help the sick sheep, but she did. The woman examined the ewe in a very expert way. She knew what she was doing. She knew about animals. She knew about sheep. She wanted to help this animal recover and be well again. She got to work.

She gave instructions, as crude as they were, to Timotei about what she needed. She communicated to the man who owned the hut that she had to have supplies to be able to help his sheep. He seemed to understand, and although it was a struggle, she finally gathered the rudiments of what she thought she needed to save the ewe. The woman needed a clean, sharp knife. She needed hot water. She needed antiseptics, which Timotei did not have. She needed something she could sew with, some kind of needle and thread. She needed clean strips of cloth to use as bandages.

Timotei knew the ewe had an infected cyst on her abdomen, and he had resigned himself that his sheep would probably die. He could not afford to lose an animal, but he had no access to professional veterinary care for his flock. He'd brought the sheep to the house to make her more comfortable until she expired from the massive infection he knew would overtake her. But the woman who was living in Timotei's house refused to accept that the ewe had to die a slow, painful, and inevitable death. She was going to try to save the animal's life. Timotei found the things he thought the woman said she wanted, and he watched with fascination while this woman from the sea attempted to save his animal.

She boiled water on Timotei's primitive outside fire pit. She sterilized the knives and cleaned the area around the abscess on the sheep's abdomen. She cut into the abscess and allowed the pus and blood that had swollen the animal's tissues to drain away. The woman worked quickly and expertly. She knew what she was doing. She continually wiped away the infectious substances that oozed from the opening she'd made, and she kept the area of the wound scrupulously clean with hot water and clean cloths. Timotei watched, mesmerized, as this person who had invaded his existence carried out her lifesaving magic.

Finally the woman had cleaned the infection to her satisfaction. She sterilized the needle and used fishing line to sew the ewe's skin back together, leaving a small drain in the incision. The woman kept wiping the wound clean with hot water, and she finally wrapped strips of clean cloth around the sheep's belly. The woman smiled as she looked up at Timotei. She said something in English that he did not understand, but he thought she was trying to tell him that his animal was going to be all right.

As she'd worked to cut open and drain the enormous abscess on the sheep's abdomen, the woman realized she was experiencing pleasure for the first time that she could remember. She loved doing this, and she knew what she was doing. She worked quickly and professionally. She worked automatically. She had done this before, and she knew that she had done it many times before. This was what she had been made to do, what she had been trained to do. She still had no memory of the person she had been in her previous life, but now she knew that she had probably been a veterinarian. She realized she knew how to save the lives of animals.

Timotei and the woman took care of the sheep in the kitchen for several days and gave her food and water. In less than a week, the ewe was able to stand on her own two spindly legs and walk. Soon she was able to go outside and join the rest of the sheep. The woman removed the bandages, and it looked as if the wound had healed. A few days later, the woman carefully removed the fishing line she had used to sew the sheep's skin back together. The sheep recovered and returned to the flock.

After the woman had saved his sheep, her host's attitude towards her changed. Timotei began to smile at her. He fed her more often. He tried harder to communicate with her and to understand what she was trying to say to him. Timotei knew the mysterious woman must be a trained veterinarian or a doctor of some kind. She clearly was a professional, and she had gone all out to save the life of his animal. She had earned his respect. Timotei knew he had to find a way to return her to the life she'd had before Boiko had found her floating in the Black Sea. He also felt in his bones that he had to be discreet about how he delivered her back to where she belonged.

Timotei made a satchel for the woman from pieces of sheepskins he'd cured and saved. Crafting the satchel was a way for him to say thank you to the woman for saving the life of his sheep. He cut the skins and sewed them together into a bag that the woman could put over her shoulder. It was a simple bag, but it was serviceable. Timotei knew she had nothing to put in the satchel. She had no possessions at all, but he was proud of the gift he'd made for her.

The woman was thrilled with Timotei's gift. She kept asking him if she could keep the satchel. She had nothing to put in it. It smelled like the sheepskin that it was, but the woman loved it. It had a strap, and when she was awake she always kept the bag with her, with the strap across her body. At night, she slept with her head on the satchel. It became her pillow.

The woman continued to recover her strength and stamina. She did not know how old she was, but she knew she was not a youngster. She made an effort to help Timotei around the hut and with his property. They developed a kind of friendship although they were mostly unable to speak to each other. The woman learned a few words of the man's Bulgarian dialect. She learned that the hut in which she was living was close to the shores of the Black Sea. Timotei was a fisherman. He left on fishing trips, and the woman was able to take care of things for him at his house while he was away.

Word of her skill with animals had spread among the inhabitants of the tiny village near where Timotei lived. He had been so impressed with the way the woman had taken care of his ewe that he had not been able to keep her existence and abilities a secret. When Timotei spoke of her, people asked where she had come from and who she was. Timotei said she had come from the sea and that Boiko had saved her life.

Those who knew Boiko ignored that explanation. Boiko was known to hallucinate and to tell elaborate tales about things that had never really happened. His word was unreliable. Anything he said was suspect. If Timotei said that the woman had been brought to him by his brother, and Boiko said he had dragged her from the sea, the truth remained elusive. No one could count on Boiko's story, so no one really had any idea at all where the woman had come from. Everyone who knew Boiko and Timotei could not help but wonder why the woman was content to stay with Timotei in his small hut.

The woman didn't know if her memory would ever return, if she would ever know her real name or what her life had been like before she had been rescued from the sea. What had she left behind in the existence she had known before Boiko had saved her? She had no papers, no money, and no passport. She knew of no life other than the simple one she had in the hut with Timotei. She knew that if her memory ever returned, she would be forced to do something about herself. She would have to do what she could to reconnect with the life she'd had before the one she was living now outside this small, obscure Bulgarian fishing village.

She tried to learn the language. Languages had never been her strong suit, and she struggled. She was an intelligent woman so she was able to learn enough words that she was eventually able to communicate s little bit with Timotei, even though it was a very primitive level of communication. She helped to take care of the animals he had on his property. This seemed to come naturally to her, and she wondered if she might have also been a farmer in her former life.

One day, Timotei came to her and asked her to go with him to a neighboring farm. A mule had been struck by an automobile on the road, and the woman who owned the animal was trying to decide whether to shoot the beast or try to save it. Timotei had told the owner of the mule, his friend Giselle Marinov, about the woman who lived in his hut and how she had saved the life of the ewe that had developed an abscess. Giselle wanted to enlist the help of Timotei's mystery woman and asked him to bring her to the farm to examine the mule.

They walked two miles to the farm where the injured mule lay beside the road. The woman hoped to be able to save the mule. She was not used to walking long distances and was exhausted at the end of the journey. She was eager to have a look at the mule which had suffered a broken leg. The woman knew that if the animal had been a racehorse, it would never be able to run again. A racehorse would have been euthanized. The mule's broken leg was not a bad break, and because the mule was a beast of burden and important to the work on this farm, the woman thought the mule was worth trying to save.

She fashioned a splint for the injured animal. Timotei and the mule's owner held the animal as still as they could while she deftly and skillfully repositioned the bones in the animal's leg. Then the woman attached the splint to the broken leg and made a kind of primitive cast of hay, candle wax, and cement to hold the splint in place. It was a very make-do kind of a job, and the woman was communicating what she needed and what was happening with sign language. She tried to warn the mule's owner that the animal might never be able to walk again. If the splint did not work and the mule's leg did not heal properly, the animal would have to be put down. Giselle, the animal's owner, agreed to give the splint and the hay and cement mixture a chance. The woman with healing powers was able to let Giselle know that she would visit again in a few days to determine if the broken bones were going to heal themselves enough to allow the mule to walk.

Walking two miles each way to care for the injured mule built the woman's strength and stamina. During her second visit to check on the mule, the woman realized she knew how to speak some French. Giselle spoke a little bit of French, as well as her native Bulgarian. When the woman heard Giselle speak a few words of French, the recognized that she understood almost everything Giselle was saying. The woman knew she must have studied French in school, and she still remembered a lot of the vocabulary words.

The woman who knew how to heal animals had finally found someone with whom she was able to communicate. No one in the remote area knew any English, but at least the woman had found someone with whom she shared a little bit of a common language. The woman spoke to Giselle in French, and Giselle was able to convey the woman's words to Timotei in Bulgarian. In an odd way, Giselle Marinov had become a kind of Rosetta Stone.

The woman looked forward to the trips to see her patient and the opportunity to visit Giselle with whom she could have a very rudimentary conversation. The mule's leg healed, and within a couple of weeks, he was walking again. The woman removed the cast from the mule's leg. He would never be as fast or as sure as he had been before he'd been struck on the road, but he was once again able to pull a plow and a cart. Giselle was very grateful to the woman who had healed her mule. They became friends.

The animal healer revealed to her French-speaking friend that she had no idea what her name was and had no recollection of the person she had been or the life she'd had before Boiko had pulled her from the sea into his fishing boat. Giselle insisted that the woman who had healed her mule be given some kind of name. The French word for healer was *guérisseuse*, and one of the words in the Bulgarian language for healer was *lekar*. Giselle decided to call her new friend Guerlek. This made sense to the woman who had come from the sea.

Guerlek was as good a name as any. She began to think of herself as Guerlek. Timotei was glad at last to have a name for the woman. He also began to call her Guerlek. Throughout the weeks of summer, people in the area called on Guerlek when one of their animals was ill or injured. Guerlek loved being asked to help heal an animal. It brought joy to her heart that she was able to do this.

CHAPTER 38

2022

One day a car arrived at Timotei's hut, and a man asking for Guerlek spoke to Timotei. The man with the car had a sick horse and wanted help from the woman who had helped others when their animals needed care. Guerlek had not ridden in a car for many weeks. She and Timotei rode with the man to a neighboring village to see about the horse. Too much time had gone by before the owner of the horse had come for help. Guerlek recommended that the horse be allowed to either recover on its own or be allowed to die.

If a laboratory have been available for tests, and if a source of medications had been available to treat the horse, Guerlek might have made a different decision. None of these resources were available to Guerlek, so she made the only possible decision under the circumstances. She regretted not being able to help the horse, but the owner of the horse accepted her decision. He would allow the horse to either recover on its own or die.

The trip in the car had taken some time, so the owner of the horse invited Guerlek and Timotei into his home for a meal. This man's house was larger and better equipped than the huts in Timotei's village. This man had books and magazines and newspapers on a table in his dining room. The man was able to read. Guerlek looked at these printed materials with interest. She recognized them for what they were, and if she had been able to read Bulgarian, she could have read the news. Bulgarian uses a Cyrillic alphabet, and the printed words on the papers and periodicals were a mystery to Guerlek. She gave the publications a cursory look, knowing she was unable to read anything they said. Then she saw the photograph on the cover of the magazine, and she almost fainted. She recognized the man whose face appeared on the page in front of her.

When she saw the evil face, everything came rushing back to her. She almost collapsed with shock. She had trouble catching her breath. The memories that had been suppressed flooded over her and threatened to overwhelm her. She remembered the life she had left behind and the reason she had left it. She remembered her mission and how she had put herself at great risk. She knew that she had been successful. She had accomplished her mission.

But her escape had not gone as planned. Something had been wrong with her parachute. She didn't know if someone had deliberately tampered with her equipment or if something had gone wrong by accident, but she remembered that she had landed in the waters of the Black Sea with tremendous force. She should have died in the fall, but she had survived. She had not been recovered by the minisub that had been sent to pick her up at a designated longitude and latitude in the Black Sea. She'd lost consciousness, and she had not been able to make the rendezvous.

It could all have been a terrible accident, but it also might have been an attempt to eliminate her. She would never know exactly what had happened. Of course she realized that everyone who had been associated with her secret mission must now believe that she had drowned. She realized she had been gone from her home and her family for so long that everyone she loved and held dear probably also believed she was dead.

The epiphany had shaken her. She was breathless when the sudden memories rushed back to reunite her with her former existence. She now knew without a doubt that she was trained as a veterinarian. She knew she had a family and a ranch in California in the United States. She was overcome with sadness when she thought of her daughter and her grandchildren and the loyal staff who worked on her ranch. She cared about her workers like she cared about her family. All would have had to assume by now that she had died.

At that moment, it became clear to her that she had to get back to her previous life and the people she loved and who loved her. She had just begun to accept her existence in this primitive place. She was beginning to accept that she would never know anything about the life she'd led before Boiko had pulled her from the sea. She was adjusting to her life in the remote and rural seacoast village of Bulgaria and becoming comfortable being known as Guerlek. Now she realized without a doubt that she was really Henley Breckenridge of Paso Robles, California.

Henley Breckenridge had made a choice to undertake a very dangerous assignment. Some might have said from the outset that it was indeed a suicide mission. Henley had put herself in great danger. The mission itself had gone off without a hitch, but her escape had been compromised. If her escape had been deliberately sabotaged, she realized she no longer knew whom she could trust.

Anonymity had been one of the conditions of her joining the group that had put together the outrageous and impossible operation to assassinate a very bad man. No one who participated in the complex and very secret undertaking had been allowed to tell anyone her or his real name or where they lived in their real lives. No one was permitted to share anything personal about themselves. This was the only way to protect their individual identities and to protect the mission as a whole. Presumably, everyone who had participated, except for Henley, had now gone back to their previous lives. Not one of them would ever speak about the events in which they had participated. They would resume their real names and become their former selves as if nothing untoward had happened.

This was true for most of the participants in the operation, but it was not true for the woman who had actually pulled the trigger. She had almost died. She had not been able to return to her previous life, to her home and her family. Until today, she'd had no memory at all of what that former life had been. Henley now longed to see her daughter and her granddaughters again. She longed to see her ranch and the loyal staff who ran the place for her. She acknowledged that she was homesick.

Henley realized she would have to be extremely careful as she made her way back to her existence in California. Would it even be possible for her to go back to that life? Many things were still a mystery to her. Had someone tried to kill her? Had someone tampered with her parachute? Did someone associated with the mission feel that the assassin could not be trusted and should not be allowed to escape with her success and rejoin her family? Did anyone who had participated in the mission know her real name or anything about her real identity? These were questions that haunted Henley, and she didn't know any of the answers.

As she contemplated the overwhelming task ahead of her, finding her way back to being Henley Breckenridge, she realized she would have to move mountains in order to return to California. And she would have to do it all in secret. She did not trust anyone and did not feel she could reveal anything to anyone about what she now remembered. She realized she had no resources that would allow her to leave Bulgaria and travel back to the United States.

Henley didn't know to what extent she dared use her real name. She decided she would continue to keep her name a secret. She would remain Guerlek as long as she was in Bulgaria. She had no phone. She had no money. She had no credit card. She had no passport. She could not call and make a plane reservation to fly from Sofia to Los Angeles. She had no way of contacting anyone. She had nothing.

If she was wanted by the authorities or if she had become the target of someone who had gone rogue from the recent mission, she did not want to put her family at risk. There were many things to be considered, and Henley realized she needed to be very careful as she longed for her reentry into the life she used to have.

All of this newly-discovered knowledge about herself, as well as the blow of seeing the photograph of the man she had killed, had knocked her for a loop. It was as if she had been kicked in the stomach when she'd seen the man's face on the magazine and her memory came rushing back to her all of a sudden. She was already completely worn out by the trip in the car and the long day with the horse.

She could not wait to get back to Timotei's hut where she could think. The bed of straw in the kitchen had become her home. The shock of remembering had almost paralyzed her. How was she going to be able get herself out of Bulgaria? How was she ever going to explain to her family what had happened and where she had been all these months? She could never tell them the truth about what she had done. She would have to give them some kind of an explanation, but she would have to be very guarded about whatever she decided to reveal.

Her mind was racing. Now that she knew who she was and what she had done, she felt tremendous pressure to get away from the Black Sea. She was frightened that someone would find it curious that Boiko had dragged her from those waters. She had begun to earn something of a reputation because of her ability to heal the neighborhood animals. She had become a curiosity. How long would it take for someone to begin to put the pieces together? Regaining her memory had brought some relief, but her new knowledge had also brought with it a tremendous urgency to get herself very far away from Bulgaria.

A part of her had begun to enjoy the simple existence she had living in Timotei's hut. But with her new-found knowledge, those aimless days had already come to an end. A part of her felt some sorrow, some regret that she would have to return to her complicated life in a complicated place. But she realized that, because she now knew who she really was, she could no longer retreat into the simplicity of ignorance. She could not live in denial any longer.

Timotei lived a primitive life. He had no money or credit card or passport. He would not know how to help her, even if she was willing to confide in him and ask him for his help. Boiko was an even simpler human being than Timotei was. Of the people she knew, only Giselle might be able to help her. Giselle was more sophisticated than Timotei, but she had no resources. Henley would have to figure out whether or not she felt she could trust Giselle with part of her story. She did not want to put Giselle in any danger, and she knew she could not reveal much of anything to her new friend.

Henley needed a cell phone in the worst way, but she had no money to buy one. Even if she'd had the money, she had no idea where she would go to make the purchase. She did not know where the closest town was that had a store that might sell cell phones, or sell anything. Even if she could buy a cell phone, would it be safe for her to use it? Even if it was safe for her to use a cell phone, was there any cell phone service in this backward place?

Even though Henley had once believed that almost everyone on the planet was the proud owner of a cell phone, she now knew that neither Boiko nor Timotei nor Giselle had a cell phone. Henley wondered if they might be the only three people left in the world who did not own them.

Henley knew that Bulgaria belonged to the EU, but she also realized that Bulgaria was still a primitive country. Neither Boiko nor Timotei was literate. Henley was certain that neither one of the brothers could read or write the Bulgarian language. She doubted if either of them had ever attended school. Even though the Soviet Union had ruled over Bulgaria from 1945 until the USSR collapsed in 1991, Henley doubted that the rural fishing village where she was now living had ever been touched by any part of the Soviet education system.

Neither Boiko nor Timotei had plumbing or electricity in their huts. Giselle did not have indoor plumbing, and she had no electricity in her four-room house. But Giselle somehow had electricity in her barn. Henley remembered there had been a lightbulb burning in the ceiling of the barn when she had made visits to check on the progress of Giselle's mule. If Henley somehow found a way to buy a cell phone, she would have to have a way to charge it and to keep it charged. Electricity was a necessity.

CHAPTER 39

2022

Henley needed to be rescued from Bulgaria, but she had no idea how she was going to make that happen. She knew she did not want to involve her daughter or anyone who was a part of her life on the Paso Robles ranch. They were innocent of anything Henley might have become involved with, and none of them deserved the complications that might arise if Henley called on them to help her. Henley had no way of knowing if anyone considered her to be some kind of a threat and wanted her eliminated.

No one in California or in the United States could ever know that Henley Breckenridge had been anywhere near the Black Sea. No one could ever know that Henley Breckenridge had been pulled from those waters and had lived in a remote fishing village in Bulgaria. Because of the potential danger to her family and to herself, no one could ever know that Guerlek was the same person as Henley Breckenridge. She needed help, but she had to be certain that help arrived in a completely anonymous way.

The only person she could think of who might have the courage, the resources, and the discretion to get her out of the situation in which she found herself was her friend Elizabeth Carpenter. Few people were aware that Henley and Elizabeth knew each other. Henley trusted Elizabeth and knew that Elizabeth would try to help her. She had to somehow find a way to get in touch with Elizabeth, the friend that Henley was certain would not let her down.

Before Henley had left her home in California to train for the mission, she had left a letter in her safe deposit box addressed to Elizabeth. Henley had also left a letter for Elizabeth to give to her daughter, if Henley died. After Henley had been missing for a year, her lawyer had instructions to contact Elizabeth, retrieve the letters from the bank, and give both letters to Elizabeth. Henley had left it to Elizabeth to decide if and when to give her daughter the letter she had written to her. That year would come to an end in a few weeks. Henley knew she had to get in touch with her lawyer before a year had passed. Henley had to tell her lawyer not to give the letters to Elizabeth.

Henley needed a plan. Most importantly, she knew she had to remain discreet. She would continue to present herself as Guerlek. There was no need for anyone to know that Guerlek had regained her lost memory or for anyone to know that Guerlek had ever had another name. Henley decided her first step was to ask Giselle if she could move to her house and live with her. She would say she was concerned about what people would think of her if she continued to live with Timotei. Henley would tell Giselle that it did not seem right for her to keep living with a man to whom she was not married. In reality this didn't bother Henley at all, but it seemed like a good reason to give to Giselle to explain why she wanted to move out of Timotei's hut. It made sense as an excuse for Henley to ask to stay in Giselle's house with her and her electricity in the barn.

The next morning Henley walked the two miles to Giselle's farm. She made her case to Giselle as well as she could in her schoolgirl French. Giselle understood the situation and was actually quite pleased that Guerlek wanted to live in her home. Guerlek had earned a reputation because of her veterinary skills, so Giselle felt Guerlek was something of an important person in the neighborhood.

Henley didn't want to hurt Timotei's feelings by suddenly moving out, and Giselle understood this. Giselle said she would ask Timotei if he thought Guerlek could be convinced to move to her farm. She had more animals than Timotei had and would explain to him that she really needed help from Guerlek. She would also stress that she had more rooms in her house and that it would be more comfortable for Guerlek to stay with her than it was for her to continue to sleep in Timotei's kitchen.

Giselle in fact had heard Timotei lamenting many times about what in the world he was going to do with this woman he had inherited from his brother Boiko. He did not really have enough food to feed her, and he certainly did not have room in his two-room hut for her to live there. She slept under the kitchen table. Giselle knew it would be a great relief to Timotei to have Guerlek move to her house. Henley moved her few belongings out of Timotei's house that afternoon, and with many thanks and head-nodding to Timotei, she moved in with Giselle.

Henley wasted no time bringing up the subject of the cell phone. To her surprise, Giselle told her she already had a cell phone. Someone had given her a flip phone, but Giselle had never learned how to use it. She was not even sure she would be able to find the phone. They searched and finally found the ancient flip phone. The phone's battery was dead, and they were not able to find a charging cord. Henley's hopes had risen, and then she had been nearly crushed with disappointment. She had quickly realized that, even if they'd found the phone's charging cord, the old flip phone would not have been able to make an overseas call. Henley realized she was going to have to find a landline to be able to make an international call. Even if she was able to find a place to make the call, she was going to have to call collect.

Miraculously, Henley remembered Elizabeth Carpenter's cell phone number. The number was basically Elizabeth's birthday. That made it easier to remember. When Elizabeth had given her phone number to Henley nearly two years ago, when Henley had been caring for Sui Wai, they had discussed the fact that Elizabeth had been able to get a cell phone number that consisted of the numbers of her birthday. Of course, the area code was from Maryland, but that also was easy to remember. Because cell phone numbers are programmed into their phones, many people do not even know their own spouse's cell phone number. It was beyond serendipitous that Henley remembered Elizabeth's phone number; it was literally a life saver.

Henley told an edited version of her predicament to Giselle. Even though Henley had previously told Giselle that she did not recall anything about her former life, she now decided to tell her friend a different story. Henley told Giselle she had to make an important emergency phone call. Henley told Giselle that she was from New Zealand, and it was critical that she call her sister who was currently working in the United States. It was urgent. Was there a post office or a hotel of any kind close by where she could make that call to the U.S.? Giselle understood that Guerlek had an emergency and told her that the next day they would ride the mules to the post office which was fifteen miles away. Giselle would translate and help Guerlek place her call. Henley knew she was taking a chance with Giselle, but it was a chance she had to take. She had no choice this time.

Henley felt she was safe calling Elizabeth's phone number. Because the number she would be calling was a cell phone, the area code of the phone number didn't really matter. The actual phone could be anywhere within the country she was calling. Henley had friends in California who had kept their cell phone numbers from when they had lived in Arizona, in Alaska, in New York City . . . from anywhere in the U.S.

She knew she was putting Elizabeth at some risk, but Henley intended to be very careful about what she said over the phone. Henley knew the NSA in the United States would be listening in on an overseas phone call. What she didn't know was if Bulgaria had a similar agency that listened in on phone calls. Henley's international phone call would be placed from a very remote part of the country. Would a Bulgarian version of the NSA be listening? Who else might be monitoring overseas calls from fishing villages on the Black Sea, obscure and primitive places that were also very close to the border with Turkey?

Henley was an expert horsewoman, but it had been years since she had ridden on a mule. It was not comfortable to ride bareback, but the two women eventually reached the post office in the nearby town. The post office was in the back of the town's only store that sold groceries, animal feed, plumbing parts, and who knew what all. Giselle explained to the postmistress that her friend needed to make a collect phone call to the United States. It was arranged, and Henley could only hope that Elizabeth would answer the phone call that was coming from Bulgaria. Henley guessed that there was an eight-hour time difference between where she was calling from and the East Coast of the United States. Maybe it was seven hours.

The first time the postmistress placed the call, Elizabeth did not pick up the phone. The second time the call was placed, Elizabeth still did not answer. The postmistress was losing her patience, and she said she would place the call one more time. The phone rang and rang, and finally, thankfully, Elizabeth answered. The international operator said in English, "I have a collect call from D.J. Aluminum. Will you accept the charges?" Elizabeth was momentarily stumped, and her first thought was that J.D. Steele was playing a joke on her. Her curiosity was piqued. Puzzled and intrigued by the bizarre phone call, she agreed to accept the charges.

Henley had carefully prepared what she intended to say to Elizabeth. She wanted to give Elizabeth as much information as she could in as short a period of time as possible. She wanted to make things completely clear to Elizabeth, but she had to keep her secrets from the postmistress and from Giselle. Both woman were listening to Henley's every word with great curiosity. Henley was depending on her assumption that neither woman understood English.

"This is your friend with the beautiful concho belt, your friend who took care of Johnny Cash's son. I am alive, but I am in trouble. I desperately need your help. I am in the Balkans. I have no phone and no money. I need for you to send me a cell phone that I can use to make international calls. I also need lots of euros. I need to be able to communicate with you and tell you what has happened. I need your help getting back to civilization. Please don't tell anyone where I am or that I have contacted you. Say nothing to my daughter or to anyone else. Don't ask any questions. I can't answer them. We will have to communicate in code somehow. Will you help me?"

Elizabeth immediately recognized Henley's voice, but was stunned by her message. She quickly pulled her thoughts together. "I know who this is, and I understand the situation. I need to know where to send you what you need, but I do not want you to give me that address on this phone call. I have another number for you. Wait ten minutes and place another collect call to the number I am going to give you. Someone will pick up and accept the charges, but they will not speak to you. Just tell whoever answers the address where I can send you the things you have to have. Then hang up." Elizabeth had been frantically searching on her own phone for Sue Keely's cell phone number in Ojai, California. She knew Sue Keely always kept her cell phone with her. Even when she was in the shower, Sue's phone was on a counter within reach. Some people never wanted to be out of touch. Elizabeth knew that Sue Keely was one of those people.

Elizabeth finally found the number she was looking for and gave the numbers slowly and distinctly to Henley. "This number will connect you with that Johnny Cash household. I will get to work immediately planning your extraction. I will say nothing to your family. I'm so glad you are alive. I will be sending you a package wrapped as a gift. It will be a music box. Open the gift. Think inside the box. Rewrap the music box and give it to someone. I will expedite the package. Come back to the post office in five days. Everything should have arrived there by that time. Anything else?" Elizabeth ended the phone call.

Elizabeth knew that the longer she stayed on the phone, the greater the chances were that someone, if indeed anyone was listening in, would be able to trace the call. She had ended the call as soon as she possibly could. She hoped she had said everything she needed to say to Henley. The reference to Johnny Cash was his song, "A Boy Named Sue." Henley and Elizabeth had met trying to save the life of a young Chinese woman whose name was Sui Wai. Sui was pronounced like the English name Sue. Sui Wai now lived in California with a woman named Sue Keely. It was Sue Keely's phone number that Elizabeth had given to Henley. Elizabeth was now calling Sue Keely's cell phone. It was very early in the morning in California, and Elizabeth hoped Sue Keely would be awake enough to pay attention to what she had to say.

When Sue Keely answered, Elizabeth immediately said. "Don't say anything. You know who this is. I will explain everything later. In a few minutes you are going to receive a collect phone call from the Balkans. Please accept the charges for the international call. Don't say anything when the caller comes on the line. That person will give you an address. Please fax that address to me ASAP. I am now going to give you the fax number for my local FedEx Office Print facility. Address the fax to Johnny Cash." Elizabeth gave the fax number over the phone and paused, but Sue Keely didn't say anything. "Just be sure to pick up your phone when you see a weird overseas number calling. It's important." Elizabeth hung up.

Elizabeth felt she had done everything she could to obscure her connection with Henley's location in the Balkans.

Some risks had to be taken. Once Elizabeth had the mailing address, she could send Henley the satellite phone and the money she needed. Once she had the address of that post office, she would also have a rough idea about the longitude and latitude of Henley's location. With that information, Elizabeth could begin to plan to get the woman with the beautiful concho belt out of whatever trouble spot she now found herself. Once Henley had received the satellite phone Elizabeth was sending her, they would be able to speak securely and make more specific plans.

Henley followed Elizabeth's directions exactly. Henley had known Elizabeth was a quick thinker, and her instantaneous grasp of the situation and her reaction to it confirmed that Elizabeth could still think on her feet. But Henley was surprised when Elizabeth used the word "extraction." Elizabeth had done this before. Henley knew that her friend would not let her down. The package with the phone and the money would be sent to her c/o Giselle Marinov.

Henley had set things in motion. She would now have to be more on guard than ever. After they had made the overseas calls, Giselle became more curious about Guerlek than she'd been before. The two women made the difficult return trip to Giselle's house. Henley was very sore after hours on the back of a mule, but her heart was lighter. She now had some hope that she might be able to get out of her situation and out of Bulgaria. She had put her life in Elizabeth's hands. She had to wait five days for the phone and the money. They would be the longest five days of her life.

CHAPTER 40

2022

Elizabeth was on her way to her local FedEx Office Print and Ship to pick up the fax that had been sent from California to Johnny Cash. She would be there when the business opened its doors in the morning. The next couple of days would be hectic ones for Elizabeth, but she knew what she had to do. She was determined to use her considerable, if rusty, skills to try to rescue Henley Breckenridge. Although Elizabeth had no proof, she was quite certain in her own mind what Henley had accomplished. The woman was incredibly brave, but the extent of her courage was no surprise to Elizabeth. Henley was a hero, a hero who would never be able to take credit for what she had done. Elizabeth would have gone all out to save Henley no matter what. Elizabeth thought she knew why Henley now found herself in the Balkans. Because of these suspicions, Elizabeth was more than willing to put herself at some risk to save her friend.

The young woman at FedEx was more than confused when Elizabeth hobbled up to the desk with her cane and asked for the fax that had been sent to Johnny Cash. The woman's eyes grew large, and she looked around . . . as if searching for that craggy-faced man with a guitar. Elizabeth quickly paid for the fax and was out the door. The millennial woman at the desk wondered if she'd dreamed the odd interaction. She knew old people were strange and lived in a different world from hers. Johnny Cash???? Elizabeth definitely would have agreed with the young woman about their living in different worlds.

Elizabeth had the address. Now she knew that Henley was in Bulgaria, of all places. When Elizabeth checked Google maps, she realized the address of the Bulgarian post office, where she was to send the package to Henley, was very remote. It might take an extra day for the package to reach that very out-of-the-way place. Elizabeth knew she had to get to work quickly. There was a great deal to arrange.

After she left FedEx, Elizabeth drove to three different states and to many different stores of all kinds to purchase twenty-five prepaid cell phones. Cost was not the issue. Security was the issue. Elizabeth probably would not need all twenty-five burner phones, but she did not want to be caught short. Most of the newly-purchased phones would be used only one time.

It had taken Elizabeth all day to buy the phones. No two phones had been bought at the same store. She felt as if the phones would be safe to use. She'd taken the first phone she'd purchased out of its package, installed an encryption app transferred from her own personal cell phone, and began making the many calls that would be necessary to save Henley, to rescue her from wherever the heck she was in Bulgaria, and to bring her home to Paso Robles.

The satellite phone was the first thing Elizabeth had to send to Henley. If the phone hidden inside the music box was going to reach the rural Bulgarian post office in time, it had to be in the mail and on its way to Henley before tomorrow. Elizabeth had a contact who could make the satellite phone thing happen for her. After her retirement from government service, Elizabeth had stayed in touch with her former colleague, but she had never, until this moment, asked him for any help. He was also retired, but he'd let Elizabeth know that he still had his hand in things and could help her out if she needed him. Her contact was surprised when she called and even more surprised when she told him what she had to have.

He said he could have the phone she needed in his hands in less than an hour. He would also have the necessary encryption software and the very special, very secret SIM cards that would fool anyone and everyone about the real world location of where the satellite phone was actually being used. Elizabeth's former colleague had been surprised to hear from her, but he was even more surprised at the level of sophistication she required for the satellite phone set-up. But he asked no questions. He listened carefully to what Elizabeth had to say to him, and he immediately got to work to procure what she'd told him she needed. They had used the music box thing and the wrapped gift thing many times before. The SIM cards, instructions about how to use the phone and how to use the encryption software, two charging cords, an adaptor so the cords could be charged using local electrical outlets, and all the other necessary phone accessories would be included with the music box package.

Elizabeth's former colleague would arrange for the phone and the music box, as well as a stack of euro bills, to be delivered to Zurich in Switzerland by noon the next day. Someone would hand carry the package from Zurich and mail it in Sofia, Bulgaria's capital. It would be expensive to go to these lengths to obscure where the package was actually coming from. All of this technology and security and subterfuge would cost a lot of money. Elizabeth had the money, and she did not mind spending it. The most important thing was that Henley receive the package when she returned to the post office in five days.

It was midnight when Elizabeth finally returned home. She was worn out. She often stayed up late, but she was not usually driving around from state to state and store to store, buying things and making encrypted phone calls. Her handicap tag had come in handy, and she had been able to park close to the entrances of most of the stores she'd gone into to buy the prepaid phones. Several high curbs had been challenging, but somehow she had managed. The world was not designed for people who used a cane and could not negotiate steps and curbs. Curbs were being made higher and higher and therefore increasingly less accessible for somebody like Elizabeth.

She had called home earlier in the day to let Richard know she would be late so he wouldn't worry. She couldn't share with him anything about what she had done that day. She would not be able to tell him anything about Henley's situation until everything had been resolved. Elizabeth was protecting Richard and Henley and herself by keeping everything confidential. Richard understood this. He had lived with her and loved her for more than fifty-five years. But until today, he'd thought the days of secrets and middle-of-the-night phone calls were behind them, as they both were close to eighty years old. Richard realized that Elizabeth had not completely given up her covert activities. Richard worried about her, but he knew his wife had a mind and an agenda of her own.

Elizabeth trusted that the satellite phone and all of its accessories was on its way and would be delivered discreetly and on time. It would appear to be a gift sent from someone who lived in Sofia, Bulgaria's capital. It would be addressed to Giselle Marinov and would be wrapped on the outside in such a way that it would not raise an eyebrow when it arrived at the rural Bulgarian post office.

The next day Elizabeth turned her attention to making arrangements to get Henley out of the-middle-of-nowhere Bulgaria. The language barrier was a problem. Elizabeth needed someone who knew how to speak Bulgarian and Greek and English. She needed boots on the ground in Bulgaria. Elizabeth had been retired for a long time. The people she had once worked with had also been retired for a long time. Some of them had died. This part of the operation was not going to be as easy as getting money and a satellite phone into Henley's hands. Elizabeth got out one of her prepaid phones and began making more calls.

Finally she thought she had located the help she needed in Bulgaria. It had not been easy, and of course Elizabeth did not personally know the people on whom she was forced to depend for this part of her plan. She had been out of the business for too long. She'd been aware of that for some time, but her attempts to pull things together for Henley were further proof to Elizabeth that she was no longer at the top of her game. She realized that, going forward, she would have to call on her smart and capable friends to help her. She trusted her friends, and she knew they would be able to do the things she was going to ask of them.

Cameron had a private plane and his own pilot. Both Cameron and Sidney traveled often to Europe and all over the world. They would be willing to help, but Elizabeth absolutely did not want Cameron to use his own plane or his own pilot. Cameron agreed with Elizabeth that was out of the question. But Cameron knew the private plane business, and his personal pilot had contacts. Elizabeth spent a long time on the phone with Cameron, explaining what she needed to have happen. Of course he was curious, but he was more than willing to set things up for Elizabeth. She told him exactly what he was to do, but she gave him very little explanation about why she needed any of it. She felt Cameron understood her insistence on obscurity and security. He may not understand why these things were so vital in this far-out, even outrageous, request from Elizabeth. Cameron knew she had a past, and he did not ask her any questions she could not answer. He promised to help. He would arrange for the flights to Greece and Italy that Elizabeth had requested.

J.D. Steele, aka D.J. Aluminum, knew what Henley looked like, and Henley knew what J.D. looked like. Elizabeth would have to convince J.D. that she needed his help in the worst way. Only J.D. would be able to play the vital role of picking up Henley from the train station in Greece and driving her to the closest airport. This critical part of the plan could only be undertaken by someone who knew what Henley looked like and whom Henley would recognize. Only J.D. Steele was able to satisfactorily fill that role.

Elizabeth's friends were a big help to her with the final stages of her planning. Sidney Richardson just happened to be going to Italy for Milan's 2022 fashion week. Sidney would be attending fashion shows in Italy from September 20th through September 26th. Sidney was an investor in and a buyer for an exclusive woman's clothing store. She would be buying merchandise for the store when she was in Milan.

It would be fairly easy for Sidney to arrange to rent a car and stay a few extra days to drive around Italy. Sidney was younger than the others in the reunion group, and she was always game for an adventure. She was more than willing to move Henley from an airport to a safe house. Sidney's participation would be an enormous help. Elizabeth knew Sidney would perform her duties to perfection. Best of all, Sidney knew how to keep her mouth shut.

Elizabeth called her good friend Antigone Wells who owned a villa in Umbria. Elizabeth hoped Antigone's villa would be available as a safe house where she could stash Henley for a few days. Elizabeth had rented the property in the past and had stayed at the villa several times. It was in a beautiful and obscure location. Definitely off the beaten path, the villa would be the ideal place for Henley to rest and recover her strength before she made her journey back to the United States.

Elizabeth contacted Matthew Ritter in Palm Springs and told him what she needed from him. He did not immediately have a solution for her, but he promised to ask around. He assured her that he would be able to find the right place and the right person. He thought he would be able to figure out a way to prove, if anyone ever seriously looked into her whereabouts, that Henley Breckenridge had spent almost twelve months at a medical facility in the Southern California desert. If she made it back to California, Matthew would arrange for her to have a complete medical evaluation and whatever medical care she required. Henley could not return to Paso Robles, her family, and her ranch until she was healthy.

Bailey MacDermott knew all about disguises. Elizabeth called him for a consultation. If he'd known how to speak Bulgarian, he himself would have been on the next plane to the Balkans, in disguise, to escort Henley on the most perilous part of her journey home . . . the trip by automobile from the meeting place at the abandoned Eastern Orthodox church to the train station in Svilengrad and the train ride that would take her across the border from Bulgaria into Greece. Fortunately for all concerned, and especially for Gretchen, Bailey did not know a single word of Bulgarian and could only give his advice from his home in Dallas. Dallas was thousands of miles away from the places where Henley would eventually be wearing the wigs and the disguises.

CHAPTER 41

2022

Documents were next. Henley had no papers and no passport. She had no proof of who she was. She had no proof that she was anybody. It is impossible to travel almost anywhere in the world today without some kind of ID. Henley had to have counterfeit papers if she was going to get out of Bulgaria and if she ever hoped to return to the United States. These travel papers and passports all had to be in names other than that of Henley Breckenridge.

Henley could not use her own name during her escape from Bulgaria. As far as everyone else in the world knew, Henley had never left the United States during the October 2021 to October 2022 time period. She had never traveled to the Balkans. She had never been anywhere close to the Black Sea or Bulgaria. Elizabeth knew the person she needed to call to take care of fabricating the papers she wanted for Henley. The passports and other documents that required photographs could be ready as soon as Henley sent a selfie to Elizabeth.

The documents Henley would need for her journey from Bulgaria back to the United States would require even more care and attention to detail than the travel arrangements Gretchen was putting together. Elizabeth knew a documents specialist, a friend she had worked with years earlier and with whom she had kept in touch since her retirement. Elizabeth knew that the documents specialist and friend had never really retired, even after she had left government service. They never discussed what Katherine Noble did with her time or how she had been able to afford the beautiful and expensive waterfront home she'd bought in Lewes, Delaware. Elizabeth and Katherine met for lunch a couple of times every summer.

Elizabeth knew she was going to have to go to Katherine for help to provide Henley with the papers she needed to leave Bulgaria and make the journey back to California. Henley currently had nothing—no passport and no identity papers. When all was said and done, the ironclad story would be that Henley had never left the United States. She had never spent any time in Bulgaria or Russia or Greece or anywhere other than the USA. She had never in her life been anywhere close to the Black Sea. Henley would have to travel nearly halfway around the world as someone other than herself, and Elizabeth would arrange it all.

Elizabeth would have to speak frankly with her friend Katherine Noble. Elizabeth was going to let her friend know that she knew about the documents business that continued to pay Katherine's bills. Elizabeth had to ask for Katherine's help, and in spite of their being friends, Elizabeth knew that help would not be cheap.

They met for a long lunch at a favorite restaurant in Lewes. Over lobster salad, cheese popovers, and several glasses of iced tea, Elizabeth laid it all out for Katherine and told her everything she needed. They put their heads together and made a great many decisions. At the end of the day, their friendship was still intact, and Katherine was going to be able to afford to finish renovating the bathroom in her Lewes home. She intended to put in a walk-in tub and a roll-in shower thanks, at least in part, to the complicated documents Elizabeth Carpenter required.

Henley would need two simple identity cards with a priest's picture on each one to allow her to travel from Bulgaria to Greece. Elizabeth would soon have a recent photo of Henley, the one she'd asked Henley to take of herself with the satellite phone. But Elizabeth and Katherine decided that any old Eastern Orthodox priest's photo would do for these identity cards. It would not be necessary to use Henley's photograph on these simple IDs. All Bulgarian and Greek Orthodox priests looked alike to Elizabeth and Katherine, dressed in black vestments and black hats and wearing long gray hair and scraggly gray beards. Who could tell one from the other?

Henley would have one identity card that identified her as a Bulgarian priest. She would present this card when she boarded the train in Svilengrad, Bulgaria. She would carry another identify card to use when she changed her hat and crossed the border and became the Greek Orthodox priest that rode the train to Alexandropolis in Greece. Because both Bulgaria and Greece belonged to the EU, the two priests who traveled on the train would probably not be asked to show their identification. Clerics were sometimes given special treatment. But just in case, Elizabeth wanted to be certain that Henley had everything she might need. If, in the end, she didn't need all of these identity cards, that would be a blessing.

Henley would not need any ID on the next leg of her journey until she arrived at the airport in Milan. In Italy she would become Glinda Southey, a humorous nod to Henley's love of the famous movie with Judy Garland. Henley would have a Canadian passport with her own photograph on it. The passport would be in the name of Glinda Southey, ready to present to the authorities, if she was asked, when she landed in Milan. Because she would be arriving from another country in the EU and because she would be arriving on a private plane, she probably would not be required to show her passport.

This was serious business, but Elizabeth and Katherine enjoyed the laughs they had about Glinda. The two doubted that Henley would ever have to use her Canadian passport, so they felt secure in having some fun with it. Glinda would fly from Greece to Milan. Was that "somewhere over the rainbow"? Just in case, Glinda Southey would have a passport that she would be able to show in Milan . . . if anybody asked.

The part of Henley's journey that took place on the overnight train through Europe and on the boat train to London's Heathrow Airport would be made on a South African passport in the name of Joan Merriweather. Joan's passport photo would be a ringer for Henley, but Joan had dark brown hair cut in a becoming bob. Katherine handed the dark brown wig she had selected to Elizabeth, so she could send it to Henley. When Henley used Joan Merriweather's passport, she would have to wear the wig. Joan would be traveling by train, and she would not interact with many people. No one would look closely at her hair. The dark brown wig would be photo shopped onto Joan Merriweather's passport photo.

When Henley was in the Heathrow airport, she would have to retire the dark brown wig and replace it with a longer blonde one. Henley's own hair was still quite short, white and gray, and growing back in patches. It was not ready for prime time or for presentation in public. Katherine and Elizabeth consulted Amazon and agreed on the most appropriate blonde wig. Katherine had a picture of the wig, and Elizabeth ordered the wig to be sent to her in Maryland. It would arrive in two days.

Henley would have a British passport in the name of Tolliver Lawrence when she wore the blonde wig and left Heathrow Airport for Montreal. Her British passport would have all the expected entry and exit stamps. All of the paperwork that Katherine was preparing would have the proper visas and stamps that even the most particular customs agent would be looking for. Henley would be covered in all of her identities.

The British don't pay much attention to outgoing travelers with British passports. They pay a great deal of attention to people with British passports as well as to people with other kinds of passports who want to enter the country. Tolliver Lawrence, with her long blonde hair, would not be carefully scrutinized when she left the UK. Likewise, travelers from the British Isles who visit Canada did not have their British passports inspected too meticulously. They were all members of the English-speaking Commonwealth and therefore kind of one big family. Tolliver Lawrence would hate wearing her blonde wig for eight plus hours, but nobody would look too closely at her passport when she flew into Canada, even into French-speaking Montreal.

The last plane flight Henley would have to make would be as an Australian woman with gray hair. She would fly from Montreal to Los Angeles as Rowena Williamson from Canberra, Australia. Her gray wig would also be compliments of Amazon and would be photo shopped onto

Henley's photograph that was on Rowena Williamson's Australian passport.

Henley would hate all the wigs she had to wear, but she would agree to wear them. Henley knew she had to reenter the United States as someone other than herself. Because she had never left the USA, she could not ever be seen or identified as arriving back in the USA.

Katherine promised that all the identity cards, passports, driver's licenses, and accompanying credit cards would be ready in a week. As soon as Elizabeth received the selfies from Henley, she would send them on to Katherine. The two women would meet again for lunch the following week. One medium-sized manila envelope and a second medium-sized manila envelope full of some serious cash would change hands.

Elizabeth would have to send the priests' identity cards to her contact in Zurich right away to be certain the IDs made their way promptly to Sofia, Bulgaria. She had to be sure all the passports and other paperwork that Katherine Noble had prepared reached Henley in time for her to be able to use them. This would depend on J.D. Steele who had to have the envelope that held Henley's documents in his hands so that he could give them to her when she arrived on the train in Greece. It was complicated.

Gretchen MacDermott made the elaborate and intricate plane and train reservations. Gretchen knew what to do. The itineraries were designed to confuse and distract. Gretchen now had the correct names from all the passports and other documents she needed to coordinate the complex travel plans. Some of the arrangements were downright byzantine. Gretchen was not really a travel agent, but she traveled so much herself, she knew the ropes. Gretchen was a person who could do anything she wanted to do, and she always did it well.

There were the wigs, and there were the clothes that Elizabeth had purchased and hoped would fit the much thinner Henley. Elizabeth had tried to select outfits that Henley would actually be willing to put on her body and would not attract attention.

These were the many pieces that Elizabeth had to keep moving on the board. It had been years since she had juggled an operation like this. She was more than willing to do it for Henley, and she was hoping against hope that she had not forgotten anything. It was a lot of time, a lot of work, and a lot of money. Elizabeth had plenty of money, but time was short. Elizabeth wasn't getting any younger. The effort that was involved didn't seem like work to Elizabeth. Although she was out of practice, she was good at this. She didn't have the energy she used to have, but doing it all for someone she cared about had energized her.

Elizabeth knew Richard was curious, and she was able to tell him a little bit about what she was doing. She was not willing to tell him things she could only speculate about. He knew she was helping Henley Breckenridge with something, but he also knew better than to ask Elizabeth for details. He trusted that she would tell him all she could tell him, when the time was right.

Elizabeth prepared a suitcase for Henley with the wigs and the appropriate travel clothes. Sidney Richardson would take the suitcase with her to Fashion Week in Milan. She would give the suitcase to Henley when she left her at the villa in Umbria. Because Henley was not really South African or British or Australian, Elizabeth urged her to say very little to flight attendants, conductors, and other passengers during her travels. Flight attendants and others who frequently dealt with international travelers were able to recognize accents. Elizabeth could only cross her fingers and hope that Henley would comply with her instructions and wear the wigs and the designated clothing. Her life might depend on her willingness to do as she was told.

CHAPTER 42

2022

GISELLE AND GUERLEK MADE THE fifteen mile journey on the backs of the mules to the store that was also a post office. Henley was nervous about whether or not her package would arrive on time. She was not certain she could make this ride bareback on the mule again. At first the postmistress seemed unable to locate the package. Henley's heart was in her throat. It seemed as if the woman was moving through molasses. If she moved any slower she would not be moving at all. Henley tried to get herself under control. What if the package had not arrived in time? The package had to be there.

Finally the postmistress found it. It was larger than Henley had expected it would be. After Giselle signed for it, Henley took it from her hands. "It's a gift for you, but I want to be sure it's the right thing first. You will love this. I promise. I will open it to be sure it's what it's supposed to be, and then you can have it." Giselle was suspicious of this plan, but Henley had the package and was not about to give it up until she'd had a chance to open it. They rode back to

Giselle's farm on the mules. Henley was exhausted after the round trip and all the anxiety and worry about whether or not the package would arrive. But she knew she had to give the music box to Giselle tonight. Giselle was too curious to wait any longer.

Henley retired to the privacy of the room that had been made into her bedroom and was also a storage room. Giselle had put a mattress in one corner of the room for her. Henley opened the package quickly. She found the Euros and the satellite phone inside the music box. There were two charging cords in an envelope that held several other things that went with the satellite phone. Henley quickly hid the phone and all of its accessories. She hid most of the Euros and put a few of the bills back into the music box. She rewrapped the gift she would give to Giselle.

Giselle was thrilled with the music box and even more thrilled with the money. Henley thought Giselle probably suspected that there had been something else—something Guerlek did not want Giselle to see—in the package when it arrived. But Giselle was sufficiently distracted by the beautiful music box and the euros. It was more money than Giselle had ever had in her entire life. Although Bulgaria did not yet use the euro and still used its own currency, the leva, usually referred to as the lev, the lev was pegged to the euro. Banks were happy to exchange the euro for the lev. Giselle was delighted to have money of any kind.

Henley was able to find some private time to read the instructions about how to use the satellite phone with its encryption software and the multiple SIM cards. The instructions were very clear that when she had used a SIM card once, she had to discard it. The SIM cards were designed to fool whatever network she might be using. Each SIM card was intended to show the satellite phone being used in a different location around the world. When Henley placed a call on the satellite phone with one of the SIM cards, the phone might show that the call was coming from Johannesburg, for example. The next SIM card would show her call was coming from an entirely different place. Henley didn't need to understand any of this technology. All she had to do was destroy each SIM card after it had been used one time. When she had destroyed the used SIM card, she was to replace it with another one. There were twenty different SIM cards included with the satellite phone package. She could safely use the phone twenty times

There was already an email from Elizabeth on the satellite phone. Elizabeth was still being discreet, in case the NSA was listening. Elizabeth asked that Henley send several selfies to her as soon as possible. Henley assumed these photos would be used to invent an ID for her to use to make her exit from Bulgaria. She knew the photos would be terrible.

Henley had never put a great deal of effort into her physical appearance. She was a very attractive woman, and she never wore any makeup. She had shaved her head several months earlier, and her hair had begun to grow back, mostly white with some gray. Her hair now looked nothing like it had before she had shaved her head. The hair had not grown back evenly over her whole head. It had grown back in wisps and patches. It was not a flattering look.

Henley thought she looked a bit like a cancer patient on the mend. She had also lost a great deal of weight while she had been living on meager rations at Timotei's hut. Her face was much thinner, and her entire body was slimmer than it had been in years. Only her face would show in the photos she would send to Elizabeth, but with the changes in her face and the changes in her hair, she looked very different from the way she had looked when she'd been all dolled up for the wedding's rehearsal dinner at the Woodbrier. That was the last time Elizabeth had seen her. Henley realized the wedding and her trip to the Woodbrier had been almost a year ago.

Henley fixed her hair as best she could. It wasn't a very good fix, but it would have to do. Elizabeth needed the photos immediately. Henley took several selfies with the satellite phone, and finally sent three of them to Elizabeth. She cringed as she looked at them and cringed as she sent them. She thought they made her look very old and haggard.

When Henley used the satellite phone, Elizabeth knew the exact longitude and latitude of Giselle's farm. Henley confirmed these co-ordinates in an email when she sent the selfie photos to Elizabeth. After she had sent everything, including an email to Elizabeth, Henley removed the SIM card from the phone. She crushed it with a rock. Then she walked to the pasture where Giselle kept her mules, dug a hole, and buried the SIM card in the dirt. It seemed like a waste to Henley, but she was determined to follow Elizabeth's directions exactly. She put a new SIM card in her phone.

Elizabeth was thrilled to receive the photographs from Henley. This let her know that the satellite phone had arrived and was in Henley's possession. Elizabeth was shocked to see how thin Henley's face was, and she was very surprised at the state of Henley's hair. But the email with the selfies let Elizabeth know that Henley had learned how to use the phone and had read her email. Elizabeth immediately forwarded the selfie photos to Katherine Noble. Katherine needed them for the documents she had promised.

Elizabeth trusted that Henley would discard each SIM card and replace it every time after she used the satellite phone. In case the NSA was listening, they would only see a very bad photo of a good looking woman. They would have no idea why someone had sent a selfie from Johannesburg, South Africa to a burner phone in Louisville, Kentucky. Elizabeth had gone to extra trouble and expense to make sure that the SIM cards in the prepaid cell phones she'd purchased for herself would show that they were someplace where they were not. It would remain a puzzle to the Puzzle Palace. Or, at least it would remain a puzzle for a while.

Even though the satellite phone was secure and even though their emails were encrypted, Henley and Elizabeth were careful about the communications they exchanged. Henley admitted to Elizabeth that, although she had never told anyone in Bulgaria her real name, she had told Giselle, out of necessity that she was from New Zealand. Elizabeth was concerned but felt she could do something to cover Henley's claim of New Zealand residency.

Henley kept the satellite phone turned off and hidden in Giselle's storage room. Each evening she walked to Giselle's barn and charged the phone. Henley checked it several times a day to see if there were any emails from Elizabeth. She hoped to hear soon that there was some kind of plan in place for her to leave Bulgaria. Henley was increasingly worried that her presence in the small fishing village was becoming suspicious.

Giselle was asking more and more questions. Because Henley had told her she was from New Zealand, Giselle wanted to know all about the place. She'd wanted to know why Henley hadn't told anyone right away that she was from New Zealand. Why had Elizabeth told Giselle at first that she didn't remember where she was from? If Guerlek knew she was from New Zealand, why didn't she know her real name? Giselle was curious about where exactly Boiko had pulled Guerlek from the sea. Giselle had too many questions. Guerlek pretended not to understand some of the things Giselle was asking her about. When she didn't want to answer a question, Henley claimed that her French vocabulary let her down from time to time. Things were coming unraveled. Henley's gift of the music box and the money had raised even more questions about who she really was. Giselle was relentless. Henley was no longer able to keep up with explaining away the inconsistencies in her stories. She needed to leave the country.

One of the many travel arrangements Elizabeth asked Gretchen to make was an effort to cover for Henley's revelation to Giselle that she was from New Zealand. The fictitious Danika Greenberg was created. Danika was a native of New Zealand who had lived in Middlebury, Vermont for the past twenty years. She would become part of a tour group that was flying from Philadelphia to London. Danika, having previously spent some time in the Balkans, would join the tour in London and would set off with the group, on paper at least, for a three-week bus trip through France and Spain.

Danika's name would be on the roster for the tour, but no one would ever see her. She would leave the tour at the end of September to fly back to the United States. Danika held a New Zealand passport. There would be a travel history that would show she had flown from London to Montreal where she would connect to a flight for Los Angeles. A woman using Danika's passport would be listed on the manifest to continue her flight from Los Angeles to New Zealand. This was all arranged on paper because Henley had mentioned to Giselle that she was from New Zealand. If anyone ever questioned Giselle about the woman who had briefly lived with her, that mystery woman who had appeared in Giselle's life would become Danika Greenberg who was from New Zealand and had now returned to her home in Wellington.

It was a lot of trouble to go to for a false trail, a trip that happened only on paper and with computerized reservations, an elaborate tour for a person who did not exist. Elizabeth had asked for Gretchen to arrange this ruse just in case anyone ever tried to find the woman who had told Giselle she was from New Zealand. Elizabeth had tried to attend to every detail and loose end and cover every base.

Elizabeth had been putting pressure on J.D. She needed his help more than she needed anybody else. He wanted to help her but was taking his time making a commitment. Henley had once threatened him with her shotgun when she thought he was involved in human trafficking. In fact, J.D. had been trying to save a life. Things had eventually been sorted out, and J.D. had forgiven Henley for pointing her gun at him.

Elizabeth was asking J.D. to put himself at some risk to help rescue Henley. It was not a huge risk for J.D. to do what she wanted him to do, but there was a small risk. Elizabeth was physically not able to make the trip that she was asking J.D. to make. Henley would be able to recognize J.D. when she saw him at the railway station in Greece, and that was the critical piece of Elizabeth's plan.

Finally, J.D. contacted Elizabeth with the news that he and Olivia had just signed on for a last-minute cruise of the Greek Islands. Olivia had always wanted to travel to Greece, and J.D. had scored a terrific price on a cruise. The Admiral's Suite had just become available on a luxury ship on a luxury cruise line. J.D. was in the transportation business. He was in the trucking business, not the cruise line business, but he had connections everywhere. How he had put the cruise and the Admiral's Suite together on the spur of the moment was a mystery to Elizabeth, but she was delighted to hear it.

Elizabeth later heard from Gretchen that it was no accident that the Admiral's Suite on that particular cruise had suddenly become available. Gretchen knew J.D., and she knew Elizabeth had to have him in Greece on a certain date. Gretchen had made that happen, but J.D. would never know exactly how he had been able to book such a wonderful stateroom on such a wonderful trip and at such a wonderful price. Elizabeth was incredibly grateful to the very resourceful Gretchen MacDermott.

Olivia and J.D. would fly to Athens on September 20th. After seeing the sights in the capital of the country for several days, they would fly to the quaint Greek village of Alexandropolis on the Aegean Sea. They would stay overnight at a hotel in Alexandropolis on September 26th and join the Aegean Sea cruise the next day. Their cruise included 10 Greek islands and would last for fifteen days. Olivia was thrilled with the surprise trip and was already packing.

Elizabeth would be forever grateful to J.D. She had counted on him, and he had not disappointed her. He would rent a car and make the short trip from his hotel in Alexandropolis, Greece to the railway station. J.D. would pick up Henley at the station and drive her to the small airport outside town.

Cameron Richardson had assured Elizabeth that the private plane would be waiting there, just as she had requested.

J.D. would give Henley the important package from Elizabeth that held the various passports, travel documents, and important IDs that Henley would have to have. J.D. would put Henley on the private plane. He might never tell Olivia about the car he had rented and the errand he had done for Elizabeth. It would take him less than an hour. His mission would have been accomplished, and he and Olivia would join the Aegean Sea cruise the next day. They would enjoy a first-class voyage in their first-class accommodations. Gretchen MacDermott had taken care of it all.

J.D. had been the keystone in the entire plan. The rest of the schedule depended on if and when he could meet Henley at the Alexandropolis train station in Greece. Now all the rest of the pieces of the operation could be confirmed. The timetable and the itineraries were set. The private plane would fly into the Alexandropolis airport on September 26th, and J.D. would meet Henley at the train station that day. She would be in Italy by the early morning of September 27th. Sidney would be finished with fashion week in Milan and would rent a car. She would drive her rental car to the spot where all the private planes landed at the Milan airport, the part of the airport where Henley's plane would land. Sidney would pick up Henley on the tarmac.

Sidney had flown privately in and out of Milan a number of times. She knew her way around the airport. She knew where to go and exactly where to find Henley. She would drive Henley to the villa in Umbria. Then Sidney would continue her drive through Tuscany. She would buy some wine, and she would fly home commercial, first-class of course, a few days later. In theory it would all proceed smoothly.

Elizabeth laid it out in great detail and sent a long email to Henley. Henley had to be ready to leave Giselle's house in eight days. Henley would not be able to tell Giselle goodbye or thank you. Henley would have to slip away. She would have to walk five miles to an abandoned church from where she would begin her long journey home. She could only bring with her what she could carry in her shoulder satchel. She had little else to bring with her anyway.

The next week seemed endless. Giselle constantly asked her what was wrong with her. Giselle wanted to know why she was so quiet. Henley claimed she was not feeling well and stayed in her room. Now that she knew she was about to embark on her journey, she was eager to leave. In her own mind, she had already left her friends in Bulgaria. She would never forget them. She owed them everything. She owed them her life, but she had already said goodbye to them in her heart. Someday she would find a way to repay them for all they'd done for her. Now that things were finally moving forward, Henley realized she could not wait to rejoin civilization.

Elizabeth had sent Henley directions and a phone map of how to find the abandoned Eastern Orthodox Church. Henley had memorized the directions and the map. Every night before she went to sleep, she mentally walked the five miles to the abandoned church. She knew the way with her eyes closed. She counted down the days until she would leave at four o'clock in the morning to walk to the meeting place. When Giselle woke up at six o'clock on the day Henley left, Henley hoped she herself would already be in the trunk of a car and on her way to the railway station in Svilengrad.

CHAPTER 43

2022

She woke up early that morning. She hadn't slept much at all, even though she knew she had a long day ahead of her and needed to get a good night's sleep. She was anxious to begin her journey. She had prepared everything the night before and laid out her clothes. She had also laid out a piece of bread and a hunk of cheese for her breakfast. She dressed quickly and left Giselle's house without a sound. She ate her bread and cheese as she walked.

Her satellite phone was charged. She knew the way. She had the phone and everything she needed to bring with her in her leather satchel. It was still dark, and she walked and walked. She did not need to look at the map on her phone. She knew every step she had to take and every turn she had to make to reach the meeting place. The building was an abandoned monastery, the Cloister of Saint Cyril. The church was in ruins, and Henley was supposed to hide herself until she saw an old white car approach the building.

The sun was just coming up when she arrived at the monastery. She found a place to hide where she was able to see the road but no one could see her. She had not intended to fall asleep, but she drifted off as she lay in an alcove of the ancient building. She heard the car before she saw it. The sound of the car on the road roused her from her nap. The man dressed as a Bulgarian cleric stepped out of the sedan. There was no one else around to see him. The road to the monastery had also been abandoned for some time. It was bumpy and muddy and overgrown with weeds and grass. No one was likely to find this place by accident. The man dressed as a priest approached the monastery. Henley left the place where she had concealed herself and walked towards the man wearing the robes and the hat. He had a long white beard. Henley thought the beard looked like a fake, but she had never liked beards in the first place.

The priest did not say a word to her. He handed her a pile of clothes that included a wig, a beard, sandals, and socks. The cleric indicated that she should put the disguise on over her own clothes. She put down her leather satchel and dressed herself in the religious garb. She put on the gray wig, and she attached the scraggly gray beard to her chin. Now she knew she really despised beards, especially those that she was forced to put on her own face. She pulled on the socks and fastened the sandals. She placed her own worn-out shoes in her satchel. She adjusted the Bulgarian orthodox priest's black hat over her wig. She was now a man and a religious man at that.

The priest who was driving the car opened the trunk and helped her climb in. The trip to Svilengrad would take a little more than two hours. She would travel most of the way in the trunk of the car. Just before they reached the railway station in Svilengrad, she would join the priest and sit in the passenger seat. She was playing the part of an elderly cleric who was deaf. The affliction would explain, if anyone spoke to her, why she didn't answer. Henley did not understand or speak Bulgarian. It was necessary that the priest she was pretending to be not be able to hear or speak.

Riding in the trunk of the car was hot and uncomfortable. Henley was thirsty. She had not had anything to drink that day because she did not want to have to use the bathroom. She would relieve herself before they got on the train, just before they reached the station. Of course, she realized she could not go into either the women's restroom or the men's restroom . . . if there even was a restroom at the train station.

She remained silent as she sat in the passenger seat of the car. The beard was scratchy and itched like crazy. It was all she could do not to tear it off her face. The priest parked the car in a field outside the train station. He handed Henley a cane that she was to use as part of her disguise, a way of making her look older and more helpless. The priest helped her out of the car. Their tickets for the trip to Alexandropolis had already been purchased. All they had to do was board the train.

Because both Bulgaria and Greece are members of the EU, the two clerics were not supposed to have to show paperwork to enter Greece. But Greece had been badly burned in the past few years with immigrants and refugees from Syria and other places trying to enter their country illegally. They had increased their vigilance about who could get into Greece and who could not. Because they were dressed as priests, these two probably would not be asked for their identification, but one never could count on that when crossing international borders. Both priests had old identity cards with blurred printing and hazy photos on them. Elizabeth Carpenter had gone to a great deal of trouble to be sure these two had the authentic-looking identification they might need.

The two Bulgarian clerics boarded the train and found their seats. Neither one spoke. No one approached them or spoke to them. Religion was out of fashion in many places in the world these days. Old priests were of little interest to anyone and were to be ignored. The conductor came around and stamped their tickets. He scarcely looked at either priest. He had seen these two before, several times, or at least he had seen two priests before who looked exactly like these two. Henley was thankful for the lack of interest.

Finally the train was on its way. After several minutes, the man who was accompanying Henley spoke to her for the first time. His English was fairly easy to understand. She wondered why he had not spoken aloud until now. He handed her a different black hat, and he replaced the hat he had on his own head with another hat. "Put this hat on your head, and put the other one in your satchel."

"This hat looks exactly like the one I'm already wearing. Why do I need to change it?"

"Trust me. It's different. We were Bulgarian clerics when we boarded this train. We wore the headdresses of the Bulgarian priests. We have just crossed the border into Greece. It is imperative that we now are both priests in the Greek Orthodox Church. Bulgarian priests and Greek priests have different hats. These black hats might look the same to you, but they don't look the same to the Greeks." Henley did as she was told. She put the Greek religious hat on her head. She folded the Bulgarian priest's headdress and put it in her satchel.

It seemed as if the train ride from Svilengrad, Bulgaria to Alexandropolis, Greece took forever. It stopped at every small village along the way. It seemed to Henley as if they stayed for a long time in each of these tiny towns. Even if no one got off or got on, the train remained unmoving in each empty station. Would they reach their destination before dark? Henley was not certain she would be able to recognize J.D. Steele in the dark.

At last the train reached its final stop. Henley's fellow priest helped her step down from the train car onto the platform. She walked away from the train, still using her cane and pretending to be an elderly man. She could not wait to get rid of the entire outfit, but she especially could not wait to get rid of the beard. The priest who had been with her for the entire day said nothing as he left her alone on the station platform and got back on the train. Henley knew that they had not been together as friends. The man dressed as a priest had been paid to do a job. He had done his job. He had delivered Henley safely to the railway station in Alexandropolis. Now it was someone else's job to take care of her and guide her through the next phase of her journey. She was in Greece and no longer in Bulgaria, but she did not feel any safer or any more secure than she had felt before. She wondered if she would ever feel safe again.

She waited at the entrance to the station. She'd found a bench to sit on. There were more people coming and going here than there had been in Svilengrad. She was nervous. People were staring at her as they walked in and out of the station. Finally,

Henley saw a person she recognized. It was J.D. He looked right at her, but he did not show any sign at all that he recognized her. She shouted to him, but he apparently did not hear her. He was leaving the station and heading for the parking lot. Henley could not let him get away. He was her only hope, her only chance to escape from this place and see her family again.

She knew it would look suspicious for her to run, if she even could run in the long skirts she was wearing while pretending to be a priest in the Greek Orthodox Church. She grabbed her cane, lifted the skirts with her other hand, and took off after J.D. She didn't care who heard her here. She didn't care if she had blown her cover. She ran after J.D. as fast as her age and her long skirts would allow her to run. She overtook him just as he arrived at his car.

"J.D. It's me! Henley Breckenridge. Aren't you supposed to be here looking for me?" J.D. stared at the strange person in the black robes and the black hat. Henley stripped the beard from her chin and took off the black hat and the wig. She knew she looked different from the way she'd looked the last time J.D. had seen her, but she was determined to make him acknowledge her. "What's wrong? Don't you recognize me without my shotgun pointed at you?"

J.D. had searched everywhere. He knew Henley was going to be dressed as a priest, but her disguise, added to the fact that she was wearing a wig and a beard and had lost so much weight, had completely fooled J.D.

"Oh, my God! It really is you. I walked by you sitting on that bench and holding the cane a bunch of times and didn't even look at you twice. You were part of the woodwork. What a convincing disguise. It was the beard that I wasn't expecting. That really makes you look old . . . sorry. I mean, it really is convincing."

J.D. knew he had his passenger, and he realized he had to stop blabbering and get her inside the car. She'd shed her beard and wig, and she was standing there in the disappearing light for all the world to see. "Get in the car. Get in quickly. I'm sorry. I thought I had missed you completely. The plane is waiting. We are wasting time. I need to deliver you to the airport and get back to Olivia at the hotel."

"I guess my disguise was just too good." Henley was struggling to reattach the beard to her chin and put the wig and the hat back on her head. Her instructions had been that she was to stay in her disguise until she was safely aboard the private plane that was waiting for her at the Alexandropoli Airport Dimokritos.

"The package from Elizabeth with your passports and other papers is here in the console. Take it now, and put it in your satchel. You won't need a passport while you are in Greece, but you may need one when you get to Italy." J.D. concentrated on finding the right road to the airport. The GPS in the car was giving directions in Greek, of course, so J.D. was trying to look at his phone for directions in English.

"It isn't very far. The airport is tiny. You will need the disguise. Every private plane that lands here is an object of great curiosity. Everyone wonders what rich tycoon has just landed and where they are planning to stay. I will do my best to get close to the plane. I'm supposed to drive directly onto the tarmac and stop as close as I can get to the foot of the plane's steps. You are to get out quickly and go straight up the steps. As soon as you are inside the door and the door is closed, the plane will begin to move towards the takeoff runway. The pilot will not wait for you to take a seat or put on your seat belt. You will be on your own to get into a seat and strap in as fast as you can. You are the only passenger of course. It's not a tiny plane, but it's small enough. It's also big enough to attract a lot of attention here in this little seaside town."

Within a few minutes, they were at the airport and driving onto the tarmac. Henley gathered her satchel and her long skirts. She knew she ought to take the cane, too, as a part of her outfit, but she decided it was more important to move quickly out of the car and up the steps into the plane than it was to maintain the ruse of the cane. She left the cane for J.D. He pulled up very close to the stairs, so close that Henley could almost not open the car door. She slipped out of the passenger seat and was up the five steps and at the airplane's entrance almost before J.D. could put the car in park. She briefly turned around to wave a thank you and goodbye to J.D. before the plane's door closed behind her. She hurried to take a seat and had just fastened her seatbelt when the plane took off into the darkening sky over the Aegean Sea. She was alone in the passenger compartment. She was on her way to Italy.

It was more than a five-hour flight to Milan. Henley was exhausted from all that had happened to her that day. It was seven o'clock in Alexandropolis, and she'd had nothing to eat all day since the scrap of bread and the piece of cheese for breakfast. She'd had very little to drink. The thing that was uppermost in her mind at that moment was to rid herself of the dreadful beard as well as the hat and wig and all the rest of her Orthodox religious outfit. She wondered how in the world a real priest was able to stand all that hair and all those skirts. She removed the thick socks and sandals and replaced them with the worn-out shoes she'd brought in her satchel.

As soon as the plane was in the air, she used the restroom. She folded the priest's garments and left them in the cubicle. Somebody else could decide whether to throw them away or keep them. When she looked in the mirror at the clothes she'd been wearing underneath the religious vestments, she realized how really disreputable she must appear to others. Her clothes were ragged and didn't really fit her. She was not nearly as well-dressed as the supposedly penniless immigrants who were fleeing the countries of the Middle East and storming the borders of prosperous European countries. Henley had never been a slave to fashion and had always chosen clothes that were practical for the life she led on her ranch. She had to admit to herself that right now she looked really terrible after her weeks in Bulgaria.

She washed her hands and face. She hoped no one would ask for her passport when the plane landed. Henley had opened the package from Elizabeth and looked over the passports she was to use on her journey. Glinda Southey's hair and clothes would never pass muster in a fancy place like Milan.

Henley knew there was no flight attendant on this private flight, but she'd been told there would be bottled water and some food in the plane's refrigerator. The galley was compact to say the least, and Henley had no trouble finding the water. There were also bottles of V-8 juice and wrapped sandwiches in the refrigerator. A few bags of chips were piled on the galley's one square foot of counter space. The sandwiches looked great. The V-8 juice looked even better to the thirsty and famished Henley. She hadn't seen a bottle of V-8 juice in months. These little bottles of V-8 looked like heaven to her. She could drink them all.

Henley helped herself to a turkey sandwich on rye with lettuce, tomato, and Swiss cheese. There was plenty of mayonnaise on the sandwich, and Henley devoured her sandwich and went back to the fridge for a second. She downed two small bottles of the V-8 juice. The mayonnaise on the bread tasted so delicious to Henley. She hadn't realized until now how much she had missed the condiments she'd taken for granted in her everyday California life. She promised herself that she would never take anything for granted again.

Henley fell sound sleep shortly after she finished her second sandwich. Milan was one hour ahead of Alexandropolis, Greece. The flight would take about five hours, so Henley knew she would not arrive at the Milan airport until well after midnight. This was a good thing as there would be fewer people around to be curious about the private plane that landed. In the dark, no one would be able to get a very good look at who disembarked from the plane.

Sidney Richardson would be at the Milan airport with a car to pick her up and whisk her off into the night. Henley allowed herself to fall asleep. The farther away she traveled from the Black Sea, the safer she began to feel. Elizabeth had assured her she would be able to stop running and rest at the villa in Umbria.

CHAPTER 44

2022

Sidney was waiting in a black four-door Mercedes sedan when the plane came to a stop. She pushed open the passenger door. Henley quickly exited the plane, sat down on the seat, swung her legs into the luxury car, and pulled the door closed. They were on the autostrada before the pilot of the private plane could begin his post-flight check. It was two o'clock in the morning, and there was little traffic on the road. Sidney's GPS was speaking English and giving her good directions towards Umbria.

Sidney loved to drive, and she was relatively young. She did not mind driving at night, and she did not mind driving fast. She had a cooler with water and soft drinks for Henley. Henley expressed her thanks and immediately dropped off to sleep again. Sidney understood. Elizabeth had warned her that Henley had been through a difficult time and had urged Sidney not to ask Henley any questions. Henley slept all the way to the villa outside Umbertide.

Sidney gently tapped Henley on the shoulder to let her know they had arrived. It was 7:30 in the morning. The driveway that led from the secondary road to the stone house was more than a kilometer long. No one was going to accidentally stumble on Henley while she was in Umbria. She had been told that Sidney would help her into the house which would be unlocked. Sidney would give her a very important suitcase, and then Sidney would leave. There was no need for Henley to make small talk or any kind of talk at all with Sidney.

Henley thanked Sidney for what she had done. Sidney handed Henley the suitcase Elizabeth had sent and told Henley that she had loved every minute of being in on the escape. She said she would do it again any time. Henley knew Sidney meant what she said. Henley knew that Sidney was cut from the same cloth that she was cut from. Henley smiled and waved as Sidney sped away from the villa in the black Mercedes.

Henley was still tired although she'd been sleeping off and on for hours. She wanted to fall right into the very inviting bed in the villa's main bedroom. But she had not had a shower for weeks, months really, and the warm water that flowed out of the shower in the newly renovated bathroom at the villa was too enticing to ignore. Henley washed her hair, and then she washed it a second and a third time. She didn't have much hair right now, but it was wonderful to have the little bit of hair she still had on her head feel clean. She scrubbed and scrubbed her body with the expensive soap she found in the bathroom. Other things she had taken for granted were hot water and soap. She luxuriated in both and promised herself she would never again fail to appreciate either one of these things.

She'd been told there were clean clothes and nightgowns and robes in the bedroom someplace. She was so exhausted, and she was really clean for the first time in such a long time. She didn't have the energy to look for a nightgown and put it on. She lowered herself into the clean, crisp sheets, naked as the day she was born. It felt wonderful to have any kind of sheets on her bed. Having them be clean sheets was a definite bonus. She knew there was no one else in the villa, and there would not be anyone on site as long as Henley was there. She was asleep before her head hit the pillow. She was eternally grateful to Elizabeth. Henley finally felt safe in this hundreds-of-years-old stone house with vineyards and fields of fruit trees all around it. No one would be able to find her here.

Henley was hungry again when she woke up in the late afternoon. She admitted to herself that she had been hungry the entire time she'd been in Bulgaria. She'd known that Timotei was sharing the little bit of food he had with her, and she had tried not to eat too much of it. But Henley had always liked to eat and had an appreciation for good food. She knew that she was the major investor in an outstanding restaurant in Paso Robles, California. Elizabeth had told her there was food for her in the villa's kitchen. It was cool when the sun went down in late September in Umbria, and Henley chuckled when she saw herself walk by a mirror in the bedroom. She found a robe and went to explore the villa.

Henley loved pasta, and it had been forever, or so it seemed, since she'd had a big plate of spaghetti. There was a container of what looked like homemade marinara sauce in the refrigerator. She also found a nice chunk of aged Romano cheese that she could grate. Henley found a pot, the olive oil, boxes of dried pasta, salt, and everything she needed to make herself a meal. There were several bottles of local wine in the kitchen, and she'd been told to help herself. She cooked her spaghetti al dente and warmed up the marinara sauce. She grated the cheese. It was a meal fit for a queen. Henley ate every bite. She drank two glasses of wine with her dinner and indulged in a third which she enjoyed with an entire pint of outstanding dark chocolate gelato she found in the refrigerator's freezer.

She did not understand how she could be so tired. She wondered if she'd contracted some bad disease in Bulgaria. She knew she was malnourished and probably anemic. There was no one here in Umbria to tell her what to do. There was no one here at the villa that she had to fool or with whom she had to pretend to be someone she was not. She could be herself here. If she was tired, even after having slept all day, that was fine. She had no schedule to keep. Her main job here at the safe house in Umbria was R&R. Bless Elizabeth for building this week of rest into the travel schedule. Henley had pushed for being allowed to return to Paso Robles as soon as possible, but Elizabeth had known that Henley would need time to decompress and become herself again. Elizabeth had understood that Henley had been through a very traumatic time and needed rest and the opportunity to get her mind set and ready to face her former life.

Henley did not know if she would ever again be the same person she had been a year earlier. So much had happened. She had volunteered to do things she'd never dreamed she could do. She had nearly lost her life. She had been forced to live in a world for which she'd had no preparation or training. No one in that world had spoken her language or knew anything about her. It was as if she had been dropped into the middle of a different planet and been expected to survive. She would always be grateful to Boiko and Timotei, and to Giselle. As kind as they had been to Henley, they were indeed from another planet in terms of what Henley's previous history had taught her to expect from life.

But she had survived and was on her way home. Forever changed, she hoped she would be able to find the joy and contentment that her family, her ranch, and her restaurant had once brought her. She knew the comfortable jeans that awaited her in her closet in Paso Robles would no longer fit, but she looked forward to putting her beloved concho belt around her waist and hearing it jingle and clank when she walked. She would soon be mentally and physically ready to get back to being a rancher.

The villa had a heated swimming pool. Henley spent the rest of her week in Umbria swimming and eating pasta and drinking the delicious local wine. The bottles she'd found at the villa were the good stuff, the stuff they didn't export. The clothes that Elizabeth had left for her to wear hung loosely on her much thinner frame. She knew she had to wear a respectable outfit for traveling first class on the train and for flying on a commercial airliner back to the Western Hemisphere.

She hated the wigs and dreaded putting them on her head, but she knew they were necessary. Henley looked at all the different passports that had her photo on them. Elizabeth had gone to a lot of trouble to provide her with a variety of identities. The least Henley could do was to wear the clothes and the wigs as Elizabeth asked her to do. Henley fully realized that all of this was for her own security and safety.

A car and driver were scheduled to arrive at the villa in Umbria at the end of the week. Elizabeth had insisted that Henley have two suitcases with clothes and toiletries in them. People who traveled without luggage were suspect. Most people traveled with too much stuff and too many suitcases. Elizabeth did not want Henley to attract attention because she didn't have the expected quota of luggage for traveling first class. Sidney had already provided one of the suitcases that contained the wigs and some of Henley's travel clothes. A matching suitcase was in the closet in the villa, ready to be filled with more of Henley's outfits. Elizabeth had thought of everything. Henley wondered how she had managed to get the matching suitcase and all of the additional clothes to the Umbrian villa in time.

The driver that picked Henley up at the villa put her two suitcases into the trunk of the limousine. Henley was wearing the dark brown wig and the outfit that Elizabeth had suggested, but she hung on to her leather satchel. It had been her only possession for many weeks. It did not really fit with the upscale clothing choices Elizabeth had made for Henley, but at least the satchel had lost its smell. It no longer reeked of the sheepskin that it was actually made of. The limousine drove Joan Merriweather to Firenze, and the driver helped her carry her suitcases into the train station. After her week of relaxation at the villa, Henley felt as if she was finally on her way to becoming her old self again.

Henley would be Joan Merriweather from South Africa when she traveled alone on the sleeper train to London. Her first class ticket included an overnight sleeping compartment and had been arranged for and purchased by Gretchen MacDermott. Elizabeth had not been able to find anyone to watch over Henley while she was on the train. But because Henley planned to stay in her compartment for the entire trip and have her meals brought to her, Elizabeth felt she would be all right traveling by herself.

Except for the wig, Henley loved being Joan Merriweather and having her own compartment on the sleeper train. Joan's meals were delivered, and she looked out the window and slept most of the way through Italy and France. She crossed the English Channel and rode on the boat train to London. All travel arrangements so far had worked as they had been intended to work. Joan Merriweather had not spoken to anyone except the attendant on the train who had brought her meals and made up her bed. Henley eventually found herself and her two suitcases at Heathrow airport.

Henley would not know it, but Tyler Merriman would be on the plane with Henley when Tolliver Lawrence flew from Heathrow to Montreal. The MacDermotts would be on the plane when Rowena Williamson, an older woman with gray hair, flew from Montreal to Los Angeles. Henley would not know she had someone watching out for her, but Gretchen and Bailey would make sure things went smoothly for Elizabeth's friend. Bailey was disappointed he would not be able to see the Bulgarian Orthodox priest's beard and outfit. But he loved to travel and would enjoy keeping an eye on Henley.

Her journey would be almost complete when she arrived in Los Angeles. She would travel from the airport to a medical facility in Palm Desert, California for a complete check-up. Elizabeth knew that Henley wouldn't take very good care of herself once she got busy with her ranch and her former life. Henley didn't go to the doctor unless she was really, really sick, and she only went to the dentist because he was an old friend and insisted she make an appearance at his office twice a year. It was important that she be checked out before she returned to her usual routine of not taking care of her health.

CHAPTER 45

2022

ELIZABETH HAD WANTED SOMEONE TO watch over Henley as she made her way back from whatever her ordeal abroad had involved to her home in the United States. Elizabeth would never know exactly what had happened with Henley. Elizabeth knew Henley would never tell her everything. Henley had called on Elizabeth for help, and she'd told Elizabeth a great deal about what had occurred in Bulgaria. But Henley had never breathed a word about how she'd found her way to Bulgaria. Elizabeth had strong suspicions and felt she had a good idea about how and why her friend had ended up where she was. But Elizabeth was not going to broach the subject with Henley, and if in fact what Elizabeth suspected was true, she hoped Henley never told her the whole story.

Elizabeth was worried that Henley was still fragile, especially physically. She was also worried that Henley might be at risk because of the mission she had been engaged in. Elizabeth didn't want to take any chances. She didn't want anyone to put themselves in danger by actually traveling with

Henley on her journey home, but she wanted somebody to be close by to keep an eye on her while she was traveling.

Gretchen had agreed to make all the complicated ship, train, car, and plane reservations for the various actors and in all the various names . . . at Elizabeth's directions, no questions asked. Elizabeth paid for all of Henley's considerable and convoluted travel. When Tolliver Lawrence boarded her flight for Montreal at Heathrow, Henley did not know that Tyler Merriman was sitting behind her in first class, keeping an eye on her. Tyler had just enjoyed a two-week biking trip in Portugal. Gretchen had made a minor adjustment to his plane reservations so that he could be on the same plane with Tolliver Lawrence when she flew to Montreal. When Tyler arrived in Montreal, he would take a plane directly to Denver. From Denver, he would drive to his home in Bayfield, Colorado.

The flight from London to Montreal was about an eight-hour flight. Henley was still recovering from her ordeal. Tolliver ate a meal when the flight attendant woke her and slept for most of the rest of the flight. When she arrived in Montreal, she changed her blonde wig for the gray one in the airport restroom. She changed her British passport for the Australian one. She made her connection to fly to Los Angeles.

Gretchen and Bailey MacDermott had just spent a wonderful week in Montreal. The weather had been delightfully cooler than Dallas was in September. Gretchen had always wanted to visit Quebec, and she and Bailey had eaten their way through the French restaurants of the province. The MacDermotts were seated in the front row of the first-class section. Rowena Williamson was seated in the second row. Neither Rowena nor Henley recognized the MacDermotts, so she had no idea that they were her secret guardian angels on this last leg of her journey.

When Rowena arrived in Los Angeles, she presented her Australian passport and went through customs. She told the officials that she was in the U.S. as a tourist and planned to stay three weeks. She had nothing to declare.

Henley was met by a limousine that drove her to an expensive medical clinic in Palm Desert, California. Elizabeth had insisted that Henley allow herself to be given a complete check-up before she returned to Paso Robles. This was not Henley's style. She didn't want expensive, and she didn't want a check-up. But she'd agreed to Elizabeth's terms. Elizabeth had convinced her that, after everything Henley had been through, she owed it to herself to have a physical examination and some lab tests.

The doctors at the McIntyre Clinic in Palm Desert were all first-rate. They had been trained at the best medical institutions in the United States. The clinic served the rich and famous, many of whom were well-known Hollywood names and faces. When the actors and actresses needed medical care of any kind, they often chose the McIntyre Clinic. It was discreet and allowed its patients to sign in and receive care under assumed names. Henley would also be admitted to the clinic under a name that was not her own.

Henley had taken off the last wig, and it was now in one of her suitcases. She'd wanted to throw every one of the wigs in the trash as soon as she'd removed the itchy thing from her head. But Elizabeth had told her to put them away in her suitcase. If someone found a discarded wig in a trash bin, questions might arise. Nobody wanted that.

Henley now had only her own hair on her head. She was going to the McIntyre Clinic as Dominique Trevellian. Both names sounded fake to Henley. Elizabeth had told Henley that many people who went to the McIntyre Clinic were there under assumed names. Dominique Trevellian was indeed a fake name, but it was the fake name of the person who had chosen it when she had checked into the clinic's long-term facility months earlier. Elizabeth and Henley were locked into the name Dominique Trevellian. Henley would have to undergo her few days of physical examinations as Dominique to maintain the cover story that she had been a patient in the McIntyre Clinic's long-term care facility for most of the previous year.

Matthew Ritter had tried hard to find just the right person whose name and medical history could be used to give Henley a convincing cover story for her whereabouts during the past twelve months. But in fact it was Isabelle Ritter who had found Dominique Trevellian. Elizabeth had asked Matthew Ritter, M.D. to find someone who was about Henley's age and Henley's size who had checked themselves into any Palm Desert or Palm Springs facility for long-term care. He had tried and come up with nothing. He'd expressed his frustration to Isabelle, and he had shared with her the characteristics of the person he was looking for and had not been able to find.

Isabelle had a famous Hollywood client who had checked herself into the McIntyre Clinic under an assumed name and had spent nearly a year in the clinic's long-term facility. Isabelle had been redecorating the client's home, knew her cover name, and had stayed in touch with Dominique Trevellian during her extended stay in what was essentially a stint in rehab. Isabelle told Elizabeth about Dominique, and Elizabeth had investigated her. Elizabeth was delighted with the details of Dominique's appearance. She somewhat resembled Henley. They were not clones, but they looked enough alike to fool enough people. And Dominique's medical history was perfect for what Henley required.

Elizabeth knew this part of Henley's story would be the most difficult and the least reliable. But it was also the most important. Isabelle gathered the information that Elizabeth needed, and Matthew arranged for Dominique Trevellian to be readmitted for a full diagnostic work-up at the McIntyre Clinic's short-term facility. Many of the short-term facility's patients were famous actors and actresses who were recovering from plastic surgery. They often used pseudonyms when they signed in for the several days' stay it took for their faces and tummies and saggy arms to heal from the surgical repairs.

A patient who was being admitted for tests and a complete physical exam would not raise any eyebrows. Hardly anyone staying at the clinic was using his or her real name. Dominique Trevellian was perfect. Henley was admitted to the McIntyre Clinic's short-term facility as Dominique.

If anyone ever suspected that Henley had been out of the country during the past year, records at the McIntyre Clinic would show that a person calling themselves Dominique Trevellian had been a resident in the long-term care facility for the past eleven months. She had never left the grounds of the clinic. Henley, or so the cover story would go, had checked herself into the facility under the name of Dominique Trevellian in November of 2021. Her family had not known where she was, and she had not wanted her family or anyone to know where she was. It was all top secret stuff, and this secrecy was exactly what Elizabeth was seeking for Henley's cover story.

In fact a woman whose name was not Dominique Trevellian and who had checked herself into the McIntyre

Clinic's long-term facility under that name in November was a television personality. The woman who had called herself Dominique Trevellian was a well-known actress who drank too much. She wanted to kick the habit once and for all and had made a commitment to stay in rehab until the demon rum had left her forever. She had been somewhat successful in her detoxification, and after many months, she had left the clinic the previous week.

Matthew Ritter had arranged for Dominique Trevellian to be readmitted for a battery of tests and examinations at the short-term care facility of the McIntyre Clinic. Matthew was retired and had never had any connection with the McIntyre Clinic. But he had a friend who had a friend who had a friend who had been able to arrange for Henley Breckenridge to be readmitted to the clinic under the name Dominique Trevellian.

In the short-term medical facility where Henley now was a patient, she would receive the full range of excellent medical care that Elizabeth insisted she needed. After she had been checked over, she would be free to return to Paso Robles and her ranch and her family on her own schedule. Henley and Elizabeth and Isabelle and Matthew and everybody else assumed Henley would pass all the exams with flying colors and would soon be on her way home. But there would be a further complication before Henley would be able to resume her previous life and see her much-loved people and her much-loved ranch again. Dominique Trevellian was diagnosed with having a tapeworm.

Everyone who had helped Henley on her journey to leave Eastern Europe and return to the United States, had been kept in the dark to a certain extent. J.D. knew who Henley was because she had scared the you-know-what out of him when she'd pointed her shotgun at him at her ranch in Central California the year before. Cameron had seen Henley briefly on that same occasion. Because Cameron had been sitting in the car, Henley had not really seen what he looked like.

Everyone else in the Camp Shoemaker crowd had seen Henley in person at her excellent restaurant in Paso Robles. But Henley had not paid much attention to her fellow diners at La Buona Ricetta. She had not recognized any of them on the plane.

Only J.D. and Sidney had actually spoken with Henley. The others in the group knew what she looked like, and they had heard about how she had gone all out to take care of Sui Wai. Some of them had seen Henley briefly a couple of times when she'd appeared at the Woodbrier for her niece's wedding. Henley had looked very different dressed in her jeans and concho belt than she had looked dressed for the wedding's rehearsal dinner. Unless they had known Henley well, no one would have imagined that these two very different-looking women were actually one and the same.

Some of the reunion crowd knew they were helping a person from Paso Robles. Some knew they were helping a woman whose first name was Henley. Others knew only that they were watching out for and making plans for a woman who was a friend of Elizabeth's. Her real name and exactly what she looked like remained something of a mystery to most of the Camp Shoemaker friends. They wanted to help Elizabeth, and they had done an excellent job for Henley. None of them knew exactly why Henley had needed their help. It was enough that she was important to Elizabeth. If Elizabeth needed their help to save this mystery woman, the Camp Shoemaker crowd was all in to help her do that. They knew not to ask too many questions. They just tried their best to do what was asked of them.

CHAPTER 46

2022

The complication in Henley's timetable to return to Paso Robles occurred because Dominique Trevellian had acquired a parasite in her gut. An MRI had shown a suspicious shadow in her abdomen. When she'd had her blood drawn, she was told that her B12 values were abnormal. After further tests, Dominique had been diagnosed with a tapeworm. The medical name for this particular fish tapeworm was *Diphyllobothrium*. Dominique was not going to be allowed to leave the McIntyre Clinic until this parasite had been treated and defeated. It might be a minor problem if treated at once. If allowed to persist and left untreated, it could become something much more serious. Immediate treatment was necessary.

Dominique, of course, could not admit to being out of the country. The tapeworm she had in her intestine was known to be found in undercooked fish, often found in Russia and Eastern Europe. Ooops! But Dominique had been a patient at the clinic's long-term facility for all of the previous many months. How could she possibly have acquired this type of tapeworm? Would this be the part of Henley's cover story that could not be explained away?

Dominique Trevellian's case was perplexing. Her doctors knew she could not possibly have acquired the fish tapeworm abroad. She had been a patient in their own clinic for most of the previous year. She'd not left the grounds of the clinic for that entire time. It was finally determined that Dominique acquired the parasite when she admitted to having indulged in eating raw fish at a sushi bar after she had left the long-term care facility a few days earlier.

Henley was furious at this turn of events. She was furious that she had a tapeworm in her intestines. She'd thought the reason she was losing weight was because Timotei had not fed her enough, but apparently that was not the only reason. Henley knew exactly what had happened, given where she had been and the life she'd been living there, but she could never tell anyone the truth about how, why, or where she'd probably acquired the nasty thing. Henley was afraid that the evidence of the fish tapeworm in her body might be the one thing she was not able to lie about. Elizabeth had urged her to admit to eating at a sushi bar. The story about the sushi was not true, of course, but with all the other stories Henley had told, this one was a very minor fabrication.

Henley had counted on being home in Paso Robles by now. She had prepared her own cover story to explain her year-long absence to her family and her employees. They could never know the real reason why Henley had been gone for such an extended period. Henley had a story to tell them. It was all false, all a lie. But it was convincing and necessary, and she would be able to sell it. Everyone would be so happy to see her, Henley hoped they might not grill her too closely about the details of her disappearance.

A tapeworm! For heaven's sake! She told herself she should be thankful that a parasite was all she'd brought back with her from the months of living in the middle of nowhere in Bulgaria. She told herself she should be thankful that she was still alive. She almost hadn't lived to tell the crazy made-up tale she was going to tell.

She decided to have to have the parasite treated at the McIntyre Clinic. The doctors were not able to tell her exactly how long it would take to fix the problem. If the worm had attached itself to Henley's intestinal wall, it would be more difficult to get rid of. Or something like that. Henley was so angry about the tapeworm and being held up in a medical clinic, she hadn't noticed the date. She had forgotten all about the instructions she'd given to her lawyer about going to her safe deposit box on November 1, 2022. Henley had told him that if she'd not contacted him and had not returned to Paso Robles by that date, he should assume that she was dead. There was a letter in the safe deposit box addressed to Elizabeth Carpenter and another letter there addressed to Henley's daughter. Both letters were to be sent to Elizabeth Carpenter.

Elizabeth had heard from Henley about the tapeworm and had urged her friend to tell the story about indulging in sushi. Elizabeth thought this would be an adequate explanation for the fish tapeworm. Hopefully no one would have the tapeworm analyzed. If it was analyzed, Elizabeth prayed the tapeworm would not be able to give up any secrets about its true origin. Elizabeth was not going to have all of her intricate and secret plans to bring Elizabeth back into the United States thwarted by a worm!

Elizabeth begged Henley to be patient and allow the doctors to treat her. Elizabeth had commiserated but agreed with Henley's doctors that she should not try to return home to Paso Robles until she was healthy. She agreed with Henley that this was a bummer. Henley did not want to let her family know she was coming home until she was actually on her way. Elizabeth suggested that she call her daughter ahead of time and warn her that she was returning so her daughter didn't collapse from shock when Henley finally appeared. But Elizabeth was worn out trying to tell Henley what to do. Henley had come up with her own story to explain to her family and the people who worked for her why she had been gone for a year. Henley's life was her own responsibility from now on. Elizabeth had done her best for her friend, but her job was done.

Elizabeth and Richard had just completed their yearly transition from the East Coast to Arizona. They'd enjoyed the five-day drive across the country and were always delighted to be reminded what a beautiful and wonderful country it was. They had arrived in Tucson and were excited to see their friends and neighbors in the Old Pueblo. They were settling into their house and making sure the swimming pool in the backyard was in good working order. They were looking forward to the winter in southeast Arizona, and they were looking forward to the reunion with the Camp Shoemaker crowd the following week at The Mimosa Inn in Paradise Valley. It was early November, and they would make the two-hour drive to the Phoenix area in a few days.

Elizabeth was surprised when the mailman appeared at her door and asked her to sign for an overnight envelope from California. She knew Henley was fine and could not imagine who in the world was sending her overnight mail from the Golden State. When she saw that the envelope had been mailed from a lawyer's office in Paso Robles, she knew exactly what it was. This was the letter that Henley had told her about, the letter that was to be sent to Elizabeth only if Henley was dead. But Elizabeth knew Henley wasn't dead . . . at least she hadn't been dead the day before yesterday.

Henley must have forgotten about the letter she'd left in her safe deposit box. Or maybe Henley had lost track of the date when she'd been forced to stay a few extra days in the Palm Desert medical clinic to get rid of the tapeworm. Whatever had happened, she hadn't contacted her lawyer to tell him she was still alive and that he should not go to her safe deposit box to pick up the letters. Apparently Henley's lawyer thought she had died. He had retrieved the letters from Henley's bank and sent them to Elizabeth as Henley had directed him to do.

Elizabeth knew Henley did not want her to open the letter she'd written to her unless Henley was dead. Henley wasn't dead, so Elizabeth told herself she was not going to open the letter Henley had written. Elizabeth was going to reseal the envelope and send both letters back to the lawyer with a note informing him that Henley was alive and would soon be back home in Paso Robles.

But Elizabeth's curiosity was getting the better of her. Every time she walked by the envelopes that lay on the table in the hall, she was tempted to reach out and open the one addressed to her. She resisted her impulse to read the letter for a few hours. Then she could not stand it any longer. She opened the letter. It had been hand-written by Henley. Elizabeth began to read:

Dear Elizabeth,

You must realize that if you are reading this letter, I have died. I suspect you know what I have done and therefore why I am dead. I knew going into this mission that I might perish in the attempt, but I felt so strongly that I had to try. I have explained to you why I have chosen you to tell or not to tell my story. I want to protect my family at all costs. I will leave the decision up to you about whether or not to give the accompanying letter to my daughter. I am not ashamed of what I have done. I am proud of it. I want you to be able to understand the depth of my feelings about this mission that has taken my life.

My husband's mother was Jewish. Her name was Hannah, and she was the kindest, sweetest, most wonderful woman I have ever known. I sometimes wonder if I married Edward partly because I loved his mother so much. Hannah's entire family died at Auschwitz. Hannah was sent to England before the war. She survived the holocaust because she was living with a family in Northumberland while Hitler murdered all the other Jews he could get his hands on. My beloved Edward often talked about the Nazi scourge and the evil that it is possible *for mankind to unleash upon the world. He used to say that he wished he had been able to destroy Hitler before he'd had a chance to destroy six million Jews and his mother's heart. He swore that he would have been willing to sacrifice himself, to give up his life, to save his mother's family. We used to talk about the ethics and the morality of this pledge when we'd had a few glasses of wine.*

Edward died too young, and now I have taken up his cause. Adolph Hitler is long dead, but there is another dangerous man who has come to power in the world. This evil man is the Hitler of the new millennium. He is even using Hitler's own playbook in his quest for who know what.

Elizabeth put the letter down. She didn't want to read any more. She felt guilty that she'd even begun to read a letter that she should have opened only if Henley Breckenridge really was dead. Elizabeth folded the two pages of the letter that she'd already read and put the letter back in the envelope. She sealed the envelope the letter had arrived in, and she sealed the larger envelope that had held the letter addressed to her and the letter addressed to Henley's daughter. Elizabeth would take the letters to the post office and send them back to Henley's lawyer with a note informing him that Henley was still alive, that he should not have sent the letters. Elizabeth's intention was not to scold the lawyer or to blame him. Of course, he didn't know. Elizabeth would tell the lawyer that she had not opened the letter addressed to her because she knew Henley was still alive. Elizabeth would suggest that the attorney return both letters to Henley's safe deposit box.

Elizabeth had not known about Edward's mother Hannah. Elizabeth had wondered why Henley had been willing to put her own life at risk on a mission that had so little chance of success. Now Elizabeth knew why. In fact, Henley's very risky and uncertain mission had been successfully accomplished. Henley never spoke of her late husband, but Elizabeth sensed that Edward Breckenridge had been the love of Henley's life and that he had been a wonderful and extraordinary man.

Elizabeth knew everything she needed to know. The rest of the story was in Henley's hands. Elizabeth had played her part. She had done all she could for her friend. Now it was up to Henley. Elizabeth was looking forward to the long weekend with her friends in Paradise Valley. She would thank them for everything they had done to help her. She would tell them that Henley was about to return to her family in Paso Robles. Some of the Camp Shoemaker crowd might guess what had transpired and why Elizabeth had gone to such lengths to rescue Henley. The people in their reunion group were the best of people. They had given their all to help her save Henley. They would never ask Elizabeth the difficult questions because they knew she would not be able to give them answers.

Epilogue

2022

Elizabeth announced at dinner, the first night they were all together at the Mimosa Inn, that the person they had all made such a tremendous effort to save was at last in good health and had returned home. She told the group that their hero had been reunited with her family and was once again living the life she had always loved. The Camp Shoemaker crowd clapped when Elizabeth made this announcement. J.D. and Sidney clapped the loudest. They were all proud that they had contributed something to help save Elizabeth's friend. None of them knew for sure what Henley had done or anything about the mission that should have earned the woman a place in history. Of course, they had their suspicions. Henley could never tell. Elizabeth had figured it out. And she would never tell.

The world was a better place for Henley Breckenridge's successful mission. As off the wall as her friend might sometimes be, Elizabeth was thankful to know this brave and unselfish woman and to consider her a friend.

Boiko Dragomir received a license that would make his previously secret fishing expeditions legal. This license would help Boiko repair the strained relationship with his brother Timotei. Both Boiko and Timotei received significant payments in Bulgarian currency. They could have retired on the money they received, but they both loved to fish. They would continue to take their boats out into the Black Sea.

Giselle Marinov received a large lump sum payment, also in lev. She built a modern bathroom onto her home and added running water to the kitchen. She bought a hot water heater. She extended the electricity she had in her barn to provide electricity for her entire house. She bought some new clothes, a second music box, a smart phone, and a new mule.

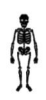

WHEN DID I GROW OLD?

When did I grow old?
    It is now so still around me.
    When did all the noise turn to quiet?
    The cacophony of busyness that engulfed me
        for so many years, has subsided.

When did I grow old?
    Did it happen slowly as the years passed by?
    Did it happen as I filled my time with immediacy …
        moving from one crisis to the next?
    Did it happen all of a sudden when I found I had to use
        a cane to get up and down the steps?

When did I grow old?
    Did I fill those years that passed with goodness and giving
        and love?
    Did I spend too many days in anger and hoping for retaliation
        for things in life that didn't go my way?
    Did I spend too many hours organizing and cleaning and
        worrying about my material possessions?
    How much time did I spend shopping? Sorting out
        my closet?

When did I grow old?
    Was it when I learned that I was deaf in one ear
        and there was no help for that?
    Was it when I realized there were so few days ahead
        and so many already gone?
    Was it when I accepted that I would die?

When did I grow old?
> Was it a gradual process as the hairs on my head
> > one by one turned white?
> Or did it happen overnight? And what night was that?
> Was it when I became a grandmother?

When did I grow old?
> Did I spend this precious time I have been given
> To make a difference?
> To make the world a better place?

When did I grow old?
> Is it today when I know that however this life was spent,
> > it cannot be respent?
> It was what it was ...
> Full of imperfections and mistakes and trying hard
> > and often struggling and falling short
> And full of joy and good luck.

When did I grow old?
I just don't know.
Or, maybe I'm not old yet.

MTT 5-7-2014

Acknowledgments

Heartfelt thanks to my readers and editors. I couldn't have done this without you. Thank you to my amazingly talented cover artist, Zoe Malekzadeh who worked so hard on this cover; to the photographer who always makes me look good, Andrea Burns; and to Jamie Tipton at Open Heart Designs. Jamie puts it all together for me. I am nothing without Jamie. Thank you to friends and fans who have encouraged me to continue writing.

About the Author

*A former actress and singer, **Henrietta Alten West** has lived all over the United States and has traveled all over the world. She writes poetry, songs (words and music), screenplays, historical fiction, spy thrillers, books for young people, and mysteries. She always wanted to be Nancy Drew but ended up being Carolyn Keene.*

More Books By
Henrietta Alten West

When Times Get Rough
Book #3 in the The Reunion Chronicles Mysteries

In spite of the COVID pandemic, the Camp Shoemaker yearly reunion was being held in Paso Robles, California at the elegant Albergo Inn. Kidnapping and torture were on the program. The group once again rallied to save a fellow guest at the Albergo and a physician whistleblower from Hong Kong who had been targeted by Chinese Communist agents operating inside the U.S. Then these seniors had to scramble to save the lives of two of their own.

Released 2021, 352 pages
Hardcover ISBN: 9781953082060
Paperback ISBN: 9781953082077
ebook ISBN: 9781953082084

Preserve Your Memories
Book #2 in the The Reunion Chronicles Mysteries

After surviving the previous fall's harrowing adventure in Maine, the Camp Shoemaker group of friends has gathered at the fabulous Penmoor Resort in Colorado Springs. In this sequel to *I Have A Photograph*, unanswered questions are addressed, and complex Russian connections become clear.

Released 2020, 362 pages
Hardcover ISBN: 9781953082008
Paperback ISBN: 9781953082015
ebook ISBN: 9781953082022

I Have A Photograph
Book #1 in the The Reunion Chronicles Mysteries

Old friends gather in Bar Harbor for a reunion. They've made it to age seventy-five this year and are ready for a party. Who knew that their annual celebration of camaraderie, food and wine, laughter, and memories would turn into an adventure of murder and revenge?

Released 2019, 277 pages
Hardcover ISBN: 9781953082947
Paperback ISBN: 9781953082930
ebook ISBN: 9781953082923

Available in print and ebook online everywhere books are sold.

MORE FROM
LLOURETTIA GATES BOOKS

CAROLINA DANFORD WRIGHT

Old School Rules
Book #1 in the *The Granny Avengers Series*

Marfa Lights Out
Book #2 in the *The Granny Avengers Series*

MARGARET TURNER TAYLOR

www.margaretttaylorwrites.com

BOOKS FOR ADULTS

Traveling Through the Valley of the Shadow of Death

I Will Fear No Evil

BOOKS FOR YOUNG PEOPLE

Secret in the Sand
Baseball Diamonds
Train Traffic
The Quilt Code
The Eyes of My Mind

Available in print and ebook online everywhere books are sold.

CPSIA information can be obtained
at www.ICGtesting.com
Printed in the USA
BVHW091945170922
647198BV00006B/18/J